Sirens in Bliss

Other Books By Lexi Blake

ROMANTIC SUSPENSE

Masters and Mercenaries
The Dom Who Loved Me
The Men With The Golden Cuffs
A Dom is Forever
On Her Master's Secret Service
Sanctum: A Masters and Mercenaries Novella
Love and Let Die
Unconditional: A Masters and Mercenaries Novella
Dungeon Royale
Dungeon Games: A Masters and Mercenaries Novella
A View to a Thrill
Cherished: A Masters and Mercenaries Novella
You Only Love Twice
Luscious: Masters and Mercenaries~Topped
Adored: A Masters and Mercenaries Novella
Master No
Just One Taste: Masters and Mercenaries~Topped 2
From Sanctum with Love
Devoted: A Masters and Mercenaries Novella
Dominance Never Dies
Submission is Not Enough
Master Bits and Mercenary Bites~The Secret Recipes of Topped
Perfectly Paired: Masters and Mercenaries~Topped 3
For His Eyes Only
Arranged: A Masters and Mercenaries Novella
Love Another Day
At Your Service: Masters and Mercenaries~Topped 4
Master Bits and Mercenary Bites~Girls Night
Nobody Does It Better
Close Cover
Protected: A Masters and Mercenaries Novella
Enchanted: A Masters and Mercenaries Novella
Charmed: A Masters and Mercenaries Novella
Treasured: A Masters and Mercenaries Novella, Coming June 29, 2021

Masters and Mercenaries: The Forgotten
Lost Hearts (Memento Mori)
Lost and Found
Lost in You
Long Lost
No Love Lost

Masters and Mercenaries: Reloaded
Submission Impossible
The Dom Identity, Coming September 14, 2021

Butterfly Bayou
Butterfly Bayou
Bayou Baby
Bayou Dreaming
Bayou Beauty, Coming July 27, 2021

Lawless
Ruthless
Satisfaction
Revenge

Courting Justice
Order of Protection
Evidence of Desire

Masters Of Ménage (by Shayla Black and Lexi Blake)
Their Virgin Captive
Their Virgin's Secret
Their Virgin Concubine
Their Virgin Princess
Their Virgin Hostage
Their Virgin Secretary
Their Virgin Mistress

The Perfect Gentlemen (by Shayla Black and Lexi Blake)
Scandal Never Sleeps
Seduction in Session
Big Easy Temptation
Smoke and Sin
At the Pleasure of the President

URBAN FANTASY

Thieves
Steal the Light
Steal the Day
Steal the Moon
Steal the Sun
Steal the Night
Ripper
Addict
Sleeper
Outcast
Stealing Summer

LEXI BLAKE WRITING AS SOPHIE OAK

Texas Sirens
Small Town Siren
Siren in the City
Siren Enslaved
Siren Beloved
Siren in Waiting
Siren in Bloom
Siren Unleashed
Siren Reborn

Nights in Bliss, Colorado
Three to Ride
Two to Love
One to Keep
Lost in Bliss
Found in Bliss
Pure Bliss
Chasing Bliss
Once Upon a Time in Bliss
Back in Bliss
Sirens in Bliss
Happily Ever After in Bliss
Far From Bliss, Coming 2021

A Faery Story
Bound
Beast
Beauty

Standalone
Away From Me
Snowed In

Sirens in Bliss

Nights in Bliss, Colorado Book 10

Lexi Blake
writing as
Sophie Oak

Sirens in Bliss
Nights in Bliss, Colorado Book 10

Published by DLZ Entertainment LLC

Copyright 2019 DLZ Entertainment LLC
Edited by Chloe Vale
ISBN: 978-1-942297-24-6

All rights reserved. No part of this book may be reproduced, scanned, or distributed in any printed or electronic form without permission. Please do not participate in or encourage piracy of copyrighted materials in violation of the author's rights.

This is a work of fiction. Names, places, characters and incidents are the product of the author's imagination and are fictitious. Any resemblance to actual persons, living or dead, events or establishments is solely coincidental.

Sign up for Lexi Blake's newsletter
and be entered to win a $25 gift certificate
to the bookseller of your choice.

Join us for news, fun, and exclusive content
including free short stories.

There's a new contest every month!

Go to www.LexiBlake.net to subscribe.

Dedication

This book is for the fans of Bliss and Texas Sirens who all know how hard life can be, and that it's only made easier when our family and friends share the burdens.

And to Jennifer Zeffer – for her generosity of spirit. Nell would approve, dear.

Dedication 2019

Sometimes in my line of work, I get to meet fans who become something more. I met Jennifer Zeffer many years ago when she was crazy enough to pay way too much to win some books I had donated for an auction. Naturally I had to see what kind of crazy lady would do that and found a lovely, intelligent woman. She was kind and funny and I enjoyed being around her.

We're years down the line and you're on the cusp of following your dreams. You've done the work and now it's time to fly, my friend.

You Are Invited

Leo &
Shelley & Wolf
are getting
married!

on the fifteen of June
at noon

THE FEEDSTORE CHURCH
BLISS, COLORADO

Chapter One

Stef and Jen

Stef Talbot looked at his longtime housekeeper, shaking his head and wondering exactly where he'd gone wrong. It was only eight thirty in the morning. How had the day gone to shit already? "What do you mean there's a child in my chandelier? I seem to recall that Jennifer ordered that chandelier to be completely child-free. Was she a gift with purchase?"

"Everything looks really cool from up here, Momma! It's like a ride!"

Stef could hear the small ball of complete chaos screaming from two rooms away.

"Olivia Barnes-Fleetwood, you get down from there right now, and you better pray that I only ground you this time." Abigail Barnes did not sound amused with her daughter.

Olivia's reply was still at a screeching decibel, though a bit more tentative this time. "I think I'll live up here now. Momma's scaring me. I think I want Daddy."

His carefully run house had turned into a circus. Over the course of a mere two days, his whole life had become all about watching and waiting for the roof to fall in. He was sure it would happen any moment and that one of the Barnes-Fleetwood children would be responsible for it.

Mrs. Truss nodded her perfect helmet of gray hair and a small smile curled her lips up. "Miss Olivia is a vibrant child. It's been a pleasure to have her around after so many years of quiet."

His housekeeper was insane. Olivia was a wrecking ball. God, he was glad they were having a boy.

The thought made him stop. Even though he'd had many months to get used to the idea, he still found himself poleaxed at the revelation. A baby. He was having a baby. Jennifer was pregnant—very pregnant. So very pregnant.

He hadn't touched his wife in weeks. He barely slept beside her, terrified that he would disrupt her sleep. He missed his wife. He missed the way their life had been. Peaceful. Quiet.

And this wedding was a pain in his ass. Why he'd thought he could handle a wedding right before Jennifer's due date, he had no idea. When he'd been asked to house some friends over the week of the wedding, she hadn't even looked pregnant. He'd thought the whole thing would be a breeze. He'd been wrong about a lot of things. "Is someone going to get her off the chandelier before it falls and kills her?"

"Aww, she's way more resilient than that." Sam Fleetwood didn't seem to be in a hurry. The blond cowboy sauntered down the hallway as though his daughter getting stuck in a chandelier was an everyday occurrence. "She fell off the roof a couple of months back. She managed to fall on top of Jack. Jack slipped a couple of discs, but Livie was perfectly fine. That girl is blessed, I tell you. Someone up there is watching out for her."

The eternally calm cowboy walked into the dining room and the door closed behind him again.

"And when are our guests departing?" Stef asked quietly. The house would be peaceful again and he could go back to only worrying about Jennifer. All day. Every day. Until his stomach was in knots. But at least he could do it in silence.

Mrs. Truss shook her head and sighed. "I believe they depart the day after tomorrow."

"What's up, babe? You're not enjoying the company?" His wife walked out of the hallway that led from their bedroom. She was gorgeous in the early morning light, her skin practically glowing. He'd thought about painting her like that, with nothing at all on her body, just the sunlight and her skin, but it was selfish to ask her to sit for a portrait when her lower back hurt most of the time.

What the hell was he going to do if he lost her? She looked beautiful, but he knew the truth. She was fragile. Life was fragile.

"I want to get back to normal." He said the words but he wasn't exactly sure what they meant anymore. He wasn't sure what normal was now.

A brilliant smile crossed her face. "I would love that, too. Normal would be awesome. Maybe we should go to the guesthouse and talk about that."

His dick twitched at the thought, hardening in an instant. It had been a month since he'd been inside his wife's pussy. One month, two days, and ten hours since she'd passed out and Caleb had hooked her up to a sonogram to prove that the baby was all right.

But all Stef had seen was his wife laid out on a hospital bed, her skin pale and her hands shaking.

He'd done that to her. He should have waited, should have simply been happy to have a wife. He didn't need kids. He only needed her. God, she would hate him if she knew how much he resented the fact that the baby growing inside her could kill her. She was excited about the entire event and Stef wanted to get it over with.

He shook his head. "I don't think we need to do that. It's breakfast time. You need to eat."

She was wearing a long, flowing dress that accentuated the curve of her belly. She was close to giving birth, her belly big and round, and he wondered how on earth she could ever have a child so large. Caleb had assured him that the baby was a normal size, but he couldn't imagine it. In his head, the baby was at least ten pounds.

She frowned his way. "I can think of some things you haven't eaten enough of lately. But it kind of feels like you're never hungry anymore. Maybe I should stop asking."

She turned and started down the hallway.

"You should wait, sweetheart. They're trying to get Olivia off the chandelier." Someone was going to have to get a ladder, and it could be dangerous. Jennifer could get hit by a flying destruction ball. "Maybe you should go back to bed and I'll bring you a tray."

He would prefer she stay in bed and let him take care of her.

Her gorgeous eyes lit up, but that joy wasn't for him. "No way. I'm going to go cheer on baby girl. I have to see this. How the hell did she get up there?"

"I'm pretty sure she pole-vaulted." Jack Barnes jogged through, carrying the ladder. "I shouldn't have let her watch the Olympics. Damn. I'm real sorry about this, Stefan. Maybe we should try going to that motel at the edge of town. There's so much here they can destroy. I'm afraid we put off buying a lot of nice things because of the kids. They're kind of chaotic."

Kind of? In the two days the Barnes-Fleetwood clan had been here, Olivia had tried to ride a snowmobile in the middle of summer, jumped into the Rio Grande because she liked to swim, and little Josh had found his way into Stef's studio and painted a mustache on his latest portrait.

What the hell had he and Jen been thinking?

"You're not going anywhere. We love having you and the kids here. They're awesome," Jen said with a laugh. "I mean it. I love your kids, Jack. I haven't laughed this much in years. And Josh is going to be an artist."

Sometimes she made him feel like a grumpy old man, but he couldn't help but pointing out a few truths. "Jennifer, it took me hours to fix that portrait."

Her gorgeous green eyes rolled. "I don't think you should have fixed it. That dude looks way better with a purple 'stache. Josh was totally right."

"I am sorry," Barnes said with a sad sigh. "Any damage they do we will absolutely pay for."

Jen shook her head. "They're adorable and the senator will survive not having a Talbot original for a couple of days. Stefan is doing this as a favor. Don't worry about it. Come on. Let's get your baby girl down and feed her some waffles. I can smell them from here." She patted her belly. "My boy is hungry. I have to enjoy this while I can. After baby Logan's here, I'll have to worry about my figure."

"I am really sorry," Barnes was saying as they walked through the double doors that led to the dining hall. Having children seemed to have put Jack Barnes into a perpetual state of apology. Stef could remember a time when every sub in The Club had feared and wanted Jack Barnes. So why couldn't he handle one small female child?

"It's perfectly fine," Jennifer said with a sassy nod. "The senator has a stick up his ass, and I'm starting to think his portraitist does, too."

Stef stared after her. She was asking for a spanking. Little brat. She was practically begging for him to turn her over his knee and slap that gorgeous ass until she couldn't sit down for a week and he had to carry her around everywhere.

"I'll go make sure the guesthouse is cleaned and ready for use." Mrs. Truss sighed as though something had fallen blissfully into place.

"Why would you do that?" he asked, staring after his wife.

"Well, Master Stefan, that is the look you have on your face before you carry the mistress off for a session."

Yeah, he used to do that. He was being a bastard for even thinking about it now. "No. I'm not going to punish her. She's cranky. I would be too if I was carrying around another human being twenty-four hours a day."

Mrs. Truss crossed her arms over her chest, staring him down. "I think the mistress wouldn't mind visiting the guesthouse. It's been a long time."

Stef shook his head. He couldn't go there. She was close to her due date and he couldn't help but remember how she'd bled in those early months. Caleb had called it light spotting, but Jennifer had been afraid she would lose their boy. She'd cried and clung to him and there had been absolutely nothing he could do, no one he could intimidate into giving him what he wanted.

Caleb had given her a clean bill of health, but she seemed fragile to Stef. Women still died in childbirth. Was it worth risking the love of his life for someone he'd never met?

The closer they got to her due date, the more panic seemed to lodge in his belly, a constant companion. There were so many things that could go wrong. "I think we're through with the guesthouse for a while."

Even if everything was all right, Jennifer would need time to recover. They would need time to figure out how they would work as a family. So many things were about to change.

He missed his wife. He missed being her Master, but he had to take care of her.

There was a loud crash and then the maniacal laughter of the evil genius, Olivia Barnes-Fleetwood.

"That was fun, Daddy! Let's do it again!"

Stef felt a tug on his shirt. When he looked down, Joshua Barnes-Fleetwood was looking up, a paintbrush in his hand. "Mr. Stef, I was looking at some of your paintings and they're just colors and stuff. I wanted to help you out so I painted some dogs on there. Now they're real paintings."

Stef felt himself flush. "Oh, god, not the Lichtenstein."

He ran down the hallway.

* * * *

Jen watched Stef go, her heart aching. She smoothed down the front of her dress. She'd tried this morning. She'd thought she looked pretty in the sunny yellow dress. It showed off her boobs, but kind of hid her belly as much as her belly could be hidden. Was she so large that he couldn't stand to look at her?

Rachel talked about how crazy Max and Rye got when she was pregnant. They were all over her. They were like that when she wasn't, but Rach talked about how good pregnancy sex was. Even Callie said that Zane and Nate loved touching her and holding her while she'd been big with their twins.

She could barely get Stef to look at her.

"Jennifer, I can't say how sorry I am." Jack Barnes had folded the ladder back up. He hadn't actually needed it. Olivia had decided that the best way to get out of a chandelier was to jump into Sam Fleetwood's arms. Jen hadn't been able to stop her laughter. Sam had been relaxed, opening his arms as Olivia jumped. Jack had nearly had a heart attack and ended up on the floor before his wife and partner got him back up.

She gave him a smile. "It's all right. I never liked that chandelier anyway. If it had all come down in a heap, I would have been okay with it. I'm just glad Olivia is fine."

She was more of a contemporary lighting girl, but Stef seemed to like it so she never said anything. It was hard to watch him walking away from her. Or, in this case, running as fast as he could.

Jack Barnes's eyes followed her own. "Don't feel too bad. He's scared out of his mind."

"Hey, Daddy!" Josh Barnes-Fleetwood ran up to the man who was obviously his biological father. He was the spitting image of Jack, but Josh was lucky enough to have two dads. "I'm hungry."

Sam Fleetwood walked up, an easy smile on his face. "Come on, buddy. Your sister has already started in on the waffles. Let's go."

Sam gave Jack a wink and there was no way to miss the easy intimacy between the two men. Jack reached out to his partner, touching his shoulder as though he needed the contact. It was the same way he touched Abby. As though he lived and breathed for his partners.

Jen was damn jealous of those three.

She shook her head. She would pay a lot to watch those two cowboys going at it. Day-um, as they used to say in her hometown. But it wasn't polite to ask one's superhot bisexual guests if she could maybe sit in on their probably fierce lovemaking sessions. She focused on his words. "What did you mean by *he's scared*?"

"Stefan. He's scared. I've known Stef for a lot of years now and I've never seen him like this. He looks like he's in control, but I know differently." Jack placed a hand on her shoulder. "How close are you to delivering?"

Not close enough. She felt like a whale. Now she knew why Callie had complained all those months, and she'd been pregnant with twins. Jen felt like she would pop any minute and there was only one inside her. "I'm due next week, but Caleb said first babies can be late."

And she couldn't wait to meet her little Logan. Logan Mitchell Talbot. He was named after the man who had saved her life and her beloved grandfather. She was excited to meet their son, but she was starting to think Stef dreaded it. He hadn't touched her in weeks, couldn't seem to stand to look at her.

Had he decided he didn't want a baby? She could still remember the moment he'd first heard she was pregnant. He'd gotten to his knees and placed his hand on her belly and they had been connected. There had been such joy in that moment, but it had faded over the long months. Somewhere along the way they'd lost that deep sense of oneness.

"Men are different, you know," Barnes said.

She was utterly fascinated with the Barnes-Fleetwood family. They had come into the estate like a hurricane a few days back and she hadn't stopped laughing since. Between the Barnes-Fleetwood clan and Julian Lodge's family, the estate was suddenly filled with laughter and baby coos and the craziness that came with kids and family. She'd always longed for a big, insane family. She had been raised as an only child. So had Stef. She wanted to change that for the next generation. She wanted her baby to have a couple of siblings they could rely on. "I don't think we're different. You love your kids. I'm going to love this baby."

She didn't say the words she was truly worried about. She didn't say that she was scared that maybe Stef didn't want their son. She tried not to even think the words.

Jack Barnes was a handsome man, but he was truly beautiful as his face softened and he leaned the ladder against the wall. "Oh, you don't understand what I mean. We don't truly understand what it means to be a dad until the baby is here. Men are simple creatures. We start out wanting sex and somewhere along the way we get caught and we find ourselves loving a woman. That one woman who can make us turn away from all the others, well, she becomes our whole damn world. We don't understand that things can change and yet still remain the same."

Stef had been her world from almost the moment she'd seen him. She could still remember the minute she'd walked into Stella's Diner and seen him sitting at the counter. He'd been beautiful. He'd taken her breath away because he was so much more handsome than his pictures. She'd loved his artwork. He was a master, and she'd come to learn from him. And then he'd been a Master and oh, she'd learned more than she could have imagined. She'd learned about love and sex and she'd become something more than she had been before. Her sweet Master who brought her such pleasure, who made her feel precious and beloved, like she was the only woman in the whole world.

Had she lost him? Had he lost interest? Her heart ached at the thought.

"I don't know about that," Jen replied. "I think some men like the hunt. Maybe they're not interested once the hunt is over."

"Stef? I don't think that he was much of a hunter." Barnes shook his head. "The way I remember it, Stef always let the subs come to him. I've been to some clubs with the man. Now, I was a helluva lot younger back then, but he never aggressively looked for anyone. He waited until he found someone deeply submissive and then negotiated a single encounter with her. He would negotiate longer contracts, but only rarely and only when the sub seemed to really need a Dom. At first I thought he was in love with Callie, but time proved me wrong."

Callie Hollister-Wright was Stef's best friend. There had never even been a hint of romance between them, merely a loving friendship. "No. He views her as a sister."

"Yeah, I got that after a while. Stef reminds me of myself. I was more about the D/s portion of the relationship than any one woman. I didn't take any woman seriously until I met that redhead who wears my ring and my collar. I knew she was the one. I knew I wanted to marry her a couple of weeks after I met her."

A bit of bitterness surged. It had taken her a long time to wear Stef down. "Stef didn't feel that way about me. He pushed me away at first."

The big cowboy grinned, a mischievous look. "Stef was a lot younger than I was. There's a certain wisdom that comes with age. Hell, Stef still isn't the age I was when I met Abby. It takes some of us longer."

"Well, I think maybe Stef is wondering if he shouldn't have taken a bit longer to get married." He'd pulled away. There were nights when he didn't go to sleep until almost dawn, as though he tried to stay away from their bed for as long as possible. He would still kiss her, but they were fleeting pecks that did nothing to assuage her desires.

She missed her Dom. She missed her husband.

"He's not." Jack glanced back at the long dining room table where his family was enjoying a breakfast. A lovely blonde entered from the opposite door. Dani Lodge-Taylor was escorted by her husbands. Julian Lodge held her hand, looking coolly elegant in a suit. She got the definite impression that Julian only wore suits and leathers. He was that kind of a man. Finn Taylor walked behind him, carrying a baby in his arms. Chloe. She was so sweet. Finn didn't seem to have a problem with being a dad. Neither did Julian. He was scary, but it was obvious he loved his daughter.

Jack caught Julian's attention with a wave of his hand. The Dom nodded, helped his wife sit down, kissed his daughter's head, and then walked toward them.

"Did you have to do that?" She was a little intimidated by the big bad Dom. Julian Lodge had a way of looking at a person that made her wonder if he was sizing her up for a tasty meal.

"He's nothing but a big old teddy bear," Barnes assured her.

A grimace marred Julian's perfect face for a moment. "I am not a teddy bear, Jackson. I still have plenty of teeth. Old age might have dulled your sharper edges, but mine are firmly in place." He turned to Jennifer and proved how charming he could be. She allowed him to take her hand in greeting. "Hello, dear. Have I thanked you for hosting us? I know it's an imposition, but we're enjoying our time here."

"Not a problem. It's been nice to have someone to talk to." She'd definitely enjoyed spending time with their wives and children.

Julian sent Jack a surprised look. "Stefan is screwing it up, then?"

"Looks like it," Jack agreed. "Julian, tell her how you felt when you first found out Dani was pregnant. Tell her all about how excited you were about the baby and how you knew that the baby was going to change your life for the better."

Julian shuddered. "I wish I could. The truth is quite different. I was completely terrified. I had no idea how I was going to handle it, but Danielle was quite insistent. Even several spankings couldn't dissuade her from trying to get pregnant."

"You didn't want your daughter?" She couldn't imagine it. Julian had been tender with the baby. Little Chloe was always held by one of them. She wondered if the baby ever touched a bed by herself.

Julian laughed. "Oh, I wanted her, but I didn't know I did. When Danielle told me I was going to be a father, all I could feel was a complete panic. My father died when I was very young. I didn't exactly know how to go about being a father, and then there was the fear of losing her." His expression turned distinctly serious. "I love my wife. She and Finn were my whole world at the time. I guess I couldn't imagine things changing."

"I felt the same way." Barnes leaned against the doorjamb. "I found out Abigail was pregnant and all I could think about was how it would change everything. We'd only been married for a year or so. I wasn't ready. It wasn't that I didn't like the thought of children, but like Julian, I didn't grow up with a father. I was afraid I wouldn't be a good one. I was afraid something could happen to my wife. Men are different. We don't get to feel that baby kicking around inside us."

"Thank god," Julian said with a grimace.

Jack ignored him. "We don't understand the parenthood thing until the baby is here and we can hold him in our arms. That's the moment we truly understand this baby is a whole human being we made with the person we loved. I think it's worse for us Doms."

"We feel out of control," Julian concurred. "Finn handled it far better than I did. I think I got through those nine months because Finn practically held my hand."

"Sam accepted it. He didn't fight it at all. He immediately started rubbing Abby's belly and talking to the baby. He brought me in." Jack sent a look toward his family. "God, I would have been lost without Sam. Stef doesn't have a Sam. He doesn't have a Finn. I'm betting that he's merely scared of losing his precious wife. He doesn't have any brothers, does he?"

"He has Max and Rye, but Stef doesn't talk about a lot of things. He's a private man." She'd kept her fears inside her for so long. "I think he doesn't want me anymore. I'm much bigger than I used to be."

Julian shook his head. "She's going to get a spanking."

"Damn, girl. I wouldn't tell your husband that if I were you." A slow smile crossed his face. "Or maybe you should."

"Yes, that would very likely bring him around," Julian agreed. "Though we certainly shouldn't be telling a submissive to poke her Dom."

"Sometimes we need a little poke. You know it." Jack gave her an encouraging nod. "Tell him how you feel. You know communication is the key to a healthy relationship. Sometimes Doms forget and we need our subs to remind us."

"But then we spank our subs for poking us," Julian pointed out.

Jack smiled smoothly. "And then we give them many, many orgasms."

"Oh, that would be nice." She kind of wished she hadn't said it out loud, but it was true. It had been forever. She needed her man.

But if she simply went to Stef and told him her fears, he would probably give her a pat on the belly and tell her she was still pretty and he still wanted her and things would go on the way they had been. He would be gentle and not at all like the husband she was crazy about, the one she'd fought for.

Of course, she hadn't always fought fair. Sometimes an indirect approach was the best plan of action.

"That is a look I know well." Jack shook his head and sighed. "That's the look my Abby gets when she's going to top from the bottom and do it well. Be prepared. Sometimes when you wake the sleeping Dom, your ass gets real tender."

"But I've been told that can be fun. Sometimes a sub has to fight. At the end of the day we can call ourselves submissives and Doms, but we're just men and women and husbands and wives. It's no different. Love, I've found, requires maintenance. If I could give Leo some advice it would be that. This wedding is only the first step. A marriage, well, that is something entirely different." Julian frowned as he turned toward the table where everyone was eating breakfast. "Jackson, your son is attempting to feed my daughter. He has got to stop that. I am told that Chase has been talking to Joshua about certain historical handfasting rituals and how he can secure himself a bride in this fashion."

Barnes's eyes rolled. "He's five. Give me a fucking break. He's not trying to get married."

"Yes, because the men of his line aren't known for their singular stubborn will. She can't eat bacon, Joshua!"

Both men took off for the children, but Jen stayed where she was, an idea forming in her brain.

Sometimes a girl needed to talk to her friends. Who else could she tell her problems to? Who else could come up with a brilliantly evil plan to solve her problems?

Yes, that should do it.

Chapter Two

Aidan, Lexi, and Lucas

Aidan took his seat at the breakfast table across from his hosts. Jamie and Noah ran the Circle G along with two men Aidan knew damn well. Trev McNamara took a long pull off what had to be his third cup of coffee of the morning. If Aidan remembered correctly, it wouldn't be his last. Trev drank the stuff all day long. Bo, Aidan's younger brother, sat down beside Trev, a plate of bacon and eggs and hash browns in front of him.

Bo looked good. His brother had truly grown up under Trev's mentorship and with the love of their shared wife, Beth. He'd gone from an obnoxious brat to a man Aidan could rely on.

He glanced over to where Lexi was pacing outside the kitchen, her cell phone to her ear and a baby on her hip. Little Jack clung to his momma like a monkey. Sometimes Aidan thought the only way to get her attention these days was to be able to climb up her body. Or to be her agent.

"Is Lexi going to come eat? I could make a plate for her." Bo looked out to the living room, a worried frown on his face.

Lexi's voice carried through the house. "No, use the second excerpt.

Yes, the one where the hero gets in the shower and finds out the heroine is already there. I agree. It's the best one and it's not so hot that it will scare off new readers. Twenty-five hundred should be enough. We only need to get through conference season."

Lucas stepped in, finding Aidan's eyes and smiling. Until he heard Lexi talking, then those gorgeous lips of his turned down. "I thought we were on vacation."

Lexi was never on vacation anymore. Since her career had taken off, she'd become a workaholic, and nothing could get her off the phone. Sometimes he wondered how she got any writing done since she was on the phone all the time.

"Her PA called. Apparently she has to get ready for some conference in Denver. She wasn't supposed to go, but she got invited at the last minute so she's hustling up books and promo material. She thought we wouldn't mind since we're already in Colorado."

"But Denver is six hours away," Lucas pointed out. "It's not like it's down the street. Are we supposed to rent a car and shove the kids in? Julian's jet leaves in two days. And we can't let the ranch run itself. I trust the hands, but you need to be there."

"I don't think she expects us to go with her. I think we're supposed to head home at the appointed time and let her go to Denver on her own." Aidan stared at his wife. "You know, it's a really big deal for her."

Those last words were spoken with a hint of sarcasm. Everything was a big deal now. Everything except him and Lucas.

"What's a really big deal?" Shelley McNamara walked in looking slightly tired.

Trev had a smile and a big hug for his sister. "You are. How was the bachelorette party?"

"Insane." A beaming smile came over her face. "Georgia brought the makeup and the booze. I'm now addicted to Chanel and Cîroc. We had makeovers and watched movies and drank too much. It was perfect. But my mother-in-law is a little crazy. I have to meet with someone today who's going to run some tests to make sure I'm not an alien queen seeking to breed with her sons. I'm worried about what's going to happen if I flunk that test. She was disturbed that I refused to eat beets. Apparently aliens are allergic to them. I understand because they taste like crap and stain your teeth. I am not getting married with purple teeth."

Trev grinned at his only sibling. "You have some interesting in-laws, sister. I've been lucky. I only have to deal with Aidan."

A cell phone trilled and Aidan would have sworn that Shelley turned white. She sighed. "It's my mother-in-law. Again." She ran her finger across the screen and brought the phone to her ear. "Hello, Cassidy. How are you this morning? What? No. No. You can't trade my champagne for beet juice. Have you talked to Leo about this? Could you please put him on the phone? If he's not there then let me talk to Wolf, please."

She walked off, her voice getting lower.

Shelley's almost husbands, Leo and Wolf Meyer, had an interesting background. Their mother apparently firmly believed that her sons were half-alien and that someday the queen would come back for them. She and some guy in a trucker hat named Mel had vowed not to let it happen. The citizens of Bliss were taking bets on whether or not the alien queen would show up to gather her mates.

It was the kind of thing that Lexi used to love.

Before all she did was work.

Lucas sat down beside him. His lips curled up slightly, and Aidan felt his hand slide under the table, over Aidan's thigh. It was a sweet intimacy he needed, but then Lucas always seemed to know what he needed. "Sweet baby girl is still sleeping."

Their baby. Daphne. She had Lucas's coloring. There was no doubt in Aidan's mind that little Jack was his, but somehow he was fascinated with the baby who didn't look anything like him. When he stared down at that precious girl, his whole heart melted. If Jack was his mini-me, then Daphne was all Lucas and Lexi. He couldn't wait to see her running around the ranch with a head full of wild black hair and a smile that could bring him to his knees.

He had it all. He had his girl and his guy and his kids. The only problem was his girl always seemed to be on the phone or at her computer.

"I'm glad. She had a long night." Daphne had been off the breast for three weeks and she still needed a nighttime feeding. Aidan liked to do it. It was just him and his daughter in the quiet of the night. He could stare down at her and she would stare back and they were so connected. He doubted she had his DNA, but she owned his soul.

She and her brother and their parents. They were his whole world.

Lucas's hand tightened on his leg, making his cock twitch. Lucas was the one who sought him out in the middle of the day. Lucas worked from home now, having turned Aidan's old crappy office into something truly elegant and beautiful. At least twice a week, Aidan could count on Lucas's sex drive. Lucas would show up wherever Aidan was and they would throw down hard. They'd done it in fields and in the pond behind the house, in the barn and in the pickup truck Aidan had been driving.

It seemed like the longer Lexi held out on the both of them, the rougher he and Lucas got with each other. He still had bruises from the last time, and he coveted each and every one. They were proof someone still wanted him.

They both missed their wife.

"Okay. I'll see you there." Lexi hung up the phone and walked into the room, a harried smile on her face. "Sorry," she said to the room. She shifted Jack on her hip. "Work is never done."

He needed to take control. Somewhere along the way, he'd lost it and he was having a hard time taking it back. "Come and sit down and have some breakfast. You only have a few hours until you're supposed to be out at the Talbot estate."

Her face tightened, lips turning down. There was a small reception for the ladies this afternoon while the men were going up the mountain to a party thrown for them. Lexi had promised him she would attend. "I want to go, but I might have to skip it."

He shook his head. "No, you don't. I already have a sitter for Daphne and Jack."

Bo grinned. "Little Jack and I are going to hang out and play. Trev and I are skipping the men's party. We would rather hang out here with the kids and keep an eye on Beth."

Trev laughed. "You have no idea how long he's been looking forward to that. He's a big kid himself. Jamie found an old trunk of his and Noah's toys. There's a train set."

"See, I took care of everything," Aidan said. He wanted her to get out and see her family and friends. Maybe it would remind her of what she was missing. "You promised Beth and Dani and Shelley that you would go. You missed the bachelorette party."

She looked at him, biting her bottom lip lightly. "I didn't mean to miss it. Something came up."

Something always came up lately. He motioned toward the seat he'd saved for her.

She started to sit down, but her cell rang again. She grimaced. "Damn. It's my publisher. Can you hold Jack?"

He settled his son on his knee as Lexi walked away again, talking into that damn cell phone that seemed to be the center of her existence. He knew he should take the phone and chuck it in the toilet, but he didn't want to cause a scene at his brother's house.

Lucas put an arm around him, his mouth close to his ear. "We have to do something, Master."

Aidan agreed. Lexi might think work was never done, but Aidan was starting to worry that maybe his marriage was finished.

And he simply couldn't accept that.

* * * *

Lexi shifted Jack on her hip as she tried to hang on to her phone. She'd attempted to leave him with Aidan, but he'd toddled into the room looking for her. Her baby boy didn't care that she had things to do. After she'd hung up with her publisher, her assistant had called. Again. "Yes, order a thousand more. That should last all the way through conference season."

She could feel their eyes on her. Oh, there might be a wall between them, but she had no doubt that both of her husbands were growing annoyed.

They seemed to be that way a lot these days.

Her assistant's voice came over the line. "But I don't have the new cover yet. The new romantic suspense is coming out before the end of the season and we should have the cover on your promo materials, but the artist is completely backed up."

Lexi held her patience. She loved her assistant. Jessica had moved from Austin to tiny Deer Run for a shot at helping run Lexi's business and she'd been a godsend, but sometimes she took her job far too seriously. "We can print some single title promo materials for it later."

Jack wiggled and his hand clutched at her shirt as though he was ready to use it as a way to climb down her body. He'd been patient, quiet, but her baby boy was restless. Since he'd learned to walk, he didn't exactly love to be carted around.

"All right."

Thank god. She could get off the phone. If she hurried, she might still be able to make part of breakfast. Maybe that would make up for the fact that she'd had to skip out on the bachelorette party in order to finish her edits.

Jessica barely took a breath before she started talking again. "One more thing."

"No." She had to get off the phone. She'd been on the phone for almost an hour, and she'd promised Aidan she wouldn't work this weekend. "I can't. I'm supposed to be on vacation and I've spent the entire time on the phone. Aidan has flown right past annoyed and into rage territory."

"I'm sorry. I'll handle it. You enjoy your weekend." Jessica's smile practically came over the line. "I will do my level best to not call again."

The button on her blouse popped open and her son started trying to crawl across her body, searching for a way down. Baby Jack wouldn't cry except as a last resort, but he would ruthlessly seek out his goal. Unfortunately she hadn't put on a bra yet, and now she was hanging out. "I've got to go."

"Hey, Lexi. How's it going?" Her brother-in-law stood in the doorway, a broad smile on his face. "Motherhood agrees with you."

She flushed. Somehow Bo always managed to catch her in her most awkward moments. Even after he'd gotten married and he no longer ogled her, he still seemed damn amused whenever he caught her in dishabille.

"You pervert." His wife, Beth, laughed as she walked into the room, her infant daughter in her arms. "Go and find something to do besides make your sister-in-law uncomfortable. Come on, sweetie. Sit over here. That boy looks like he wants down."

Bo leaned over and kissed his baby's forehead. He winked at his wife as he headed out.

"He's more of a toddler, and he takes that seriously." She buttoned her shirt back up with her free hand after shoving her phone in her pocket. Glancing around the room, she decided this wasn't the place to test her son's newfound skills. "He's also a climber."

If she set him down here, he would attempt to haul himself up those bookshelves in the corner as soon as he could toddle over to them.

Beth settled herself into a comfy chair, pulling at the side of her shirt and placing her baby at her breast. The baby's hands came up, clutching at her prize as she nuzzled and began sucking.

Jack grunted, pointing down. He was stubborn and willful, a bit like his namesake. And Daphne was off the breast now. Sometimes the only peace and quiet she'd gotten since Daphne was born had been those moments of feeding her baby, holding her to the breast.

"He's fine." Beth gestured to the perfectly clean floor. "Jamie and Noah completely baby proofed this place. We're over here as often as we are in our own house. The bookshelves are secured against the wall."

She sighed and lowered Jack to the ground. He immediately started toddling all over the place. He was going to be the death of her.

Her phone rang again.

Damn. Maybe her career would be the death of her.

"You're getting popular," Beth said with a smile.

"I'm getting insane." She pulled a magazine out of Jack's hand before glancing down at the caller ID. Her agent. If she answered that call, she would be on the phone for forty minutes. Kathy was a great agent, but she loved to talk. She shoved the phone back in her jeans.

"I would think you would be happy. I remember how happy you were when you sold that first book. I remember holding your hand the first day it went on sale." Beth's eyes were sympathetic.

And Beth would know. Beth had been her first assistant. She'd only quit when she'd married Trev McNamara and Bo O'Malley and moved to Bliss. "I am happy."

She loved her work, but she wasn't crazy about her schedule. But it was completely necessary given her current situation.

"You could slow down."

She thought about it every day. "I would lose my place."

"Your place?"

How to explain it? Beth had only been around for the first year of her career. "The industry works fast these days."

Beth nodded, her hand covering her daughter's tiny head as she continued to suckle. "You wrote six books last year. I would say it's rapid fire."

Jack climbed on the coffee table, hoisting his legs up as though he was attempting Mount Everest. Lexi sighed and pulled him back down. His tiny face frowned, but then lit up again as he found a new adventure. "It's not exactly what I envisioned."

She'd envisioned writing a book a year and making a million dollars and being celebrated for her talent.

The world didn't work that way. Every single book was a fight. She made great money—more than the ranch, but not enough that she didn't have to keep working. Not enough that she could sit back and relax every once and a while. She had to grind it out every day or people would forget about her. She had to fight for her place or someone else would take it.

And she had to pray she had enough money in the bank when the inevitable happened.

"How is the ranch doing?" Beth asked.

Lexi saved her son from taking a header off the TV stand. "It's great. We broke even last year. We'll show a profit this year."

Ranching was hard work. It had taken years to switch from traditional to organic cattle ranching and build a new client base. Aidan put his heart and soul into the land. That was why she couldn't stop.

"I heard Lucas cut back on his hours."

Lucas was a lawyer. Before they'd been married he'd worked long hours in Dallas building a client base. In the last few years, he'd given up everyone except his brother, Jack Barnes, Julian Lodge, and select friends. He did almost all of his work out of the house. Unless there was something to do in court, he was at home.

It was good since she spent a lot of her time on the road.

God, she missed her husbands. After Daphne was born, she'd promised to slow down. She couldn't tell them why she hadn't.

"He wants to be close to the kids."

"He wants to be close to his family. All of them." Lucas walked into the room and caught Jack as he fell back off the bookshelf. It might be secured to the wall, but Jack wasn't. Their son giggled as he fell into his dad's arms. "You're going to kill me, son."

"He's trying hard to kill himself."

His eyes came up, those emerald orbs kicking her in the gut. "We missed you at breakfast. Aidan went out to help Trev and Bo and Jamie with the herd. They're trying to get everything done so they can enjoy the wedding."

That was Aidan in a nutshell. He would work his ass off to help the people around him. Couldn't he see that was what she was trying to do? Her writing had started as something she wanted to do—a piece of her soul she couldn't deny. And then she realized how much she could help her family with it. She'd been a little offended when Aidan had told her he wouldn't put her money in the ranch. It was her home, too, but Aidan had been adamant that he wouldn't take her money or Lucas's. She socked it away, hoping he would relent someday and allow her to help him.

Now she needed it because her idiocy might cost them the ranch. Her stomach turned at the thought.

"Why don't you come and rest for a while? Beth wouldn't mind watching Jack." Lucas's voice was a silky seduction.

Beth chuckled. "Nope, Jack and I can watch some Disney movies. You two should rest. Resting can take your mind off a lot of things."

Sex. That was how Lucas rested. He teased and tempted her to bed and then had his wicked way with her, and after he'd wrung a couple of orgasms out of her, she could sleep for a few hours. So tempting. Aidan could join them. He could put her over his knee and spank her ass until she cried out all her tension and then he would be sweet as he fucked her senseless. She wouldn't have to think about anything but them. She could be their submissive for a few hours.

Lucas reached out to her, a sexy grin on his face. "Come on, baby. You look tired."

Horny was a better word for it.

The phone rang again.

"Ignore it and come with me." Lucas's voice had gone hard, commanding.

She bit her bottom lip. She wanted nothing more than to walk away with him, but she'd given up the right to do that. "I can't. I've been waiting on this call. Give me a minute."

Lucas sighed, his whole face tightening. "It's never a minute, Lexi. I'll take Jack out to play. Daphne's sleeping, but I'll take care of her, too. Try to eat sometime this morning."

He cuddled Jack close and walked out into the morning air.

And she was left behind. Again.

"That man is not happy," Beth said with a shake of her head.

She wasn't sure any of them were happy right now. She kept telling herself it was merely the ups and downs of a marriage, but she knew the truth. She simply wasn't ready to tell them yet. How long could she blame their problems on settling into the baby's schedule? On a million minor stresses?

How long could she fool herself into thinking she could solve this and they wouldn't have to know how much her pride had cost them?

"No, he isn't. Maybe he'll settle back down when we get home."

She would cling to lies as long as she could because she wasn't ready to face the fact that her marriage might be over. When they found out what she'd done, they might be done with her.

She answered the phone and got on with business.

Nate Wright's Shopping List

Things we need for the station	# of speeding tickets
New office chair	8 tickets
Antimicrobial desk protector	6 tickets
Detector 7000	15 tickets
K9 unit	42 tickets
Training K9 unit to hunt Max	27 tickets
Lojack for Farley brothers	22 tickets

Cam,
   This wedding is a golden opportunity. Pull over Lodge every chance you get. Milk that rich bastard!
                                          Nate

Chapter Three

Rafe

Rafe Kincaid looked down at the job offer. It was everything he'd hoped it would be. When he'd gone to bed the night before he hadn't dreamed this would come through.

It was based on a lie and it would take him away from Bliss.

"Can you take her for a minute?" Cam was standing in front of him, their daughter in his hands. Sierra Rose was the cutest damn thing he'd ever seen. He immediately held his hands out, taking the baby into his arms. Her slight weight was satisfying.

And her big brown eyes kicked him in the gut.

Sierra didn't look like any of them. They shared not a strand of DNA, but she was his girl.

And he needed to do right by her. He couldn't keep living off Cam's salary. Laura made even less. She was still working at the Stop 'n' Shop because no one had shown up to take her place and she was loyal to the man who had given her a job when she'd needed one.

Rafe needed to provide. But he wasn't sure he could do it in Bliss.

There was a job waiting for him in Miami. A good job with a six-figure salary and a company car. It was a corporate job, not what he'd wanted when he'd first joined the FBI, but it would be more than enough to take care of his growing family. He could afford a much larger place than their rundown cabin. He had some money saved up, and Laura had been hinting that they should spend it to fix up the cabin, but Rafe had put her off. When Rafe mentioned it, Cam would simply shrug and point out that the cabin was better than most places he'd lived.

Cam was smiling down at the baby, a cup of coffee in his hands. He'd slept in today. Though it was already eleven o'clock, Cam was having breakfast. Since Logan had quit, Cam had pulled a lot of late shifts. "What are your plans for the day? Nate wants a new desk. After catching Georgia and Logan going at it on his old desk, he claims there are way too many germs. So guess who gets to man the speed trap?"

Since the Bliss County Sheriff's Department was currently down a deputy, there was only one answer.

"That would be you. Tell me something. Did you pull over the club owner yet?"

Cam held a hand up, his eyes going wide. "If Nate wants to milk Julian Lodge for some cash, then he can do it himself. That dude scares me. I was in the BAU long enough to figure out who will and won't kill me. I already caught Wolf speeding twice though. What are you looking at?"

He slid the paper under a magazine. "Just another job I'm considering applying for."

He didn't mention where the job was.

Would they miss the mountains? Would they miss sitting on the porch together during the summer and having coffee in the morning and a beer at night? Would they miss cuddling during the winter as the snow fell?

Maybe they would flat tell him if he wanted to leave, he could do it alone.

Would they even listen to all his reasons for moving to Miami?

Not that there was any reason to go back to Miami other than the money. His mother had made that brutally clear. His mother's reaction to his marriage had pointed out certain hard truths about the life he'd chosen to live. He wouldn't give it up for anything, but the minute he stepped outside of Bliss, his odd marriage became a distinct liability.

Cam leaned against the fridge. "You know you could have any job you wanted if we were back in DC."

They weren't in DC. "It's different out here."

"I know, but I don't want you to feel like you've lost your touch. It's a lot harder to find a job in a town this size."

"Yes, I know. I have to be patient." He'd applied to work with the Colorado Bureau of Investigations as a consultant. They'd explained that he was highly qualified, and that they would give him the job in a heartbeat if it wasn't for the morality clause. He'd thought he'd be open and upfront, but it seemed that sharing a woman with his best friend was akin to having a felony conviction when it came to getting a job with the government.

That was why he'd lied about his marital status on the corporate job application. He'd stated only that he was married and his wife's name was Laura. He hadn't mentioned Cam at all. That was why his gut still turned when he looked at the offer.

"Can I get you anything before I head out? I'm working a double until we get the new guy in," Cam said, picking up the lunch Laura had left for him. Cam might complain about his job with the Bliss County Sheriff's Department from time to time, but he loved it. He fit in better than he had when they'd been partners in the FBI's Behavioral Analysis Unit.

And Rafael Kincaid watched the baby. Not that he didn't love Sierra, but he hadn't spent all that time in college so he could be a stay at home dad. "No, I'm fine."

Cam stared at him for a moment. "The deputy position is yours if you want it. Hell, Nate would be happy to have you. We've had trouble with applicants since Logan resigned permanently. Mel filled out an application, though he changed the title of the job from deputy to Chief Alien Hunter. He said he'll do the job for free, but he won't wear the uniform because polyester blends are alien in origin. He's our only candidate right now."

"I thought we had a couple of applicants from other towns." He knew way too much about what went on at the sheriff's department.

Cam's eyes rolled in obvious frustration. "We had two guys from Monte Vista who were interested. They were about to turn in their applications when Nell made her weekly protest."

Rafe groaned. "Well, if they can't handle Nell's chanting, they aren't suitable."

Nell's protests were a way of life in Bliss. Hell, a deputy in Bliss had to put up with any number of odd encounters.

"So what do you say?" Cam asked, his eyes hopeful.

Rafe shook his head. That was Cam's place. They'd been partners on the job once, but he needed his own identity here. "We would have to work opposite schedules if one of us is going to be here with Sierra. We would never be together as a family. And we agreed that only one of us could be in the line of fire at a time."

They had a wife and a kid. They had a future to protect, and while Cam's job was mostly ticketing tourists and making sure everyone stayed fully clothed on Main Street, there were also those moments when the bullets started flying. Bliss could sometimes be a dangerous place.

"Rafe, man, you're not going to be happy being a stay-at-home dad."

He was starting to get irritated. There wasn't anything Cam was saying that he didn't already know. "Well, once a suitable job comes along, I'll take it. I heard Cole Roberts is hiring maid staff at the ski lodge. I'll go and apply immediately if my lack of a job irks you that much."

Cam's eyes closed briefly, a sure sign that he was mustering his patience. "I didn't say it irked me. I'm worried about you. You haven't been the same since you came back from Miami. You want to tell me what happened?"

"I had a pleasant visit with my mother," he lied.

Cam's eyes narrowed. "Then why didn't she come to the wedding?"

He looked down, not willing to meet Cam's eyes. "She doesn't like planes."

"Sure," Cam shot back. "I'll tell you what I think. I think she utterly rejected the idea of the three of us being together and raising a child and she threatened to shut you out of her life."

Well, that summed things up neatly. Cam had been a damn good FBI agent.

"It wasn't a threat. My mother always means what she says. She has shut me out of her life, and my brother will do as she tells him to. Hell, he'll be happy to do it because it means he doesn't have to split his inheritance with me." Rafe looked down at the baby in his arms. She wouldn't know a loving grandmother. She wouldn't get to sit at his mother's table at the big house in Miami and smell pastelitos cooking.

He'd never felt as vulnerable as he did looking down at the baby he'd adopted. He wondered if she would thank him for it, if she would be proud that he was her father or if she would hate him for bringing her into a family that didn't fit the norm.

Cam moved in behind him. "Your mom is wrong. We're not doing anything bad. We're trying to build the best world we can. Maybe we do it outside the norm, but this is our life. We can't live it by other people's standards, not when what we do hurts absolutely no one."

He knew Cam was right, but seeing his mother reject him so completely had killed something inside him.

He hadn't bothered to contact his brother. They weren't close anyway and Miguel had always been closer to their mother than Rafe. His father was on a yearlong cruise with some twenty-year-old. They barely exchanged Christmas cards.

Sierra should be glad she had two fathers because they were going to be a very small family.

Cam put a hand on his shoulder. "Things will change when I finish the software recognition program. I've already talked to Seth Stark about giving him the first crack at it. Another six months and we could be rolling in money and all this will mean nothing. People forgive a lot of oddities when insane amounts of money are involved."

Rafe nodded and Cam gave him another reassuring pat. And then Cam was gone and it was just him and Sierra because Laura was working, too.

Cam meant well, but he didn't understand. The money wouldn't ease this hole inside him. He knew it was wrong. He had more than most people. He had a woman he loved wildly and a best friend and a kid he adored. And he wanted to matter.

Oh, he knew they loved him, and he was more than willing to give up his former ambitions. He didn't want to go back to the rat race, but he needed to contribute.

He couldn't even give Sierra a grandmother.

He rocked her for a while, his mind wandering, trying to figure out a way out of this desolation he felt. The last thing his family needed was a bitter man.

There was a knock on his door. He closed his eyes briefly. It was probably Gemma. Ever since she and Jesse and Cade had moved into Holly's old cabin, Gemma showed up from time to time with her slightly dour personality and one of Cade's loaves of bread. He rather thought Cade and Jesse were trying to soften her up by forcing her to get to know the neighbors.

He got up and crossed to the door. The slight weight of Sierra sleeping in his arms was the only thing that kept him smiling.

He opened the door, ready to invite Gemma in for what always proved to be an awkward five or six minutes, but he was rapidly getting used to his life being awkward.

And it was more than awkward because Gemma wasn't the one standing on his porch. Zane Hollister's massive body took up most of the space, but he wasn't alone. Stella Talbot was wearing her red boots with the purple fringe. Marie Warner was dressed in a pair of khaki overalls, a stern look on her face. Long-Haired Roger had a trucker hat over his bald head, and Polly, owner of Polly's Cut and Curl, was shaking her head. There was a tension among the group that was impossible to miss.

Zane loomed in the doorway, his face a grim mask. "Rafe, we need your help to stop the greatest disaster Bliss has ever seen."

Well, at least the day wouldn't be boring.

Chapter Four

Leo, Shelley, and Wolf

"Ma, I love you, but you're fucking insane if you think for a second that we're going to serve beet juice at our wedding," Leo said into his cell.

He'd been over this about ten thousand times, but two minutes ago his beautiful bride had called and used her dulcet voice to scream at him that if there were beets at her wedding, his cock was going to wither and die.

He believed her. His baby could be stubborn. Unfortunately, so was his mother. He'd figured out how to deal with Shelley long ago. He could tie her up and spank her. It usually worked quite well. His mother was still a mystery.

"Leonardo, honey, don't you want to know if she's using you for your alien sperm?"

Nope. I'm perfectly fine with my sperm being used in any capacity. But the wedding was seriously fucking with his ability to get laid. He would be damn happy when the wedding was done and he could get to the marriage. "Ma, I love Shelley. Wolf loves Shell. We're getting married to her. We're happy. She's one hundred percent human, with all the working human female parts. Be happy for us, please."

He walked down Main Street, stalking his prey. Up ahead, the man he'd been hunting was walking into the Trading Post. Excellent. He could view the subject interacting with others again. He'd discovered the man two days ago and found that studying him took his mind off all of his troubles.

He could write a whole damn book about this guy. This guy made Chase Dawson look normal.

"Leonardo, I love you and Wolfgang. Shelley seems real nice, but it's time you come to your senses. She won't take the beet. She won't even try."

The fact that his mother could use the phrase "take the beet" damn near killed him. "None of us wants to take the beet. It's not because we're aliens. It's because beets are gross and they stain everything they touch. I spent a god-awful amount of money on Shelley's dress. Someone named Monique Lhuillier believes in her own talent, and one of our future daughters should be able to wear it again because it might be her only legacy after what that dress cost me. My future daughter can't wear that dress if it's got beet juice all over it."

Not that he would ever have a child. A man had to have sex in order to procreate, and at this point he wasn't even living with his wife.

They might not have a legal agreement, but in reality she'd been his wife since the day she'd agreed to marry him. But she'd insisted on this freaking old-school, no-sex-for-a-week-before-marriage shit.

And Wolf had lain right down. He hadn't even argued with her about it.

Now they were back in their childhood cabin, in their old rooms. It was supposed to be a reminder of how far he'd come. He didn't need a reminder. He knew exactly how far he'd come from two twin beds in the loft of a ramshackle cabin. He'd worked damn hard for his luxurious condo in Dallas. Well, he'd manipulated Julian enough to get a wretchedly large salary that afforded him the best of everything.

And yet he had to admit there was a piercing sweetness to being back here. Everywhere he looked there was a reminder of how much his crazy-as-fuck mother had loved him, how much this place had molded him into the man he was. Even hanging with Wolf had been fun. They'd been fishing and gone to the Movie Motel for a showing of *Die Hard*, and they'd sat and drank and talked. Mostly about how hard up they were, but they were truly communicating.

He thought about the e-mail he'd received. It had come out of nowhere and he wasn't sure how to handle it. He hadn't told Wolf a thing about it. He sure as hell hadn't told his ma. Was he going to say a word or pretend like it didn't exist? He wasn't sure. The man who had sent him the e-mail had pretended he didn't exist for the last thirty-something years. Payback, in this case, was as easy as hitting the delete key.

"Ma? Are you there or have you vacated the premises?" He had to ask the question because on more than one occasion, his mother had simply dropped the phone and walked off when he told her something she didn't want to hear. Of course, she tended to claim that those were the times she'd been abducted by aliens.

"It's already started." His mother's voice was a hushed whisper. "You've turned your back on your upbringing. You used to love beets."

His stomach actually turned. His mother was excellent at rewriting history. He'd eaten beets half the time because they were the only things they could afford. He wasn't going there with her though. He loved his mother enough that he could rewrite history, too. "Nope, I hated them all my life. The only reason I ate them was the fact that I didn't get ice cream if I didn't clean my plate. Is there something else at work here? Some deeper anxiety?"

"Don't you psychoanalyze me, Leonardo Michelangelo Meyer. I can still put you over my knee, you know. And there is no deeper anxiety than alien abduction. You tell that alien queen that I will not attend the wedding without her beeting."

There was a quick click and Leo sighed.

His mother used beet as a verb. Yep, his condo in Dallas seemed awfully peaceful.

A loud ruckus caught his attention. The doors to the Trading Post flung open and two young men came running out.

"That is one crazy son of a bitch. He damn near took out my eye with that fishing pole."

"What the fuck is up with this place? I came here for Sasquatch, not Satan."

Both young men practically ran down the road.

Max Harper was at it again.

Yes. This was a subject he could study for days. He was actually excited again. Ever since Logan had left, he hadn't had a single fucked-up dude to fix. Leo kind of lived to fix people, but he'd started to believe that Max was that rarest of fucked-up dudes. The naturally fucked up. The "no real reason for it, just kind of crazy" idiot.

It was rather like finding the Sasquatch the young man had talked about.

Yeah, he was totally interested in Max Harper.

He stopped outside the Trading Post, not willing to get too close to the subject. He had to maintain his distance while in the observation period.

And his cell phone trilled again. He glanced down at the number. Wolf.

"Hey."

"You have to do something about Ma."

Leo sighed. "Shelley isn't going to take the beet, man."

"Ma's crying. And she's threatening to call Mel. You know what's going to happen if she calls Mel."

Mel. The craziest man in Bliss, and that was saying something because Caleb Burke was the town doc. "They go into his bunker and don't come out until after the wedding, and then the whole reason we're having the stupid thing is gone."

Frustration welled.

"Or we could convince our sweet sub to drink some freaking beet juice," Wolf replied.

Yes, that would be the reasonable reaction. "She said no."

"She said no before we made a party out of it and you presented her with some hot shoes in exchange for her drinking a cup and a half of beet juice," Wolf explained. "I have a friend and she's willing to set up the whole thing. She's going to the reception this afternoon and I'm ordering something called Prada wedges. Laura says the mint-green color is all the buzz this season. God, I feel dumb even saying that sentence, but I saw them online and they're actually pretty hot. God knows they're expensive as fuck. They should work."

Was his brother high? "Didn't you used to date Laura?"

There was a brief pause. "Once or twice. She's married now."

"Dude, you're getting advice from an ex?" Leo asked, though he knew the answer. "About our wife? What the hell do you think is going to happen when Shelley finds out? And she will find out. She won't drink the beet juice. She'll throw it in your face."

A long sigh came over the line. "Laura's not an ex. I didn't sleep with her."

That was hard to believe. "You slept with everyone."

"Not Laura," Wolf insisted. "So she doesn't count. I can still be friends with her."

He was right. It wasn't like he'd been in love with Laura. His brother had only ever loved Shelley. "Fine. You want to use a single pair of wretchedly expensive shoes to get our wife to agree to a completely bogus ceremony that will potentially placate our mother and lead our family to a certain level of harmony?"

Wolf hesitated for a second. "Uhm, yeah."

There were definitely times when having a partner made his relationship with Shelley so much easier. "I think that sounds like an excellent idea. Buy the goddamn shoes. And throw in some jewelry on top of it. We want her happy to drink that nasty beet juice. We can do it at Trio tonight."

"Why can't we do it at home?" Wolf asked.

"Because Ma has made a ritual out of it. She's calling it a beeting."

Wolf groaned. "We'll be lucky if Shell shows up tomorrow."

Leo felt a smile cross his face. If there was one thing he was sure of, it was that Shelley McNamara would be walking down the aisle tomorrow afternoon. She would be holding on to her brother's arm and smiling that amazing smile, and she would belong to them because she already did. "This is a story we'll tell our kids, brother."

He never thought he would have them, but lately, he'd been dreaming about black-haired boys and girls. He'd found out he actually had a future.

There was a pause on the line. "Yeah. We'll tell them about how screwy their parents' wedding was. I'll order the presents. Logan says his partner, Seth, can have someone fly them out from Bergdorf."

Seth was a billionaire, so he didn't doubt it. "You do what you need to do and get your ass out to Mountain and Valley. Tell me you didn't forget about our meeting with Mel this afternoon?"

Wolf groaned. "How could I forget? The invitation was carved into a beet so I will never forget it. I won't leave you alone with Mel. I'll make it to whatever the hell this is. Do you know what the hell this is?"

Leo turned, looking down Main Street. He hadn't been to Bliss in years, but it looked like nothing had changed. "He's calling it a Meeting of Men. Jen Talbot is hosting a reception for the women out at the Talbot estate. This is Mel's version. I'm sure it will be painfully embarrassing. That's all I know."

Wolf chuckled. "Then I'll see you at three. You don't think this is a way to surprise us with some crazy-ass fun bachelor party?"

Given by Mel, the alien hunter? "Not a chance in living hell, brother. Be ready for some surreal humiliation, but nothing more."

His brother sighed over the line. "See you there."

The line went dead and Leo turned, ready to get back to the task at hand. Leo nearly jumped out of his skin because he wasn't alone. It had been a while since he'd been snuck up on, but he'd been distracted.

Max Harper stared at him, a bag in his hand. "You following me?"

He could lie and make up some grand fiction, but he was too old to make shit up. The truth was far easier. "I'm a psychologist. I've been following you around and you're completely nuts. I'm thinking of writing a book about you."

Max's eyes narrowed. "Am I the hero of this book?"

"Sure, why not?" His general psychosis would likely aid everyone in the psychological world.

A broad smile caught on Max's face. "Well, hell, then let me buy you a drink. Let's go to Trio. I was headed there anyway!"

The big cowboy turned and started walking down the street. Leo followed because if there was one thing he wasn't going to turn down at this point, it was a stiff drink.

* * * *

Wolf Meyer looked across the table at Laura Kincaid-Briggs. "You're sure these are the shoes?"

The lovely blonde smiled and gave him a knowing wink as she passed back his tablet "Yep. She'll love them. It will totally make beet juice worthwhile. So I don't count because I wouldn't sleep with you?"

Shit. He'd hoped she hadn't overheard that part. "We went on two dates. It wasn't a grand love affair. You were waiting on those two FBI guys."

A flush of pink lit her cheeks. "Their names are Rafe and Cam, and I wish you had come to the wedding."

He did, too. "I'm sorry. I wanted to. Dani was traveling. Guarding her and the kiddo is my job. There are a lot of people who would love to hurt Julian, and I can't let that happen."

He was Dani's bodyguard during the day and he went to school at night. It was kind of a terrific life.

She slid a hand across the table. "I know. You look happy, Wolf. I can't tell you how glad I am. Though I seem to remember you claiming you would never be a ménage boy."

He shrugged. "I wasn't into long-term sharing back then. Shelley changed my mind."

"Yeah, well, since then I've heard a whole lot about short-term sharing."

He'd cut a wide swath through Southern Colorado after his time with the SEALs was done. He'd shared women with his friends Logan and Jamie before they'd all settled down and gotten married. Logan was sharing with his best friend and Jamie with his brother, Noah. They had all lucked out. "I found something better than short term. And I'm glad you've worked it out with your FBI guys."

A hint of sadness hit her eyes. "Yes."

She'd recently adopted a baby. She should be glowing with happiness. He liked Laura. He didn't like the fact that she wasn't glowing. "What's wrong?"

She shook her head. "Nothing." She sighed. "Rafe doesn't seem happy."

Rafe was the one from the city. Oh, both Rafe and Cam had lived in DC, but Cam was obviously a Southern, small-town boy and Rafe had big city written all over him. "He misses DC?"

"I think he misses the Bureau."

"Small-town life isn't for everyone." He'd worried about Kincaid when he'd waltzed into town. "My wife, sorry, fiancée, she couldn't live here full time. We can visit, but her ambitions are bigger than a small town can handle. She grew up in one and she needs more now. She needs theaters and art and a thousand restaurants to choose from."

"What about you? You liked it here."

He'd loved it in Bliss. But he loved Shelley more. "I'm good. Dallas is cool. We're talking about buying some land here so we can come up for summers. I want our kids to know this place, to be close to my ma."

He thought about the future all the time now. Why was Leo looking into the past? Oh, his brother didn't think he knew about that e-mail he'd received, but Wolf had seen it, read it, and thought about it endlessly.

And found his peace. Somehow, since he'd fallen for that crazy sub of theirs, his peace was easier to find. He hoped his brother had the same serenity he'd found.

Laura took a long sip of her coffee. "What do I do if he's not happy? How do I handle it if I'm not enough? We adopted a kid. I thought we would be perfect right now."

He reached out and put a hand on hers. Laura had been a good friend to him. "Kids can be hard. Babies change things. You're in transition. You're going from being a trio to being mom and dads."

God, he wanted that. He was two semesters into his business degree and he would put it all on pause for a rug rat of his own. Or two or three. He wanted a big family, brothers and sisters who could rely on each other, who had a shared history. He didn't think he would have made it through without Leo. Of course, his kids would be lucky because they would have Chloe and Olivia and Josh. Eventually Ben and Chase and Nat would have kids, too. There would be a gang of kids growing up, forming their own family of brothers and sisters and cousins.

He and Leo had been alone, but their children would have a wealth of love to call on. And so would Laura's daughter.

"What if we don't make it?" Laura had gone a tad pale.

"I can't see that happening. You grow. Every single human being does it. You all have to make the choice to grow together or to grow apart." He knew what he was going to do. He knew what his role was. He was the in between. Leo had his intellectual pursuits. Shelley had her ambition.

And Wolf was the glue. He wanted his family more than anything else. He was the bridge. If Leo and Shelley were on their own, there was a high probability that they would grow apart and find themselves with a vast distance between them after a few years.

Wolf was going to make sure that didn't happen. Not ever. He would get his degree. He was dedicated to that, but his chief job in life was to keep them all together. Love took work, and he was a hard worker.

Happily ever after was way easier to achieve with a damn fine work ethic.

"There's nothing for him to do here in Bliss. I don't think Rafe is going to be happy being a stay-at-home dad." Laura sniffled. "You know, I found this calm center of myself about six months after I got here. I thought I would hate it. I only stayed because I didn't have anywhere else to go. I'd run out of money, out of time, out of everything. Those first couple of months felt like I was in Purgatory. And then I opened my door and I really looked around. The world is softer here. I fell in love with the glow the world has. Why can't Rafe find it? Cam did. Cam loved this place the minute he walked into it."

His heart ached for her. "Maybe he needs more time."

Laura's head fell forward. "And maybe sometimes love isn't enough. What am I going to do?"

God, he felt for her. "Well, you need to talk to him, first off. You need to ask him what's going on. Have you talked to him?"

Laura's hands were in front of her, clasped together. "I'm scared to."

"You can't be. That's not the way this works. You have to be brave. You have a daughter. There's no prevaricating now. Ask him."

She nodded. "You're right. I need to talk to him."

And Wolf needed to talk to Leo. About a lot of things. "What's the whole parenting thing like?"

"I love it." Now Laura was beaming. "She's the best thing I ever did. God, Wolf, I want to cry every time I look at her. Not in a bad way. Like, in a momentous way. I hold her and I know why I was put here. I was born to be her mom. And when I see the way Rafe looks at her, I know he feels the same way. Cam laid down at her tiny feet. He's easy to love. What am I going to do if I can't have them both? I promised Sierra that her dads would always be here. I know she doesn't understand a word right now, but I do. I promised her two dads who would love her forever."

"Then you have to make it happen. He's not abusive, right?" He would have to step in if he found out Laura was being hurt.

"Of course not. Rafe is the sweetest. He's just sad and I can't stand it. And I can't stand the thought of choosing between this town and my family. What am I saying? This town is my family. I'm choosing between Rafe and my family. Why can't he see it?"

Why couldn't Leo see that their family was complete until such time as they chose to add to it? Wolf wanted kids so bad it hurt, but he wasn't going to force Leo or Shelley to move any faster than they wanted to. "I don't know, sweetheart, but you need to work it out. That's your only option."

And he had to talk to Leo. There was no other choice.

* * * *

"So you regularly go to jail." It wasn't a question. Leo was pretty sure it was a simple truth of Max Harper's life.

"He spend so much times in the jail that we have his orders for food on file. We provide the dinners. I think he get taken in because it be the only time he gets Buffalo wings." The big Russian bartender put two beers in front of them and a big basket of the aforementioned wings.

Max's eyes narrowed, and he looked around the bar. "There might be some truth to that, and let's keep this little fried bit of joy between the three of us." Max looked back at Leo. "My wife is serious about my cholesterol. I made the horrible mistake of actually following through with the physical, and apparently there's some difference between good and bad cholesterol and I have the bad shit. So Rach has decided I should be a bunny rabbit. Men need food. Men need meat."

Leo wasn't sure Buffalo wings qualified as meat, but Harper seemed to think so. He dug into the fried treats with gusto, stopping only to enjoy his beer. "How do you usually get incarcerated?"

He shrugged. "The normal way. I punch someone and Nate gets pissy about it. I rarely stay overnight. Rye comes and gets me out most of the time. Let me tell you, I like the hell out of Gemma. I don't care that she's a lawyer. She's easily bribable. Callie and Hope used to call Rach no matter what I did."

"Do you think your violent tendencies come from your childhood?" He would far rather conduct this interview in his office. It would be quiet and serene there. The jukebox was screaming out something about crashing a party, but Harper seemed to enjoy the chaos.

Harper's expression turned thoughtful. "I think my violent tendencies come from people being assholes."

"All right, I'll rephrase. What was your childhood like?"

His eyes lit up. "Awesome. Rye and I had the run of the mountain. My momma made the best cookies. Me and Rye and Stef, we were mountain men when we were kids. We used to take a tent and sleep up on the mountain. There's nothing better."

"What about your father?"

Harper sighed. "He shouldn't have stayed as long as he did."

Leo frowned. "That's an odd statement."

Harper stopped for a moment as though he was deciding what to say. "He wasn't cut out to be a father, you know. I think he tried his hardest, but it would have been better for all of us if he'd deserted our momma sooner."

Leo was confused. "You're happy he left you?"

"No. I was pissed as shit at the time," Harper admitted. "But I'm an adult now and things look differently from this side. I loved my momma. She was a good woman. She stood by her man even when she shouldn't have. Don't feel sorry for me. It's not like I didn't have male role models. I had Hiram and Mel and Bill. Sure, Hi thinks bears are out to get him. Mel hunts aliens and Bill is always naked, but they helped a boy out. I just think Momma could have found someone who would have loved her better."

"So you knew your mother and father weren't in love?"

Harper sucked the juice off a wing. "I don't know that anyone could genuinely love my father. It's not that he was a complete ass, but he was closed off. I think he cared about my momma, but he didn't know how to truly love someone."

"Your mother died when you were young?" He'd heard a couple of stories.

"I was barely eighteen. When Momma died the man who called himself my dad left. He left me and Rye with my sister, Brooke. She was seven at the time. We had to work real hard because we couldn't let the state come in and take her. But then I met my Rach. Lots of things changed after I met my Rach. Love, really loving a woman and being loved back, that's the most important thing in the world. My momma was a good woman. She deserved to be some man's whole world."

Why the hell was this man insane? He made total sense. He had all the working parts to be a functional man. So why did Max Harper insist on being an asshole?

Maybe he chose to be.

"Leonardo?"

Leo turned his head, following the sound that came from his left. A man stood there. Leo would peg him somewhere in his sixties. He was well dressed, though the clothes were of middling quality. He stared at the man trying to figure out who the hell he was.

"Yes?"

"Leonardo, I'm your father. I thought we could talk."

Harper pointed a wing his way. "Now we're getting to the drama. Nice."

Leo shook his head, hoping he was hallucinating. Maybe the strong odor of Harper's superhot chicken wings was causing him to see things. Because this shit couldn't be happening right before his wedding. He had enough to deal with. He didn't need a long-lost father.

"What do you want?" He stared at the man who had supplied half his DNA. The man didn't look anything like the father he remembered, but then a young mind could play tricks. Memory was a fragile thing. The man who stood in front of him was so much older than he remembered, his face showing decades of hard living.

A deep frown crossed Robert Meyer's face. "I told you in my e-mail. I want to talk to my son."

"I find your timing interesting," Leo replied.

Max watched the byplay like he was invested in a tennis match. His eyes went from Leo to Robert and back again as he munched down on his precious hot wings. "Do you find it interesting because he doesn't show back up in your life until you're about to get married? That's the worst possible time for extra drama."

Did he really need Max's input? "Yes. That was what I meant."

Max smiled and nodded as though giving them permission to continue. "I found that interesting, too. He's probably here to blackmail you."

"I am not." Robert shook his head, but there was something in his father's eyes that made Leo think he was lying.

The fucker.

"I only want to talk, Leonardo. I think your mother has been lying to you about me for a long time. Isn't it time to put the past behind us and be a family again?"

Max pointed a wing at Robert. "You found out how much money he's worth, didn't you?" His brow furrowed as he looked to Leo. "You are worth a lot, right? I mean you work for that crazy-rich Julian fellow so you're bound to be loaded."

"You work for Lodge? I've heard of him." Robert's face turned thoughtful. "He's an interesting man. Your job must be fascinating. You've done well for yourself."

"Cut the crap." He didn't feel like playing around. "What do you want? Look, I have no idea what you've been doing or where you've been. If you have some misconception that Wolf and I have spent our lives wondering about you, you're wrong. We grew up fine without you. If you have a deep need to reconnect, try me again after the wedding."

His father's cheeks flushed a slight red, a sure sign of irritation. This obviously wasn't going the way he'd planned.

"I think the shrink is trying to tell you to get lost or he's going to hire me to shove a baseball bat straight up your rear." Max nodded. "I'll give a real good rate on that. He was married to Cassidy, right? Real fine lady. Crazy as fuck, but nice."

"Are you threatening me, you asshole?" His father's pleasant mask dropped.

Ah, now Leo remembered him.

"Go away. I don't want to talk to you. I've moved on with my life. I suggest you move on with yours. Otherwise, I might have to take Mr. Harper up on his offer."

Max let out a long sigh. "Please do. Rach won't let me kill anyone anymore. It's been months."

Robert moved back, his mouth a stubborn grimace. "Don't think this is over."

He strode out the door.

Max leaned over. "So he e-mailed you? I don't believe in e-mail.

It's one more way for people to try to get you to do shit for them. You should be like me. Get rid of it and don't reload it again. I'm off the grid. Well, except for the cell phone. And cable. Can't miss my shows. But other than that, totally off the grid. Does satellite radio count?"

Leo felt like growling. His father might have walked away long ago, but it looked like Leo couldn't delete the fucker.

Chapter Five

Aidan, Lexi, and Lucas

Lucas waited patiently as Aidan rode in. He was sitting on top of a gorgeous brown and white mustang, his spine straight, sweat on his brow.

Working man. Cowboy. Sweat and leather. His cock sprang right up at the sight of that gorgeous man.

He needed Aidan because he couldn't have Lexi. That wasn't exactly right. He needed Aidan always, but he needed to fuck Aidan right now because he couldn't have Lexi.

Aidan's head came up and a smile lit his face. At least he could still make his Master smile.

Aidan brought the horse he was riding to a stop and gracefully dismounted, his body so long and lean that it made Lucas's mouth water.

Of course after coming close to getting Lexi into bed, his body was primed for sex. He'd been in cock hell ever since that moment when he thought she would take his hand and let him lead her away for a few stolen hours. He'd envisioned laying her out and topping her, ordering her to suck his cock before he tied her up and fucked her six ways from Sunday.

It seemed like forever since he'd gotten to top her. It had been months—since before Daphne had been born, and even then she'd been pregnant. He'd had to be tender and gentle, and sometimes he needed it rough.

"Is something wrong?" Aidan had a tight rein on the lead.

He must look ferocious. Damn. He had to keep a lid on it or he would scare the fuck out of his Master. He couldn't let Aidan know how angry he was.

Shove it down. Don't be a pain. Be helpful. It's the only way you might have a shot at saving this. "Not at all. I thought I would come out here and see how your day was going."

"Hey, I'll put up Ghost for you." One of Trev's hands took the reins. "Thanks for all your help, O'Malley."

Aidan thanked the young man and turned back to Lucas. "Come here."

Lucas sighed, Aidan's dark voice making his skin tingle. If he couldn't dominate, then he would submit. He was a switch, caught in between both worlds, as he always had been. He stepped up, and Aidan immediately threaded a hand into his hair. He kept it longish because he wanted his Master to always have a good hold.

"Do you need something from me, sub?"

He needed far more than he was willing to say. He needed Aidan and Lexi to play their parts, but he couldn't make waves. Everyone was trying. "I think I need you to clean up, Master. Would you like me to help?"

A smile creased his brow. "I think that's a fine idea. Where are the kids?"

"Beth and Hope have them over at Hope's. Their friend Gemma came by and apparently she wants to see if she can stand what she called 'tiny humans.'"

Aidan looked toward the other house. "I don't know that I want my children to be someone's experiment."

"Please, Master. Hope and Beth will take good care of them. Just an hour, please." He needed to get out of his head for an hour. Then he could get back to worrying about what the hell was going on with Lexi. His whole world had revolved around her for so long, he wasn't sure what to do now that she no longer seemed to need him.

He'd made himself indispensable in the beginning. He'd done everything for her. Her car needed gas? Lucas filled the tank. She needed coffee? Lucas ran to get it.

She didn't even bother to ask now. She had an assistant do it all.

He wasn't sure what his place was anymore.

Aidan pulled him close, bumping their chests. "Of course."

He brought their mouths together, lips rubbing before Aidan's tongue plunged deep.

One part of Lucas relaxed, the part of him that needed to submit. He let that part take over and allowed Aidan to control the kiss. Aidan didn't hold back with him. He tugged on Lucas's hair, twisting him this way and that as he devoured his mouth. Lucas felt his whole body tighten in anticipation as Aidan's tongue slid over and over his.

"Get a move on, Lucas. I want to get clean so I can get dirty again."

They hurried to the house.

Trev was riding in but simply tipped his hat, a knowing smile crossing his face.

They didn't hide. Since Aidan had come out, his Master didn't allow any of them to prevaricate about their relationship. Even in their small town, Aidan would kiss Lucas in full view of the town council and the church choir if he wanted to.

I'll kiss you because you're mine, Lucas. I'll treat you the same way as Lexi. You're both mine, and no society rules are going to keep me from my subs.

He'd said that a long time ago, right before they'd gotten married. Why had that changed? It wasn't rules that were keeping them apart. It was Lexi. Why hadn't his Master taken control and brought her back to them?

"Lucas?"

He forced the thoughts aside. Somehow they'd made it to the suite of rooms Trev had assigned them to. There were two main houses on the Circle G. The kids and Lexi were currently at the Glen-Bennett house. He and Aidan had the McNamara-O'Malley house all to themselves, and he wasn't going to waste it. "Let's see how hot the water gets."

Aidan pulled him back. "Lucas, maybe we should talk."

He didn't want to talk. Talking got them nowhere. And the person they needed to talk to wasn't here. "If you've changed your mind about wanting me, I can go find something else to do."

Aidan's eyes flared wildly. "You better rephrase that sentence, sub, because all I heard was a threat."

What was he talking about? "If you don't want to fuck, I'll go play with the kids. It seems about what I'm good for these days."

Aidan sighed. "I thought you were saying you would find someone else."

What the hell was he talking about? "Who? The ranch hands? I don't think so. If you haven't noticed, we're isolated out here."

"What's going through that head of yours?" His tone had softened.

Lucas stormed into the bathroom. His Master needed a shower whether Aidan wanted him or not. "We only have an hour and a half before we're due at the naturist community. I have to drop Lexi off first. Why don't you take a shower and meet me out there?"

He turned the water to hot. He was shit out of luck today. He wasn't sure how he was going to sit through a marriage ceremony when he felt disconnected from his wife and partner.

Aidan gripped his arm. "Lucas, tell me what's wrong."

He closed his eyes. He wanted to forget about his problems, not talk them out. "Nothing's wrong except I'm tired of being turned down. I'll get over it."

The steam was starting to fill the room as Aidan pulled him close. Aidan gripped his hips, pulling them together. There was no way to miss how hard Aidan's cock was. "I'm not turning you down, love. There's no chance of that. What did Lexi say to you?"

The same things she always said. "Nothing. I thought I had her for a moment."

Aidan shook his head. "We're going to straighten this out once we get home."

"She's not coming home with us. According to you, she's heading to Denver."

Aidan's hands went to the front of his jeans, pulling on them until he got the fly free. He felt his cock pulsing in his boxers. "When she gets back from Denver, I'll deal with her."

Frustration welled. It wasn't the first time they'd gone over this. Why was Aidan waiting? He felt the two people he loved most in the world drifting apart, and they wouldn't let him bridge the gap anymore.

"Lucas, you're right. Let's not talk about Lexi now." Aidan's hands delved under the waistband of his boxers. "We need this. I want to forget about her for two fucking seconds. I don't want to think about it. We can talk about how to deal with Lexi afterward. I'll listen to everything you have to say but give me this now."

Lucas softened everywhere except his dick. His Master needed him. And Lucas needed to be needed.

God, he needed to be needed.

He nodded, letting his hips lean forward. He groaned as Aidan's hand gripped his cock.

"Who does this belong to?" Aidan growled the question.

"You." He didn't add the rest of the answer. His cock belonged to them—to Aidan and Lexi. But Lexi didn't seem to want him anymore.

"Well then, sub, I think I'll do what I like with it." Aidan got to his knees.

Lucas's breath hitched. His Master's version of dominance dealt with a lot of service. He wasn't a Dom who had his subs constantly give without receiving. No. Aidan O'Malley had told him long ago that he would take and give, and Lucas should get used to it. If Aidan wanted to get his mouth on Lucas's cock, then Lucas would offer it up to him on a silver platter. Aidan gave now as he pulled out Lucas's cock and leaned forward to place it at his lips.

Heat enveloped Lucas. He let his head fall back as Aidan's mouth devoured his dick.

There was no teasing, no prevaricating, just one long swallow of his cock. Aidan was rough, sucking hard, pulling Lucas into his mouth from the head to the base. Aidan's tongue was a muscular presence on his flesh.

"Tell me how it feels." Aidan tugged on his balls.

The shock of pain lit him up, making the pleasurable lick Aidan gave him so much better. "So fucking good, Master. I want you. I want you to be rough with me."

"I'll give you what you need, sub." He nipped the head of his cock.

Lucas gritted his teeth and tried not to come. Pain flared along his cock and then turned into a sweet pleasure as Aidan sucked up and down. Aidan's hands squeezed his balls hard and then rolled them up. Hard and then soft and tender. A bite and a lick. That was what he needed. He needed to be on the edge, not sure what would come next except that his Master would bring him so much pleasure.

He let go of all his worries, all the needs that wouldn't be met in exchange for the one that was.

"Give it to me, Lucas. Give me everything you have and enjoy it because the next hour is mine."

Lucas felt every word Aidan said as a low rumble against his cock.

His Master was hungry, hungry to dominate him, hungry to forget about his troubles, too.

Lucas relaxed and let Aidan take charge completely. In the years they'd been married, Aidan had become his center, his core. Aidan was the strong base who provided balance for him and Lexi, pulling them back together with a masterful order and sweet discipline when they got out of line. Aidan was the one who would never let them go.

But Lucas was adrift again, and he wasn't sure how it had happened.

A sharp slap to his ass brought him back to reality.

"You stay with me." Aidan sucked him hard, and Lucas felt a tingle at the base of his spine.

The heat of Aidan's mouth undid him. His breath hitched in his chest as he came. Aidan took it all, swallowing him down, holding the cheeks of his ass so there was no mistake that he was right where he longed to be.

Making Lucas feel needed and loved and wanted.

Yes, this was what he needed.

Aidan gave his cock one last long pull before getting to his feet and slamming his mouth against Lucas's. His tongue dove deep, and Lucas could taste himself there. Aidan came up for air, a dark look on his face. "Get out of those clothes, Lucas, and get in the shower. Present yourself to me."

Just like that his cock was flaring back to life. Lucas quickly divested himself of his jeans and shirt and boots. He stepped into the shower, steam and heat surrounding him. He placed his hands on the tile and his ass in the air.

When the first smack hit him, he nearly came again.

He relaxed and finally, truly gave over.

* * * *

Aidan's hands were trembling slightly as he looked over his sub. Lucas was a fucking work of art. Every muscle in his body was toned, every inch of skin on the man a testament to his beauty. How had he held out so long against Lucas? He'd lost years with Lexi and Lucas because he couldn't handle the idea of wanting a guy. He'd never wanted a man before Lucas had walked into his life and if anything ever happened to him, he wouldn't take another man again.

For him it was only Lucas. Only Lexi. And it would never be any other way.

"Do you like what you see, Master?" Lucas asked, his head turned slightly. Those gorgeous lips of his were curved up in a playful smile that let him know Lucas was certain of what his Master's answer would be.

He still gave him the words. He wanted Lucas to always know how he felt. "I love what I see. Spread your legs further."

Lucas gave him another half-inch, far less than he needed.

Cheeky sub wanted more play time. Yeah, Aidan would give him that, too. He laid out five quick swats to Lucas's perfect ass, the sound cracking through the shower.

Lucas's breath hitched, his shoulders trembling.

"I said spread those legs."

This time Lucas's legs went wide, giving Aidan the access he needed.

He ran a hand over the cheeks he'd slapped. Muscular and smooth, Lucas's ass was utter perfection. "You know how gorgeous you are, sub."

"I know I feel that way when I'm with you." Lucas's soft words made Aidan smile.

This was exactly what he needed. He needed the easy affection he had with Lucas. He needed to sink into everything Lucas offered him. Trust. Love. Commitment.

"I love you, Lucas." He didn't say it enough. He could never say it enough.

Lucas came out of his position and wrapped his arms around Aidan, kissing him sweetly. "I love you, too, Aidan."

Aidan kissed him again, loving the way their tongues slid against each other in a lazy, lusty slide.

But Lucas had been a bad boy again because Aidan hadn't given him permission to move.

"Back in position. It's a count of twenty. If you don't behave, love, you're going to find yourself strapped to Trev's bench and I'll torture that sweet cock of yours for hours."

Lucas moved swiftly back to his position, allowing the warm water to coat his body. "Yes, Master."

Lucas had some pain slut in him. He needed the play as much as he needed the sex that would inevitably come after. And the water would prime his skin for that sweet pain.

He needed this and his Master intended to give it to him. He didn't hold back. Aidan slapped Lucas's ass hard and was rewarded by a shudder that went through his sub's body. A long huff came out of Lucas's chest and his head fell forward.

"Is that what you want, sub?"

"God, yes, Master. Give it to me. Hard. It feels so good."

Another four smacks to Lucas's flesh. Already a red sheen coated his flesh. *SMACK. SMACK. SMACK.* Aidan moved around, spreading the sensation where Lucas's flesh was the softest. He smacked the bottom of his cheeks where his ass met his powerfully built legs. Over and over. He heard Lucas cry out, but that was another part of the pleasure for his sub. Lucas kept so much inside, hid his pain well.

He smacked Lucas again, watching tears drip from his sub's eyes. They were closed. Despite the tears, his face was peaceful, almost worshipful. This was a safe place for his guy. Aidan could take him there.

Another quick five slaps and Aidan's cock was dying. He needed to get inside Lucas. He needed the connection. "See that you behave."

"Yes, Master." His voice was relaxed now, the tension seemingly gone.

But the tension was definitely not gone for Aidan. His whole body was primed and ready to fuck. He reached for the lube he'd grabbed from his shaving kit.

"Turn around," he commanded.

Lucas obeyed with a happy sigh. He knew the drill. He held his hand out and took the lubricant. "Does my Master need preparation before he fucks his sub?"

He didn't need anything. He was hard as a rock, but he wasn't going to shortchange either one of them. "Yes, love. I need some attention. On your knees."

With a sexy grin on his face, Lucas gracefully dropped to his knees, allowing the shower spray to cover his shoulders. His hair was wet, curling around his ears and falling over his eyes, making him look younger than his years. Aidan slipped his hands into that black silk and pulled his head back, lining Lucas's mouth up to his straining cock.

Lucas's tongue came out, swiping at the moisture already pulsing from the head.

His cock jumped, desperate for the attention.

Lucas wrapped his hand around the thick stalk of Aidan's cock, pumping him roughly as he sucked on his cockhead.

Aidan let his eyes drift closed as Lucas worshipped his cock. "Harder. Take more."

Lucas's hand disappeared as he swallowed Aidan's dick. He sucked him in long, hard passes, taking him to the root, letting Aidan feel the soft place at the back of his throat.

Aidan guided him, tugging on his hair, making him suck faster. Over and over Lucas sucked him down, pulling back until he almost lost Aidan's dick, only to deep throat him again.

"Stop." Aidan couldn't take another second without losing it, and he didn't want to do that in Lucas's mouth. He wanted to be buried in the heat of Lucas's ass when he blew.

He tugged hard on Lucas's hair, pulling him off his dick.

Lucas finally gave in after one last swipe of his tongue. "My Master tastes so good."

"Your Master is hungry." Starving for him. He helped Lucas back up and turned him to the proper position—hands on the wall of the shower, legs spread wide, perfect ass in the air.

Aidan lubed up his straining cock, stroking himself from base to tip. He spread the muscular cheeks of Lucas's ass, taking a moment to look at his tight asshole. Damn, but he loved the sight of it. Rosy and perfectly formed, it made his cock jump thinking of how tight it would be.

Lucas gasped as Aidan poured lube over the rosette of his ass, his thumb massaging in circles. Lucas's asshole puckered at first, but Aidan was patient. He rubbed and added lube and before too long, his thumb gained ground, spreading the slippery stuff where it was needed most.

He pulled his hand out and got between Lucas's legs, making a place for himself there. Heat washed over him as he lined his cock up.

A low groan came from Lucas's chest as Aidan started to shove his dick inside.

He gripped Lucas's hips, working his way in. He had to go slow with Lexi. Every single time he fucked her ass he had to be careful. Not with Lucas. Lucas pressed back, forcing Aidan's cock deep into his hole.

Fuck. Fuck. Fuck. It felt incredibly good. Heat enveloped him. Lucas's asshole squeezed on his cock and he felt the hard nub of a prostate dragging on him.

Lucas's dark head fell forward and he groaned in pleasure. "Yes, Master. You feel so good. Please fuck me hard. Make me feel it. I want to feel you all day long."

Aidan knew exactly what he wanted. He wanted to be sore. He wanted that sweet ache that reminded him of how good the sex had been, of how hard they had gone after each other.

He took his clean hand and wound it around Lucas's waist, gripping his straining cock and squeezing. "I'll give you everything you want, sub. I'll give you what you need."

He pumped into Lucas's ass as his hand worked over that hard cock.

Lucas fought him, aided him, got him even hotter with every thrust back that took him all the way to his root. He could feel his balls slapping Lucas's skin even as they tightened up and prepared to shoot off.

The rough sounds of their fucking clashed with the soft beat of the shower, but Aidan reveled in all of it. He loved every hard groan that came from Lucas, every slap of flesh against flesh as he took his guy hard and fast.

The cock in his hand swelled and he knew Lucas was close.

"Come for me, sub. Come all over my hand. I want to feel it."

"Yes, Master. Yes." His lean body shuddered as he started to coat Aidan's hand.

The feel of that warmth on his hand, spurting out of Lucas's dick, made him crazy. He thrust in as deep as he could go and then Lucas tightened his hold, his ass nearly strangling his cock.

He couldn't hold out a second longer. He came in long thrusts. Pleasure coursed through his system, making his eyes roll back, his brain sputter.

He fell onto Lucas, pressing his body against the tile and holding on to him for balance.

Warm water caressed his skin and he cuddled close to his guy.

Lucas turned his head slightly, just enough that Aidan could see that gorgeous shit-eating grin he got when he was really satisfied. "You're definitely dirty, Master. I think I might need to clean you up again."

Aidan moved in, kissing that mouth he loved. For the moment he could pretend all was right with his world.

* * * *

Lexi closed her eyes as the words Aidan had said washed over her. She'd been trying to process them for twenty minutes.

I want to forget about her for two fucking seconds. I don't want to think about it.

She'd stood outside the bathroom and listened in on them. It wasn't like she'd followed them. She'd walked into the room trying to find a pen that worked, but she'd been caught by the sound of them kissing, tearing at each other's clothes, making love.

And dismissing her from their thoughts.

She'd walked back out of the McNamara house without letting them know she'd been there. She'd found her way to the main house where Jamie, Hope, and Noah lived. Where her babies were playing, but she couldn't get what she'd witnessed out of her head.

Aidan had sounded tortured, as though he couldn't stand to think about her for a single second.

He would hate her even more once he found out the truth—that she would be the one to cost him O'Malley Ranch, and it had all been over something stupid.

She had one chance and that was to hope that they held out long enough so she could get her big payday and offer it to help save the ranch. Or to buy new property.

Would he even take it from her? He'd turned her down a hundred times before. It was why every dime she'd made from her writing was sitting in the bank. Aidan wanted to take care of her. Aidan wanted to be responsible.

And now he would find out how irresponsible she was.

When she'd stood outside the door and listened in, she'd heard a smacking sound, a hand hitting flesh and Lucas's low groan of pure pleasure. She could still hear it echoing in her mind.

That sound brought about a physical memory. She could almost feel their hands, slapping at the fleshy part of her ass, the sting and then the relief that followed, so hot and sweet. When that heat hit her, she could let go. Nothing else mattered in those moments except the sensations, the act of loving them.

Her skin flushed, her vision softening. How long since she'd been in subspace? How long since she'd floated along without a worry in the world? Lucas would be there soon, but then Lucas hadn't fucked up the way she had. Lucas wasn't going to cost them their home.

She would have to tell Lucas eventually. She couldn't save them alone. Lucas had money stashed, too, and they would need it. But she dreaded the fact that he would have to know.

She heard the faint sound of her daughter crying from another room.

She took a long breath and forced herself to stop the tears that were poised on the edges of her eyelids. She couldn't let anyone know what she was going through. She hadn't kept this from her husbands only to let one of her friends in on her burden. It was hers and hers alone to bear.

She hurried off to get Daphne before anyone heard her and thought to call Lucas or Aidan. Sometimes Daphne wouldn't let anyone but her parents hold her. The last thing she wanted was to interrupt their intimacy. It was all they had left. It might be all she had to give them.

She wrote happy endings for a living, but she feared she was going to cost them all theirs.

Rafe's Pros and Cons for Taking the Miami Job

Pros	Cons
Actual salary	Cost of living
Proximity to daycare and schools	Could be hard to fit in
Closer to my family	Closer to my family
Beach	No mountains
No bears	Way more people
Less protests	More corruption
Lower murder rate per capita	No Teeny's fudge
Avoid Doc's yearly exam	Colon cancer
Higher self esteem	Taking my wife from her home

Chapter Six

Rafe

Rafe walked back into the living room, a tray of coffee in his hands. Damn, but he needed Laura. She could handle this motley crew. He'd been dealing with them for almost an hour and he still hadn't figured out why they were here.

He was playing host. My, how the mighty had fallen. Once he'd stood in front of the bigwigs at the FBI, giving his advice and running meetings. Now he served coffee and tea cakes. He hadn't even realized they had tea cakes until he'd rummaged through the pantry.

He set down the tray and hoped that someone would get to the point soon.

Polly and Long-Haired Roger sat on opposite sides of the room, staring each other down from time to time. They were longtime rivals, though their businesses had nothing to do with one another. Long-Haired Roger—not to be confused with Roger, who actually had some hair and was rumored to have named himself king of Rogerville, a separate country from the US that existed only on his ten acres—was a mechanic. He had a shop and employed two mechanics, Rafe's neighbors, Jesse and Cade. Polly ran the local hair salon. As far as Rafe could tell, their long-term feud had started over the Cut and Curl's flashing neon pink lips that apparently gave Long-Haired Roger's former dog seizures. They were always clashing with each other at town hall meetings. At one point in time the town had paid for therapy, but the poor therapist had fled after the second session and refused to come back.

So the fact that they were attempting to present a united front now made Rafe curious.

Stella had taken Sierra the minute she'd walked in the door, cooing and cuddling the baby girl as if she was her own. She paced as she talked, giving Sierra comforting pats on her back. "This is serious, Rafe. Nothing like it has ever happened here before."

Long-Haired Roger shook his head solemnly. "That's because we only had one mayor. Hi's been mayor for years. Forever it seems like. We've never had to deal with anything like this."

"Something's happened to the mayor?" Hiram Jones had been the mayor of Bliss since the moment the hippies who founded Bliss had realized that they needed someone who could deal with the surrounding cities. He'd heard the stories. Apparently Hiram had been elected because he was the only one who could deal with both the hippies and the ranchers.

Marie, who co-owned the Trading Post with her life partner, Teeny, shook her head. "You could say that."

"Hiram had a heart attack," Zane explained.

The news startled him. Hiram seemed healthy for a ninety-seven-year-old with nearly every ailment known to man. He could be seen walking the streets at least once a day, tipping his hat to everyone he met. "I am sorry to hear about that. I genuinely like Hiram. How is he?"

Polly waved her hand. "He's fine."

"Polly, he's dead," Long-Haired Roger shot back. "Do you have a sensitive bone in your body?"

"Probably not." A single shoulder shrugged up. "Well, I only meant that his body is fine."

"How can his body be fine if he's dead?" Rafe was a little stunned and utterly at a loss for why they were telling him this way. Were they going from house to house?

"We got to him quick enough. We shoved him in Zane's freezer," Polly explained as though she was talking about how she'd cut someone's bangs.

Stella bounced Sierra lightly. "It's fine, Rafe. You know Zane. He has to buy everything completely oversized because he's trying to outdo the rest of us."

"Or I'm just not stingy with the cash and I like to make sure my customers get the best," Zane replied.

Zane and Stella were friendly rivals. They each ran one of the two restaurants in Bliss proper. Stella's was known for having the best breakfast in Southern Colorado and Trio was a cozy tavern that apparently had a man-sized freezer that currently served as the former mayor of Bliss's temporary resting place.

And none of this explained why they had come to talk to him. "If one of you needs a lawyer, you should go and talk to Gemma. She's licensed in Colorado now. She can help you. Do you want me to call her?"

They all looked positively horrified. Long-Haired Roger took off his hat and swiped his hand across his head. "You can't tell Gemma. God, man. That's a horrible idea."

Zane was in complete agreement. "Gemma would lick her chops at the implications. That girl loves to complicate things with silly laws and ordinances."

"Like not putting the town's mayor in a deep freeze? There has to be some sort of code against that," Rafe said.

Well, he'd wanted his mind off his anxieties. He definitely wasn't thinking about his family trouble or finding a job. He was wondering if he was going to have to call Cam in to arrest the members of the Bliss Chamber of Commerce. Had one of them killed the poor mayor? Somehow he couldn't see it. He'd profiled the worst of America's serial killers and while the five people in front of him might be clinically insane, they weren't truly violent.

Well, Long-Haired Roger wasn't. The rest…

Marie rolled her eyes. "Well, if we didn't put him in the deep freeze, he was going to start to smell. Or he would attract animals. I took a vow a long time ago to not allow another animal to take a chunk out of Hi. Oh, we were shit faced from Mel's tonic at the time, but out here a vow means something. Why do you want to let a bear eat Hi? Or a deer?"

"A deer?" He wasn't quite following the conversation, but he found himself utterly fascinated to see what would happen next.

"Oh, are you one of those bleeding hearts who think deer are all like Bambi?" Marie asked, her eyes narrowing in accusation. "Don't you believe it. You haven't stared into those doe eyes and known that if you lay there long enough, a deer will eat you, too. This is the wilderness, Kincaid. This ain't some namby-pamby suburb where neighbors don't watch out for each other. Do you know how embarrassed Hi would be if he was eaten by a deer?"

"More or less than having his body stuffed into a freezer?" Rafe asked.

"It's a really comfortable freezer," Zane explained as though that was a completely sensible thing to say. "So, look, we're kind of flying by the seat of our pants here. It was all a shock when Bambi called Polly up and told her Hi was dead."

Maybe he was dreaming. That would explain it. He'd fallen asleep, and he was having the oddest dream. "So a deer did get Hi."

Zane sent him a look that let Rafe know he was a dumbass for not following along. "No, Bambi is a hooker."

Marie shrugged. "But I think she'd probably eat a person, too."

Polly sent Marie a fierce frown. "For a woman of your persuasion, you are very intolerant of alternative lifestyles, Marie."

"Hooking ain't an alternative lifestyle. It's a way of spreading venereal diseases and body glitter all over the place," Marie shot back.

"Well, Bambi is one of my best customers and you are showing your ignorance. Bambi wouldn't be caught dead in body glitter. You're thinking of the strippers from the club two towns over. No, Bambi is all about her nails. That girl has to hook to pay for her nails." Polly looked down at her own briefly. "So much bling on a couple of little nails. I swear when the lights hit her hands it's like a disco club from the seventies pops up all around her."

"Wait. We have strip clubs?" Long-Haired Roger asked, his brows climbing up his face. "When the heck did that happen?"

"It's a rural strip club. You do not want to go there. You can't unsee that shit." Zane leaned forward.

"Could someone explain what happened?" It was like dealing with a group of toddlers. They all chased the shiny objects.

Zane continued. "So Bambi calls and Hiram's dead and Polly flips out."

"I did not flip out, Zane Hollister." Polly pointed her extremely long fingernail straight at Zane. "I had a perfectly reasonable and rational reaction to the world ending. You know damn well what's going to happen. We've plotted and planned and it all went up in smoke and cheap, knockoff perfume because no one wanted to step up to the plate and Hiram was too stubborn. I swear that man thought he would live forever."

Rafe held a hand up. "Did this particular Bambi—hooker Bambi—murder Hiram?"

Maybe she'd taken off and they needed Rafe to track her. It had been a while, but he could do it.

Stella gasped. "Of course not. Bambi is a pacifist. She would never be violent unless a client paid her to. You know you're sounding intolerant, too. Maybe we should rethink this whole thing."

It was Rafe's turn to sigh. If he didn't watch it, someone would tell Nell he wasn't honoring all peoples' rights and she would chant outside his door. "I stand corrected. Bambi is obviously a sweet woman who loves her nails and peace on earth and gives blow jobs for a living. What did she have to do with Hiram's death?"

Zane tried valiantly not to smile. His lips kept tugging up and then he would force them down. "She was, uhm, working with Hi at the time of his death."

"So the mayor of Bliss had a heart attack while screwing a hooker," Rafe surmised.

Zane finally grinned. "Yeah, I bet it was a good way to go. You should have seen the smile on the old guy's face."

"You can, actually," Long-Haired Roger offered. "We got him to the deep freeze before it was gone."

"He did look good," Polly said.

"That smile made him look like he was eighty-six again," Stella reminisced. "That was a good year for him."

If he didn't get them back on task, he would lose them again. "All right, so you put Hiram in the deep freeze to spare him the scandal of dying in the arms of a hooker."

Polly shook her head. "Oh, he wasn't in her arms. He was in a sex sling."

Zane scratched his head. "Yeah, I don't think he knew how to use that thing."

Rafe's frustration was growing. "Could someone please explain why the hell you're all telling me this? Shouldn't you talk to Nate? Or Caleb. Caleb needs to write out a death certificate and someone should contact Hiram's family."

"We can't tell Caleb because Caleb would want to put down his actual time of death. We can't have that. It's exactly what we're trying to avoid. Oh, and Hiram's family tossed him out long ago," Marie explained. "They lived here before the hippies showed up. There were about five families living here full time back then. Once the hippies formed their commune, two of the families—the Joneses and Penningtons—tried to get them thrown off the land they bought. When it didn't work, they moved. Hi was already in his forties back then, but he hadn't married. He had ten brothers and five sisters and his daddy was a minister. When he found out Hiram was helping the hippies winterize their cabins, he gave Hi a choice. He could go with the family to a more godly place or stay in Colorado and go to Hell. They went to Idaho and Hi stayed here. He never saw them afterward."

So Hiram had given up a lot for this town. "They never called or wrote?"

Stella shook her head. "No, though Hi did try to keep up with them. They rebuffed him. His momma and daddy never talked to him again. And he lost track of all those siblings."

Like Rafe would. His brother lived on the East Coast. They hadn't been close before, but Rafe had enjoyed seeing Miguel at their mother's house for Christmas. Miguel had recently gotten married. How long would it be before his brother had children? Rafe wouldn't know his nieces or nephews and Sierra wouldn't know she had cousins. "So Hiram didn't have a family."

Stella seemed startled. "Of course he did."

"Do you know who named this town?" Long-Haired Roger asked.

"I thought the hippies came up with Bliss." It sounded like a very hippie-type name.

Polly shook her head. "Oh, no. That was Hiram. He named the town Bliss because he always said this was where his happiness was. Hiram had a family. He had us."

Stella had tears in her eyes. "Hiram was everyone's uncle or brother in the beginning. He told me once that he'd fallen in love with one of those hippie girls, but she couldn't love him back. He let his family go because loving her and watching over her was more important to him than a family that would leave him behind over their prejudice."

Zane looked up, obviously interested in that bit of history. "Really? Hiram was in love? Did the girl stay around?"

Long-Haired Roger's mouth hung open. "Hiram never told me, Stella. Wow. That explains how Rye got the deputy position after his mom died and he and Max needed jobs to keep custody of Brooke."

"So Hiram was in love with Max and Rye's mom," Zane surmised.

Stella had a wistful look on her face. "Oh, yes. But he never tried to come between her and her husband. Not that Jimmy turned out great. That man better never walk back into Bliss. No, after Margie died and Jimmy left, the rest of the town took over for them and Hiram organized it all. He's been the beating heart of this town, and I don't know what we'll do without him."

Rafe sat back, moved by the story. He'd only known the man for a brief period of time and he'd seemed larger than life, the way a lot of the citizens of Bliss seemed to be. He'd been a bit of a cartoon character, but any human was deeper than his surface. It was something he'd forgotten along the way. No matter how cheerful or odd a man could seem, there was a well of loss and love beneath the surface, a well that formed a human life.

Hiram had lost one family and found another. Had he truly been happy?

"Well, we have to figure out what we're going to do without him or his entire legacy will be gone." Long-Haired Roger seemed intent on playing up his Chicken Little syndrome.

"Can we not take a minute to mourn?" Stella asked.

"Not much more than a minute," Zane replied. "Because I have a whole shipment of wings coming in Monday morning, and I'm going to have to clean the freezer out."

They all started talking at once, arguing in loud voices.

"Stop it," Rafe said in a low voice. It was the voice he used to use on the most obnoxious of informants.

Though he hadn't raised his voice, they all quieted and long looks passed between the five of them.

Polly finally gave Zane a nod. "All right. I won't fight you on it. You're right about him."

Everyone else sighed and some amount of tension seemed to leave the room.

Zane had a shit-eating grin on his face when he turned back to Rafe. "Just use that tone of voice on everyone and you'll be fine, Mr. Mayor."

Shit. His day had taken a turn for the worse.

Chapter Seven

Aidan, Lexi, and Lucas

Aidan took a long breath and stared out over the Circle G. The noonday air was warm but not hot. Unlike Texas. If he was home, the day would already be hotter than hell. It was beautiful country, so unlike the flat plains of Texas where he'd grown up and spent his life. Mountains surrounded him on every side, rising from the high plains like mammoth guardians, protecting the ranch and house and herd. He wondered what it would look like covered in snow.

He wondered what Lexi would look like in a cute parka, frolicking in the snow with Lucas. They would playfully fight, tossing snowballs at each other. He loved to watch them play like they were kids without a care in the world. He longed for a time when he was enough for both of them.

Lucas was napping. Aidan had left him in their big bed but it had seemed empty without Lexi there. Lucas had taken care of his body. However, now that he was alone again, he was thinking of his girl.

"It's different here, isn't it?" Trev McNamara was suddenly beside him. "Even the air feels different in Colorado. And the sky is so blue. I haven't gotten used to it yet. Sometimes it's hard to believe that my kids are going to be from Colorado and not Texas, you know? I always thought they would be Texans."

God, he'd given Trev hell in the beginning. He hadn't wanted anything to do with the ex-football-star-turned-drug-addict. Trev McNamara had been a friend to strippers and drug dealers until the day he'd turned his whole life around. Trev had managed to do what very few people could. He'd taken his second chance and made something of himself.

Aidan actually had a lot to say to the man who was his brother's partner. "It is different, but there's not a damn thing wrong with it. I love Texas, but I have to admit, it's easy to see why you love it here. The land is gorgeous and the people are…unexpected. I like them. They're a little crazy but a whole lot of honest. And hell, you don't have to deal with the Deer Run city council. Bunch of assholes."

Money-grubbing assholes were what they were, but he'd managed to force their hand. It would teach them to try to grab his land. It still made him angry thinking about what they had tried to do. Thank god he'd kept it from Lexi. He didn't want her worrying about something like that.

Trev smiled as he looked out over the spread he shared with Jamie and Noah. "No, but there are some drawbacks. I find Nell Flanders sometimes trying to talk my cows into forming a union. She thinks all living creatures respond to compassionate political views. I don't think she's ever watched a nature documentary in her life."

It was a weird place, but he might take some weirdness over the nasty politics of his hometown. His family was only accepted because of the money the ranch brought the town. Accepted was the wrong word. They hadn't been run out of town. They were tolerated. He had no idea what he was going to do when his kids were old enough to go to school. He was grateful he'd managed to keep Lexi out of it. "Well, Bo's happy here it seems to me. Trev, I wanted to tell you how glad I am that you took Bo under your wing. He's a damn fine man and a happy one. You and Beth have done spectacular things with him."

Trev shook his head. "Nah, all we did was give him a place to find himself. Everyone needs a place like that. It's what a Dom is supposed to do."

And that was part of Aidan's problem. He wasn't Lexi's safe place anymore. He wasn't sure he even was her Dom anymore. He started out trying to give her what she seemed to need, but what she seemed to need now wasn't him. "What if giving my submissive space means letting her go?"

Trev turned to him, a frown on his face. "I don't think Lexi wants to go anywhere. I damn well know Lucas doesn't want to. That's beyond obvious. I saw the way he looked at you. I don't have any interest in men, but let me tell you I was jealous of you this morning. He looked like he couldn't stand another minute without you. My Beth is too tired to look at me like that these days. I think she would rather cut my dick off than let me use it on her. It was like that in the last half of her pregnancy. She was tired and sick. I'm hoping it changes once Caleb lets her off the leash in a couple of weeks." Trev's harsh words were softened by an amused chuckle. "I'm praying for it because I'm dying."

"Lexi was insatiable when she was pregnant. I guess it's different for different women." It was only a few weeks after she'd given birth to Daphne that she'd moved into complete work mode. When she'd been pregnant, she hadn't shut him out. She'd clung to him and Lucas, allowing them to treat her like a queen. He'd loved that time.

"But she's not now, is she?" Trev asked. "I will admit, I was worried things wouldn't be the same after the baby was born. I hope things settle down. Beth seems happier now. She's been a little more cuddly. Damn, I missed cuddling her."

"You'll find a new normal. We were the same after Jack. A couple of months in and we found our groove again. Maybe it was too soon to have another one. Maybe she needed more time. We didn't exactly plan Daphne. She was a happy accident, but I'm worried Lexi has postpartum depression. I read somewhere it can last a long time. I ordered her to go and talk to Leo, but Leo says she's fine. I think she lied to him. She's really smart and quite good at creating a fictional tale." Fooling Leo had been the first of her many manipulations that had cut him off at every turn. Every time he tried to deal with the problem, she had another excuse. "I've tried to get her to talk to me, but she brushes me off and says nothing is wrong, that she's only trying to get back into the swing of things at work. She took a month off because of Daphne, but apparently the world of a romance novelist is very fast paced. She keeps telling me she'll lose her place if she doesn't keep up."

"Sometimes, we need to be reminded of what our place is," Trev said. "Sometimes that reminder is best served with a nice flogging. I have some stingers if you need one. Brand new. It's a hobby of mine. Drinking coffee and making floggers."

Aidan shook his head. "No. She's still too fragile. This last pregnancy was hard on her. She had a way easier time with Jack."

"And you watched her in childbirth?"

Aidan nodded. "Yes, I was there the whole time, both me and Lucas. Her blood pressure dropped in the middle of labor. She nearly coded. They had to cut her open in her room. They couldn't even wait to get her to the ER."

Trev nodded, his expression grim. "So you nearly lost her and now you're letting her run wild. I understand the impulse, but she's alive, and I have never seen a woman who was asking her Dom to take control more than your wife."

He shook off the mental image of all that blood on the floor. Lexi's blood. And he'd put her there. Oh, Daphne might not be his, technically, but he'd wanted to get Lexi pregnant again. He'd loved watching her get round and soft. "I felt like I should give her whatever she wanted. She almost died."

"I bet it wasn't as close as it felt like. Those doctors don't often lose women anymore. I'm not making light of what happened, but I've damn near died a couple of times and I know what I needed afterward. I needed control. I needed to feel safe. How is Lucas handling it?"

"He's not getting what he needs." Aidan stared out into the distance. How was the world still beautiful when his life felt like it was falling apart? "He's a switch."

Trev whistled. "Damn. He's got no one to top."

"I've tried, but he knows I'm not enjoying it. I feel helpless. I never realized how delicate a balance it is for us. I thought we were solid. I thought we had gotten through the rough stuff."

"Life is full of rough stuff. You should know that. It's why we get married in the first place, so we have someone to get through it all with. It's been really quiet and happy for me and Bo and Beth, but I don't doubt we'll come up against some bad shit. We have a long time to live, and I'm sure our kids are going to give us hell. How we deal with it is going to be the real measure of our marriage. I know we place a lot of emphasis on weddings, but that's not the end of the story. It's just the beginning. The rest might not be as pretty, but that's life."

And he was letting it pass all of them by. "I think Lucas blames me. He won't say it, but he thinks I should have brought her back in line long ago. I thought I was helping her live her dream. I don't know how I would handle it if she told me to stop ranching."

"What would you say if she asked you to cut back?" Trev asked.

He sighed because there was no easy way to answer that question. "I would say that a ranch requires what it requires. You know damn well this isn't a nine-to-five job."

"No, but you have the money to hire extra hands. You could make it a nine-to-five job. With the new baby, we've put up extra money to hire another helper so one of us is always close at hand to in case she needs us."

Aidan shook his head. "I don't have that kind of money. Everything I have is invested in the land. The free money we have is Lexi's money and Lucas's money. It shouldn't go into the…" Fuck. The truth hit him like a bull on the loose. What had he been doing? "I was about to say it shouldn't go into my ranch."

Trev nodded as though he'd figured out the problem long ago. "Yours. Not theirs. You're holding yourself apart. Do you think they can't feel that?"

Aidan groaned, the enormity of what he'd done settling in his gut. "I didn't mean it like that. You have to understand. Lucas came from money. Lexi's stepdads have more money than god. The only thing I brought to the table was that rundown ranch that Jack Barnes had to help me save. I guess I didn't think they would want it. I thought it was my burden to bear."

But Lucas had helped out every weekend. Before he'd moved his office to Deer Run, he would drive home from Dallas and change out of his fancy suit and get down and sweaty doing menial labor with him and the ranch hands. Lucas never complained. He'd sat up long nights helping with calving and rode the fences when the air was so cold he couldn't feel his hands.

And Aidan wouldn't let him put a dime into the place.

Lexi worked hard and was proud of the money she'd brought in, and he forced her to keep it in a separate account because he didn't want her hard work paying for his ranch.

How had that made them feel? Did they think he was trying to keep the ranch from them? As though it was too special to ever share?

"Do you know what Bo did with his money?" Trev asked.

When their dearly beloved asshole father had kicked it, he'd set his sons up in an impossible situation. He'd left Aidan the ranch and Bo the money needed to keep the ranch up. Aidan and Bo had been in a bad place and neither had been willing to help the other. By the time they'd settled their difference, Lucas and Lexi were on the scene and Jack had helped bail him out by bringing the O'Malley Ranch into his small co-op of organic ranches. Bo had kept his inheritance when he left Texas. "No, what did he do with it?"

"Well, first off, he gave some to Beth to fix up that house of hers, the one y'all live in now."

Aidan snorted. "Yeah, well she turned a profit on that one." Lucas had paid through the nose for the big, rambling farmhouse Beth had turned into a beauty of a home.

"Yes, and they brought every cent of it to me and demanded their fair share of our future. I bought into this place for ten million, but almost a million of that was Bo and Beth's money. I know it sounds silly. I had the ten million from my last football contract, but it was important to them that they had a stake and not something I gave them. We put the rest of the money in a safe place and now we live off what we make here and what Beth makes renovating houses. This is something we're building together. You can't take that away from them."

But he had. He'd spent years telling them they didn't matter in that one, deeply important part of his life. He didn't discuss his anxieties about the ranch with them, only telling them that everything was okay and they shouldn't worry. God, he'd gone through hell with the city council and he'd never once said a word to Lexi. He'd only brought Lucas in because Lucas was his lawyer.

He'd shut himself off from their work lives as well. In trying to honor them, he'd shut them out.

When they were safely home, he would sit them both down and fix the situation.

"Things have to change." And that started with him.

Chapter Eight

Rafe

Rafe settled Sierra down in her crib, trying to resist the urge to reach down and brush his hand across that cap of black hair. Maybe if he woke her up again, he could avoid the crazy people in the living room for another hour or so.

After Zane had pronounced those fateful words—Mr. Mayor—Sierra had conveniently pooped and gotten terrifically fussy. Stella had offered to change her but then Polly had said something to Long-Haired Roger about his new sign placement and Long-Haired Roger had started arguing about flashing lips hurting his business, and Stella had been forced to referee.

Because Hi wasn't around to do it anymore.

The whole morning was gone and now they were starting the afternoon and he wasn't any closer to getting his peaceful house back.

He stared down at the tiny baby who was rapidly becoming the center of his whole world.

He couldn't stop thinking about Hiram Jones. How hard had it been to not follow his family? Sure, Hiram had been an adult, but even adults wanted that connection to family. In making the decision to stay in Bliss, he'd given up everything he'd known before.

Had he been lonely? Had he lived all these years in Bliss wondering what his life could have been?

It was different for Rafe. He had Laura and Cam and their baby. He wasn't alone. He had a family already in place.

He needed to find *his* place. What if his place was back in Miami?

"They are awfully cute when they're sleeping," Zane said quietly. The big tavern owner leaned against the doorframe, his normally hard face soft as he looked at the baby. "I never thought that watching a baby sleep could be so peaceful."

Rafe glanced back down at his daughter in her pink blanket sleeper, her tiny belly rising and falling as her mouth sucked on some dream pacifier or bottle. "Being a parent is the most important job in the world."

He would never turn his back on her. Never. No matter what she did. Even when she was forty, she would still need to know her father was around.

Zane nodded. "Yes. I know that more than most. My father walked when I was ten and my mom was more interested in partying than raising a kid. My childhood was somewhat unstable. It's weird to think about it, but Nate Wright was the only constant in my life before I came to this town."

Zane and Nate had come to town after their jobs in the Drug Enforcement Agency went bad. Nate had become the sheriff of Bliss and Zane opened Trio. "Do you miss your old job?"

Sometimes Rafe missed the FBI. He missed the adrenaline of the chase, the mystery of the puzzles. He missed feeling important.

Zane's mouth curled up in a smirk. "Do I miss getting my ass shot at, pretending to be a drug runner, and being tortured when the people I'm investigating find out I'm not a drug runner? No."

Yes, well, their jobs had been very different. Zane had been undercover and Rafe had profiled in the Behavioral Analysis Unit. Though a couple of times he had gotten his ass shot at.

"You do miss your old job," Zane surmised.

Rafe sighed. It was more than that. "I miss having a job at all."

"Well, that's good because I'm offering you a new one, one that will definitely keep you busy."

Rafe shook his head, gesturing for Zane to move into the hall. He closed the door to Sierra's room after making sure the baby monitor light was working. "I'm still not quite sure how you can offer me any job at all."

"It's called a coup." Zane's massive body took up most of the space. "This is a good old-fashioned political coup. It's also what's best for this town and very likely what's best for you. You're drifting."

He didn't like the sound of that. Even if it was kind of true. "I'm looking for a job."

"And yet you're still here in this cabin all day long. Hey, I know about what happened with the feds. Sorry about that, man." His green eyes became grave. "If you want to work in government again, you're going to have to lie about your living arrangement. Unless you work in Bliss. I wish it wasn't true, but the outside world isn't going to accept Cam. Have you talked about keeping him a secret from work?"

Cam Briggs was his best friend and the best man Rafe had ever known. "I won't say I haven't thought about it. What am I supposed to do? Pretend Cam is some lazy friend who lives in the guest bedroom? How would I ever explain that to Sierra?"

Cam had been the one to give up putting his name on the adoption papers. Sierra was legally Rafe and Laura's. Cam trusted him. He couldn't betray his best friend like that.

And he also couldn't stay in the cabin for the rest of his life. But shouldn't the mayor be voted into office?

"I suspect that would cause trouble down the line if you decide to work outside of Bliss. Of course, you could make a difference right here in the town where your daughter will grow up." Zane was doing a reasonable impersonation of Mephistopheles. That was exactly what Rafe needed, his own personal deal with the devil.

"Explain this coup attempt to me." In the background he could hear Maric arguing with Polly.

Before Zane could say a word, Laura was walking into the short hallway. The space was starting to get cramped.

"What's going on? Why is there a town hall meeting in our living room?" Laura asked, concern in her eyes.

"Because we're trying to avoid a town hall meeting in the town hall," Zane explained.

"Hiram died." He wasn't going to keep that from his wife.

"Damn it, Kincaid." Zane slapped at the wall. "We're going to have to work on your discretion."

Laura's eyes filled with tears, her whole face softening. "Oh, I suppose that wasn't unexpected given his age. It's so sad. When is the funeral?"

"Whenever they decide to take him out of Zane's freezer."

Those tear-filled eyes went wide. "What?"

"Our friends are here because they stuffed Hiram into Zane's freezer in an attempt to take power." It was a very Blissian-style coup. No real violence, just a pacifist hooker and a freeze-dried mayor.

Laura turned on Zane, her body on full alert. "You need to explain what is going on right now, Zane Hollister, or I swear I am going to tell Callie and she is going to be upset with you."

Zane did not look impressed with Laura's temper. "Who do you think suggested the freezer at Trio? Callie's smart. She was totally in on this. And don't try to call Nate. He's backing me on this. He knows what could happen."

Laura shook her head and walked back into the living room, talking as she went. Rafe and Zane had no choice but to follow. "I can't believe this. You should all be ashamed of yourselves."

"You told her?" Long-Haired Roger asked. "Maybe we should rethink this. Rafe is not as sneaky as Zane said he was."

Rafe was a little offended. He could be sneaky when he wanted to be. He shut his mouth. It actually worked on his behalf if no one thought he was sneaky. "I don't lie to my wife."

Of course he hadn't told her about the Miami offer either.

"Stella, how could you?" Laura looked at the café owner. "Hiram was one of your best friends."

Stella stared her down. "And I'm trying to save his legacy."

Marie stepped up. "Will you think about this for two seconds, Laura? What happens if Hiram dies without a deputy mayor in place?"

"We do what every other town in this country does. We have a special election." Laura crossed her arms over her chest, a sure sign that she was irritated.

"Yep," Zane said as he sat back down on the couch. "We have a special election. How's Nell going to handle that?"

Laura sighed. "Well, she would probably run. She would think of it as her civic duty." Nell was one of Laura's closest friends, but even Rafe could see she was disturbed by the idea. "Obviously she wouldn't win."

No one in their right mind wanted Nell with real political power. She would force the citizenry to switch to eco-friendly cars. She would turn city hall into an animal refuge. Rafe tried to imagine Zane Hollister stuffing his massive body into a Prius.

"You would think that," Stella said. "But I'm not so sure. We've run several scenarios and you would be surprised at what happens. I had the Farley brothers make a computer simulation of the most likely outcome. You see, I happen to know that Stef is planning on bringing in his own candidate."

"See, Stef will pick someone good. He loves this town. He'll find the right candidate and then Nell won't stand a chance," Laura pointed out.

"Oh, but you're not thinking about the fact that Bliss has two kings now and they are battling it out." Polly shook her head with a rueful sigh. "Ever since Seth Stark came home, he's been trying to prove he's every bit as generous as Stef. Poor Gene. Stef gave him a loan to upgrade his projectors at the drive-in and then Seth turned right around and paid for new screens. And then Stef brought in new popcorn poppers and a brand-new audio system and then Seth had to pay for someone to teach Gene how to use all that stuff. He was crying, I tell you. Caught between two billionaires. It's horrible."

There were a lot of women Rafe knew who wouldn't think it was horrible, but he was starting to see the issue. "You're afraid they'll compete to put in their own mayors."

Marie shook her head. "I'm not afraid. I know it will happen. I offered to shoot them both, but Stella had a problem with it."

"I'm not going to let you shoot my son." Stella had taken to calling Stef her son ever since she'd married Sebastian Talbot. She would shrug and say she only meant that he was her stepson, but Rafe knew the truth. Stella had raised Stef.

There were odd families all over Bliss.

"I wasn't going to kill him," Marie shot back. "But I was going to make sure he was laid up. He and Seth could share a recovery room and maybe they would learn to play nice."

"No one is shooting Stef and Seth." It was time someone laid down the law. If he allowed them to go on, they would argue in circles for hours. "And Seth is spending most of his time in New York right now. Stef has a baby on the way. They don't have time to dabble in small-town politics."

Stella coughed and mumbled under her breath.

"What did you say?" Polly asked, her eyes narrowing.

Stella cleared her throat. "I said Stef already has a plan."

Marie pointed an accusatory finger Stella's way. "I knew it. And if Stef is involved, Seth won't be far behind."

"What kind of plan does Stef have? Hey, you don't think he sent Bambi to Hi, do you?" Long-Haired Roger asked.

"He certainly did not." Stella sent the mechanic a stern look. "Stef loved Hiram, but he's been waiting for him to step down and he definitely planned on installing someone who would be friendly to Stef's machinations. He hired a political consultant and he's got it between two candidates, neither of whom actually lives in Bliss right now. He's planning on moving them in."

Rafe felt a frown cover his face. He actually didn't like the sound of that plan. "Why on earth would Stef bring someone from the outside in?"

"Because he doesn't think anyone in town could do the job except himself, and he doesn't have time for that," Stella explained.

Really? Stef didn't think a man who had been educated at an Ivy League school could handle small-town politics? "If I decide to be the mayor, I assure you I can handle the job."

Laura looked back, obviously startled. "You?"

Did anyone think he could do it? "Probably not, but it's been discussed, though apparently not by Stef and Seth. So Stef intends to bring in a candidate and you believe Seth would follow by bringing in his own candidate."

Zane groaned. "Oh, he will absolutely follow. Do you honestly believe he won't? They would go all out. They would try to beat each other. We would be in for weeks and weeks of those political calls. You think you like the local radio station that plays classic rock? Well, forget about it because all we'll hear are ads for the two parties, and you know what happens at the end of all of it?"

Laura gasped at the implications. "Oh my god. Everyone gets sick of the city folks and votes for Nell. Nell will be the mayor of Bliss."

Zane gave her a thumbs-up. "Like we said—it's the apocalypse."

Laura turned to him. "Rafe, you have to save us. Please tell me you have a plan."

Yes, he had a plan. Moving was looking better and better.

How to Play Two Billionaires Off Each Other Via Email...

Rachel Harper
Re: upcoming winter festival
To: Georgia Stark-Warner; Jennifer Talbot

Hey, ladies. It's that time of year again. You know when it gets cold as shit and we all wish we were in Florida. The winter festival is coming up and I really don't want to do another bake sale because Nell is pregnant and she'll probably get hurt when I don't want to eat her vegan version of brownies. Save me.

Georgia Stark-Warner
Re: upcoming winter festival
To: Rachel Harper; Jennifer Talbot

Oh, Nell is so sweet and I'm excited she's having a little one. Jen and I just talked. Worry no more!

Georgia Stark-Warner
Re: Winter Festival
To: Seth Stark

Hey, baby. I just talked to Rachel and she's so excited about the Winter Festival! You promised you would take me and I can't wait to spend the holiday season with you and Logan. It's going to be such fun. It's sad though that the carnival rides are so out of date, but I'm sure it will be fun. Rachel said something about Stef changing things up this year. Can't wait to see what he does. It's so nice to have someone looking out for the town. See you tonight!

Jennifer Talbot
Re: He's at it again!
To: Stef Talbot

I just talked to Rachel and Seth is pushing to upgrade the carnival rides. Isn't that fun? I know you love the old ones, but sometimes we can't stop the march of progress. I guess little Logan will have a whole new experience.

Seth Stark
Re: don't change a thing
To: Rachel Harper

Stef wants to change the carnival rides? We've had those carnival rides since we were kids. If they're worn down, we need to fix them or find viable alternatives. I'm writing you a check for ten thousand. Let me know if you need more. Do not let Stef "fix" something that doesn't need to be fixed.

Stefan Talbot
RE: winter fest
To: Rachel Harper

I understand that it's tempting to walk into a town and change things. Especially when you're from New York City where everything changes all the time. But this is Bliss and we have traditions. If the carnival rides need fixing, I will handle it, but we're not letting Seth freaking Stark come in and force some monstrosity of a ride on us. If you let him we'll be overtaken by neon lights and the whole festival will be sponsored by a corporation. No. Over my dead body. I'm transferring ten k into the festival fund. Tell me if you need more.

Rachel Harper
Re: budget surplus
To: Callie Hollister-Wright; Hope Glen-Bennett; Beth McNamara-O'Malley

Ladies, let's have some fun....

Chapter Nine

Stef and Jen

Jen stepped out onto the balcony and looked down at the gorgeously decorated party space below. The morning had flown by and now the afternoon was here and the party had begun. She'd done pretty well if she did say so herself. The backyard was elegantly decorated. The manicured lawn was filled with beautifully dressed people eating the best food and drinking the best wine she could afford. The mountains in the distance lent the scene a gauzy, soft feel, like the world was one big well-painted landscape.

All the men were on the mountain at their party. She wondered if Stef was smiling and having a good time.

"Everything is beautiful," Shelley McNamara soon-to-be Meyer said as she looked around the balcony. The bride-to-be was wearing a pretty summer dress that set off her dark hair. She had been out on the lawn talking to the guests who had come to her small Bliss pre-wedding reception. She looked even prettier up close.

Jen felt like a watermelon around the radiant bride. Shelley McNamara had a lovely sense of style. With her raven black hair and stylish dress, she was rapidly making Jen feel like a big old cow.

"Thanks. I love throwing parties," Jen murmured. She wished she could have a sip of wine, of tequila, of anything.

"Well, this is one I'll remember for a long time. I wanted to say thank you." Shelley waved to someone on the lawn. "I'm going to go downstairs. I see my friends. Thank you again."

She hurried along, her heels clacking against the floor. Jen couldn't wear heels right now. She couldn't fit into that svelte, sleek dress Shelley was wearing.

"I know that look. I've had that look on my face many times." Rachel shook her head as she glanced over the crowd. "I hate her."

Jen had to smile. Rachel was always ready to lend a hand. There was no one in the world more loyal than her friend Rachel. It had been a blessing to find her. "No, you don't."

"Yes, I do. I hate whoever you hate."

Callie walked up, a margarita in her hand. "Who do we hate?"

They were her girls. Callie and Rach always had her back. Her dour mood began to lift and she couldn't help but tease her friend. "Honey, we hate you because you're the only one of us who can booze it up. I hired two bartenders for this pre-wedding reception and all I can ask for is a Shirley Temple."

Callie put her drink down. "Well, I'm the only one who's not pregnant. And I'm not going to be for a while. I'm taking a break from gestating. There are four men living in my house. Can you imagine the mess when my babies get to be teenagers? My whole cabin is going to smell like feet. I totally need the tequila."

Rachel was pregnant again, but she was barely showing. And she had to beat her husbands off her even when she was round as a beach ball. A few weeks before, Rachel and Max had gotten locked in a closet at the art gallery where they were sneaking away for some fun in the afternoon.

Stef wouldn't touch her now. How did she talk to her friends about it when they seemed to never have problems tempting their husbands? Max and Rye were all over Rachel, and Nate and Zane liked to bring the babies over to the estate so they could spend some time in the guesthouse. Callie liked to talk about how sore she was.

Jen was perfectly unsore except for her back and her feet, and that was the baby's fault. She wanted some aches and pains that went along with remembered pleasure.

Stef rubbed her feet and her lower back and then he would turn out the lights because "she needed her rest." She needed her husband, but it seemed like her husband didn't need her.

"What's going on, hon?" Rachel asked. "You look sad."

Suddenly she knew she couldn't share this. It was stupid. She should be able to share anything with her friends. They loved her and she loved them, and she couldn't tell them that her husband didn't want her anymore. She still had some small amount of pride. What the hell was she going to do?

"I'm just tired," Jen said, staring out over the lawn. Everyone seemed to be having a wonderful time. They were all relaxing. She was a ball of anxiety when she wasn't perfectly content. She swung from excitement about her son's impending arrival to a deep worry that Stef wasn't happy.

"Well, you should be." Callie patted her back. "You're breathing for two, eating for two, living for two."

"Don't be hard on yourself," Rachel said. "It's your first baby. You need to eat like there's no tomorrow and sleep like you never will sleep again, because you won't. I don't care if Stef stays up with the baby, you'll still get up because he's your boy."

Her baby might be her only boy now. She'd gone through a thousand scenarios—from Stef telling her he'd been joking all along, to their inevitable divorce where she ended up raising a baby over Stella's in that tiny one-bedroom apartment she'd first lived in when she'd come to Bliss.

"It's all going to be better in a few months," Callie offered. "The first couple are hard, but you'll see it gets back to normal. Or you find a new normal. Stef will settle down."

They all looked out over the lawn. In the distance, a single Jeep was flying down the drive.

"Oh, no. I think I see Cassidy coming up the drive." Rachel's eyes narrowed as she looked out over the estate's long road. "I thought she was going into the bunker. She put it out over the radio earlier today."

Callie took a long swallow of her margarita. "I heard she and Shelley are struggling about the whole alien queen thing. Shelley won't eat beets. Something about the color of them apparently sets her off."

"Or it could be that beets taste like ass," Rachel murmured.

Jen wrinkled her nose. "I can't blame her for that. Do you know how they can stain your teeth? Nell gave me a beet smoothie and I had purple teeth for days."

It was supposed to lower blood pressure, but hers had only risen at the idea of purple teeth.

Rachel crossed her arms over her chest. "I don't think Cassidy is going to care that Shelley doesn't like the taste. She genuinely believes that beets stave off the alien invasion. It looks like she's pushing her point home. We should go and head that off."

Rachel and Callie practically ran back down the stairs.

And Jen was left alone again. Why hadn't she talked to them? They would talk to her. Callie reached out when she was struggling. And Rachel yelled for a while. Either one of them would listen to her and help her find a solution. So why did she feel so damn alone?

"Can I get you anything?" a masculine voice asked.

She turned and tried to place a name with the startlingly handsome face. She'd never met him but she'd seen those emerald-green eyes on another face. "You're Jack's brother."

The man smiled. "Lucas O'Malley. Jack and I are half brothers. If I hadn't married Lexi and Aidan, I would have changed my name to Barnes. I'm afraid I'm not close to my father. Especially since he went to prison."

"I'm sorry," Jen said.

A satisfied smile crossed Lucas's face. "I'm not. It was the best gift he could have given me. I framed his mug shot. So, is there anything I can help with? I came with my wife, but she's taking a phone call. I was going to kiss her good-bye and go and wait for my partner, but she's busy."

That was said with a hint of bitterness. Not all was right in the O'Malley household, but, then, everyone had their problems. Lucas looked out over the lawn where a black-haired woman was pacing as she spoke into her phone. Jen hadn't met the woman. She hadn't come to any of the gatherings before now. "Is everything all right?"

Lucas didn't take his eyes off his wife. "Oh, I've been told everything is nearly perfect, at least as far as my wife's career goes."

Lexi O'Malley was a writer. From what Jen had heard, she was becoming very popular. A couple of women in Bliss read her works religiously—including Jen. Lexi was very prolific. She wrote books that combined BDSM and romance in a way Jen completely understood. "She works a lot, huh? I'm married to an artist. I know how they can get. It's hard to get them to notice you're alive when they're focused on the work."

Jen was an artist, too, but somehow she never got lost the way Stef did. She could always pull herself away. It might have been different if she hadn't married another artist, but she had and she needed to be the grounded one. It never bothered her when Stef was focusing on his work. She'd always known he would return to her, but now she wondered.

Lucas stared out at the woman pacing on Jen's lawn, a hollow look on his face. "Yes, I suppose so." He turned around and his face cleared. He was right back to being charming and handsome, without a hint of worry in the world. "I'm a big fan of your husband's work."

Jen gave him a smile. "And I have to admit, I've read all your wife's books. So we're both married to successful artists. Why do I have the feeling neither of us is very happy with them right now?"

Somehow what she couldn't admit to her friends was easy to say to Lucas.

"I'm not good at hiding it anymore." Lucas sighed. "I used to be quite good at hiding my dissatisfaction. Maybe because it didn't mean as much."

"I was always terrible at hiding anything at all. I think I might have been born without the patience to prevaricate." It had gotten her in trouble on many occasions. "I'm afraid I can be a bit of a brat."

Jack Barnes was firmly in the lifestyle. Lexi wrote lifestyle romance novels. It only made sense that Lucas was in the lifestyle, though she couldn't figure out if he was a Dom or a sub. He didn't seem to fit either title completely.

"A little brattiness never hurt anyone. Sometimes it's the only way to get what you need." His handsome face grew contemplative. "The question is what to do when the brat loses interest."

A deep sympathy welled. She knew that feeling except it was her Dom who seemed to be losing interest. "It's funny. I thought once I'd gotten that man to collar me and put a ring on my finger that the rest of it would be a breeze."

"You too, huh? It must be something about the whole wedding thing. Watching someone else starting a life makes you think about the state of your own marriage. It makes me think about a lot of things. I watched my parents be utterly miserable for most of their lives. Oh, my father wasn't unhappy. Marriage made it easier for him to cheat. My father wouldn't have been truly happy without someone to cheat on."

Jen knew the feeling. "My mother kind of rambled through life. She wasn't a bad mom. She just never settled down. We lived all over the place."

"When the going got tough, she got going, huh?"

God, she didn't want that life for this baby. She wouldn't have it. She would do what she needed to do in order to make sure her baby had a stable home and family. And that meant Stef couldn't pull away every time he got scared. Babies were scary. Kids were even scarier. Kids didn't necessarily follow the plans their parents set out for them. Stef couldn't always be in control. It was easier for Jen. She'd accepted that control wasn't an option a long time ago. "Yeah, I don't know that she honestly knew who my dad was. She always said he was a military man, but she never gave me a name. The father's name on my birth certificate is mysteriously missing."

She wasn't sure why she was being so open with Lucas O'Malley, but he seemed easy to talk to and they seemed to have many of the same problems. All around them people were happily talking and toasting the bride and she and Lucas were the only two who were standing apart. And she was the hostess.

Though Nell seemed to be doing a fine job. Her friends picked up the slack. While Rachel and Callie dealt with the chaos that tended to follow Cassidy around, Nell and Holly were making sure the guests all had what they needed. Holly was walking around the lawn talking to all the guests. She was wearing killer heels and a smile that went on for days. Nell was dealing with the caterers. God, she hoped Nell wasn't convincing them to change her crab dip for tofu, but it was wonderful and it left her with a whole lot of time to think. And she thought way too much.

It felt good to talk.

"I know where you're coming from. Not that I didn't know who my dad was, but the rambling part." Lucas seemed to relax as though he was happy to have someone to talk to as well. "I spent a lot of time in various boarding schools. I was very good at getting kicked out of them. It was all an attempt to get my parents' attention. It didn't work. They had a list of schools. I got sent on to the next one. I didn't stop trying, though. I finally did something shitty enough to get someone to notice me."

"Who?" She was curious. His story wasn't far from her own. She'd acted out trying to get Stef to notice her.

A smile curved his mouth up. "Jack. I tried to blackmail Jack. He threatened to kill me and bury my remains all over the ranch and I very nearly crapped my pants."

She shook her head, laughing at the thought. Lucas O'Malley was a brave man. "I can't imagine anyone threatening Jack. I have to admit, Stef can be intimidating, but Julian and Jack are a one-two punch."

"Oh, I threatened Julian, too," Lucas admitted, his eyes soft with the memory. "Julian didn't do anything so gauche as tell me how he was going to kill me. He would have simply had me brutally murdered by a well-paid contract killer so he wouldn't have to get his suit dirty. Lucky for me, Jack likes a challenge."

"He took you in?"

"Oh, yes. It was the first time my bad behavior got me the attention I wanted and it was pretty much the last time I behaved poorly. Jack's been more like a father than a brother to me, though he's not that much older. I learned everything I know about life and love and making a home from Jack Barnes. I married his stepdaughter." His eyes had gone wistful. "She's trying to make everyone proud. This was her dream, you know. Jack or Julian could have made it easy for her, but she wanted to do it the hard way. She wanted to earn it."

"I can understand that. I paint, too. I'm not as ambitious as Stef, though. I do it for myself. I don't care if the world knows I can paint. But Stef does. He won't admit it, but art critics get to him. I can imagine it's the same for reviewers with your wife."

"Oh, Aidan ordered her to stop reading them a long time ago. She can have ten great reviews and one bad review, and guess which one she remembers? No, I want her to have her career, though I wish she would take a breath every now and then." The longing was right there in his eyes as he watched his wife.

"Do you ever feel like she doesn't see you anymore?" It was how she felt about Stef.

"That's a good way of putting it." Lucas's face settled into a grim mask. "And I spent most of my life trying to get someone to see me. I guess I never thought she would stop looking."

"Lucas?" A tall, ruggedly handsome man with dark blond hair stood in the doorway, a concerned look on his face.

Lucas's expression cleared and the sexiest smile crossed his face. "Hello, Master."

God, she needed to visit Texas more often. All of the threesomes here were about the girl. Texans seemed to be more open in their sharing practices. Despite the fact that she loved her husband, she couldn't say that the idea of two hot guys going at it didn't do a little something-something for her libido.

Lucas's Master joined him, putting a familiar hand on his partner's shoulder. "Do I even need to ask where our sub is?"

Switch. That answered her question. Aidan O'Malley was the Master and Lucas was the switch and Lexi was the well-topped sub.

"She's busy. But it's fine. Everything is fine. Aidan, please meet our hostess, Jennifer Talbot. She's married to…"

"Stefan Talbot," Aidan finished, offering a hand.

Jen shook it. "That's my man. Are you staying out at the G?"

"Yes, my brother is Bo O'Malley, Beth and Trev's partner," Aidan explained. "They're hosting us. We're ranch people so we're certainly used to being around cows. It's nice to meet you. Thank you for throwing this party for Shelley. We've been more than pleased with the hospitality. But now we have to go to the men's reception. It's at someplace called Mountain and Valley. The invitation said it was clothing optional. That was a joke, right?"

Oh, what she wouldn't do to be a fly on that particular wall. The men were having their pre-wedding party at the naturist community. "Nope. It's a nudist resort. Expect to see a whole lot of man parts. Didn't Mel organize it?"

Aidan nodded. "Yeah, uhm, is he a comedian or something? Because the invitation said no aliens allowed."

"Oh, he's serious about the aliens," Jen replied. "Don't even joke about them. Apparently he gets probed on a regular basis, and some of them aren't very gentle, if you know what I mean."

Aidan stared at her like he was trying to figure out if she was teasing him. Jen kept her face perfectly serious. Doms were fun to fuck with.

Aidan shook his head and turned to Lucas. "All right, then. Let's get going."

He said good-bye and stepped out.

Lucas bit back a laugh. "Doms are fun to tease, aren't they?"

Jen smiled. Lucas would be a great friend if he lived in Bliss. "I couldn't help it. Though Mel really won't take well to pro-alien talk. Just say you're against them and you'll be fine. And don't drink the tonic. It's rotgut whiskey. Mel makes it himself. It's been known to get a man shitfaced in three sips."

Lucas sighed. "Thank god. Something's going right today. I could use some shitfacedness." He reached out a hand gallantly. "It was lovely to meet you, Jennifer. And if your husband isn't paying attention to you, perhaps it's time to turn the tables on him. If he won't listen, make sure he has no choice except to. It's certainly what he would do to you if he's half the Dom I've heard he is."

Lucas walked away as his words sank in.

Oh, she'd been thinking about talking to the wrong friends. All her friends would do was hold her hand and curse Stef's name.

But Stef's friends…they were another story altogether. They could be complete bastards, and that might be what she needed.

After one quick phone call to Rye Harper, she knew she'd made her play. One way or another she and Stef would have it out today.

She took a deep breath, calming her nerves, and looked out across the lawn. Lucas and Aidan were walking toward the drive. Lucas tried to get his wife's attention, but she gave him a dismissive wave of her hand. Even from her place on the balcony, she could see the way Lucas's shoulders slumped and anger flushed on Aidan's face.

Lexi put her phone to her chest and said something to them. She took a few steps toward them and then looked back down at her phone.

Lucas walked away. Aidan said something and followed him.

Lexi brushed away tears, but she answered the phone anyway.

Lucas might have solved her problem. Perhaps it was time she helped him. She caught a glimpse of metal as the light shone in the right place to illuminate the party crashers who were hiding in her bushes, no doubt listening in on all kinds of interesting conversations with one of

Sirens in Bliss

their ingenious and slightly evil inventions.

Yes, a hint of devious genius was called for and the Farley brothers were always up to the task.

She marched right across the lawn, and sure enough, there they were. They were hidden in her barberry bushes. Bobby and Will were hunkered down, a computer in one's lap. They were perfect twins, and Jen didn't even try to tell them apart. They talked quietly, but they had a friend who didn't know how to be quiet.

"If you want to know what people are saying, why don't you ask them?" Olivia Barnes-Fleetwood asked.

The one Jen thought of as Bobby hushed her. "Keep your voice down, kid. This is a secret mission. And adults never tell you the truth. When you ask what's wrong, they always say nothing and it's always a lie."

"I'm not a kid," Olivia shot back. "I'm eight. That's practically a teenager and being a teenager is practically being an adult. I'll be nine in four months so I can't be a kid."

Oh, dear. She knew that tone of voice. It was the tone of voice she'd used all through her childhood when she'd had a crush on someone and was trying to get his attention. Hell, she'd used that sassy voice on Stef back before she'd gotten him to give in.

"Yeah, well, uhm, shouldn't you be out at the party? Isn't your mom looking for you?" Will asked in a soft tone. "We're kind of working here. We're getting paid to record conversations that may or may not reveal the presence of aliens."

Poor Shelley. Jen wondered briefly what Cassidy was paying the boys, but they likely would have eavesdropped for free. It was kind of their hobby. They were the only kids their age for miles around. She was so happy her baby would have Paige and Charlie and Zander.

"I know all about aliens. I saw one once. It was at our ranch and it took a couple of our cows," Olivia proclaimed.

Whatever Cassidy was paying them, Jen would pay more, and she had a new job for the twins.

"All right, playtime's over, boys." She got a genuine thrill when the boys nearly jumped out of their skin. She was going to love motherhood.

Bobby scrambled out, laptop in hand. "Sorry, Ms. Jen. Uhm, we didn't know there was a party going on. We were working on a new science experiment."

"In my barberries, Bobby?"

Olivia wormed her way out. She looked like her momma, with auburn hair and green eyes. She was going to be gorgeous one day. "He's Will."

Will shrugged. "She can actually tell us apart. It's kind of weird."

Olivia shook her head. "It's not hard. They're very different. And they were performing an experiment about leaves for school. Do you want to make them flunk their science class? That's awfully mean of you. I was helping them."

Olivia would make a great accessory some day. It was a bold play that would have worked on a lesser woman. Jen had to give the kid credit.

Bobby crawled out. "She's not going to buy it. She was probably listening. Look, Ms. Jen, if we didn't do it, Cassidy was going to call the NSA, and we've already been in trouble with them over our very innocent hacking of their web site."

Will grinned. "He bet me I couldn't do it."

"I was totally wrong," Bobby admitted. "He did it really fast, and it made some people mad. And now our parents are ticked because we're apparently on some sort of watch list. When we tried to go to Tampa to see mom's sister, we all got patted down and questioned. I think that was what Mel meant by probing except it wasn't an ET. It was a hairy dude from the TSA."

Will shook his head. "Dad didn't like his probing."

Bobby shuddered. "Yeah, I could avoid it for the rest of my life. I'll stay here in Bliss. So we were kind of hoping to keep the whole town off the radar by helping Cassidy out. Here's the good news—unless aliens are really into shoes, I think Leo and Wolf's girl is okay. I heard aliens actually struggle with their arches. She's wearing crazy heels, so I think she's a regular human girl."

"With nice cans," Will said with a grin.

God, they'd finally discovered girls. Olivia took a moment to thrust her completely flat chest out. It was good to know the younger generation was already well on their way to being a soap opera all on their own.

"Stop looking at my guests' cans and put your thinking caps on. I have a mission for you." Lexi was Olivia's sister. Maybe she shouldn't talk about her plans in front of her.

Olivia shook her head, and while it was easy to see she got her smile from her biological dad, Sam Fleetwood, it seemed she'd inherited Jack Barnes's stubborn will via osmosis. "I am sorry, Ms. Jen. They're going to work for me. I'm going to pay them my allowance to get them to cut off my sister's cell phone. I tried to steal it, but she keeps it too close. Whatever job you have for them will have to wait because my sister is going to ruin her life and I have to save her."

Jen smiled and held out a hand to the kid. She hoped her son was as devious as this girl. "Oh, Miss Olivia, we're going to get along just fine."

* * * *

Stef looked around the lawn and sighed. He wondered what Jen was doing. The women's reception and the men's gathering were scheduled for the same time in the day, but he hoped Jen was having more fun than he was.

This was supposed to be a fun day. He didn't have any problem with the fact that everyone was naked. He preferred it. It wasn't like he enjoyed watching a bunch of dudes walk around with their junk hanging out, but he actually didn't have a problem with nudity. It felt nice. He'd started coming to Mountain and Valley when he was eighteen. He and Max and Rye had met a woman who lived there and been introduced to the nudist lifestyle.

He looked across the lawn and found the man who had introduced him to the BDSM lifestyle.

Julian Lodge wasn't naked. He was wearing his customary three-piece suit and his hair was slicked back, not a strand out of place. At his side was a man with dark hair and a ready smile. He was naked, and every now and then Julian would stare down at him, pointing out the differences between Julian's threesome and the ones Stef was surrounded by. Julian was interested in Finn Taylor's nudity while the Bliss partners sort of completely avoided looking at each other's junk.

At least Julian was honest.

And he'd been through what Stef was going through.

He found himself crossing the space between them without thinking it through. Julian had been his mentor. Stef had been going to The Club in Dallas from the time he'd been eligible to have a membership. Julian had taken him under his wing. He'd spent long hours discussing the philosophies and realities of D/s. Maybe it would be good to be around Julian when his whole damn life seemed out of control.

Julian held out a hand. "Stefan, it's good to see you. I find it interesting that I'm staying at your house and you seem to manage to avoid all of us."

Or maybe not. Julian was damn good at making him feel like a five-year-old who had fucked up. He shook the outstretched hand. "Sorry. I'm working on a project right now. It's taking up a lot of my time."

Julian's head shook slightly. "Yes, I'm sure you're always working on a project. Finn, love, would you mind grabbing me a cocktail while I talk to Stefan?"

Finn grinned up at his Dom. "Of course, Master. Would you like a beer or the stuff from the still?"

Julian shuddered lightly. "Are those my only choices?"

It might be fun to watch Julian attend a Mel-sponsored event. "The tonic is something Mel makes himself. It keeps away the aliens."

"Yes, your people seem to be very distracted by aliens. I noticed that when I walked in and was frisked for alien technology. They seemed disturbed that I wouldn't disrobe. I don't disrobe unless I want to. You understand that, correct? I will not be talked out of my clothing because some insane person wants to make sure I don't have extra parts."

Dear god, he needed to get Julian together with Mel. "I think you'll find Mel won't care as long as you pass his tests."

"I already swallowed a beet tablet. I took it because I can use the vitamins. This place is strange, and I'm not sure I like it."

"Because you can't control it." Julian was used to being in control.

Finn was grinning as he looked up at his Dom. "I'm enjoying our vacation, Master."

Julian's lips tugged up in an intimate smile. "I'm sure you are, Finn. Don't get used to it. We'll be back in Dallas soon, and I'll be in control again."

The dark-haired man sighed, and there was no way to not notice how his cock twitched. But then, Finn was used to being naked at The Club. "I look forward to it. I'll find you a beer. Preferably something imported. Be back soon."

"And put on more sunscreen, pet!" Julian watched as Finn walked away. "He burns fairly easily, but I couldn't convince him to not join the locals."

"Convince? I didn't think you convinced your submissives of anything. I thought you simply told them what to do."

Julian snorted lightly. Somehow he turned it into an elegant sound. "I thought you had been around long enough to know that complete control never works. I suppose it might for some, but I must confess I would find that perfectly dull. It was exactly what was wrong with my life before I met my Danielle and my Finn. I preferred to maintain perfect control because I didn't love anyone enough to be bothered with their pesky human flaws. That's not entirely true. I maintained a few friendships that didn't always go my way."

"Jack Barnes?"

"Yes," Julian admitted. "I was rather upset when he left The Club and took Samuel with him. I liked having them around. And Leo was always obnoxious, but I found his company oddly soothing. Now I am laid back. I have to be or I would kill Chase on a regular basis. Though I do think about it. I can't now. My security firm swears they can't replace him, and he has a wife. For some reason, Natalie loves him."

Stef wouldn't exactly call Julian laid back, though he was certainly calmer than he used to be. "I heard you had a hand in that."

"I don't know what you're talking about."

From what Stef understood, Julian also had a hand in the wedding that was taking place tomorrow afternoon, but apparently he didn't want to admit to playing matchmaker. And an admission of meddling wasn't what Stef was looking for anyway. "So how's fatherhood treating you?"

"Ah, I wondered when you would go there." A smug satisfaction took over Julian's expression. "What happened with Jennifer?"

Damn. Julian never liked to play all the polite games that might have spared Stef the embarrassment of admitting he had no fucking clue what he was doing. "We had a scare a couple of months back. She was bleeding."

Spotting is what Caleb had called it, but it was bleeding in Stef's head. Sometimes he had nightmares that she bled and he couldn't stop it.

Julian nodded as though he'd expected something like that. "It's a terrifying position to be in, I'm sure. Pregnancy is not something any Dom is going to handle well because of the absolute loss of control. It would be easier if we were the ones to deal with the pain that comes with it. Watching our submissives struggle is difficult when we can do nothing to ease them. Danielle had morning sickness in the beginning. Terrible nausea. It was hard for me to watch her go through that. I couldn't control the situation. She would be so sick and I couldn't help her. I definitely remember that feeling. I do not like being helpless."

Jennifer had been pretty healthy through her pregnancy, but the one time she hadn't been still haunted him. "I'm afraid of what's going to happen in the delivery room. I won't be in control of anything."

He couldn't stand the thought. Other people would control her fate, make decisions about her care.

"No, you won't. It's hard, but that is your submissive's burden to bear, unfortunately. Danielle wouldn't scream. She didn't want to scare me. She tried to pretend it didn't hurt, that she could take the pain. She fought me on the epidural and then she begged me for one. I was happy to drug her up. I rather thought about taking one myself. I swear, that was the longest day of my life. And then I saw my Chloe and I fell in love. But it was weeks before I felt settled again."

Stef stared up at the perfect sky. There wasn't a cloud marring the glorious blue. "Then why do we do it? God, I've been asking myself what I was thinking. Our life was good. Why are we messing it all up?"

Julian chuckled. "Because I believe our submissives would insist on it. I will admit, I wasn't excited at the prospect of change. There was a part of me that wondered if I would even be capable as a father, but this is something that no one can prepare you for. There is no book you can read or friend you can talk to that will make you ready for the moment when they place a seven-pound bundle of humanity in your arms and tell you to take care of it. If you think you feel out of control now, wait until that happens."

"It's going to change everything." He wasn't ready for it.

Julian put a hand on his shoulder. "Yes. Your son will change everything and there will be days when you wonder why you didn't simply remain the same. But I've discovered something. My life would have been incomplete without Chloe. And when the time comes, and I know it will, I will grit my teeth and go through it all again."

Stef looked at Julian. "Are you kidding me? You would give up control again?"

"Life is about more than control. If you try to tell my wife I said that I will deny it, and I am an excellent liar. The best things that ever happened to me happened when I gave in to what life offered me. You can cocoon yourself and pray that nothing bad happens. You can mitigate the risks. You can hold on with both hands, and things will still go wrong. And then you'll never learn the true joy of having a child."

"And what's that? Because I'm not seeing it."

A sympathetic look crossed Julian's face. "Like I said, I can tell you, but you won't understand now. The real joy of having children is seeing the world through their eyes. I've done almost everything deviant a human being can do, but I feel clean when I look in my daughter's eyes. The world is fresh again."

Stef couldn't see it. Julian was right about that. "I still don't think it's worth risking my wife's life over."

"But she does. You'll find your wife becomes a tiger when it comes to her child. If I'd had things my way, Danielle would never have discovered that piece of herself. Finn wouldn't have had this experience. I wouldn't have grown. We would have gone through our days, but for us, something would have been missing. Jennifer could die on you in a hundred different ways. Are you willing to give up everything you could have with her today because you're frightened that it could be gone tomorrow?"

Stef took a long breath. Was that what he was doing?

"It's funny," Julian continued. "I think about my parents a lot these days. They died when I was very young. I wonder if they regretted that much of their married life was spent taking care of me rather than enjoying each other. I wonder if they were happy to go together."

Stef knew far too much about his parents' bad marriage. "And what did you decide?"

A peaceful smile lit Julian's lips. "Oh, I know that they would have fought to stay with me. My parents loved each other, but they would have wanted one of them to stay with me. They would have sacrificed if the opportunity had been there. I'm a grown man, and yet something settled inside me when I realized that. Our childhood can seem far away, but it is always bubbling under the surface."

His father had left. He'd thought he was doing the right thing. And Stef wouldn't have left Bliss, but now he wondered if he was simply waiting for something bad to happen. He was happy. He loved his wife. Why was he waiting for the other shoe to drop?

"Master? I managed to find some Scotch." Finn had a softness to his eyes that made Stef wonder how much he'd overheard. "And I also found some sunscreen."

Julian took the drink. "Excellent. I'll help you with the sunscreen. We'll be back in a bit. And Stefan, you should talk to your wife. We Doms forget that our subs can hold our hands, too."

Julian stepped away with his sub, a hand on Finn's shoulder.

He was restless, anxious. He hated the feeling. And now he had to wonder if he was being fair to Jennifer. She was carrying his child and he was pulling away from her. Oh, sure he took care of her, but was he giving her what she truly needed? He wasn't in the moment with her. He hadn't been able to take joy in feeling the baby kick. He certainly hadn't enjoyed these last few months with her.

She'd asked him in a hundred different ways to make love to her, but he was afraid.

Was he going to be this weak every time something went wrong?

"Talbot! You son of a bitch!"

Stef looked up and Max Harper was stalking across the lawn, his shoulders set in an angry line. Rye was walking beside him, his face every bit as stern.

What the fuck had he done now? Max hadn't thrown down with him in almost a year. And Rye never joined in their fights. Rye always talked about how stupid they were.

His hands squeezed into nice fists. Yeah, it had been a long time since he'd had a little exercise. Maybe thrashing Max would clear his head. Pounding him into the ground would feel damn good.

"Don't you think for a second that you being nekkid is going to stop me! I ain't afraid of your junk." Max was in his normal boots and jeans. It put him at an advantage.

"I am afraid of your junk," Rye declared. "No one warned me there would be man junk swinging in my face. There is only so much I'm willing to do for a friend."

Stef ignored Rye. Max was the dangerous one. "What is your

problem, you freak?"

"You know exactly what my problem is!"

Max had been one of Stef's closest friends for over twenty years, and for as long as he could remember, they had beaten the crap out of each other every so often. Though most people believed it was due to Max's insanity, Stef knew the truth. He'd needed it for a long time. He'd been so shut off that he'd required the twice a year throw downs with Max as a release valve.

But he wasn't like that anymore. He was an adult with a baby on the way. He couldn't fist fight his best friend. He forced himself to relax. "Max, come on, man. We're not going to do this here. I am not going to fight you while I'm naked."

Max was a mean shit. God only knew what he would do. Stef wouldn't put it past Max to use his junk against him.

Max stopped in the middle of everything. He frowned as though that was the last thing he'd expected to hear. "But you've been itching for a fight."

He had. He'd actually kind of been baiting Max for a month. It was stupid and childish, but he relied on those damn fights.

And he had to stop because he was going to be a dad. Max already was a dad. Like it or not, understand it or not, his world was changing and he had to change with it. And that meant no more throw downs with Max Harper.

Who should really be more of a damn grown-up. His second kid was on the way.

"We're not twelve anymore."

Max's eyes rolled. "Obviously."

"We have to start acting like responsible adults at some point in time."

"Says the man who's standing around nekkid."

Stef gritted his teeth and forced himself to respond. "It's a naturists' resort, asshole. Now tell me what imaginary shit you've come up with this time. And you, Rye? What the hell did I do to you?"

Rye and Max exchanged a long glance, the anger in Max deflating at once.

"I thought you had a reason," Max said.

Rye shook his head. "No, I thought you did."

Max threw up his hands. "Rye, you're the brains of this operation. I'm the pretty one. I was supposed to beat the shit out of Stef and you were supposed to come up with a good reason why. What are you here for anyway? What are we going to do now? Jen is going to be pissed."

"Jen?" What the hell did his wife have to do with any of this? His wife usually rolled her eyes when he fought with Max.

"Max, you dumbass." Rye whistled, a high sound he usually used on horses, but it wasn't a horse who showed up this time.

Caleb Burke and Alexei Markov showed up. Caleb was carrying his tranquilizer gun.

Stef took a step back. "Caleb, now you put that shit away. You are only supposed to use that when Mel goes insane."

Caleb sighed. "I switched to the low dose. Don't be a baby."

Had he stepped into a bad dream? "What the fuck is wrong with you? I swear to god if you shoot me with that thing, I'm going to sue your ass."

Caleb's eyes rolled. "No, you won't. That's the great thing about being the only doctor for forty miles. 'Night-night, Stef."

And the son of a bitch shot him. The tranq dart went right into his upper thigh, and Stef went down, his backside hitting the grass. Fuck. His head was already swimming.

Max's face stared at him. "It's going to be okay, buddy. And actually, I want to thank you for being naked. It makes things so much easier. Alexei, get his legs. And watch out for his junk. I think the client is interested in it."

Caleb stepped up. "Hey, as your doctor and your wife's doctor, I'm totally giving you permission to have sex when you wake up. Go for it, man. Jen's perfectly healthy. Hell, she's ready to pop. A little sex might get the process started."

He hated Caleb. Why had he ever thought bringing a doctor into town was a good idea?

As his peripheral vision started to fade, he realized something.

Responsible adult or not, he was going to kick Max's ass. He might kick all their asses. Some things could never, ever change.

Olivia's Note

To: Bobby & Will

Do you like Olivia Barnes-Fleetwood?

☐ Yes
☐ No

This note did not come from Olivia. Please give this note back to Josh Barnes-Fleetwood. He's the little one.

Chapter Ten

Leo, Shelley, and Wolf

Shelley McNamara looked down at her watch. All around her the bridal shower was moving forward, but all she could think about was the fact that in roughly twenty-four hours she wouldn't be Shelley McNamara anymore. She would be Shelley Meyer, and she intended to die as Shelley Meyer. She'd been married once before to a complete douche lord, but this time was different. This time she was madly in love.

However, the course of true love didn't always run smoothly. Sometimes it was blown wildly off course by a crazy person with a deep love of beets.

Cassidy Meyer was a sweet woman in her sixties. She'd welcomed Shelley with open arms and then she'd used one of those arms to try to shove a beet down her throat.

"Oh, no." Beth was staring across the lawn. "I don't know exactly what's happening with my brother-in-law and his subs, but it's not good."

Shelley looked over in time to see Lexi O'Malley wiping tears away as she talked on the phone and Lucas and Aidan walked away. They were likely heading out to the men's gathering, which looked to be much weirder than the gorgeous garden party Jennifer Talbot was throwing her.

Shelley watched Lucas and Aidan walk away with a heavy heart. She'd known Aidan for a long time, and Lucas and Lexi for several years. She'd watched as they had stood together even when the town they lived in disapproved of their lifestyle. They'd been so close.

The way she was close to Leo and Wolf.

"She's working too much," Beth said with a frown. "But she's convinced if she slows down she'll kill her career."

"It's hard to give up momentum." Shelley should know. "If Lexi's business is anything like mine, then the more work you get out there, the better your profits are. The design business is almost entirely word of mouth. The more clients I have, the more they multiply. You work for years and then realize that there's just more work ahead of you. And it has to be worse for Lexi."

"How?" Beth asked.

"Have you forgotten how precarious ranching is? I would be shocked if they've turned a profit yet. I know Lucas makes good money, but it's nothing compared to Lexi. Think about it. Lucas gets paid a salary. He knows what he'll make any given year. Lexi's income is only limited by how many books she sells. It's a siren song. The more books she sells, the more opportunity for her family. She can give Aidan's ranch a real shot. She can subsidize it until it's profitable. I grew up on a ranch. There were years when my momma had no idea if we would have a place to live the next spring."

Beth winced. "I don't think he's letting her put money into the ranch."

That couldn't be easy for any of them. "Then he's letting his pride get in the way. That ranch is Lexi's home, too. She's got to be scared because a ranch can go belly up any time."

"It's not so bad," Beth said with a sigh.

Shelley shook her head. "Oh, don't try to equate your experience. The Circle G was making a comeback when Trev bought in. Aidan's ranch was broke because Bo got all the money." Aidan and Bo's father was a bastard. He'd given Aidan the land, but no money to keep it up, and Bo all the money and no land to invest in. And they had been too stubborn to see the obvious solution. It had worked out for the best because Bo had found Beth and Trev and moved to the Circle G, while Aidan was happier on his own.

But how much stress had it caused Lexi? She had two kids.

Beth took a sip of her lemonade. "I guess I didn't think of it that way. There are always two sides. I can't stand the thought of them being unhappy."

Shelley hated it, too. "Does the whole Dom thing change when you have kids?"

Beth looked thoughtful. "A little, I guess. Why?"

"Because if I was working too much, Leo would put me over his lap before I could breathe." And that was pretty much how she liked it.

She was too ambitious in some ways. She found it hard to turn down jobs even when she knew she couldn't handle them. Leo had made it easy. She could do three jobs at once and if she took a fourth, she better be damn ready to give up a layer of skin. It had made it easy to find her balance.

Beth's nose wrinkled sweetly. "Well, I guess it's different. Kids complicate everything. It's easy to follow your Dom's orders when it's just you, but when they place this baby in your hands, suddenly you're not thinking about yourself. You have a whole different set of priorities, and don't let anyone tell you that you can prepare for that. No childcare class is going to train you on how to handle it. You can feel the baby kick and know that you love her, and it doesn't prep you for the utter realization that this baby is wholly dependent on you. You've brought a life into the world and you're responsible, and no amount of a submissive nature can make you give up that responsibility. I love Trev, but I'm the alpha when it comes to that baby girl. I'm her momma. So yes, it changes. I can't sit back and let Trev make the decisions, and neither can Bo. We have to decide together, and sometimes Trev has to give in. I expect it will get worse as she gets older, as we have another one eventually."

The idea scared the crap out of Shelley. "I don't know that Leo wants kids. Maybe he's right. Maybe we should concentrate on our marriage."

"You should at first, but I think he'll change his mind. What does Wolf want?" Beth asked.

Of her two men, Wolf was the sweet one. "He would have me

pregnant now."

"And you three have talked about it? It doesn't seem right going into a marriage where two of you might not ever want kids."

"I didn't say that." Shelley got an antsy feeling in the pit of her stomach. "I think I do. But then I look at how they change things and I wonder if we wouldn't be happier without them."

"Wolf Meyer picks up every kid he sees," Beth pointed out. "I only asked because I knew the answer. Wolf won't be complete without kids. And a lot of men don't know they want kids until someone puts a baby in their arms and they look at that sweet face."

"You think we're not being fair to Wolf?" She hated the idea. Hated it in a nauseating way.

And could she really go without babies? It seemed like she was surrounded by them all of a sudden. Olivia and Josh. Chloe. Here in Bliss it was multiplied by ten. There was her new niece, and the parade of kids that came through the G seemed to never end.

Could she live a lifetime without holding her own baby in her arms? Without seeing a little one who looked like Wolf or Leo? But Leo seemed indifferent to the idea. She also couldn't stand the thought that Leo wouldn't want the baby. It was perverse.

The wedding she'd been crazy about minutes before now seemed too close for comfort.

What if they were making a mistake? Aidan and Lexi and Lucas had seemed happy, and now they were miserable. What if love couldn't work out in the long term? What if people were too different to make it work?

"You're freaking out," Beth said, taking her hand.

She was. "My first marriage was horrible."

"But Leo and Wolf didn't blackmail you into this. Neither one of them is using you as a front for their drug dealing and information brokering business."

It had been a really shitty marriage.

"What if I make all the wrong decisions?" It was a thought that had crossed her mind more than once before. "I obviously don't have good instincts."

Beth squeezed her hand. "You don't make bad decisions. You got caught in Bryce's trap. Leo and Wolf are about as far from Bryce as you can possibly get, so put that thought out of your head. Now, the kids thing is something you need to work out."

But there wasn't much time left. She was getting married in roughly twenty-four hours, and she wasn't supposed to see Leo or Wolf until she walked down the aisle. It was a stupid ritual, but she'd insisted because at the time it seemed romantic. Now it simply seemed silly.

Maybe she shouldn't worry about it. Maybe it would all work out in the end.

That was exactly what she'd thought the day she'd allowed herself to be pulled into Bryce's world. She'd stood there at the courthouse and convinced herself that everything would be fine. It hadn't been fine.

Lexi was staring off into the distance, her eyes still watching where her husbands had walked away from her. It wasn't fine for Lexi.

What made her think it would be fine this time around?

"Oh, Alien Queen!"

Shelley turned. Normally she wouldn't think that a crazy voice screaming for an alien queen would be referring to her, but here in Colorado she knew damn well it was all about her. "Hello, Cassidy."

Two women she'd met previously were with her almost mother-in-law. Rachel Harper and Callie Hollister-Wright were standing on either side of Cassidy Meyer, who wore a string of beets around her neck. Yep. She might need to rethink that whole "everything's going to be fine" thing.

"I'm sorry," Callie said apologetically. "We tried to talk her out of it."

"But she's stronger than she looks," Rachel added.

Cassidy stared at her. "Please don't take my boys away, Alien Queen. Take me instead."

Shelley felt a headache start and realized that if she had any real shot at making her marriage happen, she needed to start by compromising. "Somebody get me some beets so I can prove my humanness."

Cassidy's eyes went wide. "You'll take the beet?"

Apparently there was some form of ritual. "Sure. I'll take the beet and then someone needs to hand me some whitening toothpaste because I'll be damned if I get married with purple teeth."

Cassidy smiled and showed that she didn't mind the color purple. From what she'd heard, the older woman had been bingeing on beet smoothies in an attempt to ward off aliens who would come to the wedding. "Excellent. We'll do it tonight at Trio."

"You can't just hand me a beet from your necklace and let me have a bite?" It would make things simpler.

Cassidy was all grins now, as though the weight of the world had been taken from her shoulders, and Shelley felt a hint of guilt. She'd been stubborn. "No. We have to have a whole ceremony. Your Beeting Ceremony is going to be even more beautiful than the wedding. Do you know how long I've waited for a daughter?"

Probably longer than Shelley had waited for a mother-in-law who thought she might have tentacles hidden away somewhere. But a thought occurred to her. "Do the boys have to be at the ceremony?"

"Absolutely. They play a very big part."

And then she could talk to them face-to-face. And maybe the feeling of dread would pass if she could see them.

"I have to get cooking. We need beet pie and beet stew and, oh, so many wonderful dishes. Rachel and Callie, find Nell and have her meet me at my place." Cassidy gave Shelley a sheepish grin. "She was going to protest you, I'm afraid. I'll call it off and we'll get to cooking."

Cassidy practically skipped back down the drive.

Callie pressed a margarita into Shelley's hand. "You're probably going to need this. And just so you know, all your drinks are free tonight at Trio. My husband runs the place."

Shelley took a long swallow. "Thanks. That's awfully sweet of you."

Callie turned a nice shade of green. "I've eaten the beet pie. You're going to need it."

Yep. It sounded like she would.

* * * *

Wolf looked around the well-manicured lawn of the Mountain and Valley Naturist Community and wondered, briefly, why the hell he'd ever left Bliss. Oh, he was happy he had because he would never have met Shelley, but there were times when he missed this place.

"Why the hell is everyone naked, brother?"

Yeah, this was totally one of those times. Leo's eyes were as wide as saucers as he stared at what Mel thought a reception should be. There was a cooler of beer, and it looked like he'd bought a bunch of cold cuts and put them on a tray.

Shelley was at the Talbot mansion, likely sipping champagne and eating a spectacularly catered meal, and they got cold cuts Mel had picked up at the Stop 'n' Shop and a sea of naked dudes.

"He forgot the bread," Chase Dawson said, walking up to them. He was in the altogether and it didn't look like he minded. "But there's something called tonic and Ben is already shit-faced. He only had one drink. I promised Nat I would be the designated driver, thank god. I think it might have affected Ben's brain. If one of us is going to be brain damaged, it should be the himbo."

Chase was eating what looked to be a rolled-up slice of ham. Ben walked up beside him, a loopy grin on his face.

"Hey, we're all naked. And there are pork rinds. I thought they would be disgusting, but after a couple of drinks, they're really good. Salty. It's nice."

Yep, Ben had gotten into the tonic. Mel made it himself. He was surprised more people hadn't gone blind from it, but Mel's tonic was a sort of rite of passage in Bliss.

Wolf was going to settle for a beer. He kind of thought his bride would be pissed if he had to have his stomach pumped before he walked down the aisle.

"This place is completely bat-shit crazy." Leo was looking around like there was some magical exit he could go through. "I spent the afternoon talking to Max Harper, and I swear he would be my next project except for one small problem. He's completely happy. He's a lunatic who's managed to find a way to get married and have a kid. It was disturbing. And then he got a phone call and he said something about a kidnapping. I'm worried he's actually going to hurt someone. Should I call the police?"

"Harper? The one with the twin?" Chase asked.

Ben huffed. "They're weird. They finish each other's sentences and stuff. It's annoying. Hey, are you going into the weird teepee thingee? I crawled into it, but it was hot."

Leo shook his head. "No. We're not going in there." He turned to Wolf, a desperate look on his face. "Tell me he didn't."

"Yep, I think he set up a sweat lodge for us. What did you expect, man? Did you expect Mel to hire a couple of strippers? He wouldn't. Apparently stripping as a profession is high on the alien preference list. Nope. We're stuck with naked Mel and an ancient Native American tradition."

"Huh. That's funny." Ben started laughing. Wolf had no idea what he was laughing at. Ben kept up his giggles as he started to stumble off toward the volleyball court saying something about finding a beach.

"I'll make sure he doesn't kill himself," Chase said with a smile. "I'll also probably take a couple of videos. I like trashed Ben. He's fun."

He followed his brother.

"Why didn't we go to Vegas?" Leo asked.

"Because Shelley wanted a big wedding and this is the only time Ma is ever going to get to watch her sons get married. Because we make sacrifices for family and that is a very good lesson to learn right before our wedding day."

Leo's shoulders slumped. "Where do I change?"

He was totally missing the point. "Into what, brother?"

"Fine. Where do I leave my clothes?"

"Oh, they're free and easy up on the mountain. Anywhere you like. I think there are some lockers in the gym. Dude, you do not want to use those facilities without a towel, I'm telling you."

Leo turned, a worried look on his face. "We need to talk."

Thank god. Wolf had been worried Leo wouldn't talk about it. "About the fact that dear old dad's been calling?"

Leo's eyes closed briefly. "Has he called you, too?"

Wolf shook his head. "No. You left your computer on. I used it to book our movie tickets a couple of weeks back. So what does the fucker want?"

Their father had left long before Wolf was capable of truly remembering him. He'd been a toddler when their father had walked out. As far as he could tell, the man hadn't actually divorced their ma. He'd simply disappeared one day.

"What do you think he wants?" Leo asked, his tone sarcastic.

"A renewed and loving bond with his sons?" Yeah, he could be sarcastic, too.

"Money."

That was pretty much what he'd expected. "How does he expect to get it?"

"Blackmail, naturally."

That didn't make sense. "What's he got on us?"

"Nothing on us. He's threatening to call Ma."

Fuck. A whole lot of their mother's history was wrapped up in her firm belief that their father never actually existed and that both he and Leo were the result of her alien abductions and the aliens' love of the deep probe. "How do you think she would handle seeing him?"

Leo's brow creased in obvious worry. "Look, Ma is great, but I worry in this case."

"Because all the shit with that man is what broke her in the first place?" He didn't want to call the man "dad."

"I think Ma has some carefully constructed walls that allow her to be happy, and I would hate to see them fracture," Leo explained.

"So where is the bastard?" He could take care of this small problem. There were numerous places to hide bodies in Southern Colorado. And he hadn't killed anyone lately. It had been a long dry spell.

"So you can murder him and hide the body?" Leo asked, proving his brother knew him pretty damn well.

"It's a solution to the problem." A nasty thought struck. "You didn't already give him money, did you?"

Leo snorted. "Of course not. I'm not going to either. I threatened the fuck out of him if he didn't leave. Harper actually helped with that. The man is inventive when it comes to threats. And he's not skittish about threatening another dude's junk."

Wolf could believe that of Max. "But that man is not going away. He needs something, and he figured out we can give it to him. Why the fuck now?"

"I suspect he looked us up, or he's been keeping tabs on us."

He'd never imagined this would be a problem. "How much did he ask for?"

"We didn't get that far." Leo ran a hand through his hair. "Has Ma ever talked to you about what happened?"

Wolf huffed. "Oh, many times. I've heard far more than I want to about probing. Apparently I came out jumbo sized because she got a double shot of Reticulan Gray DNA. Why do I have to be from the creepy looking grays?"

Leo's eyes rolled. "I was talking about what really happened."

"Oh, no. All I got out of her was probings."

"All right." Leo turned away. "I thought he would look like us. We don't look a lot like Ma. I guess I always thought if I ever met the bastard, that he would look something like me. But he was short and looks like he was probably a blond before he went gray."

Wolf was happy he didn't look anything like the fucker. He was also happy he didn't look anything like the Reticulan Grays. "You know there's one person she might have talked to."

Leo's shoulders slumped. "Damn it. We're going to have to go into the sweat lodge, aren't we? Is there any way Mel's fully clothed?"

"No way in hell." They couldn't possibly be that lucky.

Leo shuddered and began making his way toward the main building. His brother wasn't as comfortable with walking around in the altogether as he was. Wolf glanced around. Julian was fully dressed, but Finn was playing naked horseshoes with a very comfy-with-himself Sam Fleetwood.

Wolf felt his eyes widen as he watched Max and Rye carrying a passed-out Stef Talbot across the lawn. "Hey, did he have too much tonic? Should we call Caleb? Because I'm worried that it could actually make a person blind."

Caleb walked out from behind the trees, a rifle resting against his shoulder. "He's fine. Pissed off, but fine. But hey, he's going to wake up as Jen's sex slave, so it will all work out in the end. It's a damn fine day, Meyer. Damn fine."

"He's going to kill us," Rye was complaining.

"Probably," Max agreed. He smiled at Wolf. "Hey, Wolf. Your brother is cool. He's writing a book about me."

"Dumbass," Rye shot back. "His brother is a psychologist. He's writing a book about how fucked up you are."

Max's grin widened. "Yeah, and I'm the hero."

Rye groaned. "Move it. He's heavy. Hey, where are we going to stuff him? Paige's car seat is in the back. I don't think I like the idea of a naked dude riding on Paige's car seat."

"No way, brother," Max said. "No naked dudes get to touch our baby girl. We can dump him in the flatbed. Do you think anyone's got some rope so we can tie him down? Oh, and we should totally take some pictures."

Rye brightened. "I think someone in this group can help us out with some rope."

Max and Rye carried Stef away.

Stef was totally going to kill them.

"This place is fucked up, man. I think that dude got sniped." Chase was suddenly standing beside him, watching as Stef Talbot's limp body got carried away.

Chase was always worried about snipers. He was sure they were everywhere. Wolf needed to let him know the possibility was small. "I think it was tranq darts. Caleb likes to shoot people, but he doesn't actually kill them."

"A sniping is a sniping, brother." Chase had his quirks. He also had his extreme talents.

And one of them was finding out any information a man could possibly need. "Hey, could you do a quick job for me?"

Chase perked up. "Sure. Ben passed out in the volleyball pit. I made sure he could breathe and shit, but I am not reapplying his sunscreen. His ass is going to be bright red for that wedding tomorrow. I'll be surprised if he can sit in the pew. Nat is going to be pissed."

Wolf was going to have to drag Ben's naked ass into the shade. Why had someone thought this was a good idea? "I need you to find out everything you can on Robert Meyer."

Chase's eyebrow quirked up. "Your dad? I already have a file. McKay-Taggart worked one up a couple of years back. I update it twice a year."

There was only one reason Chase would already have a file on Robert Meyer. "Julian. Of course."

"Of course. Julian doesn't do the whole 'wait until people trust me enough' thing. He finds shit out and holds the info until such time as he needs it. Are you sure you want to find that asshole?"

"No. I don't." Wolf sighed. "The trouble is he seems to have found us."

Chapter Eleven

Aidan, Lexi, and Lucas

All around her Shelley's bridal shower continued, everyone looking politely away as though they hadn't witnessed the tense scene that had played out in front of them. They pretended they hadn't watched as her marriage took a nose dive. God, she wished she could take the last few minutes back.

Lexi was utterly miserable as she stared at the place where Lucas and Aidan had tried to get her attention. She'd been in the middle of listening to the details of a deal that would potentially turn her novels into audiobooks and it had been hard to hear her agent. The cell reception wasn't the greatest out here.

Of course it was probably perfect compared to the reception that would be waiting for her when she got back to the ranch. She glanced around and everyone was going on with their lives. There were women all over the beautifully decorated lawn sipping champagne and margaritas and talking with friends.

When was the last time she'd simply sat down and talked about anything but business? When she got together with Jessica, they talked about upcoming conventions. She had made friends in Dallas with some writers and she loved to talk to them, but they inevitably spent their long phone conversations helping each other with plots and problems with their characters.

She used to talk to Lucas about things like that, but somewhere along the way she'd lost touch even though he was only in the next room.

And now she was a jealous hag because she'd watched Lucas talking to their host, and for a minute, his whole face had lit up and he'd been her Lucas again, smiling and charming and witty, and that smile had not been for her.

Her heart had tightened, and she'd been ready to march straight up to Lucas and ask him what the hell he was doing smiling at another woman when his wife was standing not a hundred feet away.

And she'd forced herself to stop because she didn't have that right anymore. She sure as hell didn't have the right to complain about Lucas's lack of attention when she didn't have a minute to spare for either of her husbands.

Why couldn't they understand? Aidan had shot her a look of pure anger when she'd shooed him off. Contracts were important. She had to make as much money as she could. If things went poorly, they would need every dime to fight to save the ranch. That land had been in Aidan's family for a hundred years. She couldn't let them lose it. It was her children's legacy.

She glanced down at her phone. She had to be resolute. Her men weren't thinking in the long term, and if they didn't, then she had to.

"Don't you dial another number, baby girl!"

Shit. Her mother was marching across the yard, a stubborn look on her face. She was dressed beautifully in a designer suit, but she was carrying her heels in her hands as she stalked toward Lexi.

This was why she'd been more than happy to find out they were staying with Trev and not Stef Talbot. The whole Dallas gang was at the Talbot estate where none of them could lecture her on how her career was ruining everything.

God, when had talking to her mother become a chore? When had she started avoiding anyone who had an opinion? She hadn't been to the ranch in Willow Fork in almost a year. She got annoyed when her parents descended because they were a drain on time she should spend working.

Guilt settled into her gut.

"Alexis Ann, you have been avoiding me and I want to know why."

"I haven't been avoiding you, Momma. I've been working." The words sounded weak even to her own ears.

A single brow rose over her mother's green eyes. "You're always working. Did you talk to Lucas before he left?"

She wished her mom hadn't seen that. "I was on the phone. I waved."

Her mother stared at her, judgement plain in her expression. "Do you understand what you're doing to him?"

She did not want to have this conversation. "To Lucas? Momma, I'm not trying to hurt Lucas. He knows I have to deal with problems as they come up. And I need to call my agent back. Those contracts won't wait forever."

Her mom threw her hands up. "If you're talking to your agent, he should be on that call with you. Does Lucas look at your contracts? Why are you dealing with this? Lucas is your lawyer."

"I'm not going to bother him with something I could do myself. Lucas has enough to deal with." She looked down at her phone. No bars. What was happening? Despite the fact that they were in the mountains, she hadn't lost coverage once. "Hey, do you have a signal?"

"Lexi, I am talking to you."

Lexi didn't look up. "I know, Momma, but this is important. My cell phone isn't working."

A long sigh came from her mother's voice. "Well, thank the good lord. Maybe you'll get your head out of your ass long enough to understand that you are treating Lucas like he is meaningless and it's going to kill him."

She was startled by the words. "Lucas? Meaningless? That's insane. I love Lucas."

A pause came between them. "Then why are you treating him the same way his father did?"

The truth hit her like a baseball bat to the head. Lucas's father had treated him horribly by shoving him to the side in favor of his other children. And she could see where Lucas might feel the same way now. She'd marginalized him even as she was trying to build a better world for them all. She'd shut them out. She'd tried to take it all on without any help from anyone.

Because it was what she'd watched her mother do. Her mother had worked her ass off, but she'd had to. Her mother hadn't had a Lucas or Aidan. Her mother had been on her own and not by choice.

"I'm trying to live up to you."

Her mom shook her head in confusion. "What are you talking about?"

She felt light in the head, the revelation having an actual physical effect on her body. "All my life I looked up to you because you took care of things. You didn't complain. You didn't whine. You did what had to be done. You made sure everyone had what they needed."

Her mother's eyes went soft. "Oh, honey. Everyone was you and me, and I didn't have a choice. Trust me, if your father had lived, I would have leaned on him. Adam took damn good care of me before he died. Your stepdad cared for me. I might have still gotten a job, but I certainly wouldn't have expected to take care of you alone."

"Lucas and Aidan have their own concerns. They have to take care of the ranch. You know how ranching is. It's precarious. It could all go under with one bad winter." Or with one bad choice.

Her mother shook her head. "No, it can't because Jack's made sure of it. Why do you think he brought Aidan and Trev and James Glen in as partners? They share the reward and they share the risks. If one has a bad year, the others help out. No one is going under. Honey, why are you worried about this? Lucas makes good money."

"He doesn't make enough to cover us if we go under. Or if someone tries to get rid of us." The minute the words were out of her mouth, she wanted to take them back. She'd kept the secret inside for so long that it felt odd to say the words.

Her mom's eyes widened. "Who is trying to get rid of you?"

The question wasn't asked with a breathy curiosity, but rather an undercurrent of potential violence. Her mother wasn't exactly the world's most docile human being. She fought for the ones she loved. She sheltered them, and she'd taught Lexi to do the same.

The way she was trying to shelter her husbands from the truth.

Lexi shook her head. It would do no good to involve her mother. "It's nothing. It's just some stupid shit. You know how the town can be."

Her mother was still considered a woman of ill repute in Willow Fork, though everyone was too afraid of Jack to say it to her face. Deer Run was another version of Willow Fork.

Would they go through with it? Would they really take away her husbands' home because they didn't approve of her lifestyle? God, she couldn't be the reason Aidan lost his ranch.

The only thing that would make them safe was money and a whole lot of it. If they had the money to buy off the damn city council, then no one would come after O'Malley Ranch.

She looked back down at her phone. Why didn't she have any damn bars? She had a book coming out in two weeks and everything depended on it. The city council would take their vote in a month, and she needed time to get her fucking bribes together so Aidan might never know how close they came.

"You need to start talking now, baby girl." Her mother was a dog with a bone. This was why she'd avoided her, why she'd avoided her dads. Jack and Sam had become her fathers over the years, and she didn't even try to call them stepdads anymore. DNA didn't matter. Only love did.

"Mom, it's nothing. I'm more worried about my cell phone not working. Can I see yours?"

Her mom pulled her cell phone out of her pocket and looked down. "I have three bars."

"Can I borrow it?"

Her mom frowned her way. "No."

Olivia ran up. She was wearing her version of her Sunday best, a pair of clean jeans and a T-shirt without stains on it. "Hey, Momma. Hey, sis."

Lexi's heart swelled. Her baby sister was a ball of chaos, and Lexi loved her so much it hurt. And she hadn't seen Olivia since she'd started avoiding her mom. God, how much was she going to give up to try to save the ranch? "Hey, Liv. How are you doing?"

Liv's face turned up. "I'm good, but I need to find a dress. I think I should start wearing dresses, and I want to take a bunch more science classes."

Her mom's eyes widened. "You hate science."

Olivia shrugged. "No. It's kind of fun."

"Oh, god, who's the boy?" Lexi asked. No tomboy ever hung up her jeans for anything other than a boy. She wanted to meet the boy who could handle Olivia Barnes-Fleetwood.

Olivia frowned. "There's no boy. Ewwww. I was only talking to Will and Bobby."

The names were said with the casual tone of a girl who didn't care. Which meant she cared. A lot. Her baby sister was interested in boys. It was the best thing that had happened in years.

"Oh. My god, she's going after the twins." Lexi couldn't help it. She'd never had a little sister before and teasing her was totally fun.

It was far better than ignoring her. She wanted to be close to her sister. Not far away.

Olivia put her foot down, stomping on the ground. "I am not going after anyone. I was only talking to them because they're real nice." She stared at Lexi's phone. "Are you going to make a call? You're always on the phone."

It was true, and now she felt naked without a working phone. "I can't call anyone. I don't have a signal."

Her mom got to one knee. "Livie, baby, can you go and find Aunt Danielle? I need to talk to your sister."

Olivia got a brilliant smile on her face. "Sure, Momma. Gee, sorry about your phone, Lexi. I guess it doesn't work anymore."

Lexi felt her eyes narrow. Olivia wasn't merely a ball of chaos. The older she got the more sneaky she was. "Did you do something to my phone?"

Olivia simply grinned and ran off toward the main house.

How the hell had she managed it? Lexi stared down at her phone. It was seventy-five percent charged. One minute it had been working perfectly and the next the whole thing had shut down. It was as if someone had found a way to cut her off from the grid.

She turned to her mother, feeling more like a teen than she had in years. "Momma, I think she somehow got my account canceled. Olivia, you come back here!"

Her mother rolled her eyes. "God, I am so glad I had you two twenty years apart. You still fight like siblings. And if Livie managed to get your phone turned off then I'm raising her allowance because she's the only one who's had the guts to do it. Now tell me what's wrong in Deer

Run."

But her mind was flying through the scenarios. "I have to go. I think the closest place I can get a new cell is Alamosa. Damn it. Lucas and Aidan took the car. Maybe Beth will run me into town."

Her mom stepped in front of her, blocking her way. "Lexi, if you walk away from me now, I'll explain to Jack that I need him to figure out what's going on."

Lexi stopped in her tracks. Damn it. Jack was the one threat she couldn't counteract. "Please don't tell Dad."

Her mom smiled. "You know he melts a little when you call him that, but it won't make a damn bit of difference. You're lucky that Lucas has been hiding this from him or he would have already gotten involved."

She did not want to bring her father into it. She didn't want Jack to know how stupid she'd been. "Please don't tell him."

Her mother's foot tapped against the ground, a sure sign of her growing impatience. "Then you should get talking."

"Promise me you won't tell him."

Her mother shook her head shortly. "I can't, baby girl. You know I can't make that promise. I promise I'll try to help you without involving him."

Lexi took a deep breath and finally confessed to her mother.

Chapter Twelve

Leo, Shelley, and Wolf

Shelley stepped out on to the porch and looked over the grounds of the Talbot mansion. It was almost dusk. Her shower was winding. She closed her eyes and tried to memorize the moment. The afternoon had been sweet, filled with friends old and new. She wanted to remember everything.

Except the crap with her mother-in-law.

She enjoyed the silence for a moment and then her eyes got wide as she opened them because a big black truck pulled up, carefully maneuvering its way through the multitude of cars parked on the driveway and lawn. It drove past the circular drive and up to what looked to be the guesthouse.

Jennifer Talbot hurried across the lawn as though she'd been expecting that truck to show up. She stopped when she got to the truck bed, looked down, and then began to unleash holy hell on the men who stepped out of the truck.

The cowboys held up their identical hands as though pointing to each other to take the blame.

Shelley couldn't hear the argument, but there was no way Jennifer was happy with whatever they had done.

She turned away and wondered if Leo and Wolf were having fun at their party. She loved spending time with all the women from Bliss and her friends from back home, but she was craving a couple of minutes to herself. The wedding had become the whole center of their world, and she couldn't wait to get back to focusing on her men. She missed their mornings together.

Leo would get up first, putting on the coffee for her while he went on the balcony and practiced some yoga. She would get up and watch him, his lean and limber body moving with such grace.

Then Wolf would walk in, scratching his belly. He would lie down on the couch, put his head in her lap, and go back to sleep for a while.

She missed those sweet mornings. What would mornings be like when she had some kids? Would it be hectic and chaotic? Or would she find a deep peace in sitting down with her family and eating breakfast?

The way she had with her momma and daddy and Trev. Her mom and dad were gone now, but there had been a piercing sweetness to sitting across from her brother and having him pass her the syrup.

And now Trev was a dad. He had a baby girl. She was an aunt. It was a responsibility she didn't take for granted. She had a place in that girl's life. She just wasn't sure it was a good one.

Was she still afraid of her choices? Had Bryce damaged her so badly that she was worried about what she would do to a child?

"Ma'am?" A masculine voice pulled her out of her thoughts.

She turned and saw a man walking across the porch. He was dressed in jeans and a Western-style shirt. His hair was gray and cut in a severe style. She didn't recognize him at all. "If you're looking for the men's party, you'll have to go up the mountain."

He shook his head. "No, I'm afraid I wouldn't be welcome there, but I might have better luck with you."

"With me?" She kind of didn't like the sound of that. Had Cassidy sent another crazy to plead her case?

"Yes. You're Shelley McNamara, ain't you?" His eyes narrowed, looking her up and down.

Yeah, she didn't like that look. And now Jennifer Talbot was gone and there was no one on the lawn. She definitely didn't like how quiet it was. She could hear the party going on in the back, but she'd been through enough crap in her lifetime to know when it was all right to be alone with a man she didn't know.

Never.

"I think I saw her in the back. I'll go get her for you." He might be the kindest man on the planet, but she wasn't taking chances.

She started to move toward the door to the house, but he stepped in her way.

"I know you're Shelley and I know you're marrying my boys."

That stopped her in her tracks. A chill pierced through her. "You're Leo and Wolf's dad?"

The one who had walked away and left them alone? The one who had forced them to grow up way too soon? Her husbands hadn't hidden their past from her.

He shrugged. "Not that they acknowledge it. Probably best for them, but I'm afraid I'm going to have to insist on a little family time with them. Leo is being real stubborn about everything. He's like his good-for-nothing mother."

Tears pricked at the back of her eyes, but they weren't about sadness. Anger started to burn through her. She knew exactly what it felt like to be told she was useless. Bryce had tried to make her feel utterly worthless. She'd wasted years on him, trying to be a good wife when there was nothing she could do.

Had Cassidy's husband done the same?

She would take that damn beet. She would make sure her MIL knew she wasn't alone. Cassidy had somehow managed to raise the best men she'd ever met.

"What do you want?"

He put a hand on his hip and stared at her for a moment as though trying to assess the best way to answer the question. "I want what's coming to me. Now the way I see it, you three have yourself a mighty nice setup. You all work for that fancy city slicker, the one with all the money."

"Are you talking about Julian Lodge?" Julian, who loved Leo. Julian, who would likely find a man to kill the dude in front of her. Taggart would give him a discount on his services and be happy to cause this man a whole lot of pain.

"Yeah, that fellow. I read about him. He's got a pretty wife."

He was setting off her every ick factor. If the man in front of her knew exactly what Julian Lodge would do to him if he laid a hand on Dani, he wouldn't think she was so pretty. He would think she looked like his painful death. "What about Julian?"

"My boys both work for him, right? When I heard about this wedding, I did some checking because I thought it was weird that Stef Talbot would be hosting my white-trash boys. Turns out they ain't white trash anymore."

She hated the term. She'd grown up fairly poor and in the South, so she'd been called by that name more than once. "They've been very successful."

"Real rich now. Leo's got some sort of fancy degree. He was always a smart kid. Must have got that from me. Wolf is as dumb as his momma, though. If I went to him, he would probably try to kick my ass. I have to think you're going to be the reasonable one. I mean, you like your life, dontcha, girl?"

Yep, her rage was getting pretty volcanic now, but she put a blank face on. Leo had been keeping this from her, and maybe from Wolf. She knew why he was doing it. He was trying to make sure their wedding was as happy as possible for her, but it looked like she would be the one handling this small problem. Because there was no way she was letting this asswipe anywhere near her men again. He'd done enough damage. She needed to find out what his plan was. "I like my life a lot."

His eyes roamed up and down her body, making her wish she had a turtleneck sweater on and maybe a suit of armor. How this man had produced the two kindest men she knew, she had no idea.

Except she suddenly did. Cassidy had made them kind. Cassidy had raised them to be gentlemen and true friends to all those around them. DNA had nothing to do with it. Cassidy's will and perseverance had ruled the day.

His eyes narrowed, his mouth turning cruel. "Well, the way I look at it, you should probably want to keep that nice life with your pretty clothes and shoes and such."

"I intend to." She would do anything she needed to in order to make sure her men didn't have to worry about this asshole.

"What would that fancy boss of yours say if he knew where Leo and Wolf came from? It looks to me like my boys have him fooled. I don't know how they know Talbot, but they probably have him fooled, too. You're moving around in high society, but that society won't keep you for long once they find out that Leo and Wolf come from a man who spent more time in prison than he did out of it."

If Julian Lodge didn't already know that, she would eat her Jimmy Choos. But she played along, letting a horrified look cross her face. "Prison?"

Mr. Meyer nodded solemnly. "Yes, girl. I done a nice bit of time and for some pretty ugly crimes. That Julian fellow might be open-minded when it comes to you sleeping with both boys, but how is he going to feel about a criminal's son watching over his daughter?"

Wolf's job was security for Dani and Chloe. He also watched over Finn when Julian was worried about one of his cases. It was obvious that Robert Meyer hadn't done his homework. He'd looked up Julian Lodge and seen exactly what Julian had wanted him to see—an upscale businessman with a beautiful wife and daughter. It was the image Julian presented to reporters. The last thing the very private Julian would want was newspaper stories about his ménage lifestyle.

On the surface, Julian might look like the type of man who would be horrified to discover his seemingly steady bodyguard actually had a dark past. Many businessmen in his position would immediately fire the bodyguard and find someone more suitable.

Julian Lodge would shoot Robert Meyer and consider the world a better place.

She managed to sniffle. "What are you saying? You're going to tell Julian?"

She knew how to handle the problem. Give the man everything he thought he would want and let her men deal with the situation. She trusted them on every level.

"All I'm saying is a man like that would probably rather fire a problem than deal with it. I don't think it would look too good for Leo and Wolf if I showed up on Julian's doorstep. Or if I started talking to the papers. Tell me something, is that bitch still crazy?"

"I don't know who you're talking about."

He sneered her way. "Their momma. What kind of medication does Leo have her doped up on so she could meet with these people?"

"These people" all seemed to accept Cassidy for who she was.

Maybe if Shelley had been around "these people," she wouldn't have stayed in a terrible marriage for as long as she had.

God, she had so much more in common with her almost mother-in-law than she'd dreamed of. And she owed her. She was starting to realize that. She'd thought, in the beginning, that Cassidy was someone she had to put up with. Maybe Cassidy was someone she could learn a whole lot from.

"He doesn't have her on any medication."

Robert snorted, a wholly nasty sound. "Now I know you're lying. She was crazy when I married her. And I still hear the rumors all over the county. Everyone talks about her. She was lucky no one took those kids from her. Everyone knew how loony she was. She's the biggest joke around."

Shelley wanted to slap the son of a bitch, but she'd already decided on her plan of action. It required a little more acting. "What do you want from us?"

"To stop me from going to Lodge or from going to the newspapers and making you the laughingstock of the country? Wouldn't that be a good story? Woman sleeps with two brothers. You don't want everyone calling you a whore, do you?"

Once they got a look at her men, most women would high-five her. And she didn't care who called her what, but she liked her privacy. "No, I don't. What do you want to keep quiet?"

She could only imagine what Leo had threatened him with. And he was damn lucky he hadn't gone to Wolf. Wolf wouldn't have talked. Wolf would have shot first.

"I'm thinking ten thousand would keep me pretty quiet."

Not for long, though. It wasn't her only experience with blackmailers. Her first husband had used her decorating business to gain entry into high-powered officials' homes so he could bug them and use what he found out to drain the politicians and businessmen dry.

So she was pretty sure Robert Meyer would take his ten grand, spend it, and show back up in Dallas looking for more.

Unless she proved to him that this scam wasn't worth his while. She sniffled again and placed her hand over her mouth as though she was trying not to cry.

"You can take care of this, Shelley," he said, standing far too close to her. "You can go and get me a check and then you don't have to see me again."

She managed to nod and step away. "I have a checkbook in my purse."

She stepped around him, keeping her eyes on the floor so he didn't see the burning hatred she was pretty sure was in her eyes. She stepped back into the house and immediately ran into Rachel Harper.

"Hey, I'm sorry about the whole Cassidy thing. She's actually quite sweet. She has this thing about aliens. I promise to have tooth whitening mouthwash waiting for you."

She wasn't even thinking about that right now. She was only thinking about the fact that if she didn't explain to that fucker what the real situation was, he might show up at her Beeting Ceremony, and apparently that meant a lot to Cassidy. She wasn't about to allow her crazy, prove-you're-not-an-alien-queen party to be interrupted by a douche lord. "Do you have a gun?"

Rachel's eyes went wide and then her mouth turned down. "Of course not. That would probably be silly."

"Because I need a gun and I don't carry one."

Rachel looked back up, her eyes assessing. "Is this one of those 'make fun of the country people' things?"

Shelley wasn't sure what she meant, so the truth was all she could offer. "No, this is one of those 'I need to shoot someone' things."

Her mouth curled up in a happy smile. "Oh, thank god. Yeah, it's in my purse. Do you know how to use it? Who are we shooting? Because I've got one in the car, too. If we can wait a couple of minutes, I can call Marie and we can get the whole crew out here."

"Crew?"

Rachel nodded. "The 'I Shot a Son of a Bitch' club. We meet every second Tuesday. I do take it we're shooting a son of a bitch. Wait. We're not shooting Wolf, right? I don't know the other one. I could probably shoot him."

Shelley shook her head. "No. We're not shooting my men. We're shooting their no-good, blackmailing, criminal, nasty-ass father who looked at my boobs the whole time he was threatening to ruin my life."

Rachel got her purse from the bar. "Oh, we can totally shoot him. Should I call the crew to hide the body or are we going to go with self-defense?" The strawberry blonde, who looked to be about four months pregnant, pulled a nice-sized revolver out of her baby bag. She blushed as she wiped off the handle. "Sorry. Paige's diaper rash cream comes open sometimes. Here you go."

Luckily, Wolf had been taking her to the shooting range. She snapped the safety off, checked the bullets, and was ready to go. "And I'm not actually going to hit him. I only want to be sure he won't come back."

Rachel followed her to the door. "I'm just saying that killing is usually the way to go. They don't normally come back no matter what Nell says about restless spirits and murder bringing about bad karma."

Shelley took a deep breath. She hoped she didn't actually shoot the man. Something told her it would be bad to have to get married in the Bliss County jail, but she was willing to take that risk.

She threw open the door and he was still standing there, a smug smile on his face. He was incredibly unhandsome, his character somehow showing through the lines and planes of his body.

"You got my money, girl?"

Shelley took great delight in aiming that revolver right at his head. "I got everything I'm ever going to give you right here."

He gasped and took a few steps back, his hands coming up. "Now, we should talk about this."

"Oh, I am done talking with you, but I will make a few things plain."

He went an unnatural shade of red. "You don't want your nice friend there to call the police on you, do you?" He pointed behind her, indicating Rachel.

"Oh, I'm not going to call the police. I'm going to help her. I told her she should totally kill you and we could make up a good story about it. Lexi's in the back, isn't she? She's a writer. She can make something up real fast. And there are about a million places to bury your body up on my mountain." She looked out over the yard. "Hey, Max! Rye! Come on over here. We might need you to carry some shit for us!"

Robert Meyer was sweating, his feet shuffling. "You don't want to shoot me."

He obviously hadn't researched her well enough. "Oh, I totally want to shoot you. And if you ever come near my family again, I will. And you should be glad I'm the one delivering this message and not Julian Lodge. I have no doubt in my mind that Julian knows more about you than my husbands do, and he won't hesitate to take you out if you threaten any member of his family. And trust me, he considers my husbands family."

"Hey." One of the twin cowboys from the truck came walking up. He pointed to Robert. "You're that motherfucker from Trio this morning. I thought for sure the shrink and I had scared you away."

Rachel stared at her husband, one hand on her hip. "What the hell were you doing at Trio? I thought I smelled Zane's wing sauce on you!"

The big cowboy shook his head, going pale. "No, baby. I was getting myself shrunk. I was talking to that Leo guy about all the things that are wrong with me. I know I have mental problems."

"You liar." Rachel held her hand out. "I'm going to need that gun back, Shelley."

But she hadn't made her point yet. "In a minute."

She planted her feet the way Wolf had taught her, took careful aim at a place to his left, and fired.

There was a loud scream and Robert Meyer covered his faced and dropped to his knees, though not before Shelley saw the front of his pants suddenly stain and turn wet.

Yes, she'd made her point.

"You told me you had oatmeal at Stella's." The other twin didn't seem at all bothered that she'd nearly killed a man. He was only concerned with yelling at his brother. "Goddamn it, Max."

Max held his ground. "Well, it's not fair that you get to eat fried foods and I don't. I don't understand why I got the bad cholesterol DNA. It should have been you."

"Please don't kill me." For a man who had apparently spent a lot of time committing crimes, Robert Meyer seemed really scared of guns.

"That's up to you." Shelley took a couple of steps his way, standing over him. "If you come near me or mine again, I'll shoot you, and I won't miss next time. Am I understood? The next time you threaten my life, I'll take yours. And if you think you can go to the papers, think again. Julian will buy them all and shut the fuckers down. Now get out of here."

He got shakily to his feet and managed to run down the stairs and across the yard.

"And I hate oatmeal, Rye. It tastes like cardboard even when I put a cup of sugar in it," Max was yelling.

"And I hate the thought of you having a heart attack." Rachel was getting right up in her husband's face. "So I'll shoot you now and put myself out of my misery."

She sounded serious. Shelley watched as her nemesis ran into the woods and disappeared. Maybe he would get eaten by a bear and all her troubles would be solved.

That man had hurt her mother-in-law. She didn't need to hear the story to know. It was plain that this was a man who enjoyed hurting others. He would have loved hurting his wife. He was a man who likely would have enjoyed hurting his kids.

They would have been vulnerable, small and easy to hurt. A man like Robert Meyer would have felt powerful having small kids to torture.

Unless someone had fought back. Unless someone had loved her children so much, she found the strength to break out of her cycle.

She was going to eat that beet. She would eat it down and thank her mother-in-law for the chance to enjoy it.

"Shelley, I need my gun. My dumbass husband wants to die," Rachel said.

"I don't want to die," Max shot back. "I just wanted to eat something tasty. You've fed me salad for two weeks. I'm wasting away. A man needs meat."

The door to the house flew open and most of the garden party was suddenly on the porch.

"We thought we heard gunfire." Callie looked down at the revolver in Shelley's hand.

"No one's dead," Shelley explained. "Though I think Rachel might kill one of her husbands." It was time to help out her new friend. She walked up to Rachel, handing her back her gun. She was pretty sure the blonde wouldn't actually kill her wing-loving hubby. "I have a great cookbook. It's low-salt and low-cholesterol versions of comfort foods. Wolf used to eat like a five-year-old. It gave him high blood pressure. Trust me. After not being able to eat anything but salad and fruit for a couple of weeks, those recipes seemed heavenly to him. He never even realized that his new mashed potatoes were cauliflower."

Rachel turned back to her. "Really?"

She pulled the last ace in her deck. "And I lost five pounds."

A smile hit the blonde's face. "That's sounds perfect. And if you ever decide to kill your son of a bitch, we'll help you hide the body."

"Rachel, I've already had one body in the back of my truck today because Max had to do a favor for Jen. I just got it detailed," Rye complained.

The Harpers were an interesting family.

But she needed to focus on her own. As the Harpers started to argue about whether or not Rye's precious truck should be used in criminal activity, Shelley turned back to Callie Hollister-Wright. She seemed like a woman in the know.

"Hey, can we talk about Cassidy?"

Callie's eyes widened. "Sure. You're not going to shoot her, right?"

"Not at all, but I would like to understand her better. After all, she's going to be my momma after I prove to her I'm not using her boys to propagate an alien race."

Callie smiled and led her back to the bar. A good stiff drink was definitely called for.

Chapter Thirteen

Rafe

Rafe moved through the door to Hiram's cabin with only the slightest trepidation. He'd left the crazy crew behind with his daughter, but the insanity of the day wasn't anywhere close to being over. After all, it was his first real foray into breaking and entering, but then he had the law on his side—or rather at his back. Cam was right behind him.

"Where do you think he would have left it?" Cam asked.

"I suspect it should be somewhere on his desk." Rafe looked around the small cabin. The walls were covered in fishing equipment and photographs, each lovingly framed.

"I'll take a look through the drawers." Laura pushed her way in. She had vigorously protested the whole breaking and entering idea. "I don't see why we can't simply print out another form."

He'd been over this. Zane had been explicit about why they needed the original letter of intent Hiram had signed a few months back. Unfortunately, Zane had been called back to Trio. After a long argument in which the group had explained that the world would end if he didn't get that letter, Rafe had given in. Hence his current dilemma. "It's because the town seal is on the document."

"All right, we can get a new seal," Laura suggested.

"Stef is the only one with a seal stamper. Hiram claimed a moose ate his so Stef, as the county's chief engineer, has the only one left," Rafe explained. They were a very small government.

"What a clusterfuck. So Hiram named a successor and we have to find the paperwork?" Cam had been a little slow on the uptake since he'd been called home from work. He'd hung up before Rafe could explain why they needed him, so he'd come charging in expecting something was wrong with Sierra. He'd actually had his lights and siren going.

Cam needed to chill.

"No, Hiram was supposed to appoint a deputy mayor, but he left the name off," Rafe explained. "They were all in discussion about who it would be. Apparently Hi never made decisions without taking everything into account."

Cam picked up on the conversation. "And we're going to find the document and forge your name, thereby stealing all the political power in the town and setting ourselves up as the first family of Bliss. Does the mayor get a mansion?"

Laura rolled her eyes. "Look around you, babe. This is it."

Hiram's cabin was small but well built. There was absolutely nothing about the place that screamed political power. It was kind of a temple devoted to fishing and hunting.

"And we're only going to find the document," Rafe insisted. "I'm not going to be the mayor."

Cam turned. "Why not? It seems like a pretty sweet gig if you ask me."

"It seems like a pain in my ass." He'd been to more than one town hall meeting. And despite what Zane thought, there would eventually be elections.

Although Hiram never faced one. No one ever ran against him. He was utterly beloved.

Rafe looked around the cozy cabin and again wondered if Hiram ever regretted his decision to not leave Bliss.

"I'm only saying that it would be helpful to have someone more friendly to law enforcement in the mayor's office. Hiram was a total radical."

"Hiram was not a radical," Laura argued. "He felt like Nate

shouldn't write tickets every time he wanted to upgrade something at the station house. He was scaring off the tourists."

"Well, then he should open up the town's pocketbook. We needed that fridge. The old one was from the sixties. Hiram tried to tell Nate that the sixties were the height of refrigeration technology. Though at least he wasn't a hypocrite." Cam put a hand on Hiram's white, had-to-be-fifty-years-old Frigidaire. "If Rafe was the mayor, we could upgrade the bed in the overnight room. I swear that mattress is so lumpy my back aches for days."

"I wouldn't write you a blank check." He would be careful with the town funds. He would more likely spend the money on training the citizens in fire containment and prevention. Bliss was surrounded by national forest land and the threat of wildfires was always around. Yes, he would allocate funds to the volunteer firefighters.

There was also talk of a school. Bobby and Will were homeschooled, but if Sierra was going to go to school, there would be a forty-five-minute bus ride both ways. Bliss needed a small school, an innovative, multi-grade learning institution.

That was where he would use Stef and Seth. He would casually mention some of the things he would need, perhaps even indicate that he was having some sort of bake sale as a method of raising money. Stef's eyes would roll and he would tell Rafe what a waste of time that would be, and suddenly Rafe would have a six-figure check in his hand.

And then he would mention Stef's amazing generosity to Seth. He would go on and on about how the King of Bliss was investing in its future.

Seth would then cut him an even bigger check.

Sierra would have the best of all worlds—the beauty of the mountains, the close-knit family of a small town, and a world-class education. All it would take was a man who knew how to work the Bliss system. It would be good for everyone. There was a baby boom happening in Bliss and someone needed to be prepared.

"I think it would be a cool gig," Cam said. A frown suddenly crossed his face. "Except for all the Nell and Henry interaction."

"I'm worried about them actually," Laura said. "Something's off. Nell seems fine, but Henry is anxious about something. He hasn't been throwing himself into his protests the way he used to."

Cam looked around, his eyes perfectly innocent as he took in the room. "He seems fine to me. They were protesting Jack Barnes yesterday. Apparently even though he's organic, he still kills cows and that's bad. I don't know. His burgers are pretty tasty."

Something about the eyes gave him away. Cam never looked that innocent unless he was hiding something. Laura sighed and mumbled something about male hormones being involved, but then she wandered off to look through Hiram's office.

"What's wrong with Henry?" Rafe asked quietly.

Cam looked through the mail on Hiram's small bar. "Like I said, absolutely nothing."

He was not buying it. "You figured out his past."

There had been rumblings about it in town ever since the incident with Gemma and her ex. Caleb had told a few people that he didn't believe Henry's story about how the man had tripped. Caleb thought Henry had taken him down and in a very calculated way. A professional way.

A single shoulder shrugged up and down.

"Since when do you hide information from me?"

Cam's eyes came up and there was an unfamiliar hardness there. "Since I took an oath to protect and defend the citizens of this town."

A shiver went up Rafe's spine. He'd always, always known that Henry wasn't what he seemed. He'd never doubted that Henry loved his wife, but there was an undercurrent of danger that ran beneath Henry's placid surface.

Rafe had profiled for a very long time. He'd been damn good at it. If he was profiling Henry Flanders, he would put him in the predator category. It was in the way he moved, the way his eyes hardened when he thought no one was looking. It was in the way he quickly surmised he was being watched. Rafe was also good at quietly studying people, but Henry always felt his eyes and turned on his laid-back charm. "Has Henry's past caught up with him?"

Cam's jaw tightened, and Rafe knew that whatever secrets he had, they were bad—potentially very dangerous. "I can't talk about it outside of the station."

"Does Stef know?" The King of Bliss knew everything.

"Yes, but you can't blame me for that. Hiram knew, too. Stef and Hi are the only political figures in this town. Stef holds an office. If you take the mayor job, I'll immediately fill you in. Other than that, you're on a need-to-know basis and you don't need to know."

"If something is going to happen in Bliss, I should be informed." Everyone should be informed. The town had been hit by everything from biker gangs to a serial killer. Rafe didn't believe it was a hot spot of alien activity, but Mel still ran around town with a bullhorn informing the citizenry when probing season began.

Cam's blue eyes came up and there was a steely anger in them. Rafe braced himself because that look told him Cam knew something he shouldn't. "Yeah, well, I would like to be informed when you're planning to move us all to Miami, but I didn't get that courtesy, so I guess you'll survive like I did."

Fuck. "I haven't taken the job."

"I hear the 'yet' in those words, partner."

"And I'm wondering why you've taken to spying on me." He could turn this around. He hadn't said a word because he hadn't decided what he was going to do. Cam was pushing him, and he didn't like it one bit.

"Well, you've taken to hiding whole fucking life decisions from us."

"What's going on?" Laura was standing in the doorway, a piece of paper in her hand.

"Did you find it?" Maybe he could avoid this conversation.

She turned her eyes up to his. "Yes. I also found a list. I think it's a list of potential deputy mayors. Would you like to know who was at the top?"

It didn't matter now, but he would say anything to not have to answer her original question. "Who?"

She looked back down at the lined piece of paper she was holding. "It's a list along with pros and cons. Nell is at the bottom. Her pro is *hard working and makes excellent bread.* Her con is *will make everyone in town blow their own heads off.* He has Cade Sinclair in here. He's smart and hard working. Cons—*why can't that boy wear a shirt?* But at the top of the list is Rafael Kincaid."

Did he want to hear this? He carefully schooled his expression. "And what are my pros?"

"*One of the smartest men in the county. Good family man. Could handle the craziness and keep everyone in line. Best man for the job.*"

"What are his cons?" Cam asked, a deep frown creasing his brow.

"*Rafe could be the best mayor, if only he opened himself up. He likely won't stay. He'll take his family back to the city in the end.*" Laura looked up. "Is that what you're planning?"

It looked like they would have it out here and now. "You know staying here was always contingent on me finding a decent job. How are we going to raise our daughter if no one is making any money? Right now we're living off the money we had saved up. We won't have money for her college fund. We won't be able to fix up the cabin. If we choose to adopt again, where will we put the child? You two don't seem to think about these things, so I am forced to."

"The money is there to build onto the cabin. You've been holding off on it because you don't want to stay here," Laura accused.

"And screw the money part, man." Cam jumped in. "Where do I fit in when you start your corporate job in Miami?"

"You already have a job?" Laura's question came out on a breathless huff.

"I've been offered a job with a six-figure salary, a company car, and the best insurance we could possibly get." Perhaps she would see it was for the best.

Laura shook her head. "So you expect us to move to Miami where you have a job and we don't."

That was one argument he could shoot down. "Laura, you work at a convenience store."

She frowned his way. "I help out the people of my town, and as soon as we find someone to take my place, I'm going to start working on some projects. You know Georgia Stark is talking about a school."

"That school should be under the purview of the mayor's office." He wanted to control the project. If he let Georgia handle it, school uniforms would be provided by Prada and walking in five-inch heels would be a requirement of graduation.

Except he wasn't going to handle it.

Laura's face had gone a stunning shade of pink. "Well, that's not up to you because you'll be in Miami. Tell me something, Rafe. Did your mother put you up to this? Can she not stand the thought of her precious boy being stuck in some back-road Colorado town?"

"Laura," Cam warned.

Laura's well-shod foot came down. "No, I've had it up to here. If Rafe isn't happy, he can run right back to his momma. She doesn't like me anyway. She hasn't even asked to come out and see Sierra. She doesn't care about her own granddaughter. That's what you're trying to choose over us, Rafe."

"Laura, you need to stop," Cam commanded.

"No," Laura shot back. "I won't. He loves his mother so much? He can live with her. I'm not moving. I'm staying right here. I made it clear to you in the beginning that I wouldn't leave Bliss. I gave you every opportunity to go back to DC and keep your job with the BAU, but you want to have your cake and eat it, too. This is my family. I'm not leaving. I'm not raising my child, our child, in a world that would ridicule her for the type of family she has. Or did you expect that Cam would stick to the background? Maybe we shouldn't tell Sierra that Cam is her father at all. We can call him Uncle Cam and pretend like he doesn't sleep with us. You probably have this all figured out."

Every word stabbed at him because it was all true. She had told him she wouldn't leave. She had made her wishes clear, but he wasn't sure there was a place for him here. Cam had slid naturally into the role of deputy and hero and small-town good guy.

Rafe still enjoyed expensive wine, and he'd never gotten into fishing. He'd spent most of his time since getting married looking for a job or working with Caleb to adopt Sierra. He hadn't fit in around town. He hadn't tried because he'd needed the job first. How could he introduce himself without a job?

And he would never have one in Bliss.

Unless he took what his crazy neighbors were offering.

"I haven't figured out anything at all." It wasn't worth throwing her misunderstanding in her face. He wasn't mad. A deep sadness weighed him down. His mother had rejected him, and now it felt like his wife and partner were doing the same thing.

"Well, I'll leave you to it then. I'm going home to take care of our baby. Maybe you should think about her. I'll get this to Zane. He needs to talk to Cade so we can get this thing done." Laura stormed out, her blonde hair flowing behind her.

He loved her, but now he wondered if love alone was enough for him. Perhaps it would be better to leave Bliss, to let Laura and Cam stay where they obviously belonged. He slumped down on Hiram's couch. At his feet was a bearskin rug complete with head and claws attached. The story was Hiram had fought with the bear and eventually won and cackled with glee every time he stepped on his rug.

Rafe wasn't colorful, not like Laura and Cam. Not like Hi.

"She doesn't know, man. I'm really sorry, but she doesn't know about the rift with your mom because you haven't talked about it with us. You hold yourself apart." Cam sat down beside him. "It makes me wonder if you're going to leave. And I don't think for a second that you're planning on shoving me to the side. You would never do that."

At least Cam believed him. "I didn't know how to tell you."

Cam stared straight ahead. "Well, I'll tell you I feel some guilt about it. It's me your mom truly has a problem with. She would get over the small town and your lack of prospects. It's the weird marriage she won't accept. I suppose that's one reason you wouldn't tell us."

His heart ached. "Yes. I knew how it would make you feel."

"But, god, Rafe, I'll take the guilt to get you to talk to me. If you don't want to talk to me, then at least tell Laura. You were a momma's boy. I don't mean that as an insult. I know how close you were to her. I loved my mom, too. And I know how hard it was on her to raise a kid in a place that didn't accept her." Cam continued as he crossed to the kitchen, opening the fridge. "My town didn't accept her because she was unmarried when she had me. Do you even know what it would be like for us in Miami? I've lived this life. I don't want it for our daughter. At the same time, I know how you feel. You had the rug ripped out from under you."

Because his mother was always supposed to be there. Because she was supposed to stand beside him even when she thought he was wrong. She wasn't supposed to tell him he was dead to her. She wasn't supposed to cut him out of her life.

She wasn't supposed to abandon him.

"I knew she would take it hard." Rafe began speaking slowly, forcing the words out. "It was why I put off telling her the truth. I only told her that we'd found Laura and we were working things out. I knew how she would take those words."

"She took the 'we' to mean you and Laura," Cam surmised.

Rafe nodded.

Cam sat down, passing him a beer. "Well, I suppose that's only to be expected." He popped the top on his. "Her brain isn't on the Bliss wave station. It must have been a surprise to her."

Rafe looked down at the beer. "I don't know about this. It feels wrong to go through the man's kitchen."

Cam chuckled. "Hi doesn't need it anymore, and while he was stingy with money, he was always quick to offer a beer. So tell me what happened, and not the craptastic, two-second version."

"Fine." He took a long draw off the beer. There was something soothing about sitting with his best friend, enjoying a cheap beer. "I tried to explain it to her gently. I thought showing her some pictures of Sierra would soften her up. She wanted to know why I couldn't get a kid who looked like me. She said we should have gotten a surrogate because Sierra didn't have her blood."

Cam sat back, a thoughtful look in his eyes. "She was always concerned with her bloodline."

"We have a long family history." He'd heard about it endlessly growing up. He and Miguel were the latest in a long line of Spanish royalty who came to the new world centuries before. They had a duty to be the best, to continue the line.

He thought he had. He had a daughter and she was beautiful and sweet and he intended to raise her to know all of her heritages. His daughter would be the quintessential American—a child of the world, raised with American idealism.

His mother had only cared about the blood that ran in Sierra's veins.

Sierra's blood meant nothing. The love he and Laura and Cam would pour into her, that was what would bind them together as a family.

Cam sent him a sympathetic look. "She could change her mind. Living in Miami so close to her might bring her around."

He shook his head. "That's not why I was considering the job in Miami. It was a coincidence. I simply have contacts there. I was considering the job because it's the only one that's been offered to me."

"That's not true." Cam stood up and gestured around. "It seems to me you've been offered another job."

He knew the score. "I've been offered up as a sacrificial lamb to keep Nell Flanders out of political office."

Cam's lips quirked up. "That seems like a mighty important job to me. You know she thinks the sheriff's department should switch to nonviolent methods of…well, everything. She wants to ban all firearms in the county and teach the citizenry to talk to bears so we don't kill them."

Rafe had come into close contact with a bear two months before. It had been attracted to the hummingbird feeders Laura had placed around the house. He'd been scared shitless. "They'll eat us."

"And Nell would say we deserved it. Do you understand the chaos that Nell taking over city hall would bring? I think you are underestimating how important the office of mayor is to Bliss. And I think you would do a hell of a job. It's up to you. Laura will come around. I can work on her. If you want to give Miami a shot, I'll make sure it happens. Nate has connections with the DEA, and I'm sure he can give me some serious recommendations. I can try Miami PD maybe."

He didn't like the thought of Cam on the streets. He didn't like it at all. "But you love it here."

Cam sat forward, a sad smile on his face. "And you're my partner. You gave it a shot. I won't have you miserable. We'll find a way. We'll compromise because we're a family. I'm going to go talk to our wife. You think about it for a while. We're supposed to be at Trio for some weird ceremonial thing that proves Wolf's girl isn't an alien queen. I have to go fire up the Detector 6000. Stef made it special for the wedding. You won't want to miss it."

He walked out the door, leaving Rafe alone in Hiram's tiny cabin.

There would be no Detector 6000s for Cam in the Miami PD. There wouldn't be Big Game Dinners or Winter Festivals where Sierra could ride ponies. There would be no crazy town hall meetings.

He looked around. Hiram had lived alone for the last fifty or so years, but Rafe couldn't tell from the pictures on the wall. He stood up and stared at that wall. Forty or so pictures hung in cheap frames, but somehow they made a rich canvas of the man's life. There were old black and whites, one of a very large family. The man who was obviously the father had a grim look on his face, and the others were crowding in, looking similarly stoic. Only one boy was grinning like a loon.

Hiram. Maybe he'd never fit into that large, serious family, but he'd kept the photo. There was a picture of Hiram and a woman who looked a whole lot like Max and Rye Harper. They were dressed in late seventies clothes. She was smiling at the camera and holding up a trout she'd caught, but Hiram's face was toward her and he practically glowed.

There were pictures of Hiram with Stella and a young Stef, with Jamie and Noah's dads and mom out at the Circle G. He recognized some of the locals who had been here long before him because Stella had taken him through her albums one night. There was a picture of Hiram handing out diplomas to Max and Rye and Stef and Callie.

The last one caused Rafe's throat to tighten. It was a picture of Hiram holding up Sierra Rose.

Hiram had come to the small party that welcomed his daughter. Hiram had picked her up, pronounced her perfect, and welcomed her as the newest citizen of Bliss.

Tears filled Rafe's eyes because he finally realized something.

Sierra had already lost a grandfather. And if Rafe took his family out of Bliss, she would lose a whole family.

Blood. All his life it had been pounded into his brain. Blood made a family, a long line of DNA that connected him to ancestors who the history books talked about.

But here was a whole life laid out in faded pictures and knickknacks, and suddenly it was lovely to him. Hiram's history didn't span Europe. It was all about a lifetime spent in Bliss. It was about a world of friends who became family. They didn't need blood. Hell, half the time they didn't have anything in common with the singular exception of where they lived, but somehow it had worked for Hiram.

Because he'd been open. Because he'd made his decision and he hadn't looked back. He'd moved forward. He'd forged his own life, his own path.

Wasn't that all a father could ask for his child?

Rafe sat back and allowed a wealth of history to play in his brain.

Invitation to A Meeting of Men

MELVIN HUGHES CORDIALLY INVITES YOU TO A

MEETING OF MEN

IN HONOR OF

LEO AND WOLF MEYER

Join me in a celebration of masculinity and humanness in honor of my beloved stepsons, Leo and Wolf, as they prepare themselves for the marital bed.

JUN 14 — 3 PM

THE MOUNTAIN AND VALLEY NATURIST SOCIETY

BEER, SWEAT LODGE, AND SEXUAL HEALTH LECTURE PROVIDED

CLOTHING OPTIONAL

NO ALIENS. IF YOUR BLOOD IS GREEN STAY UNSEEN.

Chapter Fourteen

Leo, Shelley, and Wolf

Leo needed a drink. Or five. But he was pretty sure he should stay away from the tonic, because in about three minutes he was going to be brutally dehydrated. This afternoon seemed to never end. He would glance at his watch, but he'd left it behind with his clothes.

He pulled the flap on the sweat lodge and steam threatened to overtake him. He crawled through anyway, his eyes blinded momentarily by the intense heat.

Leo made it through the steam and found the sitting area. He sat back on the bench Mel had thoughtfully provided. In the center of the lodge was a small fire and a bunch of rocks covering it. Mel had a bucket next to him. He took the ladle from the bucket and doused the rocks with water, sending heat into the already humid air.

"Welcome, my spiritual sons."

God, he wished his "spirit dad" had some clothes on.

Wolf leaned over and whispered. "You know for a skinny dude, he's got an awfully big—"

Leo elbowed his brother. He was not going there. He did not want to know what his momma saw in Mel. "Thank you for hosting this get-together."

He couldn't call it a party. A party wasn't a bunch of naked dudes drinking rotgut whiskey while only Julian and Jack maintained their dignity. It was more like hell.

Mel smiled. "It's my pleasure. Your friends seem real nice. Except that Julian fella. He's got the look of a hunter about him. There are natural alien hunters in the world, you know. Born to protect our Earth. I think I should talk to him about taking up the fight."

"You should totally do that," Wolf said encouragingly.

Wolf loved the surreal.

Leo loved reality. "I think Julian is busy with his businesses. Mel, we wanted to talk to you about something else."

Mel nodded. "I figured you would. That's why I wanted us to spend some time in the sweat lodge. This is a place for men. Now, I know you don't have a daddy around to talk to you, so your momma asked me to explain some things to you."

"Actually, that's what we wanted to ask you about," Leo began.

"Sex is nothing to be afraid of, boys," Mel said with a grave seriousness.

"Oh, god," Wolf whispered, his eyes going wide. "We're going to get the sex talk."

Mel leaned forward. "You see, when you marry a woman, she's going to expect certain things of you, including physical affection. I want to make sure you boys understand how to bring a human woman to pleasure. It's different than what your alien instincts will tell you. Women have different parts than men. I brought some magazines to show you."

Leo held out a hand. He was not going to sit in a tent with Mel and look at seventies porn magazines. "We know about sex."

"God, you're no fun," Wolf grumbled.

Mel nodded sagely. "I tried to tell Cassidy that you two probably understood, but she was real insistent that you were both pure."

"Mel, I've been married before," Leo pointed out.

"Oh, well, then you understand."

"But I'm totally pure," Wolf said quickly. "I could use some pointers."

"You've fucked your way through half of Southern Colorado. I don't even want to know what you did overseas." He wasn't going to indulge his brother's deep love of the surreal. "Mel, we do need your help, though it's not with sex."

"Alien issues?" Mel asked.

Leo managed to not scream. Maybe he should switch his psychological efforts from Max to Mel. "No. It's a family issue, though it turns my stomach to call that man family."

Mel's eyes narrowed. "Are you talking about Robert?"

Well, at least they were off the aliens. "Yes."

"If you're thinking about reuniting with your father, I'm going to ask you to reconsider. I know you missed having a daddy, but he's no good."

Well, Mel proved he could be sane from time to time. "I don't want to have anything to do with the bastard. He found me, not the other way around."

Mel's eyes closed briefly. "If he's back then he wants money. You should know he's going to try to blackmail you. Whatever he comes at you with, tell him no and I'll take care of the situation. You boys don't have to worry about anything. You concentrate on your wedding."

"He's done this to Ma before?" How much had his mother kept from him?

Mel sighed. "Every now and then he gets out of jail and he comes looking for cash. When you two were kids, he would threaten to have her institutionalized so she would lose custody unless she gave him everything she had. She would save up money for years at a time, and he would walk in and take it all because she didn't have anyone to lean on."

"I'm going to kill the fucker." Wolf practically growled beside him.

Mel gave Wolf a hard stare. "No you are not because if anything happened to either one of you, your momma would lay down and die. She spent her whole life protecting you."

"Did he hit her?" His mother would never talk about those years before his father had walked out. Leo was almost certain there had been some physical abuse.

"Yeah," Mel said, taking a deep chug off his water bottle. At least Leo hoped that was water.

Well, he'd always wondered why his parents had split. His mother wouldn't talk about it, preferring to discuss alien invasions when he brought the subject up. He'd had a couple of theories. He'd always worried that she'd driven him away with her special brand of crazy, but now he was pretty sure he knew the truth and it made him love his mother all the more. "She took it until the day he hit me."

Wolf sat up, his head brushing the top of the tent. "Leo?"

It was a dream he'd had since childhood, but now he realized it was more like a memory. His father standing over him, a shadowy figure with no real substance. His mother screaming and then telling him everything would be all right.

His mother had been stronger than he'd ever given her credit for.

Mel reached out and put a hand on Leo's shoulder. "You made her strong, Leonardo. Her love for you and Wolfgang made her real strong, and you have to honor that by staying away from the bastard. It's what she fought all her life to do. She gave up everything so you wouldn't have to know the truth about the man who calls himself your father."

"Shit." Wolf let his head drop to his hands. "How could we not have known about this? Chase told me about the police report, but I didn't think it was this bad. She only filed the one."

Leo hadn't seen the report McKay-Taggart had compiled for Julian a few years back. When he'd come out of the main building feeling completely vulnerable because his junk was hanging out, he'd found Chase and Wolf discussing the facts of the case. It hadn't surprised him that Julian already knew everything. But hearing it from someone close to his ma somehow made it more real. "Mel, we can't let him hurt her anymore. We're not children. It's time we took care of her."

"No."

Leo waited for a moment, but Mel didn't say anything more. "You can't say no."

"I sure can," Mel replied simply. "Your mother belongs to me now, and this situation is something for me to take care of. And I am serious about that."

If he knew Mel, Mel would probably handle the situation by calling aliens down on the asshole. "I don't want Ma to know he's here."

"She won't. I'll take care of it before the wedding. Don't worry about it." Mel sat back. "Now, are you sure you two know about orgasms? Because they're very important to women. They get real twitchy when they haven't had one in a long time. And the women around here have guns. They ain't afraid to use them on a selfish son of a bitch."

"Mel, you can't just throw that information out there." They needed to talk about this.

One of Mel's surprisingly muscular shoulders shrugged. He actually didn't look as skinny out of his normal coveralls. "Sure I can because I have it handled. Don't you go worrying about it. I told him what would happen if he came back."

The hits kept coming. "He's come around since we grew up?"

"Sure," Mel replied. "He got out of prison after doing a stretch for bilking old ladies out of their social security checks. It was right after Wolf had come home from the Navy, and Cassidy was real worried about him. Robert showed up and mentioned that maybe he should reconnect with his poor injured kid."

Wolf huffed. "I wasn't so injured I couldn't have shot the shit in the face."

Wolf had been a little lost after his injuries cost him his SEAL career. Leo knew exactly why Robert's threat would have scared his mother. Wolf had been vulnerable, looking for something to make his life meaningful. A good con artist could potentially have worked Wolf over. "Did Ma pay him off?"

"Nah." Mel waved that thought off. "She came to me. She wasn't alone this time, and she was smart enough to not try to hide it from me. She knew I would take care of the problem for her."

"Okay, well, he never contacted me, so I have to assume you did something," Wolf said.

Mel nodded. "Sure, I did. I sent the fucker back to jail. He was on parole. I made sure he missed a parole meeting. While he was my guest, we talked about a couple of things, including what would happen if he ever approached my woman again. It looks like I should have been more detailed about the consequences. Cassidy says I get too focused on one thing and forget about how important the details can be."

Leo found himself staring at Mel, perfectly shocked. "You distracted him so he couldn't get to his meeting with his parole officer?"

Mel shook his head. "Oh, no. Distraction isn't the right word. He was real insistent about making that appointment. So I tied him up and we had a nice long talk. But I'm not a horrible son of a bitch. I also told him about the alien invasion. This time I'm going to let the fuckers take him, if you know what I mean."

Mel was crazy, and that was kind of cool. Maybe Mel and Julian had more in common than either would admit.

"You totally kidnapped him," Wolf said, respect plain in his tone.

Mel waved that off. "Nah, not according to some very carefully selected alibi witnesses. And there were plenty of people at Hell on Wheels who saw him drinking. That Sawyer fellow is a good man no matter what Nate says. He's been good to our whole hunter society. He also sets up a real nice sweat lodge."

Leo laughed. He'd spent a whole lot of time being worried about his mother and crazy Mel and it turned out that crazy Mel took damn fine care of her. He looked over at his brother. "What do you think?"

Wolf smiled, wiping a hand across his hair. "I think we're getting married tomorrow and we should trust our Ma to know what she wants."

And she wanted Mel. Mel had been the one standing beside her and taking care of her. Leo turned to him and gave him a deferential nod. "Thank you for taking care of this, Mel."

Wolf held out a hand. "Thank you."

Mel shook it. "That's real nice, boys, but I'll always take care of your momma. I love her. I've loved her since I saw her across the crowded medical examination room the aliens were holding us in. She was so beautiful in the stark white lights. You see, they think they can blind you with those lights, but we hunters have trained ourselves to be able to see through it."

Mel started in on how he'd met their ma on an alien research ship.

And Leo forced himself to listen because sanity, he'd learned, was sometimes in the eye of the beholder.

And his mother had more than earned his respect and love and tolerance.

If he could show her that by accepting her nutty, loving, protective boyfriend, then Mel had just become family.

Chapter Fifteen

Stef and Jen

Jen stared at her sleeping husband and wondered why she asked a man to do anything. She'd asked them to bring him in and help her get him tied down. It was a simple operation. No fuss. No muss. There were two Harper twins and only one Stef. It should have been easy.

They had shot him with a tranq gun. That was their brilliant solution. To shoot him. With drugs.

And then they'd tossed him in the back of Rye's truck. Naked.

She was going to give Holly and Rachel an earful about their dumbass husbands. There wasn't a brain among the four of them. Next time she would call the women together. Marie would have been humane about bringing Stef in. Maybe.

But she had a decision to make and she needed to do it before he woke up.

She stared at her gorgeous husband. He was tied to the bed, his arms and legs spread. Every inch of his tanned skin was on display. How long had it been since she'd simply stared at him like the work of art he was?

She tugged at the silk straps of her nightgown. She'd been surprised to discover that there was a whole line of sexy maternity nighties out there, but the one time she'd been brave enough to wear it, Stef had wrapped a robe around her because he didn't want her to be cold.

He was still the perfect man she'd married and she...wasn't.

Her gray-eyed boy. God, she loved him. And he was going to be so mad at her.

Maybe she hadn't thought this through.

"Jennifer?"

Her heart skipped a beat. "Stefan."

She hated the fact that she was nervous. He was her husband. They were married. She shouldn't be nervous about trying to sleep with her husband.

"Would you like to explain to me why the doc shot me and my friends dragged my naked body home and apparently tied me to the bed?" His head had come up and those glorious gray eyes were arctic as he stared at her.

She actually swallowed. She could blame it on pregnancy brain. Yes, that's what she would do. Hormones. Lots of hormones. "Well, I didn't expect them to shoot you. I merely asked for Max and Rye to bring you here and tie you up. I guess I didn't think about the fact that you would be naked, though I do like the view."

Maybe flattery would help.

"Why?"

That should be apparent. "Come on, Stef."

"Jennifer, I asked you a question. I intend to have the answer, so unless you are going to keep me tied up here for the rest of our lives, or you're planning on playing out a Lifetime movie, I would suggest you begin your explanation. Every second you delay is another set of very nasty punishments. You should understand, my love, that these punishments are not erotic treats for you."

Shit. Well, she'd wanted her Dom back. It looked like he was in the house and he was pissed. Honesty was called for. "I wanted to get your attention."

"Consider my attention wholly focused on you."

She'd forgotten how intimidating he could be. He hadn't used that dark chocolate voice of his on her in forever. He hadn't stared at her with pure dominance on his face since he'd discovered she was pregnant. She had to take a deep breath, and not simply because she was nervous. Her pussy had tightened the minute he looked at her. This wasn't simply her husband. This was her Dom, and she wanted him.

With shaking hands she pushed at the straps of her gown. "I love you."

"You have an odd way of showing it." He wasn't giving an inch, and she couldn't tell a thing from his eyes except that he was angry.

"You didn't leave me a choice. If I didn't make a stand now, how long would it take? It could be another three or four weeks before I have this baby. Sometimes first babies are late. And then it's six weeks after that before I can have sex. I don't want to wait another two or three months to be with my husband."

"And rather than asking me to make love to you, you chose to take away my control."

God, how did he manage to put things in the worst possible light. Her gown slipped down, her breasts on display now, but Stef kept his eyes on her face. She felt her skin flush with embarrassment, but she wasn't giving up yet. She couldn't.

She reached out and touched his leg, running her hand up the powerful muscles there. "I wanted to play. We haven't played in so very long. I don't know how much time we'll have once the baby is born. I don't want to lose this part of our lives."

His face was like granite. "You lost it the moment you chose to put me in this position. What is in our contract, wife?"

"This is about more than a contract." Her voice was shaky because she was losing him.

His words came out clipped and sharp. "You said you wanted to play. Our play is defined by that contract, or are we going to throw everything away because you've decided you want something? Is that how this works now? Our contract is meaningless because Jennifer Talbot isn't getting what she thinks she deserves? That gives you the right to humiliate your Dom?"

"You tied me up before. I didn't feel humiliated."

"I asked you. Everything was consensual. Putting me in this position is not consensual. Having my friends go after me was not consensual."

Tears blurred her eyes. She hadn't meant to humiliate him. She'd meant to show him how much she wanted him. She'd meant to show him that she would fight for them.

But he didn't want her. She pulled the straps of her gown up and reached for her robe. She would cover herself properly. He didn't like her body now. She knew she should be angry, but the dull ache that filled her crowded out everything else.

"I'll have you out in a second." She pulled on the ties Rye had made, tugging until his feet were free. She moved to his hands, and he was out of the bonds in moments.

She wouldn't look at him, couldn't. She simply got up and found his robe. She laid it out on the bed. "I'm going to get dressed. Rachel and Callie have been handling the party for me. I think I'm going to go to my room. I'm very tired."

She would wait until she made it to her room and then she would cry. She would wail. She would mourn because he didn't want her anymore and he might not again. She could try to get her body back, but it couldn't be the same. In a few weeks, she would be a mom and nothing could change that. She wouldn't be Stef's hot sub ever again.

And maybe then it would only be a matter of time before he started looking around, before he started wondering what he'd given up to marry her. He was rich and gorgeous and could have any woman he wanted.

How long would she be able to keep him? How long would she even want to keep a man who didn't want her?

She took a deep breath. All that mattered now was getting out of this with as much dignity as she could muster. "I apologize, Stef. I thought I was being cute and spontaneous. I won't do anything like this again. I'm going to the bathroom to get dressed. Please don't blame Max and Rye. I asked them to help me."

"Oh, I have plans for all of them, pet." He was on his feet now, but he didn't bother with the robe. "It might take years, but I'll have my revenge. I'll be creative, and this town will never forget what I do to those four men. I'm thinking of running Max up the town flagpole suspended only by his boxers. I won't let him down until he cries a little. And Caleb Burke is going to get a dose of his own fucking medicine. I'm going to roofie the bastard and maybe get a tramp stamp of a butterfly tattooed above his ass. Yeah, we'll see how he fucking likes that."

"Stef, you can't do that."

"I don't see why not." His eyes rolled slightly. "It's not like it would be permanent. Not that I would tell Caleb that. I have to figure out what to do to the big guy. I bet Alexei's nasty with the revenge thing. I'll think about it. Why are you dressed?"

She was confused. And her heart was still aching. "This was a stupid idea. I told you I'm sorry. You can't run around plotting revenge."

"Oh, I'll have it. You see, I realized something in those moments right before the tranquilizer took effect. I've been going about this all wrong. I've been thinking I needed to figure out how to be a proper father to the boy. I've been thinking I needed to change everything about myself so I can teach our son. But our son is going to live here. So the first lesson he's going to need to learn is how to beat the shit out of Max Harper's kid because that rat bastard is going to have a son one of these days and I'll be damned if our Logan doesn't know how to handle him. They'll be best friends. It's important they understand how to fight. Now, I am only going to ask one more time, why is my submissive wearing clothing in our playroom?"

She sniffled and stood her ground. "You made yourself plain. I said I was sorry."

"And now you'll accept your punishment." He looked down. "Oh, thank god. I thought for a minute the damn drugs were going to make this difficult. That's a plan. I'll sneak some Viagra into Doc and Alexei's coffee right after I've made sure Holly is totally unavailable to them."

His cock was working again, thrusting up from his nest of perfectly trimmed dark hair. "Stef?"

"I'm going to be gentle because of our child, but you should understand that you'll take the spanking I'm about to give you. And you'll take the fucking that's going to come afterward, and as soon as Doc clears you for sex after the baby is born, I'm going to strap you to the St. Andrew's Cross and you won't come off of it until I'm satisfied. You will never, never wrest control from your Dom again. Are we understood, Jennifer?"

She couldn't help it. Tears were still right there, leaking from her eyes. "I don't understand anything."

He softened, making his way across the room toward her. He stopped in front of her, his hand coming up to cup her cheek. "You've been heard, love. I'm sorry, too."

"I don't want your pity."

His eyes hardened. "No, but you obviously want the flat of my hand on your ass. We're going to talk this out, but we're going to do it my way."

He could be deeply unfair. "I've tried to talk to you."

"And it didn't work. So we'll do it my way. Off with the clothes. Find a comfortable position, but I want your ass in the air. You wanted your Dom back, you have him. But you know what happens when you wake sleeping bears, love."

She shuddered a little. People who woke sleeping bears tended to get eaten.

And it had been so long since he'd made a meal of her.

She pushed the robe off her shoulders.

"Show me what you're offering. Show me how beautiful you are." He stared down at her, a hungry look in his eyes.

And for the first time in forever, she felt beautiful again.

* * * *

When his wife decided to get his attention, she went all out. It made a man puff up.

Thank god he was hard. He'd woken up, seen his wife sitting there in that gossamer gown that barely contained her breasts, and he'd gotten nothing, very likely because he was still processing whatever the fuck Caleb had dosed him with.

The minute he'd seen Jennifer's face, he'd known what a coward he'd been and that he had to get his marriage back on the proper footing. And that included his dick.

Which was working fine again. Not that he wouldn't get his revenge on his asshole friends anyway. It was going to be a long-term labor of love.

Jennifer blushed slightly as she began to move the straps off her shoulders.

"I'm not getting any younger, love." Now that he was here, he had to wonder why he'd been so stubborn. He craved her, and he'd been away for far too long.

"They're so big."

"Because they're getting ready to feed our child." He'd been an ass. She'd needed him and he'd retreated because of fear. She'd needed to know how beautiful she was and all he'd told her was that she was fragile. "Let me see them. I love your breasts. I love them when they're small and fit perfectly into my hands, and I'm going to love them now that they're ripe and overflowing."

Her breath caught. "Will you like them when I take my bra off and milk shoots across the room? Because Rachel told me that can happen."

Oh, she made him smile. "Yes, love. I will adore them."

She tugged the straps down just enough to tease him with the sight of the tops of her breasts.

Yes, his cock was working fine. It was twitching now. How much discipline did she need? Because all he could think about was the fact that he was letting himself off the leash and he couldn't wait to get inside her.

He was impatient. God, it felt good to be impatient. It felt good to want something and know he could take it.

He reached out and let his fingers glide from her cheek to her neck to the round globes of her breasts. They were so much bigger, the ivory of her skin marked with blue veins. He traced them, reveling in the changes of her body.

"I was very scared, love. When you passed out and you were bleeding, my world shifted, and I haven't quite come back from it yet."

Her hand reached out to touch his cheek. "It happens to a lot of pregnant women."

"All that matters is it happened to you." He cupped her breast gently. "Are they sore?"

She shook her head, her eyes closing in pleasure. "No. It feels so good."

It felt good to be connected. He knew what she was saying because he felt it, too. He ran a thumb across her nipple, tweaking it lightly. This was different than rubbing her feet. He did that for her pleasure. This was mutual. This was connection. This was what they had both been missing for months.

And he'd missed talking to her. Jennifer knew him better than anyone. Jennifer had been the one to teach him it was all right to talk to her. "I had nightmares about you bleeding."

Her hand came over his. "Babe, I didn't know."

"I didn't tell you. I didn't want you to know because in those dreams

I wasn't worried about our son. All I cared about was you. I don't want you to think I don't care about him. He isn't real to me yet."

Her face softened, those innocent eyes catching his. "Of course not. It's all right. He doesn't kick you in the ribs twelve times a day. He'll be real to you soon enough. I'm not worried about your fathering skills."

"I am." He didn't feel like a Dom in that moment. He felt like a man who was about to have a baby, and he had no idea what would happen.

Jennifer wrapped her arms around him, drawing him close. He had no idea how she always managed it, but she made him feel safe. She made him feel loved. When he was wrapped in her arms, he was home. "You are going to be the best dad in the world, Stefan Talbot. You're going to teach our boy everything you know, including how to take down the Harpers. You have everything you need to be a great dad."

Yes. He did. Because he had her. He held on, doing what he'd needed to do every day since she'd fallen over in his arms and he'd carried her to Caleb. He held her, praying he never had to let go.

He wound his hands in her hair. It had thickened during her pregnancy. When he looked at his wife now, he could see how she'd bloomed. How could he have allowed one bad moment to ruin watching her glow and grow?

"God, you're gorgeous." He caught her mouth against his.

Stef ate along her lips, reveling in her touch and scent. He kissed her sweetly for a moment, but that was never enough for him. He plunged his tongue inside, dominating hers as he pulled her close.

Her belly was in the way, but he didn't avoid it now. Now he kissed her and let his hand rest there. He felt the baby kick, a strong motion against his hand.

Stef stopped, looking down in wonder. "Take it off. I want to watch."

Jen frowned at him, but her hands were already going to the stretchy waist of her gown. "Fine, but I'm serious about sex. This better not devolve into you spending hours watching my belly jump."

Oh, she was asking for it. He twisted slightly and was able to get a nice hard smack across her ass. Jennifer jumped, but the gasp that came out of her mouth was breathy and her nipples had perked up.

His sub had missed her Master.

He laid a quick ten gentle smacks across her ass. No matter how hard she pushed him, she wasn't going to get what she wanted. He would make her skin sting, but it would be nothing she would feel tomorrow. Despite Caleb's permission, he was going to be gentle with her. Well, as gentle as a spanking could be.

"God, I missed that."

"I missed smacking your ass, too." He ran a hand across the globes of her ass. Like the rest of her, she'd gained a little weight there. Stef loved how she'd rounded out, how luscious she was. He'd fallen for her slender frame, but he had to admit, he also loved her like this.

He simply loved her. She was the world to him.

"He's kicking again." Jennifer reached out and brought his hand to the swell of her stomach.

His son, the child he'd made with Jennifer, moved against his palm, something small and round. A foot or an elbow.

God, there was a baby in there, and it was a combination of him and his wife.

"Stef, it's going to be okay."

"I'm terrified. How can I be terrified of my own child?"

"Because you've seen the kids around here, babe. They're pretty intense." She was grinning at him.

He got to his knees and placed a kiss on her belly. They would get through it. And he wasn't about to let Caleb shut him out of the delivery room. No matter what. He would be there for his wife.

And his kid.

But for now he would concentrate on her.

He took hold of her hand and moved them back to the bed. He adjusted the pillows so she would be comfortable. "Lay back."

He kissed her as he helped her to the bed, settling her back so she was elevated, but he could get to that part of her he longed to taste.

"Spread your legs, love."

"I thought you were punishing me."

"That happens later. After the baby is born and you're completely healthy again, I intend to take it out on your backside. That sting I gave you is nothing compared to what I intend for you in a few months. And you should enjoy all the orgasms I give you now because you're going to have a long dry spell."

It was a fairly empty threat. Oh, he would spank the hell out of her.

He would whip that gorgeous ass, but he struggled with denying her pleasure.

Giving her pleasure was his job.

He pulled her ankles apart and settled himself between her legs. Silky skin surrounded him. The smell of her arousal made his cock tighten.

He rubbed his nose right in her labia, loving the way her thighs tightened around him.

She was his favorite dessert. He licked her in long, loving passes, gathering the honey of her core on his tongue. He sucked and licked, laving every inch of her pussy with affection. He pulled her labia apart and fucked her with his tongue, moving into her channel with a singular purpose. Over and over he surged into her, feeling her body starting to shiver and shake. Hot moans came out of her body.

"Please, Stef. Please."

She was pleasing Stef. Every gasp and plea loosened something deep inside him. Keeping her at arm's length had hurt them both. He needed her close. He needed every moment he had with her.

He found her clit and sucked it into his mouth, using his tongue to send her flying.

Jennifer shouted out as she came all over his tongue.

He flipped onto his back, the soft comforter against his skin. But he didn't want the silk of the bed covering him. He wanted his wife. "Come on, baby. Ride me."

He stroked his cock as she moved into position, straddling him carefully. Her belly was so round, her breasts ripe, her skin glowing. She was so fucking beautiful and she was his.

Forever.

They could have a baby and he would love her. They could go through life's ups and downs and he would love her. The whole world could change and only one thing would remain steady—he would love her. He would love her until the day he died and long after.

"Forgive me."

She shook her head, but he could see how emotional she was. "There's nothing to forgive. You got scared. You came back to me."

He couldn't help but smile. "I was drugged and dragged back."

"And I'll do it again, Stef, because you're mine. You belong to me.

You said I belonged to you, well, it works both ways."

He let his hands find her hips, his cock already pressed to her pussy. "I belong to you heart and soul, love. Always."

She lowered herself onto him. She wasn't as graceful as she normally was, her body made unwieldy by the child growing there, but he'd never seen anything so gorgeous as his pregnant wife taking his cock into her body. She was so careful, biting that gorgeous bottom lip as she took him in inch by glorious inch.

Heat enveloped him, wrapping him up in Jennifer's unique essence. No matter how many times he had her, it would never be enough.

He held himself still, giving her time to get comfortable, to work her way down. He watched her face, the way her eyes closed in pleasure as she worked her hips.

He was dying. His cock was going to burst, but he wouldn't take this from her.

"You feel so good."

"You have no idea, love. You're killing me."

A hint of a smile curled her lips up. She always had that smile. Julian had talked about seeing the world anew through the eyes of his child, but Jennifer was the first one to make him look at his life in a different way. She'd been the one to force him to see how much beauty there could be in the world. That smile of hers had been the doorway. "We can't have that, now can we?"

She sighed in pleasure as he joined them fully.

Stef gritted his teeth as she stopped and then dragged her pussy back up his cock. Tight, wet heat threatened to send him over the edge. Jennifer moved herself up and down, a slow, grinding penetration. Over and over she lifted and descended, dancing on his dick.

He gripped her hips, pushing up into her.

She wiggled, her head falling back as a breathy moan came out of the back of her throat and she tightened around him, her orgasm calling his own.

He lost it. He held her firmly and thrust up, his cock finding her sweet spot, and she screamed his name.

His balls pulled tight against his body and he shot off, the pleasure coursing through his body. He ground upward, giving his wife everything he had.

Sweet peace. Jennifer slid off his body, turning slightly away so her belly rested against one of the pillows. Stef turned, spooning her body, unwilling to break the connection. He might never break the connection again. He'd been so stupid. He needed to hold her when he was worried. He needed to wrap himself around her. He slid one arm under her shoulders and the other on to her belly, resting right over the fullest part.

Jennifer sighed. "Now we know how to get him to sleep. He's been kicking like a soccer player all day. He's finally still."

A shock of worry shot through his system. "Did we hurt him? Is that why he's not kicking?"

Jennifer slid a hand over his. "No, babe. Like I said, he's sleeping. Our lovemaking rocked him to sleep." She yawned. "It might have rocked me to sleep, too. Hmmm, we need to do that more. I feel so good."

She snuggled back against him. She was soft and sweet in his arms and his cock was already stirring again.

"You don't need to sleep, love." He didn't want to sleep. Once the baby was born, it would be a while before he had her to himself again. Jennifer wouldn't allow her child to be raised by a series of nannies. She had already placed a crib in their bedroom so she could have baby Logan close at hand.

He wasn't ready to share his wife yet. Sometimes it felt like he'd just found her.

She moved out of his arms. "I should have known I was waking a sleeping bear."

Not a bear exactly. A sleeping Dom was more like it. "Come back here."

She turned slightly as she sat up. "I will, but my bladder is smaller than it used to be. Or has less space than it used to. I'm going to get cleaned up and then we'll see if we can keep this baby asleep for a little while. I think I'll find another burst of energy somewhere."

She hauled herself up and walked toward the bathroom, leaving him with the sight of her fine backside. She shut the door and he relaxed.

His whole body was humming, but his head was right back to worrying.

Jennifer seemed so sure of herself. She was a natural mother. She didn't question anything, simply expected that they would be able to handle everything. She didn't sit up anxious about all the things that could go wrong.

She didn't worry that she wouldn't be able to love her child as much as he needed to be loved.

Stef loved his father, but years of neglect had played hell on his confidence in this arena. He had no real memories to pull from, no place to start.

He took a long breath. He still had some time. He could talk things out with Jennifer, maybe sit down with Max and Rye after he'd beaten the holy shit out of them and figure out how they had dealt with it. If Max Harper could be an effective father, there had to be hope for him.

He had a week or two to figure it out.

The door to the bathroom slammed open and Jennifer was standing there, a shocked expression on her face. "Stef?"

His heart nearly stopped. He shot to his feet. "What's wrong?"

"My water broke."

His time was up.

Chapter Sixteen

Rafe

Rafe let himself into the small cabin he'd called home for the last year. It was blissfully devoid of the businessmen and women who had been arguing when he'd left.

He glanced up at the clock. Five. Only a few hours until he was supposed to be at Trio. He'd skipped the men's party, so he had to make an appearance at Trio. He didn't know Leo or Shelley and he kind of still wanted to punch Wolf, but Laura had made him promise.

If she was still talking to him.

Cam was sitting at the kitchen table. He looked up when Rafe walked through the door. "Hey, man. I kicked everyone out. I told them you would get back to them. It should work for a couple of hours. The good news is Jen Talbot went into labor, so they'll be preoccupied with that for a few minutes."

Another friend for Sierra. "How's the baby?"

"Stella fed her while we were gone and she's asleep again. Laura's in there with her now. You know she likes to stare."

Rafe did, too. He liked to stand over her crib and look down and watch her sleep.

"Rafe?" a feminine voice asked.

He turned and his breath caught. God, he loved his wife. He loved this family they had made together. "I'm not going to go anywhere."

Laura's eyes went soft and she rushed to him, her arms winding around his waist. "We need to talk. I need to ask your forgiveness."

So Cam had told her about his mother. "It's all right, *bella*."

Her head shook. "It's not. I was mean. Oh, Rafe, I was scared. I can't stand the thought of losing you, but I can't make dictates and draw lines in the sand without talking to you."

He let his hands find her hair. "I'm all right."

"I'm so sorry I said those things about your mom. You have to be devastated. I know how close you are."

"Were, my love. We were close, but she's chosen to no longer be close to me."

Her arms tightened as though she was trying to hold him to her. "Are you mad at us?"

"Never." He forced her head up. "Oh, *bella*, I'm not even mad at her. I'm sad and I feel a bit lost."

"Because of the job stuff? I promise we're going to make this all work. Once Cam's done with the software, we'll have a million options. You don't have to work for a while."

Sure they would. "I would prefer to work, but I'll take care of Sierra."

Sometimes a man had to sacrifice his dreams. *And sometimes,* a voice inside him said, *a man found new dreams, new hopes, new battles to fight.*

Tears were shining in Laura's eyes as she looked up at him. "Or we can sit down and figure out how we would live in Miami."

Cam was suddenly standing beside him. "We can talk about it over dinner. We have to be at Trio in a couple of hours. Nate's going to be at the hospital. He's called in some backups to run the stationhouse. I need to hang out at this weird ceremony of Cassidy's. Caleb is on doctor duty, so I might have to take care of Mel, if you know what I mean."

Another thing he wouldn't have to worry about if they went to Miami. No one would have to be on standby in case Mel went a little crazy and needed to take a nap via sedative.

Laura's hands were on his waist. "We could talk about it now."

His body started to heat up at the seduction in her voice. They'd only had Sierra for a few months. All of their time had been spent watching their new daughter, sitting up with her, feeding and loving her.

He missed his wife. "Or we could not talk, *bella*."

He knew of only one way to make his wife be quiet. He dropped his mouth to hers and kissed her with everything he had.

This was his safe place. This was where he could relax. When she was in his arms, he knew exactly what he'd been born to do. He'd been born to love her.

His tongue surged inside, and she made no move to stop him. Oh, no, she softened underneath him, her lips parting eagerly and meeting him with the silky glide of her tongue.

He heard her sigh as Cam moved in behind her.

"Kiss Cam." He didn't want to leave his partner out. Cam had his back. Cam had been the one to bridge the gap between them. Without Cam, they would still be fighting. He would have been too stubborn to explain himself. She would have been too angry to ask questions. Cam bridged them.

And if he were gone, Cam would let Laura walk all over him. They needed each other.

And they definitely needed her. He'd known it from the moment he'd seen her all those years ago. They'd lost five years along the way. He wouldn't allow them to lose another second.

He watched as she kissed Cam. Cam pulled her body close. He was taller than Laura, bending over to get at her mouth. Cam devoured her. Watching them had Rafe's cock twitching in his pants.

They were going to have her. They were going to take her pussy and her ass and he would feel like he was a part of something incredible.

Cam turned her back to Rafe, his hands pulling at her blouse. He brought it over her head and leaned in. "Take off that bra. Show us your breasts."

Yes, this was what he needed. He needed her compliant. He needed her soft and sweet. His wife would never be truly submissive. Some of the trios in Bliss played that way, but Laura needed her control. Still, his cock did a dance as she obeyed Cam, her hands undoing the front clasp of her bra and those perfect breasts of hers spilling out.

Perfect and round, with tight brown and pink nipples. His mouth watered as he looked down at her tits. His hands came up and he palmed her, feeling the hard points of her nipples against his skin.

Her eyes closed and she sighed, her head rolling back to Cam's chest.

And then there it was—a soft sound that came through the baby monitor. Sierra cried and the whole world stopped.

They all froze as though they could halt the horror that was occurring. Not a single sound was made, not a breath passed between the three of them.

One second and then two. A third passed and then Laura looked up at him. "You need to fuck me now. She is going to wake up and I need an orgasm. Hurry, Rafe. Hurry."

A quickie. Yeah, he could do a quickie. Anything to get inside her. It had been so long, so damn long. He was aching for it. He let go of all his worries, all his cares. Only one thing mattered—being with his wife.

He picked her up, her slight weight nothing against his strength. He swung her up into his arms, like he had on their wedding night, like he would when they were eighty and he could barely handle her. He would find a way to carry her around because she was his. Maybe it would take them both. Perhaps that was how they would manage it. It would be him and Cam, loving Laura forever.

"Quietly," Cam said, a grin on his face. "If worse comes to worse, I'll take the baby, but I expect you to pay me back."

Always. A deep well of love for Cam welled up. He didn't want to kiss Cam or make love to his nasty ass, but he loved him all the same, and despite what his mother believed, it was good and right and perfect. He always had backup. He never had to worry that Laura would be alone, that his daughter would be alone.

Family. His mother had been alone when his parents split up, and it had turned her into a bitter woman. He wouldn't be allowed to make the same mistake. Cam would kick his ass if he tried to leave. Cam would call him home.

He hurried through the door to their small room. They needed at least two more, and Laura was right. He had the money to do it, but he'd been hedging his bets. No more. This was their home. This was the best place to raise their baby. He would open up the wallet and get them what they needed, including a wraparound deck where they could sit and watch Sierra run around. And her brothers or sisters.

More. He wanted more, but it had nothing to do with more money or choices. He wanted more children, more family, more love. More responsibility.

He tossed her on the bed.

"Out of the clothes now." Rafe wanted to see her, every inch of her.

She hustled, pushing at her slacks and shoving her shoes off her feet. They were cute wedges, but he wanted her naked. Her skin was shown off inch by inch, from the slight, feminine curve of her belly, to the swell of her hips, to her perfectly shaven pussy.

"Fuck. Spread your legs. I want a taste." He hadn't licked at her pussy in months. There had been too much to do. Despite the fact that Sierra hadn't come from her womb, Laura was a mom now, a mother with an infant, and she was so tired, but they needed this connection. Sierra needed them to have it. She needed her parents to be passionate about each other.

He tore his own clothes off. He couldn't stand the thought of a single centimeter of cloth between them. He shoved his shirt aside, pulled off his pants, and shoved his boxers down, freeing his cock. He was pulsing with need, desperate to get inside.

"Come on, baby." Cam had shed his uniform. He strode into the room completely naked and utterly confident. "He needs to get his tongue on you. We both do. It's been far too long. We don't know how much time we have so spread those gorgeous legs for your men."

She laid back and slowly brought her ankles apart, every centimeter a flirty seduction. She licked her lips, tempting him to play with her. "My legs are spread. I'm ready for you."

Rafe dropped to his knees and shoved his face toward her pussy. He loved her smell and taste and the soft skin of her labia against his tongue. He dove deep, spreading her with his fingers and licking up every ounce of cream she had.

He parted her labia, sucking one and then the other side between his lips. So fucking sweet. The shells of her sex were petal soft and getting damp with arousal. It coated his mouth, filling him with her essence.

He let his eyes drift up, and Cam was busy at work. His mouth was at her breast, pulling and tugging on her nipples. His left hand was flicking her other nipple, keeping it on edge. Laura's head was thrown back, her mouth open on a keening cry.

He played with her clit, pressing down on that nubbin and dragging it in slow circles. He speared her with his tongue, fucking up inside her in long strokes. He covered her whole pussy with his mouth, his thumb on her clit. He pressed down and felt her start to shake, her hips shimming with the dawning orgasm.

She came all over his tongue, coating his mouth and filling him. Perfection. He spread her wide, getting every drop he could.

His cock was pulsing, desperate. He shoved her knees apart. "Cam, get the lube."

He wanted inside her, but he didn't want to go alone. He wanted Cam with him, the three of them together.

Cam was grinning as he got to his knees. "Already on it." He had a blue tube in his hands. "What do you say we get creative?"

Laura was sighing. "We don't need creativity. I'm happy to be right here. Do you know how good that felt? Months and months and I haven't felt anything like that."

Neither had he. He'd had little kisses, fleeting things as they passed the baby to each other or as she ran out of the house for work. This was what he'd been missing, the deep connection between the three of them.

This was what he could never explain to his mother, what a person simply had to accept—that they were connected, together, that they would never be whole apart.

It was odd and weird and it was theirs.

Rafe opened himself. That was what Hiram had claimed he refused to do. He opened himself and suddenly he was full. Full of love. Full of hope. Full of them.

"Let's play."

Cam lubed up his cock. He laid back on their bed, his hand running up and down his dick. "Those are the words I want to hear. Come on, baby. Sit on my dick. Work that hot ass on my cock."

Laura's eyes lit up, and he saw the moment she stopped being a mom and gave herself permission to be a woman. They'd been parents for the last couple of months and had forgotten to be lovers. Her skin flushed a pretty pink and her nipples stood at attention. Such pretty nipples.

Rafe reached out and grasped her hands, giving her the balance she would need. They hadn't tried this particular configuration before, but Rafe was feeling as adventurous as Cam obviously was.

Cam was holding his cock in his hand. "Help us, Rafe."

That was his job. It was Cam's job. They were partners. Other people could call themselves partners, but Rafe truly understood what it meant. It meant sharing a life. It meant sharing their wife and kids. It meant having someone's back.

He held her hands as he lowered her down. Cam's fingers circled her hips, gripped her.

He watched her face as she grimaced. "Do you have to have such good aim?"

He grinned. It had been a while since her pretty asshole had been invaded. "Oh, my poor darling. Is he too big?"

Her eyes rolled back as she sank onto Cam, releasing Rafe's hands as she found her balance. "He's too big. You know that's why it feels so fucking good."

He did. At least on an intellectual level. "You take him. You take every inch he has to give you. You let his cock into your ass or you won't get anything else."

Laura might not be a sub, but she responded to dominance.

She whimpered, a sound that went straight to his dick. He was dying, pulsing, blood flowing to his cock and making the world shift to one reality. Her. He needed to be inside his wife. He had to get into that pussy or die.

"God, you feel so fucking good." Cam groaned as he worked her down his cock. "Take more."

Laura wiggled, her eyes flaring as she sank onto Cam's dick.

She was trapped, her body naked and soft. Cam held her hips. Her legs spread wide, welcoming Rafe in.

He stepped back, taking in the sight. Perverted? Perhaps. But there was no doubt in his mind that while what he shared with them would be considered perverted and weird, it was also love.

"Rafe? Come here. I need you." Laura's voice called to him.

He stepped up because he needed her, too. Cam and Laura. They were his family.

He moved in and kissed his wife, pressing her back against Cam. His cock was aching, rubbing against the soft flesh of her pussy.

His body anchored hers and her hands came around his waist, clutching at the cheeks of his ass.

"You're teasing me," she accused.

"You're killing me," Cam shot back with a low moan. "Come on, man. Baby girl could wake up any minute. Get this bus moving."

He wanted to play forever, but Cam was right. Their time was no longer their own, and that was how it should be. They were more than a trio now, and they would always be Sierra's mom and dads.

Always. And always partners and spouses.

Rafe reached down and guided his cock where it always wanted to be—inside her. He worked his way in, thrusting in little forays because she was so damn tight. Cam's massive dick in her ass made her all the tighter, all the sweeter.

Heat suffused him, threatening to make the experience a short one. He forced himself to focus on her, to make it last as long as it could.

"You feel so right." She felt right and perfect and good. There was nothing wrong with loving her the way she needed to be loved, and she needed them both.

Hell, he needed Cam.

"Are you ready?"

Cam gave him a steady grin. "Brother, I was born ready for this."

Rafe surged in as Cam retreated.

Laura gasped, her head falling back as she gave over to them.

Rafe pulled out almost to the tip. He found his rhythm, the partnership with Cam so ingrained that they simply knew what to do, as though their bodies were in synch.

Over and over he dove in and rode back out. She was tight on the way in, as though fighting him, but the sensation was fluid, changing as he pulled out, fighting as hard to keep him inside.

Laura's arms were around him, holding him close. Though he was on top, she surrounded him, but it wasn't merely her arms that pulled him close. This small cabin that had seemed so tiny an hour before was big enough to hold them all. It was big enough to hold his whole world.

Rafe knew he was close. They couldn't last too long. She felt far too good. Already his spine was tingling, his skin lit with pleasure. Cam's skin was flushed. He was close, too. They had to make sure their wife went first.

He shoved his hand between them, finding her clit and pressing that button that always made her scream.

Her breath caught, and her whole body tightened as she came.

The tight muscles of her pussy milked him, sending him over the edge. He gave up any semblance of control and gave over to the feeling. He pumped himself into her, giving up everything he had.

Cam shouted and held her close as he pressed up inside.

Peace, a pulsing sense of peace, invaded his very bones.

He fell to the side, pulling her with him.

He had some big decisions to make, but nothing mattered now. His wife's arms were around him. His partner was close.

All was right with his small world.

But he knew he would soon have to decide if he was going to take his small family and make it much bigger.

Probed by Cassidy Meyer

PROBED BY CASSIDY MEYER
A podcast that lifts you up and explores dark places.

TRANSCRIPT OF EPISODE 413

Welcome. My name is Cassidy Meyer and I like to start these podcasts with an explanation. I was probed and impregnated by alien forces. Now I'm not saying some of it wasn't nice because it was. My alien lover was a lovely male complete with extra parts designed to enhance womanly pleasure. But I rapidly discovered that sex and love are two separate things. I intend to stay true to my human lover, Mel. If you are listening to this from the Zandar galaxy, you know him as Xitilhup, the great hunter. That's right. He's watching you. Now I know my boys were born to rule planetary systems but we have chosen a quiet life here on earth and I would appreciate it if everyone both human and alien will respect that particular life choice. So this is Probed with Cassidy and on today's show we will talk about beets and the historical reasons behind why aliens are allergic. Hint – it has something to do with how Lincoln beat back the Reticulan Gray invasion of 1889. Now some people will tell you that he was dead by then, but we know the truth...

Chapter Seventeen

Leo, Shelley, and Wolf

Wolf looked around the bar, hoping to catch sight of his fiancée. He needed to find her, hold her, reassure himself that the whole freaking world hadn't upended.

Some bastard out there had used him to torture his mother. He'd put a good face on with Mel and Leo, but he fully intended to have a nice discussion with his "father."

God, his father had hit his ma and Leo. If his mother hadn't found the strength, they might have grown up very differently.

He remembered all the times some asshole in his class had told him he took after his ma. It was their way of telling him he was crazy and an outcast, but he was never more proud to take after his mother than he was tonight.

Even if she was wearing a headdress made of beets. She looked like the vegetable version of Carmen Miranda. He wasn't even sure how that thing was staying on her head. She turned from the table she was at, a bright smile on her face. "Wolfgang."

God, no one in Dallas ever called him Wolfgang, and he kind of liked it that way. Still, he forced a smile on his face. "Hi, Ma. Looks like we're getting set. Isn't this a whole lot of ceremony for one drink?"

God, he prayed it was only one drink. A small one. Shelley might run if there was a tumbler involved.

His ma shook her head. "It's so much more, Wolfgang. Shelley's agreed to make her pledge tonight."

"There's a pledge?"

"Of course."

Well, naturally. "Ma, I'm going to ask you to go easy on Shell. Please."

"No need, babe." An arm wound around his waist, and she was suddenly at his side.

He practically sighed. He hated being away from her, and he'd been away far too often lately. He pulled her close, reveling in how soft she felt against him. "Hey, baby."

She tilted her face up, offering those gorgeous lips of hers. "Kiss me hello."

He wasn't going to refuse that offer. He bent down, covering her lips with his, his tongue delving briefly inside her mouth. "Hello."

She smiled up at him, a peace to her expression he hadn't seen in a while. She'd been a bit manic lately, but now she was relaxed. "Your mom and I spent the afternoon going over my pledge, so don't you interrupt us tonight."

"Shelley was real sweet. She helped us make the decorations and everything. You got a real good girl there." His ma looked at Shelley like she was a shining light in the darkness.

Wolf's heart damn near skipped a beat. This was not what he'd expected.

"Well, this is a special day, Ma." There was a quiver to Shelley's voice that told him she was emotional. In a good way.

What the fuck had happened? For the first time, he wondered if aliens had taken his sweet baby and replaced her with a pod person.

"It certainly is." His ma gave Shelley a quick hug. "This should all be ready in an hour or so."

She turned back and went about her work with an energy he hadn't seen from her in a long time.

Wolf looked down at Shelley, his eyes wide. He couldn't talk to her here. Out of the corner of his eye, he caught sight of Leo walking in the door and waved him over. The place was starting to get packed. He saw Logan, Seth, and Georgia in a back booth laughing with Gemma, Jesse, and Cade. Laura was talking to Cam, but Rafe didn't seem to be with them. God, he hoped that went all right. He liked Laura and couldn't stand the thought that one of her men might leave. The Circle G contingent was in full force. Shelley's brother, Trev, had a cup of coffee in one hand, his other arm slung around his pretty wife, Beth. She sat in between him and Bo O'Malley. They were having an animated discussion with Jamie, Hope, and Noah. His boss was standing in the back, watching Dani and Finn on the dance floor, a smile on his face.

Even Kitten had shown up with her brand-new Dom, Cole Roberts, who owned the ski lodge. She was vibrant in a lovely baby-blue dress and high heels, but he could tell they were still awkward with each other. While Kitten laughed with some of the Dallas girls, Cole held himself back.

It wasn't all hugs and kisses though, Wolf noted. Aidan and Lucas were sitting with the Circle G crowd, but Wolf didn't see Lexi anywhere.

And then there was Michael Novack. Why the hell the former US Marshal was here he had no idea. He was sipping a beer and he seemed to utterly ignore everything that went on around him with one exception. His eyes were like lasers on Lucy, the pretty brunette waitress. Well, he stared at her until she actually tried to get his attention and then he pretended to ignore her.

But then she was ignoring Tyler Davis, so it kind of served her right. That was an interesting threesome.

"Hey, why is Ma wearing a vegetable garden on her head?" Leo asked as he walked up, pulling Wolf out of the Trio soap opera happening in front of him.

"She's a Priestess of the Beet," Shelley informed him. "It's very important. If I ever want to become one, I have to take it seriously. No beet tablets for the Priestess. She told me beet tablets could be easily manipulated. It's where she and Mel diverge. They had a long argument over it. She thinks he might have been brainwashed at his last probing. He claims she's crazy. Like he should say that. And then they made out for a long time. It's all very complex."

Wolf forgot about everyone else and decided to concentrate on the changes that had come over his bride-to-be. The last thing he wanted to think about was beets and his ma making out. "We all need to talk."

He took Shelley's hand and started to lead her toward the back, behind the bar. There was a kitchen and freezer and tons of closet space. Wolf had taken bartending shifts when he'd first come home. He knew exactly where to go to get away from all the noise and hubbub.

"Where are we going?" Shelley asked.

"Someplace where I can hear myself think." Once he got her behind the bar, they could talk without shouting. He pulled her along and Leo followed.

He walked them past the bar. No one was standing behind it. Lucy passed them with a tray full of drinks, and Alexei stepped into the back. Wolf led Shelley into the dark recesses of the bar.

"What the hell happened tonight?" The last time he'd talked to her, she was so pissed at his ma she couldn't speak.

Shelley turned into his body, her hand coming up to cover his chest. "Tonight? Not a lot. I helped your mom out. I drove her here. Her car needs a tune-up by the way."

"You drove Ma?" Leo asked.

At least someone got it. "She and Ma seem real tight all of a sudden."

Shelley's laugh rang in his ears. "Well, we are now. I finally figured her out. I think we'll get along really well. Your mother is a great lady."

"Did she feed you some of Mel's tonic?" Leo asked, his eyes searching her face.

Shelley huffed. "No. No, I just found a few things out about her, about what she went through. I met your dad today."

Wolf's heart clenched. "He came after you?"

Leo turned her toward him. "What the fuck did the bastard do?"

Shelley didn't seem at all fazed by his and Leo's freaked-out anger. She simply smiled and ran a hand along Leo's chest, leaning her body back toward Wolf. "We had a talk and it pointed out a few things to me. He tried his damnedest to scare me, but I took a couple of shots at him and he ran away."

Shelley had taken a shot at him? "With what? You barely managed to shoot my gun."

"You shot him?" Leo asked, but there was pride in the question.

"I didn't shoot him." Shelley leaned over and ran her nose along

Leo's neck. She turned and her hands found Wolf's waist. "He came to me at the Talbot estate this afternoon. I listened to his very disgusting rant and then I went inside, ostensibly to get him a check for ten grand. I went in the house and found Rachel Harper and she loaned me her revolver. I made sure the asshole won't ever come near my mother-in-law again. If he comes anywhere close to Cassidy, I swear I will shoot off his balls. It might take me two or three tries because I'm a horrible shot, but I'll make it happen."

Wolf brought his hand to her face. "He threatened you?"

Sweet brown eyes rolled. "Like he could. He told me he would go to Julian and tell him about you and Leo's past. He has a mistaken impression of Julian. He thinks he's some high-society drone who would be horrified to find out that his bodyguard had a bio dad who spent time in jail."

Leo snorted. "Julian knows everything. Julian knew more than we knew. If that fucker had gone to Julian, he would be six feet under now."

"I thought so, too, but I wanted him to be afraid of me." Shelley got on her tiptoes and pressed a kiss to his jaw. "I wanted to make sure he never got anywhere close to your momma."

His skin was lighting up everywhere she touched him. He had to wait until tomorrow night? It seemed like forever since he'd sank his dick inside her, found his home. "You tried to protect her for us?"

Shelley shook her head. "No. I protected her because she's going to be my mother tomorrow. My mom died. The only other mother I intend to have is Cassidy Meyer. And what I discovered about her today is that she's brave and strong and she is going to make one hell of a grandma if you two want her to be."

Leo moved in, not willing to go along with the seductive explanation Shelley was playing with. He had to be an impatient asshole. "Shelley, what happened today? Tell me right now."

Shelley didn't seem to be worried about his gruff tone. She pulled at Leo's shirt as she backed up past the kitchen. "I told you. I shot at the bad guy. He peed himself and ran away."

"I got that. I meant with Ma."

She stopped and seemed to get serious for a moment. "I realized we have a lot in common, Cassidy and I. We both picked crappy first husbands. We both got into horrible relationships that should have made us unwilling to ever try to love again. And we both survived and we both found great guys who love us. She did an amazing job raising the two of you. If she managed to be a great mom after everything she went through, then maybe I can be, too."

Wolf got behind Shelley, wrapping his arms around her. "Baby, you'll be a wonderful mom. How can you even question it?"

Leo's hands moved, cupping her face. "Is this what's been worrying you?"

"I thought it was the wedding." Had she been stressed about babies? He'd known she was worried, but he'd thought it was the stress that came with getting married.

Shelley nodded. "Sort of. I guess it's been a worry in the back of my mind. I know I said I wanted babies, but I've been afraid that maybe I didn't deserve them. And I'm definitely afraid that you don't want them, Leo."

Leo didn't ever want kids? He hadn't heard that. How could that be possible? "Leo?"

Leo's head shook. "Hey, that was before we got engaged. And yes, it had a lot to do with my dad. I still remember him. I remember how rough he was on Ma, how nasty he could be with me. I guess I've been afraid I might be a little like my dad, but that's bullshit. I didn't learn anything from that man except what not to do. My mother taught me everything. And watching Julian and Jack has made me think I could handle it. And I know Wolf can. He's practically my momma right now."

Wolf sent his brother his happy middle finger. "Fuck you, brother. I make sure you have lunch. You forget it half the time. And I could say you're practically my maid, and a nagging one at that."

Leo shuddered. "Well, you could pick up your clothes every now and then."

"No, I can't. The minute they hit the floor, you're diving to catch them and then bitching at me about what a slob I am." He totally wasn't. Not much. Maybe a little. Leo had an obsessive-compulsive need to see every inch of the floor at all times.

Shelley put a hand on each of their chests. "Both of you, stop."

And they did because Shelley was kind of, sort of the boss of them no matter how sweetly she submitted in the bedroom.

She smiled, a sexy expression that had her lips curving up. "So we're all in agreement about the babies thing?"

He'd never known they weren't. "I want lots of babies."

"I want babies that look like Shelley," Leo said, his face softening.

She turned her head, looking between them both. "You know I thought it was weird that neither one of you looks a thing like your father."

Wolf shrugged. He was happy about that. "Guess we took after Ma's side."

"Nope. I spent the afternoon looking through pictures of Cassidy's family while we played with beets. They're all small. She said Robert's people were, too."

Leo sighed. "We're not aliens, Shell."

Oh, god, had his mother gotten to her? "No alien DNA here."

She shrugged, a teasing smile on her lips. "I don't know. You seem smarter and faster and more agile than the normal human. And hey, I wouldn't mind if my kids got an edge because their dads had some freaky genetics."

She laughed and threw her arms around Leo, kissing him soundly. She turned and gave Wolf the same treatment.

He could actually see several play scenarios where being half-alien might be fun.

"Hey, I have about thirty minutes before I have to drink beet juice. Why don't we have one last crazy fling before we're boring old married people?" Shelley asked, a glint in her eye.

Wolf knew just the place. "There's a big closet where Zane keeps the dry goods."

He started to lead them back, finding the door and hauling them all in. He shut the door and turned on the small light. Thank god Lucy, Zane's waitress, was as obsessively, compulsively clean as his brother. The storage room was pin neat and had enough space for what he needed to do.

"Shouldn't we turn the lights off?" Shelley asked.

Leo stared at her. "Shouldn't you take your clothes off?"

Yep, he was already in Dom mode. That was plain to see. "Hurry, baby. He'll spend all his time spanking you and then we won't get to the part where I feel some small amount of relief for my aching dick."

It was only the truth. He'd been hard for days. Well, the whole sweat lodge thing had actually been a blessing since his cock had shriveled up at the thought of being alone in a sweaty, naked place with his brother and de facto stepfather, and his stepfather had been talking sex. It had been damn funny until he got a picture of it in his head. He was actually happy now that he was hard again. For a couple of minutes, he thought his cock might be dead.

"Well, we can't have that, can we?" Shelley pulled the tie on her wrap dress and was handing it to Leo in no time at all. Her gorgeous curves were on full display in a sexy black bra and some killer heels. No panties. His girl had learned that lesson long ago.

Leo sighed, his hand covering her shoulders and sliding down to her breasts. "Do you have any idea how much we've missed these breasts?"

Wolf flicked the back clasp of her bra because the situation was far too desperate for a ton of playtime. His brother liked to warm up, but Wolf was already on fire. "We sat around drinking beer last night and moaning about how long it had been since we've seen you naked, baby."

A shake in Leo's voice gave away the fact that he was on edge, too. "It's been eight days, thirteen hours, and twenty-four minutes."

Her head fell back against Wolf's shoulder as she laughed. "Well, you two certainly know how to make a girl feel wanted. Don't waste another minute. It's been that long since I saw you naked, too."

The closet was too small, but Wolf managed to get out of his clothes pretty damn quick.

Leo shrugged out of his shirt but put Shelley's hands on the fly of his jeans. "Take me out."

Damn, why hadn't he thought of that. "Me, too."

Shelley grinned as she got to her knees. "You're already out, Wolf."

He was. His cock was already pointed straight at her, pulsing and desperate. He couldn't help it. He was tuned in to her. She was his wife. They were as alone as they ever got and she was naked. His cock wasn't as patient as Leo's.

She unzipped Leo's jeans, drawing his cock out and lowering her head for a kiss. Wolf's cock strained, waiting for its turn. Shelley put a hand on him, firmly pumping his cock as she kissed Leo's.

Wolf let his eyes drift closed. This was where he'd needed to be for days. He'd needed to have her hands and mouth on him. He'd needed to remind himself that she'd chosen him and he had the family he wanted.

He looked down when he felt the heat of her mouth start to envelop his cockhead. Already he could feel a pulse of arousal wetting the tip.

Leo put his hands on her hair, pulling her dark head back. "Suck him, baby. Suck him hard. We don't have a ton of time before you have to prove you're not an alien queen, so prove to us that you're our queen."

She was. And she was damn fine at giving head. Her gorgeous lips slid down his dick, encasing him in spine-melting pleasure. Over and over she sucked at him, one hand coming up to play with his balls while her breasts jiggled and got him even hotter.

"That's perfect, baby. Take me deeper."

She obliged, opening her jaw and letting her tongue whirl over his cock.

Pleasure threatened to overtake him, but he stared down at her. Her eyes were up, watching him, too. Another connection. He watched as her mouth sucked his cock deep and then she pulled back almost to the tip before starting the journey again.

"Don't come, Wolf." Leo was on his knees behind her, one hand holding her hair while the other played with her breasts, tweaking the nipples. Leo pulled on them and Shelley groaned around Wolf's cock. The sound sent vibrations all over his skin.

His brother was so fucking bossy. "Dude, I don't think we can double-team her in here."

Not unless he wanted to get far too close to Zane's stash of paper towels. This was really more of a quickie-type situation.

"I don't think I'm that flexible, guys," Shelley said, coming off his cock.

A sharp slap sounded through the room. Shelley gasped, but Leo frowned. "Did I tell you to stop sucking? We might be in a storage closet, but I'm still the Dom, sweetheart."

Wolf was going to protest, but he shuddered as Shelley started in on his cock again. "So why can't I have my happy ending hummer?"

"Because how are you supposed to get a baby up in her? Maybe I should have let Mel explain the birds and the bees to you. See, it only looks like the baby is in a mother's belly. Let's talk about the uterus."

Fuck. He almost came at the thought. He had to step away, his cock popping out of her mouth. Because now he so didn't want her mouth.

"I would like to point out that I didn't stop. Wolf did. Are you going to spank him, too?" Shelley asked.

Leo twisted her nipples between his fingers. "I'll have you tied up and begging me, brat. But not right now. Right now we should all be thinking about the fact that I don't have a condom on me, and I'm betting Wolf doesn't either. We packed them all for the honeymoon, but I think we could better use that luggage space."

Shelley turned to him. "Are you sure?"

Leo nodded. "Yeah, I'm not getting any younger. And neither is Ma. I want her to see her grandkids. Coming home, it's meant a lot to me. I also think I could work a raise out of it. Ben and Chase haven't gotten Nat pregnant yet. We need to beat them."

His brother was a competitor to the end. "We can crush them. Our sperm can beat their sperm's ass. Besides, I think after all the tonic he drank today, Ben's sperm might be brain dead."

"Another thing to thank Mel for."

Shelley stood up. "Hey, no one asked me if I want to pit my womb against Nat's."

There was a smile on her face. God, how could he look at her face when all he could think about was getting inside her bareback? He'd never touched her without a condom on. The idea of nothing between them was making him a little crazy. "Shelley, if you're going to say no, say it now."

"I love Nat, but I'm going to kick her ass!"

And that was all Wolf needed. He picked her up and moved her to the wall, putting her back against it. The minute her arms and legs wound around him, he pushed his hips up and his cock found its home.

He pressed against her, his chest to her breasts, belly to belly, arms and legs entwined. "I love you. I love you so fucking much."

She was his whole world. He'd been born that day he'd met her. He could remember thinking that there was nothing for him after he left the SEALs, but Shelley had taught him how much more life there was left in him.

A whole future was laid out. A future with children and new adventures and challenges and a family he'd never imagined he could have. Emotion swamped him. He held her close and pushed up, burying his cock deep inside.

There was nothing between them. He could feel her heat and the warm depths of her pussy. It was so different, so much sweeter. There was no worry or compromise between them. They were through with that. There was only the future and everything it would bring.

Her hands came up, cupping his face. There were tears in those gorgeous brown eyes. "I love you, too. Do you have any idea how much I love you both? You give me everything. You give me everything I need. Do you know how few women get that?"

Because they loved her enough to share. But what she didn't understand was that she completed them both. It wouldn't work with just one of them. And nothing worked without her.

"What Wolf is trying to say is that we love you, too, baby."

Sometimes he wanted to punch his brother. "I love you, too."

Her head fell back, and he let himself go. He fucked up into her, not able to hold back a second longer. He pushed his cock into her pussy over and over and over again. Every muscle strained to bring her pleasure, to find his own. He used every ounce of his strength to hold her up, to move her up and down on his cock.

Shelley's breath became uneven, her nails sinking into the flesh of his back. She cried out, and the little muscles of her pussy started to grip him.

A telltale shiver began at the base of his spine.

He forced himself up, her pussy sucking at him, drawing him in and giving him more pleasure than he'd ever known.

He held her close as the orgasm engulfed him. Pleasure swamped him, coating his brain and making him shout out.

He pumped his cock in as long as he could, giving her everything he had.

Finally he was empty and he slumped against her, their bodies held up against the wall.

"Oh, my god, that felt so different." Shelley's hands moved against his scalp, pulling him close. Her mouth found his. "So different. We're going to win."

He laughed, his whole body filled with joy. He was surrounded by crazy people, and he was thrilled to be so.

He set her on the ground and took a step back. His brother immediately moved in.

Wolf knew exactly what it had cost his brother to let him go first. His brother had a dominant streak a mile wide, but in this, he'd allowed Wolf to lead. Because Leo knew what kids meant to him. And Leo had always made sure his brother got what he needed. From food to protection to being first.

Damn but he loved his brother.

"Let's take 'em down, brother," he said.

Leo high-fived him and crowded their almost wife.

And all was right with his world.

* * * *

Shelley took a long breath before Leo put his hands on her. Her body was still humming from the orgasm Wolf had given her.

"You okay, sweetheart?" Leo asked.

She looked up in his eyes. Wolf was the sweet one, but Leo moved her, too. Oh, he moved her. Her whole body went on full alert the minute he turned that dark voice on her. She needed them both. She needed Wolf's sweetness and Leo's dominance. She couldn't live without them. They were her world.

She'd made so many mistakes, but loving them wasn't one of them. Loving them had opened her up.

And she was going to have their babies. She was going to be a mom. Her sons and daughters would have such great fathers. Yes, she was giving them a unique family, but it would be full of love, full of devotion, full of hope.

"I'm fantastic." She put her arms around Leo's neck. It would likely be a while until they took her the way they had before. They wouldn't want to miss a chance to get her pregnant. They would fight for the right and then never even question who the baby belonged to. The baby would belong to them. Their baby would have two amazing dads.

"God, I'm so glad to hear that because I don't want to be selfless tonight." He kissed her neck.

She should be rung out. She shouldn't want this, but somehow her body had tuned to her heart's needs. She was only halfway there. She'd only had one of her men. She was ready for the last leg home.

She dropped to her knees. She wanted to submit to him. He was her

Dom. He needed her submission, and she longed to give it to him. She was on all fours and let her head drift down, her ass high in the air.

She heard Leo sigh behind her.

"Do you know what you do to me?" His voice had gone to that sweet, guttural place where she knew damn well she had him in the palm of her hand.

She wriggled her ass his way. "I only care that you want me."

She felt him get to his knees behind her. His hands found her hips. "You have no idea how fucking much I want you. Tell me what you learned today."

His cock was poking at her pussy, pressure making her shiver. She should have known that he wouldn't let it go. Honesty was the glue that held her to Leo. "I learned that I'm strong. I learned that I made mistakes but it's okay, and I can trust in us to build something better."

His cock pulsed at the edge of her pussy. She was tempted to shove back at him, but he would spank her ass if she did that.

"Why did you shoot my father?"

A loaded question. "He isn't your father, babe. I don't even know if you share DNA with him. I think I might go with your mom on this one."

A sharp smack hit her ass. "Shelley."

"No." She wasn't giving in this time. "A name on a birth certificate doesn't make him your dad. Biology is a chance of nature. Your mother loved you. She was your parent. Love makes a family. Nothing else. It's why I decided we should have babies. We love each other. We can make a good home. Love is all that matters. The man who signed your birth certificate means nothing. God, I think Mel might love you. He might be your real dad."

Another slap hit her ass. "I think you might be right, sweetheart."

She felt a kiss to the back of her neck. Shivers split her spine. "I know I'm right. I fought the thing with your mom, but I won't anymore. She's amazing. You're here because of her."

He sighed, a peaceful sound. "I know. I figured that out, too. He hurt me. I was just a kid and he hit me, and my ma wouldn't take that."

Her heart clenched. "He hit you?"

"Yes. She took it when it was her, but when he hurt me, she was done. I know she's got a crazy streak. I know it. Wolf knows it. But we love her. I can't thank you enough for accepting her."

Now her heart felt overflowing. "I don't merely accept her. I love her." It had happened the moment she realized they were the same. Cassidy had survived a bad marriage and produced two men Shelley loved more than her own life. "I love her. I will give her grandbabies and tell them how courageous their grandma is."

"I love you, sweetheart." His cock slid against her pussy, his hips pulling her back. "I love you so much."

She pressed against him. She didn't care whose damn sperm won. They were her husbands. Sure, it wasn't legal until tomorrow, but in her heart, she was already their wife.

The wedding meant nothing except a chance to get closer to Cassidy and Mel. Cassidy loved Mel and she was pretty damn sure Mel loved the hell out of Cassidy. That made Mel her father-in-law.

Leo's cock pressed in, filling her. God, her men were big. They stretched her and forced her to open up wide.

"Take me."

She couldn't disobey. She forced her ass back, letting Leo take her pussy inch by inch. She was already wet and wanton, ready for him. His cock forced its way in, every inch a pure pleasure against her skin.

Wolf was in front of her. She was never without both her men. He put a hand on her hair, letting him know he was there.

She was still with her men. They might take her separately for a while, but they were with her.

She felt Leo pressed against her, flush to her ass. His hips moved against her cheeks, trying to find the deepest entry point. He wanted to be as far inside her as he could possibly be—to get his semen deep inside her womb. It was what they both wanted, the chance to make a child with her, to start a family.

She wanted that, too. She pressed her backside back as far as she could go, giving Leo the chance to get high inside her.

Pressure quaked against her. Pure ecstasy ran through her veins. He pulsed inside her. She'd just come, but she was softening again, getting moist and warm around him. They had spent long hours training her to accept their pleasure.

She relaxed under his dominance, his big hand running up her spine. "Take me." She gave him his words back.

"Oh, I'll take you, brat. I'll take you every day I can for the rest of our lives." His cock surged in, filling her and making her quake.

The ground was hard underneath her, but she didn't really feel it. All she felt was Leo's cock invading her and Wolf's hands in her hair. All she felt was her crazy love for her men.

"You know I will." Leo slammed into her, shoving his cock as far as he could go. His hands held her hips hard, forcing her back on his dick.

He filled her as well as Wolf had.

And then she felt something at her ass.

"I'll fill you everywhere," Leo promised, the words rumbling against her neck. His finger pressed against her asshole.

That was Leo. He wouldn't stop at merely getting her pregnant. He would need to fill her completely.

Her asshole clenched, and she felt a sharp slap to her backside.

"You let me in."

Oh, god. It wasn't Leo's finger. It was Wolf's. He was pressing into her ass. He was dominating her. He was on his knees next to his brother so he could press his finger into her ass.

"He seems serious, baby." Leo kept up his long, slow fuck. "You should let him in."

She tried to relax, allowing her ass to flex and let that finger deep inside.

"That's right, baby," Wolf said. His free hand came up to play with her breast, plucking at her nipple. God, she loved that. It went straight to her pussy.

They both had their hands on her. Leo was pulling her back, impaling her on his cock, and Wolf's finger was fucking her ass and pulling at her nipples.

Her world was pretty perfect.

And then Leo slapped her ass. "Why did I have to find out my blackmailing father came to you after you nearly shot him?"

She should have known he would be pissed about that. "Because my phone was in my purse when he tried to blackmail me. I could go for the phone or Rachel Harper's gun. I picked the gun. Hey, should I get my own gun?"

It made perfect sense. She needed her own gun.

"I'll die first." Leo slammed into her. "You will let your men protect you. And we're not going to need protection. We're going to live a quiet happy life, and no one is going to try to kill any one of us, damn it. God, that feels fucking good."

He pulsed inside her, over and over again. He drew out and slammed back. Every inch of his cock was pure pleasure. He fucked her hard, hammering in and out of her pussy as Wolf matched his rhythm in her ass.

Wolf's fingers stretched her as Leo's cock plunged deep. So much heat, so much life.

She was full of them.

She let herself go. She moved her hips, taking them hard and deep.

Wolf stretched her, making her squirm and shake. Leo fucked her hard, hitting her sweet spot and making her scream his name. She shouted her pleasure over and over again. Every muscle worked. Every inch of skin quivered. She felt herself convulse, sending her pleasure out and clamping around him. She held him as tight as she could.

Leo bucked and his gorgeous face contorted and she felt him flood her pussy. She was warm and wet and full. Leo and Wolf's semen was hot and wet inside her.

And maybe racing toward her womb to make a baby.

That thought would have scared the holy crap out of her two days ago, and now all she could think about was how happy they would be.

Because she'd discovered that she was right. She'd been worried about her decision making, but she knew they were right. Bryce had blackmailed her into marrying him. He'd used her love for her mother and then her love for her brother to keep him close. She'd been so young. She didn't have those fears about Leo and Wolf. They loved her. They wanted to take care of her.

"Come on, baby." Leo was still panting as he got to his feet and started to haul her up. "You have to prove you're not an alien queen. Though I would still fuck you hard. You have to know that."

He would. So would Wolf. She reached out and steadied herself against them. She turned into Wolf's arms. God, she loved how big he was. He loomed over her. She could barely fit herself against his chest.

She felt Leo move behind her. He was only slightly smaller than Wolf. He bent over to rest his head against her shoulder.

"We could stay here," Wolf said. "I'll accept her as an alien queen.

She can totally take my sperm."

But Cassidy would freak out. "No. I have to take the beet."

She winced as she said the words. But she would go through with it because now she knew how important it was.

"Hush, Wolf. She's got a connection to Ma now. We have to let it be. It's a good thing." Leo's arms curled around her. "Tomorrow, we're going to be married. Then you have to obey me."

She practically snorted. Like he didn't demand she obey him in the bedroom now. He was her hardass Dom. Nothing about that would change. And Wolf would be the one who indulged her every whim. She needed them both.

"Like I don't do that now." Her ass was still stinging from the slaps he'd given her. They hadn't been enough. She'd needed more, but it didn't matter because she still felt them inside her.

Things could change, but her love wouldn't. She knew that now. She could face anything as long as their love for each other was still strong.

Faith. Sometimes faith got a person through life. She could hear her momma whispering to her about faith in life, faith in the universe, faith in herself and her love.

Faith and hope had gotten Cassidy through, and she'd had far less than Shelley had.

Leo handed her the dress she'd been wearing. "Well, then it won't be hard for you."

He leaned over and pressed his mouth to hers, softening his words.

They elbowed each other, struggling in the small space to get dressed. Leo laughed, falling to his ass as he tried to get his jeans back on. Shelley tumbled into Wolf. They all hit the ground.

"Shhh." Wolf shoved a hand over her mouth. "Someone's out there. Listen."

A masculine voice cut through the silence. "I need to talk to you before I leave."

"That's Zane," Wolf said in her ear.

"All right. What you need to tell? You go to hospital?"

"That's the Russian," Leo whispered. "Alexei. Zane's bartender."

Damn. The last thing she needed was to get found half-dressed the night before her wedding. What they had done in the closet was probably some sort of health code violation.

"Yes. I got a call from Callie. I have to go to the clinic. Jen's having the baby. Nate and Callie are already on their way, but I have to join them. Stef is like Callie's brother. She won't let Jen go through this alone," Zane said.

They all settled down, no one making a move, as though they were all praying the door didn't open.

"No problem. I take care," Alexei said. "You don't to worry about anything."

"It's more complicated than that." Zane's voice was tense. "You need to see what's in the freezer."

What the hell was in the freezer? Did they have a bad shipment of beef?

She heard the sound of a heavy door opening. A moment passed and then Alexei spoke.

"What has happened, boss?"

Zane Hollister sighed and then his voice went low. Shelley couldn't hear most of what he said to his bartender, but a couple of words stood out. Hiram. Mayor. She heard Alexei gasp in what sounded like horror when that sweet lady named Nell from her bachelorette party was mentioned.

"This is disaster," Alexei said.

"We have a plan," Zane replied. There was more whispering and then a long sigh. "So you understand why we have to keep this quiet? I'll take care of it in the morning. You need to keep Lucy out of here tonight."

There was a little sniffle. "This make me miss mother Russia, Zane. Yes. Yes. Not to worry. I take care of for you."

"Dear god, no. I'm going to handle it in the morning. Properly and through all the correct channels. I'm just waiting for Rafe to do the right thing. He needs a night. I don't want Cade as our mayor. He'll make the whole damn town a safe place to be naked. I don't want to watch Max Harper flicking his dick in everyone's face. He will do it."

"Yes, he would make me uncomfortable as well. I could burn evidence for you. I do this many time before."

She felt Wolf start to laugh. She clasped a hand over his mouth.

"Damn it, I didn't commit any crimes," Zane argued. "I only want to make things right. Don't let anyone in the freezer, okay?"

"This I protect."

They continued to talk as the voices faded away.

"What the hell was that about?" Shelley asked as she managed to get up.

"God only knows. We're not going into that freezer," Leo said. Her bra was in her hands. She pulled it on.

"I don't want to know," Wolf said. "I want to go out there and get the ceremony done and get married tomorrow."

Bliss was an odd place.

She got dressed and followed her men out, carefully avoiding the freezer.

Twenty minutes later, she made her pledge—to fight all aliens, to embrace humanity, to love the Earth. Easy promises to make.

When Cassidy passed her a shot glass filled with beet juice, she slammed it down to the roar of the crowd.

Proving her humanity and her love for two very human men.

Chapter Eighteen

Rafe

Trio was hopping. Even from the street he could hear the raucous laughter coming from the tavern.

He patted the baby who was currently strapped to his chest. Yep, he was taking his baby into a bar, but then Trio wasn't the kind of bar where people got trashed and broke things. That was Hell on Wheels, and hopefully his daughter would never see the inside of that place. No, Trio was a meeting place. Trio was filled with families and friends.

Sierra's legs and arms kicked. He couldn't quite see her face but he was sure her eyes were wide with that wonder she seemed to have for everything from the trees to the fabric of his shirt to his car keys. His baby girl took everything in and all of it seemed amazing to her.

Maybe all he needed was a little of Sierra's wonder.

He opened his eyes and really took in the town he lived in.

It was filled with family. He stepped up close to the door and Max and Rye were walking out.

"Rafe, my man, did you hear about Jen?" Max asked, slapping him on the shoulder. "Won't be long now and we'll have a bigger playgroup."

Rye let Sierra take his thumb in her hand. "Max and I think we need to start a poker night. The girls have their meetings. We should be able to have one, too, right?"

The girls' meeting was something called the "I Shot a Son of a Bitch" club. Poker night sounded practically innocent. And it would be fun to get together with the men. "I think that would be great. I'll bring the beer."

"Bring a lot," Max said. "Have you seen how much that Russian can put away? He can drink us all under the table."

Alexei? Drink him under the table? "You haven't seen a Cuban drink, my friend. Perhaps I'll bring rum instead. I think this is going to be fun."

Rye's eyes widened. "Well, hell, I'll look forward to it, then."

The Harper twins walked off, talking about Stef and how they would have to watch him for a while. Rafe wasn't so sure Stef needed someone to watch him. He thought Talbot would make a good father, but he put it out of his head as he walked through the doors.

He was immediately surrounded. Holly gave him a hug and reached for the baby.

"Cam and Laura are dancing. You should join them." Holly winked. "I need baby snuggles."

"I can give you these snuggling babies, *dushka*." Her husband Alexei, who was going to get a run for his drinking money at the next men's gathering, gave his wife a smile before turning to pour another beer for Jesse McCann.

Holly shook her head. "He's baby crazy." Holly looked a little baby crazy herself as she held her hands up. "Please?"

Why had he thought his daughter wouldn't have a family? His daughter's family was huge and sometimes obnoxious. Like a family should be.

He'd spent the last few weeks mourning his own rigid, formal childhood. Perhaps a man always longed for what he knew, but what he had now was so much better. It was messy and hard, and these people would make him crazy.

And they would really love him. They would love his daughter. They would stand by him and his wife and partner whether they always agreed or not. They would argue with him and fight with him and they wouldn't leave him.

Sometimes a man lost one family only to find another.

"Rafe?" Zane walked around the bar. "Man, I'm glad to see you. Laura told me I needed to talk to Cade. I don't think that's a good idea. He's going to have to wear a shirt to town hall meetings, and that might be hard to get him to do. And let's face facts. If Cade takes over, he's going to be Gemma's puppet. That girl scares me."

He pulled out the letter they had found in Hiram's desk. It was time to put Zane and the Bliss Chamber of Commerce out of their collective misery. "It's all been decided. I think you'll find the new mayor's name here."

Zane frowned and took the paper. "Maybe we should talk about this."

"Just read the name."

Zane's eyes went to the name and he smiled. It was written right there. The deputy mayor of Bliss, selected by Hiram Jones himself, was one Rafael Kincaid. "Thank god. You won't regret it, man."

"Oh, I'm sure I will." He was certain he would need to start drinking before his first Bliss City Council meeting. But he also knew that it was right. He did have a job. He could mold the way his town developed. "But I expect to be mayor at least as long as Hiram."

Zane held out a hand, grasping his. "That's all we can ask, man. You have no idea how happy this makes me."

Rafe sent Zane what he hoped was a very mayoral frown. "Don't be too happy. I might have something to say about your health and sanitation standards if you don't extricate my predecessor very soon."

Zane shook his head, using his thumb to point to his bartender. "Alexei says he knows what to do. I filled him in on everything. He's a great accomplice."

Alexei nodded. "This is no problem. I handle many of these situations in Russia. I am good cleaner. I take care of this."

Alexei used to be a Russian mobster, so Rafe wasn't sure he wanted to know how Alexei would clean up. "You cannot chop him up. You need to get him to the funeral home. We found his will when we were looking for the document. It lays out everything he wanted, including instructions about how to handle his funeral and his body. He wants to be cremated."

"I do this many times in Russia!" Alexei smiled like cremating a guy was an everyday occurrence. Well, if he ever needed an enforcer, he knew where to go.

"The funeral home, Alexei."

The Russian shrugged. "I do for free, but I follow orders of mayor. Mayor has seized power in smart play that has blocked all competitors. This I respect."

He'd only done what Zane had told him to. And he didn't feel bad about it. It was best for the town, and Hiram had chosen him. And left him with a legacy.

He would build his family the way Hiram had. When he'd been turned out, Hiram hadn't gone into his shell and retreated. He'd gotten kicked in the gut, and his response had been to open himself up, to offer more, to build a town.

A deep sense of responsibility settled over him. Bliss was his, his to protect, to grow, to love. His family needed him, and he wouldn't let them down.

He looked over at Sierra, who was cooing at Holly. She would be the mayor's kid and the deputy's kid. She was doomed to be hell on wheels.

And he wouldn't have her any other way.

"Will you excuse me? I need to make a call." He started to look for his cell phone. He would have to go outside. It was raucous in Trio.

Zane pointed to the back. "Use my office, Mr. Mayor. I have to go and wait for Jen to spit out a baby. We're growing, you know. We need to talk about schools. I don't want my sons taking an hour-long bus trip every day. We need a school here."

"It's on the agenda," he said, moving back toward the office. He shut the door behind him and made the call he needed to make. He waited. It rang once and then again. Three times.

A low, angry voice came over the line. "I told you I will not speak with you, son. Not until you change your life."

Ah, his mother. He had but one more thing to say. "Don't speak. Simply listen. This is important because after this, the ball is in your court, Mama. I love you. I want to thank you for raising me. I want to thank you for loving me as much as you could. I want you to know that you can call me anytime and I will come to you. I will always honor you as my mother. I'm going to start something, Mama. I'm going to take pictures, so many of them that I can fill a wall in our house. Those pictures will be our blood, our history and tradition. You say that blood is all that matters, but, Mama, blood did not teach me how to work, how to strive. You did that. Blood did not hold me when I was sick. That was you. You are always welcome here in Colorado. And I will always love you. I would love for you to be a part of those pictures on my wall, but if you choose not to, then I will move on and I will raise my children with love. The way you raised me."

There was a sob that came over the line.

And then nothing.

She had hung up.

He'd done all he could do, and now it was up to his mother. Rafe took a long breath. Pain bloomed, but relief was right beyond the door. He didn't hesitate this time. He walked out and joined his family.

"Rafe!" Cam yelled over the music. "Come on. We're dancing."

Laura smiled, that gorgeous goddess calling to him. "Dance with us!"

Holly was bouncing Sierra gently, holding her close as Alexei smiled down at them both. His baby girl was safe with her aunt.

And it was time to dance.

The Phone Tree, Bliss Style

Stefan Talbot could barely breathe through the panic that threatened to overtake him.

"You have to call Callie," his wife said.

He needed to have his hands at two and ten because he wasn't going to be the man who had an accident on his way to the hospital. Clinic. His son wasn't being born in a hospital. He was being born in a two-room clinic.

"Or I'll do it," Jen said, her voice oddly calm.

It was mere seconds before Stella's voice came over the speaker in the car. "This is Stella's Cafe."

"Stella," Jen said. "It's go time."

There was a strangled shout over the line and then it went dead.

Jen grinned at him. "Stella will handle it all from here. She'll start the phone tree."

His wife gasped, a hand on her belly. "That wasn't so bad. It's all going to be okay, babe."

He prayed she was right.

Stella pressed the number to call Trio, her hands shaking with excitement. "Callie, it's time. They're on their way to the clinic. Let everyone know."

Callie dialed Rachel's number, joy in her heart. Unfortunately, it was Max who picked up. He would have to do because she needed to get to the clinic. "Hey, Logan's almost here. Stef and Jen are on their way right now. Pick up Rachel and meet me at the clinic. Hurry. Oh, and call Marie and let her know. She'll know what to do."

Max wished he hadn't picked up Rachel's phone. He didn't want to be the one to tell Marie her son had gotten into town and apparently needed the doc's services. "Hey, Marie. Uh, apparently Logan's at the clinic. Look, I think maybe Stef thought he was involved in shooting him up and took his revenge. He wasn't. That was me, but seriously Stef has the constitution of a rutting bull if he's already given Logan a beat down...Marie? Marie?"

She'd hung up on him and he did not envy Stef when he had to explain the mistake to Marie.

"What are you doing with my phone?" Rachel asked, giving him a death stare.

He shrugged. This was what a man got for helping out. "Callie called and said I should call Marie and tell her Logan is here and half dead or something. Jen and Stef are taking him to the clinic."

Rachel's jaw dropped. "Jen's having the baby?"

Huh, now that he thought about it, that could have been what Callie had said. She should have been clearer. "Now see this is why you shouldn't name people after other people. It gets confusing."

Rachel groaned and took the phone. "I'll handle it from here."

Marie slammed into her truck as Gemma's voice came over the line.

"Bliss County Sheriff's Department. This is Gemma."

"Gemma, you should let Nate know that I'm going to kill Stef Talbot if he hurt my boy."

"Whoa," Gemma said. "I just talked to Rachel. She tried to call you back. Max is an idiot. Logan's fine. Jen's in labor with Baby Logan. Not your Logan. Not that she would be in labor with him. The point is Max isn't allowed to answer her phone anymore and you don't have to shoot anyone. She also said something about a phone tree."

Marie breathed a sigh of relief. She could take it from here.

"Nell, Jen's in labor," she explained a few minutes later.

Nell held the phone to her ear, a smile of her face. "Mel, this is Nell, I'm calling to let you know something wonderous is happening and a new era is being birthed into this world we call Earth sometime tonight or tomorrow. It's a joyous time."

"Cassidy, baby, it's Mel. You were right about Shelley. She's here to steal the boys' seed. The invasion is coming."

And that's how Bliss does a phone tree.

Chapter Nineteen

Stef and Jen

Stef Talbot held his wife's hand, but he wanted the whole ordeal to be over with. She was tired, in so much pain. She squeezed his hand tightly, but he wondered how much more of this she could possibly take.

Hours and hours had gone by and it had gotten progressively worse. At first the contractions were bubbles of pain that she'd managed to smile through, then she'd squeezed his hand and promised him it wasn't bad, and now she screamed and groaned with every single one.

And they wouldn't let up. It was midnight. A whole night of her pain had gone by with no end in sight.

He was utterly helpless. He was surrounded by friends, and he'd never felt so alone in his whole life.

Max, Rye, and Rachel, Callie, Nate, and Zane, his father and Stella were all out in the waiting room, but he didn't want to talk to them. He didn't want to tell them how much pain his wife was in, how small and insignificant he felt in that moment.

He wanted it all to be over.

She finished another killer contraction and Jennifer's head flopped back to the pillow, her hand slacking in his. She was covered in sweat, her face red from exertion.

"Please take the drugs." He'd stopped commanding her a few hours back. It hadn't worked. She'd snarled back at him and refused. She had a birth plan, she'd told him, and it didn't involve drugs.

"Okay. I'll take them," she said, her voice a tortured whisper.

Thank god. He looked up at Naomi who was calmly writing in a chart. "She needs an epidural now. Call the anesthesiologist."

He'd decided natural childbirth was for the birds. Rachel must have an unnaturally high tolerance for pain. Jennifer didn't need to compete with her. Callie had been perfectly happy with her epidural. She'd started out with every intention of getting through it and four contractions in was screaming for drugs.

When Jennifer was relaxed and out of pain, maybe he would be able to breathe.

"Mr. Talbot, she's at a nine. The time for an epidural has passed." Naomi set aside the chart and gave Jennifer a friendly smile. "I'm sorry, honey, but it won't be long now."

"I hired an anesthesiologist to be on call." He'd only agreed to her birth plan because he had a team on call. Jennifer had insisted the baby be born in Bliss and not in Del Norte, where the nearest full-service hospital was. Logan Talbot was going to be born in Bliss according to his momma, and that meant his father had to be prepared. He wasn't about to let anyone ruin his plans. "I want him in here now. I want him doping her up and making her feel better and I want it right now." He used his deep voice, the one that got people to do what he wanted.

It seemed no one had given Naomi the memo. She shrugged off his command. "I explained when she got to four centimeters that we didn't have long. She's too far in for an epidural now. Dr. Harris is still on call, but he's only here in case she needs an emergency C-section, and it doesn't look like that's going to happen. She's doing great."

Jennifer's body seized and she screamed again, reaching for his hand. He let her damn near break his bones as she rode out the wave of pain.

"Oh, god, it hurts." She sobbed. "It hurts so much. I want to push. I want it to stop."

Every word tore at his soul. Why had he ever thought this was a good idea? She was precious. He should never have put her through this.

"I'm going to fix this."

Naomi was moving to the end of the bed. "You do that, Mr. Talbot. Jennifer, I'm going to check you again. Don't push yet."

"I'll take care of it, love. I'll make this right." He hated leaving her, but he had a job to do. He stepped out of the larger of the two patient rooms that Caleb had renovated in the last several months. The Bliss County Clinic now boasted a small emergency room, one operating room for the worst of emergencies, and two recovery rooms. And one very full waiting room.

"Hey, is she holding up okay, Stef?" Rye asked.

"She's in pain. She needs drugs." He looked around. Where the hell had Caleb gone?

Rachel was shaking her head. "See, I think woman should get drugs the whole last month of their pregnancy." She pointed at her slightly rounded belly. "This baby is getting drugs. And he's not being born on a table at Stella's. You know why? Because Stella doesn't have any drugs. Caleb has drugs."

Maybe his wife wasn't so far behind in that particular competition. But that didn't matter now. His eyes caught on Caleb as he walked into the waiting room wearing green scrubs. The man with the drugs. "Caleb, get in there and tell your nurse to call the anesthesiologist, or better yet, call him yourself. And then when you're done, you can fire her because she doesn't listen to orders."

A brilliant smile crossed Caleb's face. "Couldn't get Naomi to do what you wanted, huh? That's why she's the best nurse I've ever had. And it's too late for an epidural."

"Goddamn it, Caleb. She's in pain."

"That's what happens when you try to push a baby out of your body. I keep telling you people it's a bad idea and you keep on making kids."

He wasn't about to let this go. "You owe me. You get my wife her drugs and maybe I won't sue you for shooting me with a tranquilizer gun."

Caleb shook his head sharply. "Look, I'm not sorry about that. You've been an ass. And no jury is going to convict me. As for the epidural, I could go into a lengthy medical explanation of why it's a bad idea at this late stage of labor, but I'm just going to say no and leave it there."

The door opened, and Naomi looked out. "Doc? She's ready."

Caleb slapped him on the shoulder. "Come on, Talbot. Let's go and pull a tiny human being out of your wife's vagina. Damn, I might still get a nap in today. Your son cost me a good night's sleep, my friend."

She was ready? Ready to have their baby? His heart seemed to slow down just when he thought it would go supersonic. He heard the people around him, his friends and family, wishing him well and cheering Jennifer on. Callie had tears in her eyes, and she hugged him briefly. She said something that was probably meaningful, but it didn't penetrate. The world seemed to have slowed to a sluggish crawl, and he couldn't hear much past Caleb's voice.

She was ready. He wasn't ready. Not even close.

The door opened and Jennifer was already in stirrups, her legs spread in an odd facsimile of lovemaking—but this wasn't sex. It was the product of sex. It was pain and work and creation, and he had no real place here.

Jennifer screamed, her face red as she pushed.

Caleb looked between her legs and smiled. It was a surreal moment. He settled onto the stool at the foot of the bed. "There you go, Jen. You're doing great. He's crowning. Another couple like that and we're all done here. Easy breezy."

"Easy breezy, my ass, Caleb Burke. You try shoving a bowling ball through your hoo-haw." Jennifer snarled his way.

Caleb kept on smiling. "I have never in all my life been disappointed I was a guy. Stef, take her hand. She needs to break something. Let's go."

Another contraction seized his wife and he did as Caleb asked, feeling like a zombie the whole time. He wasn't really here. It was a weird dream. Jennifer screamed as she pushed, squeezing his hand until he thought it would crack.

"Oh, there's a boy. The head's almost out, sweetheart. One more push should do it. Do you want to see, Stef? Miracle of life is right here," Caleb offered.

The miracle of life was bloody and sweaty and he didn't want to see a head coming out of his wife's vagina. He clung to Jennifer's hand. "I'm fine."

He was far from fine.

Jennifer turned her face up. "It's okay, babe. Oh, god."

She squeezed again, every muscle in her body tense as she pushed one last time. She relaxed suddenly, a bright smile on her face.

"Hello, Logan. Welcome to Bliss, son." Caleb was holding something bloody and squirming in his hands. He handed the tiny thing to Naomi, who wrapped it in a blanket and started to coo. "Stef, come cut the cord."

"No, I don't want to do it. You do it." He wasn't a doctor. He might screw something up.

"Scaredy cat." Caleb slipped a clamp in place and used the scissors and cut the cord that bound mother to child. "Show Momma her baby boy and then we'll get all the after parts done."

"After parts?" That wasn't the worst of it?

"It's nothing," Caleb said. "Just some afterbirth. As in everything having to do with this process, Jen is going to do all the hard work. All you have to do is hold that baby."

"He's not crying," Jennifer said, sitting up.

Naomi was right there, placing the baby boy on the nursery station. "Because he doesn't have anything to cry about. He's perfect, Jen. Apgar of nine. He's seven pounds nine ounces of pure Bliss baby boy."

Jennifer held the bundle in her arms, her eyes wide with wonder as she stared down at the baby they had made together. "Hello, Logan. Oh, Stef, he's perfect. He looks like you. He has your hair."

But Stef held back. He couldn't feel anything—just a numb awareness that he was glad this part was over. Jennifer seemed fine. The baby seemed fine. And he felt numb.

Jennifer looked up at him. "Hold him, Stef."

She thrust the bundle at him. It was too small for his hands. He would fumble. His wife would kill him if he dropped their son. She'd worked so hard to bring him here.

He had a son and he still felt numb. Julian had told him he would feel something but all he felt was nervous about Jennifer yelling at him if he dropped the baby.

There had been no grand revelation. No magical waterfall of feelings had rained down on him. He was tired, and he wanted to make sure his wife was all right.

He held the baby close to his body because it seemed like the best way to not drop it. *Him.* He had to start referring to the baby as him. Although Caleb was bad at reading sonograms. It wouldn't be the first time he screwed up. Rachel had thought she was having a boy her whole pregnancy. "Is it really a boy?"

Jennifer frowned. "Yes, Logan's a boy. You weren't watching?"

"Of course." He hadn't wanted to watch. He'd watched her. He'd held her hand and prayed to get through it.

Naomi was suddenly at his side. "Here, let me have him. We'll get him cleaned up and ready to meet his family."

He gave the baby up in a heartbeat.

"Follow her," Jennifer urged. "I don't want him to be without one of us."

He didn't want to leave her, but he knew damn well there were some orders even a Dom followed.

Naomi set the baby in a small bassinet and the blanket fell away. Logan cried out at the loss of his warmth, a loud roar of a cry. Naomi had cleaned him up initially, but now she set about washing him.

Stef looked down at the small thing whose eyes were still closed. His legs were kicking and his arms jerked.

It was kind of cute in a tiny human way. And definitely a boy.

"Here, wipe down his belly, Mr. Talbot. It's his first bath. Be careful of the cord." Naomi pressed a warm cloth into his hand.

Stef shook his head. "No, I don't know how."

"Sure you do." Naomi stepped away.

The baby squirmed, but he'd stopped wailing. He had a tuft of dark hair, and it was easy to see that he had the Talbot nose and the same stubborn chin he saw in the mirror every day. DNA had worked to make the baby a mini version of himself. He gently rubbed the cloth across the baby's belly.

And Logan Talbot's eyes opened for the first time. He looked up at his father and those green eyes hit Stef Talbot with the force of a lightning strike.

He had Jennifer's eyes, those same eyes that stared at him with amusement and made him look at the world in a different way. Those eyes were right there, and he suddenly understood.

Jennifer's eyes, her heart, and her soul would live on in this child. She would teach him to view the world with her amusement, her open heart. She would house her love in this boy so that when she was gone, her love would live on in Logan and his children and his children's children, a long line of hope and faith that sprung from his wife's pure heart—and from the love he felt for her.

His son. His son was kicking his legs and staring up at him, an amused expression on his tiny, perfect face.

This son would run through Bliss, likely trying to catch up with Charlie and Zander and looking for the maximum amount of trouble he could cause. He would sleep in the woods and get scared by Maurice. Mel would train him to look for aliens and Stella would finally have the grandchild she'd longed for. Logan Talbot would sit at Stella's Café, his feet not quite touching the ground, downing pancakes and feeling like a big man.

He would grow up here. He would love this place.

And Stef would show him the world.

Suddenly he knew there was only one thing that mattered about being a father. He would screw up. He would do it multiple times. He would want to pull his hair out over and over again. But now he wasn't afraid because there was only one real promise he had to keep.

He looked at his son, reaching out to touch that sweet face. Logan's hand touched his.

"I will never leave you."

And in that moment, Stefan Talbot became a dad.

Chapter Twenty

Aidan, Lexi, and Lucas

Lucas sighed as Aidan pulled the truck into the drive. "What happened to her phone again?"

Aidan put the car in park. "Abby said it died. It won't hold a charge anymore, and Lexi threw a near hysterical fit until she promised we would get her a new one. She was ready to drive her into Alamosa herself but I convinced her to meet us at the G."

"So we're taking her into town? Isn't it kind of late for that?" As far as Lucas was concerned, the phone could rot. He would never buy her another one again. He felt guilty, but there was a part of him that wished they were still back at Trio. He'd been able to forget some of his troubles with all the craziness going on there.

"No. I told Abby to bring her back to the G so we could lay out a few new rules. I've been thinking a lot about this. I've been neglectful. I haven't been doing my job because I got distracted."

"By the shit with the city council?" He'd been angry that Aidan had let it go on so long without bringing him in. "That could have gone very poorly."

Aidan's hands tightened around the steering wheel, and he stared out the window. "I don't like bringing you into ranch business."

Another thing he had a problem with, but then he'd spent the afternoon watching Jack and Sam. Sam could act like a goofball, but there was no question he was Jack's partner. "Sam is a true sub, yet Jack treats him like a partner when it comes to that ranch. Hell, Finn is as submissive as they come, but Julian never hesitates to use his skills."

If this had happened to Julian, Finn would have been in on the plans from the beginning. Julian would have dumped it into Finn's lap and fully expected him to deal with the situation.

But Aidan apparently didn't trust him.

Aidan's eyes closed briefly. "You don't understand. Sam was in on the ground floor of Barnes-Fleetwood."

Well, of course. He was tired of it, tired of being shoved to the side. He undid his buckle and opened the door. "Yeah, well, tell me how it goes with Lexi."

"Lucas, get back here this second."

But he was exhausted. "No. I'll head out to the motel. I'd like a night to myself."

The car door slammed behind him and suddenly Lexi was standing on the porch, her eyes hollow as she stared at them. "Lucas?"

"I'm not taking you into town." He brushed by her. She wouldn't care that he was leaving. She would only care that he wouldn't give her a new phone. She shut him out the same way Aidan did. She didn't even ask him to read her contracts anymore.

He wasn't even sure why he was around.

He stopped. He couldn't walk away, because Aidan and Lexi might not need him anymore, but Jack and Daphne sure as hell did.

"Lucas." Aidan stormed up the steps. "You are not going anywhere."

Once again, he'd done exactly the wrong thing and made an ass of himself. "Of course not. I apologize. I'm going to go and spend some time with Jack and Daphne."

He would hold his kids and maybe they would remind him that he had something to offer.

"They're not here," Lexi said. "What's going on? Why are you two fighting?"

"What do you care?" Lucas was feeling mean. She only paid

attention to him when he was fucking up. Come to think of it, Aidan only paid attention when either Lucas was screwing up or Aidan was horny. "And where are my kids?"

"Momma took them," Lexi explained.

So now she was sending his kids away without talking to him about it. "Tell her to bring them back."

Aidan got in between them. "Lucas, you need to take a time-out."

So he got treated like a child? "You know what? You don't get to order me around."

Aidan seemed to grow two inches. "I don't? Because maybe I don't understand the nature of our agreed-upon relationship."

"You should both stop fighting," Lexi said, her voice soft.

But he wasn't about to listen to her either. "Maybe you don't. Maybe we have different versions of what a Master should do. You don't get to let her run wild while controlling everything I do."

"I do not control everything you do."

"No, you're far too busy running your ranch and Lexi is too busy becoming a best-selling author to be actual functioning members of a marriage."

"Lucas, you misunderstood me. Calm the fuck down." Aidan stepped up, using his height and bulky body to crowd Lucas.

"Please don't fight," Lexi said, putting a hand on both of them.

"You can't step in after months of ignoring us and expect that we'll fall in line, Alexis. Go inside. This is between me and Lucas," Aidan said.

"Lots of things are between you and Lucas." Lexi sounded vulnerable.

"Don't you blame me for that," Lucas shot back, well aware that they were out in the open where anyone could be listening in, but it didn't matter. If Aidan didn't value him and Lexi didn't need him, nothing much mattered.

"I don't, babe." She hadn't called him babe like that in months, not in the soft sweet way she used to.

"Are you challenging me, Lucas?" Aidan seemed to not notice that something was different about Lexi.

"I haven't challenged you enough." He said the words, but now he was looking at Lexi, seeing the tired look in her eyes, the way her mouth turned down. He'd spent so much time being angry with her that he hadn't truly looked at her in months. He hadn't taken the time to study her. Lexi wore her worries on her face. She'd always been unable to hide from him. She could shut down, but then he would know something was wrong.

Lexi hadn't been the only one who had shut down. Lucas had stopped trying somewhere along the way. He'd allowed his own private hurts to become his world.

Marriage didn't end at the "I dos." It didn't stop being hard simply because they had decided to be together. He'd thought they would magically get along once it was all settled, but that wasn't true.

Marriages could end. Marriages could crumble. People could grow apart. They could become invested in their own worlds, believing that the people they loved would always be there because they had said some words and signed some documents.

Words didn't keep lovers together. Documents didn't make a marriage.

People grew. They changed, and he suddenly realized that they could change together or grow apart, and it was all their decision.

"Stop."

"We're not stopping anything, Lucas."

His Master was on edge, and Lucas had done nothing to help the matter. He'd broken their contract by not communicating with him. "I'm very angry with you right now, Master."

Now that he was saying the words, there was no real heat behind them. Emotion, for sure, but speaking them out loud, the simple act of being heard, lessened his anger.

And his Master's, it seemed. Aidan's angry look softened. "I know you are."

"And I'm mad at you, Lexi."

She nodded. "You should be."

"We have to be more important than your career."

Her skin had paled to a waxy color and he reached out for her, but she stepped away, shaking her head. "No. Don't. Not until you've heard what I have to say."

"And me." Aidan didn't pull away. He took Lucas's hand. "You misunderstood me, Lucas. I might have made some mistakes, but you have to hear me out."

Because that was what people who wanted to stay in love did. They listened. They talked. They forgave. "All right. It hurt when you told me that I shouldn't feel like I had a claim to the ranch because it belongs to you."

Aidan shook his head. "I didn't say that. I have never said that and never once felt that way."

Lexi's eyes were on the ground. "But the land has been in your family for years. You love that land."

"Yes, I do," Aidan agreed. "It's O'Malley land, and you two are missing out on the fact that you're both O'Malleys and so are our children. That's not why I've kept you out of the business. I've kept you out because it hasn't been much of a business up to this point. It's been a money pit and you know it. Both you and Lucas brought money into this marriage and all I brought was a place to throw it the last couple of years."

Lucas shook his head. "That's not true."

"Who paid for the house?" Aidan asked.

Lucas sighed. "I wanted to buy the house for us. The ranch house was getting too small."

Aidan took a deep breath and seemed to calm a bit. "I'm the Master. I should be the one to provide. At the very least, I should be able to pull my own damn weight. This year we should finally see a profit. Don't think I don't know that I wouldn't have made it to this year without Lexi's dad. I wouldn't have made it without you, Lucas and Lexi. So I try to keep you out of it because you've already done your part."

This was what made him crazy. "There is no part to this. I can call you Master all you like, but at the end of the day this is our life and our home and I don't have some part that you can stick me in and say this is what I'll give or let you give back to me. I want to help with the ranch because it's yours and mine and our babies'. Can't you see it doesn't mean as much if I don't help? You said Sam was in on the ground floor. Yes, he was. They didn't have a damn thing before. Well, I don't care that the ranch has been in your family. It's our family now, and if you won't rely on me, then I'm not worth much."

Aidan put a hand on his shoulder. "I know. And I'm sorry. You have to understand. I wasn't trying to cut you out. I was trying to offer you something. I wanted to turn the ranch into something that was worthy of you."

He needed to make his Master understand. "Everything you do, everything you have, is worthy. Let me help you build it. I should be the first person you call when we have trouble, not the last."

"Oh, god." Tears were pouring down Lexi's face. "Oh, god. I cost us the ranch. We're going to lose the ranch because of me."

Lucas had to catch her before she fell.

* * * *

Lexi shook her head as she started to wake up. Had she actually fainted? She seemed to be on a bed. Someone had taken off her shoes, and she could feel a hard body pressed behind her.

"The doctor is apparently dealing with a situation." Lucas's deep voice penetrated her brain. Everything was foggy.

"Well, I have a situation right here. We need to call an ambulance," Aidan said. His arms tightened around her as though he was afraid to let go.

She forced her eyes open. If she let him, Aidan would have three ambulances, the police force, and a fire truck in the front yard before she could take a breath. "I'm fine."

"You fainted," he pointed out.

She shook it off. "Because I haven't eaten in a couple of days."

Aidan's eyebrows came together in a frustrated *V*. "What? I fixed you a plate."

She shrugged. "And I couldn't eat it."

The thought of food turned her stomach. Ever since she'd gotten the last e-mail from Karen, she hadn't been able to think about anything but maximizing her career.

"Lucas?" Aidan asked.

"I'm on it." Lucas had a glass of orange juice in his hand. "I brought this with me. Drink it. I'll go and grab a protein bar."

"This has to stop, Lexi. You can't treat yourself like this. You're making yourself crazy. Drink." Aidan held the glass up to her lips.

She was forced to drink. Cool, sweet juice filled her mouth. She swallowed it down before pushing his hand away. "We need to talk. I've done something terrible."

He frowned. "What was all that shit about you costing us the ranch?"

If only it was a joke. "The city council is going to take our ranch."

"Baby, that's not going to happen." He smoothed back her hair. God, it felt so good to be in his arms. How long had it been since she'd relaxed in their arms, lazing away the hours while they talked and made love?

She was pretty sure he wouldn't want to hold her after she told him what she'd done. "You have to listen to me. I've got a plan to save us."

"I don't know what you've heard, but it's only gossip. It's nothing for you to worry about."

She had to make him listen. She turned to him, staring into his eyes, willing him to believe her. "The city council is planning on rezoning key parts of the county."

He nodded. "Yes, I know, sweetheart. It's already been taken care of."

"You don't understand. I pissed Karen off."

"Karen Wilcox?"

"She's Karen Carter now. You know, like Mayor Carter."

His eyes rolled slightly. "Yes, baby. I know she managed to get the mayor to marry her. I don't know what she has to do with this."

Because he wasn't thinking. "Right after Daphne was born, I went to a brunch at the Deer Run Women's Committee. I was going to head up the auction to raise funds for the new school. Well, Karen had me kicked off because she said there was no place for whores in her town."

"She said what?" Aidan's voice had gone dangerously low.

There was a reason she'd tried to take care of it herself in the first place. "She always calls me a whore, Aidan. But she usually does it behind my back. I got a little mad."

His eyes narrowed. "What exactly did you do?"

She bit her bottom lip. "I might have dumped a punch bowl over her head and told her to take her fake boobs and get out of my house. We own the building the meeting was taking place in. Needless to say, they moved their meetings to somewhere else. But Karen was mad. Everyone laughed at her. She deserved it. But then she walked up to me at Patty Cakes and we had a discussion."

Aidan's eyes had narrowed. "You should have had a discussion with me."

"You shouldn't have to deal with mean-girl name calling. But she took it further." Tears threatened, but she bit them back. "She's going to have her husband take a thousand acres in the east field. He's going to take our water access and he's going to use eminent domain to do it. He claims he's going to build an outlet mall."

Aidan's eyes closed, and he took a long breath. "Oh, baby. That wasn't about a shopping mall. That was a land grab plain and simple. The east pasture is sitting on what might be a ton of natural gas. I turned down a contract with the gas company to drill because I don't trust them. The mayor wants that money so he came up with the idea of taking the land."

"You knew about it?" All this time she'd worried sick and he'd known?

"The mayor doesn't want the land anymore." Lucas was standing in the doorway, a plate in his hand. "I explained that I could keep him tied up in court for a very long time."

That didn't sound like Lucas. "Is that all you did?"

"I might also have had Chase dig up dirt on the bastard's tax practices. He might owe the IRS a ton of money and he has undocumented workers working in his family's estate. I might have presented him with evidence, and he might have crapped his pants and backed down. But the official reason is we're being completely unreasonable and threatening to tie the county up in court. I think he told everyone Aidan was an environmentalist."

"Yeah, they think that's worse than being gay, which is the other thing they call me." He took her hands in his. "I didn't tell you because I didn't want to fight about the gas rights. Baby, the company that's offering is known for being sloppy and, honestly, I don't want to take the chance that we could make a quick million but lose the land in the end. Ranching is our future."

She felt numb. "But all this time I thought I was going to cost us the land."

Aidan ran a hand over her hair. "Baby, the mayor might enjoy screwing Karen, but he's not about to let her make decisions like that. He didn't marry her for her brain. He married her because she's thirty years younger than him. She was always a mean bitch. She probably heard what he was planning and decided to make herself look like she had some power. How long has this been going on?"

"That bitch." She felt stupid. "Months."

"Months? Why didn't you talk to me?"

"Why didn't you talk to me?" she threw back at him.

"Because you're both impossibly stubborn and obnoxious." Lucas sat the plate in front of her. "And you're both going to change or we're going to fall apart. Lexi, what was your plan to save the ranch and how did it involve being on the phone twenty-four seven?"

He knew her really well. "I was going to up my writing schedule so we would have the money to fight this or I could buy us new land."

Aidan shook his head. "Do you know how much new land would cost? I know you make a lot of money, but you don't make millions and that's what it would take. Lexi, I don't know what you were thinking."

She sniffled. "I was thinking I didn't want you to know how stupid I was. I was thinking I would try to save us. But you and Lucas had already done it and not even bothered to tell me something was wrong."

"That sounds a whole lot like the pot calling the kettle black," Aidan shot back. "You've kept us at arm's length for months because you weren't willing to talk about what had happened. I might not have been totally truthful with you, but I didn't push you away."

"Really?" Lucas asked, passing the plate to her. "Eat, Lexi. If you don't, I'll pull you over my knee. I haven't topped you in almost a year. Between the pregnancy and this episode, I haven't gotten what I needed in a very long time. I wouldn't test me now."

Her heart ached. She'd known that Lucas was hurting and she'd still held him away. She took the sandwich he'd made her and had a bite.

Lucas wasn't through. "As to you, Aidan, you can't say you haven't held yourself apart from me. How long did it take you to ask me for advice? How many weeks went by?"

Lexi looked back at Aidan. "You didn't talk to Lucas?"

They always talked. She couldn't stand the thought of Aidan feeling alone—the way she'd felt for months.

"I thought I could handle it." Aidan took a long breath.

The same way she had thought she could handle it.

"I'm tired of both of you," Lucas said. "I'm tired of being ignored.

When I have a problem, I come to you. I've asked your opinion on everything from what car to buy to how to handle the human resources problems at the Dallas office. I didn't do that because I thought the two of you knew everything. I did it because I trust you and love you and I need you to know what's happening in my life. Neither one of you feels the same about me."

"Or we're just very stupid," Lexi tried.

Lucas shrugged. "Either way, it has to change. I'm not saying I'll leave. I can't. We have two children who depend on me. But I will change my expectations of what our relationship means. I'll hold myself apart. I don't want that. I want what was promised to me. I want my family. Make your decisions. I'm going to go and think for a while."

"Lucas," Aidan called out as he turned to go.

Lucas didn't turn around. "No. If you want me, you'll know where to find me. Don't come looking if you can't be my Master."

He walked out the door, his boots ringing against the hardwood floors.

"He doesn't mean that." She couldn't let Aidan get mad at Lucas.

Aidan sat back against the bed. "Yes, he does. He has every right to be mad. We failed him."

The "we" gave her hope. Something had settled deep in her chest. Something that had been tight and nasty had loosened up. "I didn't fuck everything up?"

Aidan chuckled. "Oh, I think we fucked up plenty. Why didn't you talk to me?"

He pulled her back into his arms. Those big biceps surrounded her, and for a moment, she felt safe. He'd heard the truth and he wasn't pushing her away. "She has power over us. She can make life difficult for us and I still got pissed off."

"You should have clocked her," Aidan replied.

She shook her head. "I can't get us kicked out."

Oh, god. She'd never thought about it that way. She'd had her daughter and then she'd done something that could have cost them the ranch and her whole childhood had played out in some weird place in the back of her brain.

She'd always felt it. She'd felt the fact that she was the reason her mother had lost her home. She'd been the reason they had struggled and her mother had to fight for their existence. She'd been the reason her mother had married a man she'd liked but didn't love.

She couldn't be the reason her daughter got kicked out. She couldn't be the reason her son lost his home.

"Oh god, Aidan. What was I thinking?"

His arms tightened. "Baby, baby, I know what's going on in that head of yours, but it's wrong."

"I can't be the reason we fail." Tears pierced through her.

"Baby, we're not failing."

"I can't lose our home. I can't get us kicked out. I can't do it again."

Aidan sighed, pulling her so close she could barely breathe. "Lexi, that's not going to happen. We're going to be fine. No one can throw us off our land. I won't allow it. Your momma was all alone. She didn't have anyone to help her. You can't think it was your fault."

"She got kicked out because of me. What if I do the same thing to Daphne? To baby Jack?"

Aidan forced her to turn around. "How do you feel about your mother? Are you angry with her?"

Lexi shook her head. "Of course not. She's the strongest woman I know."

"Why? Why is she so strong? And don't bullshit me, because I can get her over here in a heartbeat."

Lexi let her tears flow. "She's strong because she loved me."

Her mother hadn't faltered. She'd been seventeen years old, barely out of high school, and pregnant and alone. She'd managed to pull herself up and put herself through school. She'd taken care of them both. She'd educated herself.

Because she'd loved Lexi.

"I can't be as strong as my momma."

"You don't have to be." Aidan kissed her brow. "Baby, she doesn't have to be anymore, and I bet your mother would say she's thrilled about that. You and I have been giving into our childhoods. You're trying to be your momma and I'm trying to make up for everything my father didn't give me. Lucas is the only one who's fighting it."

Because Lucas had been ignored. He'd been marginalized and he was standing up to the people he loved because he wouldn't be that way again. He wouldn't walk away because that man would never leave his children, but he would stand up for himself.

"I don't want to live like this. I don't want to hide things from you. I was stupid, Aidan."

"No. Like I said, you should have clocked her. I have plans for her. Maybe it's time to unleash Lucas's inner bastard and let him take that bitch down. Let Lucas be the man he wants to be."

She smiled. "But he wants to be Jack."

Her stepfather was known for being a man no one wanted to cross.

"Exactly. I'm not as smart as Lucas. I tend to fight my way through life when he can finesse it, and sometimes revenge requires finesse. I love you, Lexi. You're not capable of finesse. You're capable of tossing a bowl of punch over someone's head. I'm capable of punching someone. Lucas is capable of taking apart someone's life in such a way that no one even knows he did it."

That summed up her dad. "I love you all so much. I don't want to fail you."

"Lexi, baby, you can't fail us. We're your family. The only way you fail is by walking away. Don't walk away." Her Master had tears in his eyes. He stared down at her like she was precious, and she was. When he looked at her like that, she knew she was loved. Only a few humans in the world ever looked at her like that. Her husbands. Her mother. Her children.

Her family.

She couldn't fail them. Like her mother couldn't fail her. She'd been righteously strong, and she'd gained that strength from loving her child. Even though she didn't need to be strong now, her love for Jack and Sam made her that way.

The only way Lexi had failed was in not talking to her men. "I want to slow down."

Aidan's mouth curled up. "Oh, my darling, you will slow down. I've been seriously lacking as a Dom. You aren't going to the conference in Denver. You're coming home with your family."

The whole idea of going to the Denver conference had made her tired. Luckily it hadn't been publicized that she would be there. She could get out of it. It was time to stop. She said yes to everything and everyone, no matter what it cost her. She wanted to be home, cuddling with her babies. There would be time for conferences later when her men could be with her. "All right."

Aidan was taking control. She wanted it. Needed it.

"I'm never going to tell you how to write or how much to write. The writing part is a piece of your soul, but the business part is different. I think Lucas should take control. You don't like making all of these decisions. You mostly want to write. Tell me if I'm wrong."

He wasn't. "I'm not saying I won't have ideas. I'm not a doormat, but at the end of the day, I want to write my stories. I want to be successful, but I would rather someone else handled the money part. I want to do the fun part."

"And Lucas wants to help you. And I need you both to help me." Aidan rubbed their cheeks together. "I need you to support me. I know you and Lucas are smarter, but the ranch is important."

"We're not smarter, merely different." But the whole idea of helping him filled a void inside her.

"Well, I need you both. You and Lucas have so much experience that I don't have. I'm done with this whole feeling like shit thing. I'm necessary in this marriage. I love this family. Maybe I didn't bring as much money into it, but damn it, I'm valuable."

He thought he wasn't? Her heart softened. "Oh, babe, of course you are."

His lips touched hers, a fire sparking across her flesh. He only needed to kiss her to make her go up in flames. His arms wound around her. He pulled her close. Everything in Lexi responded to him. This was what she needed.

"I haven't been valuable lately." He said the words against her lips. "But I will be. I can be what you need again. Eat that damn sandwich because you're serving two Masters tonight."

Her whole body clenched in anticipation.

She ate her food because she would need her strength.

* * * *

Aidan led Lexi to the playroom. The doors were open, but he stopped them outside. His heart softened as he saw Lucas sitting in the middle of the room, his gorgeous, lean body in a sitting position. Cobbler Pose. His feet were together, his hands behind his back.

When they had first gotten together, Lucas had wanted to join him in his daily yoga. Aidan needed it to feel flexible. His muscles tended to seize up after all the surgeries he'd required to fix the damage he'd taken in Iraq. So he and Lucas had gotten up with the dawn and moved through a series of yoga poses, starting with Sun Salutation and ending with Relaxation Pose.

He missed that. He would reinstate those mornings with his guy. Lexi and Lucas liked to sit together in the mornings and have their coffee. Aidan couldn't stand the shit, but he could have his yoga time. And in the evenings he would shower with Lexi. She needed a shower before she could sleep. It could be their special time together.

They had to fight for it. Every day. Every hour.

They made the choice to be together.

All three of them. "We need to join Lucas. Are you strong enough, baby?"

"I am. I need to be with you." Tears filled her eyes. "I've missed you both so much."

And he'd missed her. He and Lucas had been together, but not with the tenderness they had needed. They'd lived a half-life without her.

"Then come back to us. Come and complete us. We've been lost without you." Aidan reached out, holding a hand to her. "We need you, baby. We don't get what we need without you, but you have to decide to come with us. I won't order you to do it."

She was the true center of their world. He and Aidan could fuck however they wanted, but they needed her. Lucas had been miserable without his girl to top. Aidan couldn't give him that.

Lexi sniffled. "You're not mad at me?"

Oh, he was plenty mad, but he also realized that both his subs could be pissed at him, too. He wasn't innocent, not by any means. He'd wanted to save face with the people he loved and now he realized that "face" didn't matter. Truth mattered. Love mattered.

He could be weak around his wife and Lucas. They would make him strong.

"How long is your mom watching the kids?"

Her lips curled up. "The whole night. We'll get them back after the wedding."

His cock twitched in his pants. "Perfect."

"Of course, we're taking Josh and Olivia the night before we leave."

Usually the thought of being responsible for those two hooligans would make him want to run out and hide in the barn, but now all he could think about was the fact that they had all night. All night alone. There was time enough tomorrow to want to tear his own hair out. "Then I think we should play, baby."

She took his hand and let him lead her up. "How rough are you going to get? I have a lot to make up for."

Her breathy tone did amazing things to his cock. She had a little masochist buried inside her. It totally called to that tiny bit of sadist in him—and the one who lived in Lucas. She was their perfect mate.

"You do. I think you might have a rough night, baby."

She shuddered softly, enough to let him know how much she wanted it. "All right."

"But I was serious about you slowing down. You have to rest. You have to spend more time with us. I know you love your writing and I won't come in the way of that, but the travel has to slow down. We need you at home. When you do need to go, we'll go with you. This family stays together, do you understand?"

She placed her hands in his. "Yes, Aidan. We stay together. And you know I can handle whatever discipline you and Lucas mete out."

His cock was pressing at the fly of his jeans. They had all night. Trev had texted him and offered him use of the playroom. No one expected anything from them until the next day at the wedding.

It had been forever since he'd taken hours to play with his subs. Lucas always wanted things to go fast. Lexi needed a long time to find her subspace. She luxuriated in the discipline, and she would need so much of it.

He led Lexi through the dungeon doors, closing them behind him.

Lucas sat in the middle of the room, his legs now in a perfect Padmasana or Lotus pose. His legs were locked together, ankle over ankle, his hips open, palms resting on his thighs. He'd taken off his shirt and switched to a pair of sweat pants, but Aidan meant to get him out of everything soon.

He'd given Lucas this. He'd taught him the same way Leo had taught Aidan. He'd given Lucas this place to go to find peace.

"He's so gorgeous," Lexi whispered, her eyes on his perfectly straight back.

"Yes, he is. And he's ours." Aidan didn't whisper because he'd never met a human being who needed to belong more than Lucas O'Malley. "I won't make him question that again."

Lucas's head twisted slightly, his green eyes opening and a soft smile playing on his face. "Yes, you will. Forever is a long time, Master. I suspect we'll all fuck up again. But it will be all right as long as we find our way back to this place."

Aidan knew he wasn't talking about the physical space they were in but rather Lucas was talking about finding their way home. They could move. They could have more children. They could love the rest of their family, but they could never forget that their world had begun with these three people.

"I'll always choose this place." No matter how lost he became, Lucas and Lexi would always be his home.

Lucas smiled again, and then turned his attention to Lexi, his gaze becoming predatory. "Why is our sub wearing clothing in the playroom? I don't think she really wants to make up for her bad behavior, Master."

Yep, Lucas was hungry. He was going to have to share some power tonight. "Why don't you help her fix that problem while I select a few toys to play with?"

He heard Lexi gasp as Lucas rolled his body up. Fuck, he was a gorgeous man and when he decided to top their sub, Aidan liked to watch. He stepped back, leaving Lexi to her second Master for the moment.

The McNamara playroom was a model of efficiency. Beth liked to build things, and she'd designed a whole wall to organize the toys. Like the rest of the room, it was discreet, and a person had to know what buttons to push to get to the good stuff. Bo had given him and Lucas a tour the first day, so Aidan knew the light switch to the side would do the trick. He flipped it up and the door slid open.

"That's cool. Oh, my god. I have to see that." Lexi was watching the doors slide away, revealing a wall of nasty fun.

"No," Lucas said in his darkest Dom voice. "No research. You should have taken the tour with the rest of us, but you were on your phone. Maybe, if you're a good girl, we'll let you take notes before we leave, but for now you need to get out of those clothes and find your position."

Lucas wasn't playing around. And Aidan could see plainly that his bossy switch was getting to their girl. Her nipples stood out against the cotton of her shirt and there was a pretty pink flush to her skin.

Lucas sank his hand into her hair, dragging it out of the bun she'd fashioned. Black silk tumbled across her shoulders. "Did you eat what I made for you?"

She answered quickly, a sure sign she was ready to play. "I ate every bite."

"Good." He fisted her hair, gently drawing her face up to his. "You're going to need the energy."

His mouth came down on hers, and Aidan watched as his partner damn near inhaled their girl. So much longing and it was finally getting fulfilled. No matter what came next, he had to make sure they got what they needed.

He regretfully turned away and looked for a few of the items they would need. Bo and Trev kept several unopened selections for guests to use. He pulled out the lubricant and an extra-large plug. Yeah, he was going to have some fun. He winked at Lucas as he walked to the bathroom, opening the plug and sterilizing it.

It was a nice-sized monster. Lexi was used to anal, but it had been a while. And it would be fun to watch her eyes go wide as he sank the plug deep.

And then he'd sink his cock in.

He walked back out and Lucas had done his job. Lexi was naked and waiting in her slave pose. Her back was straight, her head submissively down, palms up on her thighs. Her knees were wide, leaving her perfectly shaved pussy on full display.

Lucas stood back, his eyes staring right at her pussy. "It's been too long. I think I could stare at her for a while."

"More, Alexis," Aidan commanded. "You can get your knees wider."

"Sorry. I lost a bunch of flexibility when I gave birth to your children and stuff."

Aidan felt a thrill go through him at the sound of her sarcasm.

Lexi's head came up. "I'm sorry. I didn't mean to say that out loud. It was supposed to be one of those bratty things I only say in my head."

Ah, but she'd opened that door. "Hands and knees, ass in the air. If you want to keep the spanking you're about to get in your head next time, keep the brat locked up tight."

She bit that gorgeous lower lip of hers as she looked at the plug in his hand. "Please tell me that's for Lucas."

"No, my lovely, it's all for you. Lucas never gets out of practice."

"Lucas didn't have to carry our sweet babies," Lexi pointed out.

"Not going to save you," Lucas said with a wicked grin. "Ass in the air, brat."

Lexi leaned forward. "Fine, but only because I know the phone thing was obnoxious and now that it's all out in the open, I realize it was the stupidest plan ever. I deserve to have an elephant plug shoved up my poor rectum for being so naïve."

Aidan got to his knees as she made her way to all fours. Her body had changed over the years, growing a bit softer. She was still the most beautiful thing on the planet. So womanly he couldn't look at her without thinking about sex. "This is about making sure you can take us, baby."

He put a hand on her ass, feeling the warm flesh under his palm.

"Tell me you're not going to enjoy it."

Such a brat. He brought his hand up and down in a quick arc, the sound cracking through the room. Lexi moaned as he held his palm flat against the flesh he'd spanked. "You know I'm going to love it, baby. Lucas, would you like to help with discipline or do you want to occupy that bratty mouth of hers while I work?"

Lucas had his sweats off in record time. His cock bobbed as he got settled onto the floor. "I think I should make sure she doesn't get in even more trouble, Master."

He pumped his cock in his fist, getting it hard and long. Lexi licked her lips as she watched.

"Suck him. Suck him and make him come, and then and only then will I think about giving you a treat. But first"—he slapped her ass again—"it's a count of thirty. If you ever wave me off when I'm trying to talk to you again, I swear you won't be able to sit for a week."

"I don't think I'll be able to," she said in a shaky voice. "I think Olivia did something to make phones not work around me anymore. At least not the one I had. I can't prove it, but she found a way."

And Olivia was getting a great Christmas present this year. "Suck Lucas."

Her head moved forward, and Aidan watched as Lucas's cock started to disappear inside those gorgeous lips. He swatted her ass, finding a good rhythm to go with the way her head moved up and down on Lucas's dick.

Her skin, so flawless, got a hot pink sheen to it, the flesh of her ass jiggling slightly with each smack. Her knees were spread wide so he could spank every inch of her cheeks and thighs and stop every once in a while to make sure the discipline was having the required effect.

He let his hands slide over her pussy. Yes. She was getting what she needed. Her pussy was soft and ripe with cream. He let his fingers play for a moment and then dragged them into his mouth, enjoying the tangy taste of her essence.

She worked Lucas over, drawing him deeper and deeper into her mouth. Lucas's eyes were down, watching that place where she sucked him in. His hands were on her hair, and for a moment, he brought his gaze up, staring at Aidan. Pure connection sparked through him. This was what they had been missing. The three of them together, working for each other's pleasure, but most of all reveling in the connection they had.

"Plug our girl. I don't know how long I'll be able to hold out. Her mouth feels so good." He winked Aidan's way and then went back to looking at Lexi.

He'd kept a careful count. He owed his love another five smacks. He took his time, drawing it out. He slapped at her ass, holding his hand there and letting the heat sink into her skin. Then he smacked her thigh, loving the way she tensed and then relaxed. He could take her away from all her worries.

Sometimes they were too busy being parents and business owners to remember to be lovers.

Never again. He would schedule time for them to play if he had to. He wondered how Lexi would like it if he called up her assistant and asked to be put on her schedule for an hour's worth of anal play or an afternoon of applying a crop to Lexi's ass. Yeah, he needed to see what that schedule would look like.

"He's planning something evil. He's got his super-villain smile on." Lucas gave him a grin that told him he would be in on whatever plot he came up with.

Lexi moaned, but Lucas kept his promise. Not a single word left her bratty, gorgeous mouth.

Three more smacks and he was done. He placed a kiss on each cheek before reaching for the plug and the lube.

Her punishment was far from over.

* * * *

Aidan was going to kill her. Lucas wasn't helping. Her whole body was poised and ready to go off and they insisted on teasing her.

She didn't need a damn plug. She needed her men. Surely after all the times they had shoved large objects up her anus, she should still be ready to go. Her asshole should remember not to clench, shouldn't it?

But, no, Master Aidan had to play things safe. She licked at the cock in her mouth. Lucas's cock tasted so good. Clean and manly. He was dripping his arousal on her tongue, teasing her with salty goodness. She sucked him hard, but he kept pressing in and pulling out of her mouth.

She whimpered as she felt Aidan pull her cheeks apart. The spanking had sensitized her skin. Everywhere he touched lit up, making her shiver.

"Don't you stop sucking his cock. You have a job to do." Another slap sent a wave from her ass straight to her pussy. She could feel herself getting creamy and so wet she almost couldn't stand it.

But Aidan was right. She had to pay attention to the cock in her mouth. It was past time to push Lucas over the edge.

She sucked hard, letting her tongue roll over his dick. He was deeply sensitive at the *V* on the underside of his cockhead. She worked her tongue over and over it, pressing up and catching it against her teeth.

"Fuck." The curse spat out of Lucas's mouth and suddenly his hands tightened in her hair. His hips bucked.

She tried to concentrate on the cock in her mouth, but Aidan was lubing up her asshole. Now she was the one who was breathless as he rimmed her, spreading lube all over her hot hole. She wriggled. It had been so long since she'd felt that dark pleasure, known what it meant to have them both. She didn't want the plug. She wanted his cock.

But what she got was the hard press of a plug against her asshole.

Aidan worked the large piece of plastic in a circle around the rosette of her ass. Pressure, dark and nasty, worked its way up her spine.

"Don't you focus on him," Lucas bit out between clenched teeth. "I'm the one fucking your mouth, darlin'. You focus on me. Your time is coming."

She was sure it was. She would end up in between them. She hadn't been there since before Daphne had been born. She would be between her men, trapped by their hard bodies and rough desires.

But now she was caught between a hard cock and a plug that didn't seem to be going in.

A hard smack to her ass had her panting.

"Relax," Aidan ordered.

Easy for him to say. The only thing that stopped her from complaining was the fact that she'd watched Lucas penetrate Aidan. Aidan knew damn well what it felt like to have a monster shoved up his rectum.

They were different from anyone she knew. For the last few months, that had seemed to be a bad thing. Even among the threesomes they knew, they were different. Aidan was willing to give over to Lucas from time to time. Her Dom had a switch and he'd compromised.

Why hadn't she trusted him? She relaxed because it wasn't Aidan she hadn't trusted. It was herself, and that had been foolish.

She was her mother's daughter. And she might screw up mightily from time to time, but she would win in the end. She would win because she was surrounded by love.

It was more important than pride. More important than any career. More important than land.

She'd worried about her place. If she didn't write fast enough she could lose her place.

But her place was right here—pleasing and being pleased by her men.

"That's what I need." Aidan's hand skimmed up her back as the plug slid home.

It was so big. She was stretched and full. She clenched around it, feeling every centimeter deep inside.

"And that's what I need. Yes, baby. Yes." Lucas held her hair, and his hips plunged deep.

Lucas came, spurting onto her tongue. She lapped it up, drawing Lucas's semen into her mouth and swallowing him down. It coated her mouth, filling her with his essence.

He pulled his cock out of her mouth, his face flushed, his chest heaving. "Damn, that felt good. Did she take the plug?"

She heard Aidan chuckle behind her. "You impatient son of a bitch. You just came and you're already wanting to know if we can take her."

"Well, can we?" Lucas asked, proving exactly how impatient he was.

Aidan moved the plug, pulling it out and slowly, so slowly, pressing it back in. Every nerve in her backside was lit with a jangly pleasure. Her spine threatened to curl, but she had to stay still. Aidan was serious about the discipline thing, and she had the feeling if she did what she wanted to—arch back and force him to fuck her harder—she would find herself tied up and tortured for hours.

It wouldn't be the first time they had tied her up and spanked her and brought her to the edge of pleasure again and again only to hold back.

She couldn't stand the thought of that. She needed them tonight.

Lexi closed her eyes and submitted. She relaxed and gave herself over to her men.

"That's exactly what we want." Lucas put a hand on her head. "Let us take care of you. You don't have to be in control all the time."

She didn't. The last several months had been a blur of worry and work. This was the first time she'd sunk into subspace and let her cares fall away. There was nothing but safety and pleasure in this place. There was nothing but love.

The plug moved in and out of her, but Lexi concentrated on them. She focused on the hands that rubbed across her skin, gentling her, soothing her worries away.

The plug was still huge in her ass, but it moved easily now. Aidan fucked her over and over, opening her up.

"Now she's ready," Aidan said, and the plug slid away, leaving her empty and wanting.

Lexi felt Lucas lift her up. She was cradled against his chest as he walked her toward the big bed that dominated half the playroom. Solid arms held her so she didn't need to work. She relaxed in his arms and looked up at that face she loved so well. Lucas had come so far from the frightened kid she'd met in Willow Fork all those years before. He'd gone from the bad boy of the tabloids to a man who was steadfast and loyal and knew his worth.

"I love you."

His face turned up, his eyes softening. "I love you, too, baby."

He tossed his body on the bed, carrying them both down. It wasn't hard to move her body, straddling him, rubbing their skin together. She could already feel his cock stirring to life. It hardened against her pussy.

"Ride me." His hands were on her skin, guiding her where he wanted her to be. With a firm twist of his hips, he joined them together.

Her eyes closed in pleasure, but they weren't done. She felt callused palms cup her breasts. Her Aidan. Her cowboy. He'd been her first love, the man who broke her heart, the man who put her back together again. When they'd first met, he'd been so beautiful she couldn't imagine she would ever be attracted to anyone else, but the Aidan who loved her now was a man and not a boy. He bore the scars of a war, and she couldn't imagine loving him any more than she did in that moment.

She let her face turn to his, their mouths fusing lightly.

"Baby, let me get inside." Aidan pressed her down, gently forcing her against Lucas.

She was right where she needed to be. She was surrounded by them.

Something hard but warm pressed against her ass. Aidan worked his cock in and despite calling the plug too large, she was reminded that Aidan was bigger. She wiggled, gasping and trying to relax. Lucas held her hips, forcing her cheeks wide to give Aidan room to work.

"Let me in." Aidan's command washed over her. His silky, dark voice was seduction in itself. "Don't try to keep me out. This belongs to me. You belong to us."

She did. And they belonged to her. Sometimes she forgot that it worked both ways. She needed her Masters to remind her again.

She let loose a long breath and tried to flatten out her back. The pressure on her ass increased until finally, blissfully, she felt Aidan slide in.

He shuddered behind her. "You feel so damn good."

Lucas pressed up. "Yes, she does."

Lexi was suffused with heat as they moved against her, long practice making the action easy. Aidan drove into her ass while Lucas was dragging his cock out. Lucas fucked deep inside her pussy while Aidan was pulling out, his dick lighting up every nerve she had.

It couldn't last. They were too hungry, too desperate.

Lucas twisted his hips, his pelvis grinding on her clit as his cock drove deep and Lexi hurled over the edge. Pleasure crashed over her in waves, knocking her breath away and making her shake.

Aidan shouted out and held himself hard against her body. He filled her ass, whispering her name like a benediction.

Lucas's beautiful face contorted in pleasure as he found his orgasm. He held her tight, as though she was his anchor.

They fell together, Aidan pulling her to one side so she was in the middle. Her place. She slept between them so she always had an arm around her or legs tangling with hers.

Lexi settled down, finally remembering her place in the world.

Baby Logan

WELCOME TO BLISS!

STEFAN AND JENNIFER TALBOT ARE
PROUD TO INTRODUCE THEIR SON

LOGAN MITCHELL TALBOT

Born June 15th at 2:34 am
at Bliss County Clinic in Bliss, Colorado

Chapter Twenty-One

Stef and Jen

Jennifer cuddled her son in her arms as she looked up at the friends who had gathered in her room. The morning sun was streaming through the windows, giving the room a soft, gauzy feel. Rachel and Callie had been in the waiting room most of the night, and Nell had shown up with zucchini bread bright and early.

"He's so beautiful," Nell said, staring down at him. She put a hand on her still non-existent stomach. "I hope my baby looks like Henry."

Callie gave Nell a hug. "I think whoever the baby looks like, he or she will be beautiful."

Nell took a long breath and nodded.

Jen reached her free hand out and covered Nell's. Something was wrong. Maybe it was pregnancy hormones. Jen hoped so, but it seemed like something was wrong with Henry, too.

"Good lord. Nell, what the hell is wrong?" Rachel asked from her place in the comfy chair. She was bouncing Paige.

"Rachel!" Callie said, indignation in her voice.

Rachel shrugged. "Well, we're all wondering about it. She's been moping around for a month. It's like someone put moody juice in her tofu."

"That doesn't even make sense," Callie shot back.

"Neither does tofu," Rachel replied.

Nell held a hand up. "I found a gun in the house."

Jen felt her eyes go wide. Nell and Henry were pacifists. "Holy shit."

She needed to clean up her potty mouth. Her baby boy was already learning bad words. But, holy shit…

"That has to be a mistake," Callie said.

"Maybe it was left behind by someone else," Jen tried.

"No one leaves a gun sitting around," Rachel retorted. She frowned and seemed a bit more sympathetic than before. "This town can be a dangerous place. Maybe that mess with Gemma's ex scared him. A man can do some strange things when he thinks his woman is in danger."

Nell sniffled. "I think he's hiding something. I think…I think he might have been lying to me for a while now, but he won't tell me anything."

Jen couldn't believe it. Nell and Henry were solid. They had to be. "Honey, I went through this with Stef. Men get scared. First he had to deal with the fact that Gemma's ex nearly killed you, and then he had to watch the man die. Now you're pregnant. It can make a man crazy."

"What did he say about it?" Callie asked.

Nell looked hopeful suddenly. "I didn't mention it. Oh, do you think it could all be a misunderstanding? Or that he's nervous about the pregnancy?"

Rachel waved a hand her way. "Honey, men are dumbasses. You can always count on them to do the dumbassedest thing possible. For Henry, that means buying a gun. For Max, it's eating wings. You thought Henry was perfect. Well, guess what, hon, he has a penis. It was only a matter of time."

Rachel had a way with words, but it seemed to work wonders on Nell. She smiled and her naturally sunny disposition seemed to come back.

"I'm sure you're right. That incident with Gemma's ex was very scary for both of us. And my first trimester was a little touch and go. I haven't told anyone except Laura and Holly, but we actually decided to try a while back and I miscarried twice."

Jen's heart went out to her friend. "I'm so sorry to hear that. That could make any man crazy."

Stef would definitely have gone a little nuts.

Callie pulled Nell in to a hug. "Everything is going to be fine. You need to talk to him."

"And you need to take that gun away. I can't imagine Henry is any good with it," Rachel said. "He needs to leave the defense of the town to law enforcement and me and Marie."

Nell smiled brightly. "I will. It's time we talked. He's been tense. Yes, talking it out will be good."

Callie sighed. "Well, we need to start getting ready for the wedding."

Jen wished she could go with them. "Please tell Shelley I'm so sorry I'm going to miss the ceremony, but Caleb said no. You know how he says no and doesn't give you an explanation and refuses to argue in any way?"

Callie grinned. "I might have come up against that once or twice." She sat on the edge of the bed.

Rachel shook her head. "One of these days I'm going to throw down with that man. He can be unreasonable. I'll probably wait until I'm done having babies, though. The man is damn good at delivering them."

Jennifer looked down at her boy. She couldn't complain. "Doc does a good job. And he's going to let me go home tomorrow, but he's insistent about staying here for the night. Naomi even offered to stay with me but Doc said…"

"No," Callie and Rachel finished in perfect harmony.

Baby Logan was sleeping, his head on her breast. Naomi had suggested that she hold her baby skin to skin. She'd offered to diaper the baby, but Stef wouldn't have it. He'd looked a bit lost in the beginning and tossed out the first two diapers, but he'd finally managed to get it around the baby's bottom perfectly. Stef had been the one to put Logan against her breast. He'd sat and watched as their son latched onto her nipple and began to suck.

Now her baby was sleeping and Naomi had been right. Being skin to skin with her baby was perfect.

Stef walked in. He took in the scene and his eyes heated for a moment. And then he frowned. "Anyone could walk in here."

While Logan was covered in a blanket, her torso was still naked.

Rachel rolled her eyes. "We've seen her naked before, Stef."

Callie shook her head, a confused look on her face. "I've been naked with Jen lots of times. What's the problem?"

Callie was a bit of a nudist. And it was completely true. Before Callie had married Nate and Zane, Jen had felt completely comfortable shedding her clothes at Callie's house. Nate had caught them sunbathing once and said she blinded him because those boobs didn't belong to him, so now they only did it at Mountain and Valley and only where she wouldn't cause Nate Wright hysterical boob blindness.

Nell frowned Stef's way. "I sincerely hope you're not trying to discourage your wife's very healthy practices."

Stef wasn't amused. He pulled the blanket up. "I think I'm going to have to agree with Max on the whole nursing thing. I don't know that I want my wife's breasts on display for all to see."

Rachel's eyes narrowed. "Well, then you should figure out a way to make your man chest produce some milk, mister." Her face softened, but Jen wasn't fooled. "Uhm, by the way, Stef, I was kind of hoping that you wouldn't kill my dumbass husbands over the whole shooting you and carrying your naked body around town thing. And I want you to know that I have confiscated all the pictures. I also took the thumb drive Max thought he hid."

Stef's face went a little red. "I promise you this, Rachel. I'll tell the assassin I hire to not touch you or Paige."

"Stefan!" It wasn't nice to scare pregnant ladies.

The second pregnant lady in the room wagged her finger Stef's way. Nell gave him a good frowning. "That was very impolite, Stefan."

Stef shrugged. "So was shooting me up with sedatives and shoving me in the back of Rye's truck naked. I have a sunburn on my ass you wouldn't believe."

Jen stifled a smile. "Rachel, he's not going to hire an assassin. He's going to jump Max when he least expects it and beat the holy living shit out of him, because that's what they do."

Rachel breathed a sigh of relief. "Oh, thank god. He's been a pain in the ass lately. He really needs a release. Do it quick."

"I will," Stef agreed. "And don't you protest me, Nell. This is totally consensual. Mostly. I think I need a physical outlet, too, and it can't be sex. I asked Caleb if he could shave a couple of weeks off that whole six-weeks-without-sex thing and he just told me no."

Yep, that was Caleb Burke. He had zero bedside manner. And he would be the one to perform her baby's checkups. Baby Logan would have to get used to his gruff doctor, but then he was a Bliss Boy. Jennifer had made damn sure of it. She'd wanted her baby born here and not in Del Norte or Alamosa, and Caleb Burke had made that happen, so she would put up with his "nos."

"I think Logan here will keep us busy for a couple of weeks."

Stef frowned. "Fine, but I'm sleeping with you."

She couldn't help but smile. He'd talked about sleeping in the guest room so he wouldn't disturb her. "I thought you had other plans."

He turned his Dom eyes on her. "You'll have to put up with me."

What had Jack Barnes told her? Sometimes a Dom needed a good poking. Her Dom was back in charge. Well, he thought he was in charge, and that was exactly the way Jen liked it. "I suppose I will."

"Ladies, I think Jennifer needs some rest," Stef said.

Callie sighed. "It's time to get to the wedding anyway. I'll send your regards."

"And I'll be waiting for you to jump Max," Rachel said. "Do I even want to know what you're going to do to Rye?"

Stef shook his head.

"All right then." Rachel and Callie and Nell took one last glance at the baby before saying their good-byes.

And then she was alone with her boys. With her husband and her son. God, she had a son—a tiny piece of her and Stef—someone totally unique in the world. She wanted her boy to have her sense of humor and his dad's intelligence and talent. She wanted him to have his namesake's bravery and Stella's enduring loyalty. She prayed the universe gave her son Rachel's stubborn will and Callie's deep tolerance.

And that the world around him would give him such bliss.

"Hey, you're crying." Stef's voice had softened and his hand came out to cup her cheek. "Are you in pain, love?"

She shook her head. "No. I'm just so happy."

"Scoot over," he commanded. "And get rid of the blanket. It's warm enough in here."

Such a bossy man. She moved slightly, and Stef climbed on the bed and wrapped his arm around her, cuddling her close. The blanket fell away and she lay naked from the waist up. Baby Logan's body shuddered as he sighed, his eyes opening and his mouth starting to move. She brought her nipple to his mouth and he started to suck. "I thought I was supposed to be modest."

"Not around me," Stef said, his eyes going straight to where his son was nursing. "And that is a beautiful sight."

"Stef, I don't want you to think of me as just a mom." She remembered how Callie had worried that her hubbies hadn't wanted her sexually. She didn't want to get into the rut they'd been in before one long night in the guesthouse had proven to Callie that she was still a woman.

Stef chuckled and moved against her, pressing himself to her thigh. "Love, does that feel maternal to you?"

Nope. That was an erection. "God, I'm so glad you're a complete pervert."

"I'm a pervert who loves his wife. Jennifer, I love you. I love our son. I can't thank you enough for him."

"So no more pulling away? You should know that I'll pull you back." She had no intention of ever losing her husband.

"I live in fear of it." Stef touched his mouth to hers in a sweet kiss. "I'll never leave you. Either of you."

Logan kicked and started to cry.

"I think he wants his dad."

"His dad is right here." Stef gently cradled the baby. "Come on, son. Let's let your mom get some sleep."

He took Logan to the rocking chair and unbuttoned his shirt. He cuddled the baby to his chest and started to rock. "Well, Naomi said skin to skin, right? She said it would soothe him. I assume she meant my skin, too."

Sweet tears pricked at her eyes. "Yes, absolutely."

Logan settled down again and Stef was watching their son.

Jen laid back and dreamed of their future.

Chapter Twenty-Two

The Wedding of Leo, Shelley, and Wolf

Leo pulled at the bow tie of his tux.

"Don't, son." Mel was suddenly in his space, standing in front of him. "You have it too tight. Let me."

Mel knew how to tie a bow tie? He moved his hands away, allowing Mel access.

Mel quickly worked the tie into something that allowed Leo to breathe. He looked at himself in the mirror. It was damn near perfect. "Thanks."

The older man smiled. He was in a tux, too, but he was also wearing a trucker hat that sported a tinfoil lining. "You're welcome. Oh, and I took care of the problem with Robert, though I would appreciate it if you didn't mention it to your momma. I had some help from your boss. I told you that one would make a good hunter."

"If I ever decided to rid the world of aliens, I could certainly do it," a low voice said.

Leo felt his eyes widen. He turned and Julian was standing there looking resplendent in his tux. "Is he still alive?"

"Of course," Julian replied steadily. "I wouldn't kill anyone right before your wedding. I've heard the sheriff around here is quite unreasonable, but Danielle told me not to replace him."

"Replace Nate?"

"You know, with a more reasonable man. Apparently the town is happy with him. Danielle thinks I should pay the tickets he's written us, but I told Finn to do whatever it takes."

Oh, god. "I'll have Wolf talk to Nate. We'll get it cleared up. So what did you do to Robert?"

Mel smiled. "Julian talked to him."

Julian smoothed down his jacket, looking into one of the mirrors and checking his already perfect appearance. "I pointed out a few irrefutable facts of life to Mr. Meyer. It's highly likely that he will end up in jail again, and despite the fact that he's always been in minimum security prison, accidents can happen there, too."

So Julian threatened to have him killed. That wasn't so surprising. "So you and Mel found him and talked to him?"

A tiny shake of Julian's head indicated his negative response. "*I* simply talked to him. Mel gave him a sound thrashing. Apparently he's quite up on all the alien fighting techniques. He's quite good in a fight. A mean fucker. I like him."

Mel tipped his trucker hat. "A man has to stay in shape. I'm going to go see how Wolf and Jamie are doing. I doubt either one of them knows how to tie a bow tie either."

Mel shut the door behind him, and Julian's lips curled up in a grin. "This place is completely insane. I have to admit, I'm looking forward to the sanity of Dallas."

Because Julian controlled his world in Dallas. Julian preferred to control everything, but he'd learned to bend in all the right ways. When Leo had first met Julian, he'd been cold and shut down to everyone except Jack Barnes. Over time, Julian had become more than Leo's friend. Julian had mentored him, taught him how to blend into high society, gave him a place to stay, a job to do, while he sorted through his life.

Julian Lodge had been a real father to him. And now Julian was standing beside him on his wedding day.

He would never tell Julian that he thought of him as a father. Julian would very likely punch him in the face, or pay someone to do it.

But he suddenly felt an overwhelming need to do something he'd never done before. He stepped close and put his arms around his mentor.

Julian was perfectly still. "Leo, there's seems to be something wrong. You've fallen and you don't seem to be getting up."

"It's called a hug. Give me a minute."

Julian sighed, and then there was a pat to Leo's back. "I'm very proud of you, Leo."

Fuck. He was not going to cry. He stepped back and took a long breath. "Back at you, man."

The door opened again and Wolf stepped in. "Hey, brother. I believe it's time. Don't tell me you're getting cold feet."

His feet weren't cold. They were eager. Eager to begin his new life. Eager to see the whole world again, this time in the right way, with his family by his side.

Leo stepped out and joined his brother on the most important day of their lives.

The day they truly became a family.

* * * *

Wolf felt his heart clench the moment she stepped into the church on her brother's arm.

This was why people spent god-awful amounts of money on weddings. This was why they waited and went through all the trouble. They did it because there was something deep and meaningful about standing at the end of the aisle and watching the woman he loved walking toward him.

Shelley was choosing them. She was forsaking all others.

And he had his brother beside him. Oh, Jamie was his best man and Julian was Leo's, but at the end of the day, his brother had become his best friend, his partner. His brother was the one he could count on. They shared a life. They shared a past and a future. No one would ever know him the way Leo did.

The music swelled and Shelley walked toward him, Trev leading her. His ma was in the front row. Sure, there was a beet attached to her hat, but she was smiling serenely, perfectly happy with the proceedings. A tear came to her eye, and Mel slid an arm around her.

Crazy love. Who could ask for more?

"God, she's beautiful," Leo said, his eyes on their bride. "Have I thanked you, brother?"

"For what?"

"For bringing me here." Leo slid a hand to his shoulder, patting him like he had when they were children and Leo had been forced to play all the roles in Wolf's life. "We wouldn't be here without you. Shelley would still be searching. I would be alone. You brought us here, brother. Never forget it."

Shelley made it to them, a smile on her gorgeous face. "Hi."

Such a silly to thing to say, but "hi" was a beginning. And that's where they were. The beginning. A whole future lay in front of them and Wolf couldn't wait for it.

"Hi," he replied, and took her hand.

"Dearly beloved," the preacher began.

But Wolf was lost in his bride's eyes.

* * * *

Lexi

"And now," the preacher was saying, "Leo and Wolf and Shelley would like to invite their friend Lexi O'Malley up to say a few words about love and marriage."

The whole congregation seemed to stop and stare, but Lexi was ready for it. She'd worried for days about what she should say, but it had come to her the night before as she lay between her men. In the still of the night, when peace was all around her, she'd known exactly what to say about love and marriage and something equally important.

Lexi smiled as she stood, making her way from the pew to the front of the church and the small podium to the right of the altar.

She stared out at the crowded church, familiar faces everywhere. Aidan and Lucas looked completely delectable in their suits. The fact that each gorgeous man was holding one of their children made them all the sexier in her mind. Jack was climbing up Aidan's leg, trying to crawl over the pew to get to his grandmother while Daphne was sleeping peacefully in Lucas's arms.

They were balls of chaos, and she wouldn't have it any other way—except one. She wanted more babies. She'd told herself she was done, that she needed to focus on her career, but there was a whole life to be had and it wouldn't wait for her. It wouldn't put itself on pause and hope that she got back to it. It would move on with her or without her.

She would find a balance because nothing was more important.

A sweet sense of belonging swept over her. It wasn't merely her immediate family she belonged to.

"I suppose Shelley thought the romance writer would get up here and talk about romance and sexy nights spent with the ones you love. All the things you can count on right before and at the beginning of a marriage. I probably should talk about how weddings symbolize the joy of love, but I think we all know that a wedding is merely the beginning. It's an acknowledgement that you've decided to take the next step, to share a life together. What's waiting for you, my friends? What's at the end of this journey you've chosen to take together? By saying 'I do,' what do you gain? I believe you gain something more than a lover, more than a friend, though both of those things are necessary. What you gain is a family. Look around you. Most of these people aren't your blood."

She looked out at her stepfathers who hadn't raised her, didn't share an ounce of DNA with her, but they'd been there for her from the moment they'd fallen in love with her mother. They'd become her fathers. "Blood, I've discovered, is pretty meaningless in the face of real love. For some of us, our mothers and fathers and siblings are wonderful, but if there's one thing this group of people have taught me, it's that we choose who we love. Even when blood relations let us down, we can form our own families and they can be every bit as tight."

Julian came to mind. He didn't have to care about her, but he loved Jack and so he'd taken Lexi in as well. He'd taken them all into his heart. It was difficult to believe that once she'd thought he didn't have one. Julian's heart was so big, he couldn't seem to stop bringing people into it. She owed the man so much, and there was nothing between them but the choice to be family.

"So what is waiting for you, my sweet friend Shelley, is a very large family. It's so big, it covers two states, and you have a home with any of us should the need arise. We promise to annoy you, to bug you, to push you, to love you and stand by you. We promise to choose you. Every day. Marriage, family, life, they're all hard and require work. Happily ever after is a choice we have to make every day. You think you're making your choice today, but I challenge you. I challenge every single one of us. Start each day by choosing. Skip the good morning and say something infinitely more important. I do."

She looked at her husbands, her loves, the joys of her existence. "I do, and I do. Every single day. I choose this life and these loves and I choose my family. Welcome to my family, Shelley."

Lexi looked over and Shelley was crying. Hell, most of the women in the Feed Store Church were crying.

Shelley looked and mouthed the words "I do."

Everyone looked out, reaching to their loved ones, reaffirming the choices they made long ago.

Lucas winked at her. "You know I do."

Aidan put his hand over his heart. Right before he had to save their son from almost certain death as he nearly went over the top of the pew.

"Momma," Olivia was heard whispering loudly. "I think baby Jack is saying I do to climbing on top of you, but Uncle Aidan says no. Why does my family say no so much? Lexi just told us we should all say I do and I think that means yes."

The whole church erupted in laughter.

Her family. They were loud and obnoxious and sometimes they completely worked the system so she couldn't even buy a new cell phone.

And she would choose them. Every time. Every day.

I do.

From the Bliss County Gazette

Hiram Prosper Jones, aged 97, died on Thursday in the loving arms of his part-time caregiver, Bambi Lou, after a heart attack, though it should be noted, he went out with a smile on his face and his teeth in a jar by the…bed. Hiram was a giant in Southern Colorado politics, serving as the mayor of Bliss for more than forty years. He protected his town with his policies and his body when he stopped a rampaging bear. He never married but rather spent his love and time on the people. For this reason, he was preceded in death by all those who went before him and he leaves behind every citizen of Bliss. We were his family. Rest in bliss, Mr. Mayor.

Memorial Services will be held at the Feed Store Church starting at 11 a.m. on Monday and followed by a 'burial" service at the Mountain and Valley Naturist Community. In keeping with Hiram's wishes, all are welcome.

Chapter Twenty-Three

The Funeral of Hiram Jones, Mayor of Bliss

Two days later, Rafe turned his face up, letting the sun shine down on him, warming his skin, reminding him that he was alive and in the company of people he loved.

Of course, most of those people were crying.

"Hiram was a great man," Rye Harper said. He stood at the head of the party, his role as leader in this mournful act clear. Hiram hadn't wanted a preacher. He'd wanted a short service led by Rye and Max and he'd wanted a party at Trio. In his will he'd left money for beer. "He had a vision for Bliss. He wanted to make this town something special, something we could all be proud of. Hiram knew what it meant to be from Bliss. It might not always be easy. We might face hardship, but we do it together. He knew that a town is really just another word for family. He was like a dad to us all and his passing leaves a mighty big hole to fill."

Yes, he had big boots to fill. Enormous ones. He'd been named the mayor of Bliss days before. He'd stood in town hall and sworn to protect this town and to fulfill his office to the best of his abilities.

He knew how important the role was now. And he could spend a lifetime trying to live up to his predecessor. The good news was, he had a lifetime.

He looked around the cliff-top gathering spot at the highest point of the Mountain and Valley Naturist Community. The entire town had turned out for the celebration of Hiram Jones's long life. They all stood, huddled together. Callie and Nate both held a baby while Zane had his arms around Callie. Jen was leaning on Stef while Stella cuddled her grandbaby and Sebastian stood close. Holly had a hand on both her men. Caleb had been pulled into their conspiracy and Alexei had gotten sniffly and talked in Russian. Gemma and Jesse and Cade stood beside Long-Haired Roger, Liz Two, and their weird baby dog. The funeral seemed to have brought about a truce between longtime rivals as Polly stood near Long-Haired Roger and not once did she attempt to kill him. Even Roger, Liz One, and their whole brood had turned up, though they were carrying shotguns in case the apocalypse happened. Marie and Teeny stood with Seth and Logan and Georgia.

But Nell and Henry were standing apart. And Henry had a dark look in his eyes. After this was done, it was time for that meeting Cam had promised.

The mayor needed to know what the hell was going on.

But that was for after. For now, he held Laura's hand and comforted her while Rye spoke and Max held on to his wife and baby girl. For all his stubborn craziness, Max Harper wasn't a man who buried his sorrow. He loved Hiram and it showed on his face.

"Hiram Jones was loved and he loved, and he would say that was enough. He helped build this town into something we're all proud of, and it's a sad day when we have to let him go." Rye held an urn in his hands. "In his will, Hiram asked that the new mayor say a few words."

Rafe's breath caught in his throat. Wow. Hiram had wanted to push him. Well, it was time to open himself up, but this wasn't a political speech. He would make enough of those. It was time to honor a man he admired by following in his footsteps and speaking from his heart.

Laura gave him a gentle nudge and Cam smiled, bringing Sierra's hand up in a playful wave.

Rafe nodded, acknowledging that he might speak alone, but they were here with him. "I'll just say a few words about Hiram because he would be insulted if I spoke for too long. He would want to get on with the party, so to speak. We should mourn the fact that he's no longer with us, but we shouldn't mourn his life. His life was full and rich. I've been a person who counted success in terms of money and power, but Hiram taught me something different. Hiram's success came from how well he loved the people around him. He was a builder—a builder of towns and families and friendships. He didn't look outside his world for recognition. He knew that the best world possible is the one we build in our hearts. He knew that when the outside world says no, we do not have to accept it. When the outside world lays down roadblocks, we build a new road, a better, more inclusive road. We control our destiny and we build toward it with love and compassion. And we build it together. I will honor Hiram by learning the lessons he had to teach."

He had already moved into the mayor's office. The business of the town was never done. In his days as mayor, he'd already arbitrated a fight between Roger and Long-Haired Roger, had a fight with Hal the cook from Stella's over whether or not the town's health codes allowed puffer fish to be on the menu as the special of the day, and helped Noah Bennett start up an animal shelter. The days had been busy, and half the time he worked while Sierra kicked her legs in a playpen in his office.

It wasn't what he'd expected from life.

It was so much better.

He turned to Rye and nodded. Max stepped up. This was their job.

Max took a long breath as Rye opened the urn. "Good-bye, Hi. Don't think I don't know why you did what you did. And don't think she didn't know it. I hope like hell you find her wherever you're going. Find her because I think Momma knew she should have chosen you. Maybe you get another chance."

Tears slipped from Rye's eyes. "Thank you for being there for us. We love you, Hi. Happy journey."

They released the last earthly remnants of Hiram Jones's body on the mountain he loved. The wind picked up some of his ashes and took them down the mountain, a piece of Hiram to forever remain where he loved.

But another wind swept upward, to places unknown.

A man's journey was never really over.

Rafe joined his family, his whole family.

His journey had just begun.

One Night in Bliss

A special gift to my fans…

At the Talbot estate, the night of Leo, Shelley, and Wolf's wedding…

Abby Barnes-Fleetwood looked up at her husband. She sighed every time she saw those damn Dom eyes of his. "Hey, Jack."

Her husband shut the door to their room. "Hey, baby. Did I mention how lovely you were tonight?"

She was still dressed in her St. John suit, but there was a bit of sadness that draped her now. She'd swelled with pride as her Lexi had given the speech of a lifetime. And then she looked around her and realized that Lexi was on the upswing of life. She and Livie had their whole lives before them. Lexi had figured out her love and herself at such a young age. It had taken Abby years to realize the same truths.

It hadn't been until she'd come home and faced all her demons that she'd found her real world. Her Jack and her Sam.

"Thanks, hon." She tried to put some emphasis behind her words. She didn't feel them tonight. She'd looked at all the youth and beauty around her. Everyone was twenty years younger than her, it seemed.

"Abigail, I know that tone of voice. Talk to me." Jack always saw through her.

Jack was getting better looking the older he got. The years had been more than kind to her husbands. She stared up at him with his emerald-green eyes and pitch-black hair. There was the lightest dusting of pure silver at his temples, but it made him all the more dominant.

"I'm fine. There's nothing to talk about."

"I don't like the sound of that." His gorgeous mouth frowned, leaving a sexy crease around his lips.

"I said thanks," she tried. She had to because she wasn't sure she was up to a spanking tonight. She was tired in a way that had nothing to do with her body and everything with her soul.

"What are we thankful for?" Sam asked as he walked into their room. A broad smile covered his face, lifting his lips up. Such a sensual man. Sam Fleetwood oozed sexuality. At forty-two he was in his prime, and Abby couldn't help but damn near drool as he pulled his shirt over his head and uncovered perfect abs and those notches at his hips that always got her motor running.

She wasn't forty anymore. She would always be older. She'd thought a lot about surgery, but Jack always said no. He said he loved her the way she was. How long would that last?

"Abby is doing that thing where she says all the right words but I hear another meaning behind them," Jack explained.

Sam clapped his hands together. "Thank god. She's been so good this whole trip. I've been dying to watch you spank her. Let's get going."

Sam was an optimist. Abby didn't have any intention of letting that happen. She'd gained weight recently. "I'm fine. I don't know what Jack is talking about."

Jack's hand came out, tilting her chin up. "No. You're not fine and I want to know why. Tell me now, Abigail."

She hated it when he did that. He just commanded, but she heard the words beneath it. *Tell me now because I love you and I have the right to know.*

Because they shared a love and a life and babies. Because she'd promised him long ago to share all of her burdens. All of her joys. In some ways, the burdens meant more.

"I felt old today." Tears pierced her eyes. "I looked around at all those twenty- and thirty-somethings and I felt so old."

A low chuckle started in the back of his throat. "Oh, my darlin', that is the funniest thing I've heard in a while."

She frowned his way. "Thanks for understanding."

She hadn't expected that. Abby turned away. She started to work the jacket off. If Sam was in the room, then Livie and Josh were in bed. It was time for her to turn in, too. They were going back to Dallas in the morning. They would sit in Julian's jet and talk and laugh and she would be in comfortable company. Maybe she could forget how young these people were, how their whole lives were in front of them.

Probably not.

She needed a good night's sleep. That was all. Tomorrow she would get up and head home and everything would be normal again.

"Stay right where you are." The deep timbre to Jack's voice made a delicious shiver go up her spine.

They had been here for days and the whole time they had been running after Livie and Josh and trying to keep them out of trouble. She'd been worried about Lexi. They had spent the night before with little Jack and Daphne with them. She'd been playing the supportive mom and friend. They had fallen into bed exhausted every night.

Not once had she heard that dark tone in Jack's voice.

"What do you need, Jack?" She didn't move. She was well trained. He'd made sure of it.

"I need a whole lot of things, but right now what I need most is utter and complete obedience." A hand brushed across her shoulder. "I need you to believe me. Have I ever lied to you, Abigail Barnes?"

Sam moved in front of her. His blond hair fell over his eyes. He'd lost his shirt and he was past toned. He didn't have a six-pack. No. Sam Fleetwood had an eight-pack. He was ridiculous. "Has either of us lied to you? Jack wouldn't bother and I'm not smart enough."

"Oh, you are begging for it, too," Jack growled.

Sam grinned. "Probably. You know I like a little discipline."

He did. Sam was more masochistic than she was. But she had to answer them honestly. "Of course not, Jack."

Jack stared at her. "You're the most beautiful woman in the world, Abigail. You were yesterday. You are today. You will be twenty years from now."

Tears pierced her eyes. "You make me feel that way."

"I don't see through other men's eyes. I only know what I see. You're gorgeous, my Abby. And Sam and I will make your ass red the next time you insult yourself, but you know that."

Sam smiled at her. "Hell, I heard that Tyler guy trying to hit on you, baby."

"What?" Jack's face went dark. "Someone tried to hit on our wife and you let it happen?"

Abby shook her head. She'd ended up talking to the young EMT because she understood his profession. "He's an EMT at Cole Roberts's lodge. He'd heard I used to be a trauma nurse. We were trading war stories. He certainly wasn't hitting on me."

Tyler Davis was maybe twenty-seven years old. He was blond and reminded her of a slightly nerdy Sam. He certainly wasn't hitting on a woman who was closer to fifty than she liked to be reminded of.

"He brought you a glass of wine," Sam pointed out.

"He did what? Where the hell was I?" If Sam kept it up, steam would start pouring out of Jack's ears.

Sam shrugged. "You were talking to that crazy guy."

That could be any of several men, and she needed to get Jack to calm down. "He was getting a drink for himself and picked one up for me, too. He was being gentlemanly."

"He was staring at your ass," Sam pointed out.

"What!" Jack's face had gone the slightest bit red.

Abby put a hand on Sam's leg. "Will you stop it? Are you trying to give him a heart attack?"

"He should have been giving this Tyler fellow a swift ass kicking," Jack said.

Sam stifled a laugh. "I'm not going to beat the shit out of every man who looks at our wife. She's a work of art. It's inevitable. As long as he just looks and is respectful, I'll give him some leeway. After all, he's only looking and I get to touch. And every time you looked away, his eyes were on your ass, baby."

That hot EMT had been looking at her backside?

Sam nodded as though he'd heard the question. "The only other woman he was looking at was the dark-haired waitress. Lucy, I think her name was."

The gorgeous waitress with a perfect body.

"He needs to keep his eyes on the waitress and off my wife." Jack was a possessive man. Abby sometimes thought he would be happier if she never left the house. The only time he was all right with men looking at her was in the dungeon at The Club because everyone knew the rules there.

It had been so long since they had played. Their world had started to revolve around Olivia and Josh, and she knew that was the way it had to be, but she needed those pockets of time where it was just the three of them.

"I miss playing."

Jack calmed, his hand going to her hair. "I miss it, too, baby. We need to make time for ourselves. And I damn straight need to make a few things clear. I think you'll hear me better if you find your position."

She started to fall to her knees, but Sam's hands held her up.

"He doesn't want to admire your suit, Abby." Sam chuckled against her ear as he worked the buttons of her shirt.

Her skin started to hum. "But the kids…"

"Are very likely giving Lexi hell by now," Sam said. "They came by and picked them up ten minutes ago. They'll meet us in Alamosa tomorrow."

"Sam, I didn't expect Lexi to pay us back. Our kids can be a handful."

Jack frowned. "And Lexi's been a handful herself lately. She and Lucas and Aidan can handle our kids. Well, I expect them to at least live through the experience. So take the clothes off, Abigail. I'm not going to ask again."

He hadn't asked the first time, but there was no point in telling him that. She let Sam undress her while Jack watched. He looked deliciously decadent in the remains of his tuxedo. He'd gotten rid of the jacket and bow tie the minute the ceremony was over, and now she could see the way his tan skin looked against the snowy-white dress shirt. And how interested he was in watching her get undressed.

Jack's slacks tented, his cock making a firm line against the zipper. Her Dom was hungry.

Sam's hands slipped the bra off her and immediately cupped her mounds. "God, you feel so fucking good, Abby."

She let her head drift back against Sam's shoulder. She suddenly didn't feel so tired.

"Pinch them," Jack ordered.

She groaned as Sam's fingers squeezed her nipples tight and twisted ever so lightly. She was no longer thinking about how they sagged. She was thinking about how they seemed to have a direct line to her pussy. She could feel herself getting hot and wet.

"Get her out of her clothes and then deal with mine." There was a tension in Jack's voice that belied his calmly spoken orders.

Sam's hands skimmed down to her waist where he made quick work of her skirt. His fingers cupped her ass for a moment. "See, I get to touch."

And he knew how to touch her. He ran a single finger along the crease of her cheeks, reminding her of how good it was to have a man there.

He kissed the nape of her neck. "Now, be a good girl and spread those legs wide. I have to go take care of our Jack."

She got to her knees, the carpet plush under her skin. She spread her knees wide in slave pose, giving her Dom a good view of that piece of her he loved to call his own.

And watching her men together was enough to get her blood pumping. Jack's eyes held hers as Sam's hands worked to get his shirt off. Jack's perfectly cut chest appeared, tapering down to his lean waist. Jack still rode herd and fixed fences, though he could certainly pay others to do it for him. Not her Jack. He was out in the fields with the hands and with Sam.

Working kept Jack young. She'd seen the way he smiled when he and Sam were on horseback, racing across their ranch. Jack had come from nothing and turned himself into a millionaire cowboy, and he still grinned like a kid when he was working a herd with his best friend.

Sam gave her a wink as he stepped behind Jack and started to work on the fly of his slacks. Sam was ageless. He would still be young when they were all old and gray. Sam was sunshine and light. Loving kept Sam Fleetwood young. He never had the ambition Jack had, but finding his family had brought Sam everything he needed. She'd been the one to draw Jack and Sam together. Maybe Lexi had found her way to her men sooner than Abby had, but then she'd paved the way for her daughter.

And while she might claim her babies kept her young, she knew the truth. Jack and Sam kept her young. When they looked at her with dark eyes, she couldn't feel old and tired. Her whole soul lit up.

"Sam, our Abigail felt old among all the youngsters tonight. Did you feel the same?" Jack asked as Sam slid his slacks off.

Sam managed to brush Jack's cock as he removed the slacks. "Hell, no, Jack. I ain't old. Oh, these Bliss kids might be younger, but we're the originals."

A smile crossed Jack's face, his hand running through Sam's hair. "I like the way you think, Sam. We're the originals. And we do it right, don't we?"

He tugged on Sam's hair and then took his mouth. God, she loved watching them kiss. Their first kiss had been at her request, a boon for good behavior. She'd asked for Sam's sake, but over the years she'd come to realize how much their loving each other meant to her.

She'd brought them together. She'd been the catalyst to those men getting what they needed—each other and her.

She liked the sound of it. Original.

She watched her men devouring each other. Jack pulled at Sam's slacks, tugging them down so he could get at Sam's cock. He stroked it, getting it long and hard. Sam shuddered in his arms, his hands reaching for Jack.

Jack reached down, cupping Sam's balls as Sam held on to him. "Tell me something, Abigail. Are you thinking about that boy who was flirting with you at the wedding now?"

"Tyler?" Was he insane? "No. I was never actually thinking about Tyler Davis."

But Jack's needless jealously did make her grin. Why would she ever think of another man when the two most beautiful men in the world belonged to her?

Jack's hands ran over Sam's body. "You better not. That would not go well for you."

"I can't think of anyone except you and Sam." They filled her whole life.

"Go and join her," Jack commanded. "And get rid of those clothes."

Sam moved quickly. He'd taken care with Jack's clothes, but practically tore off his own. He was kneeling next to her, their knees touching. He moved his hand over her open palm so they were holding hands. Holding hands and waiting for their Dom.

It was exactly where she needed to be.

"Abigail."

She looked up and Jack was standing over her, his big cock in hand. "Yes, Jack?"

She knew what he wanted, but she loved the way he commanded her.

"Suck me."

She leaned forward and kissed that cock that had brought her such pleasure. She ran her tongue along the hard, hot flesh. She took her time, enjoying every ridge and line of him. She traced her tongue along the thick vein running along the bottom of his dick.

Jack's hand sank into her hair, pulling it out of its neat bun. "Don't stop what you're doing. Just listen to me."

She sucked his cockhead into her mouth.

"I love you, Abigail Barnes. I love you today. I'll love you tomorrow. I'll love you as long as my soul exists. I don't care what age you are. I will always see you walking into Christa's living room in a tight sweater and jeans that made my dick stand on end for days. You'll always be young to me. You'll always be gorgeous and fuckable and you will always, always be mine."

Tears blurred her eyes and Jack pulled her off, forcing her to look up at him.

"Always. I don't care who is younger than you or who you think is prettier. There is one woman in the whole world for me. And that's you. I do, Abigail. I do every single day of my life."

Lexi had told the congregation to make the choice every day. To be together. To love each other. To celebrate their marriage.

"I do, Jack. I do."

Sam sat up. "Well, I do, too, but there hasn't been a whole lot of doing going on lately, so I was hoping we didn't spend all night talking and stuff."

God, Olivia was so his child.

"Brat," Jack barked. "Ass in the air, Sam."

Sam sighed. "Thank god. I thought we were going to talk about loving each other all damn night and never get around to actually doing it."

He was so impatient. And so gorgeous. She watched as he turned, putting his ass right in the air, a sigh going through his whole body.

Jack walked across the room and pulled out his leather bag. It was his kit, the one that contained all the fun toys he never left home without. He pulled out a flogger, one with small metal tips. The one he used on her was deerskin and soft as butter, but Sam needed more.

"You have to get on a plane tomorrow," Jack warned. He looked dark and dominant as he stood over Sam, his shoulders broad and his cock still hard.

"I can handle it. Please, Jack."

The flogger made a sharp sound as it hit Sam's flesh. Red lines immediately became visible, but Sam actually relaxed.

This was what he needed.

"Abigail, if you would help me out," Jack offered.

And Sam liked a bit more than just the flogger. Abby moved to his head, staying on her knees. She sank her hands into his silky hair. Jack laid the flogger on Sam's ass and Abby tugged his hair.

Sam moaned and it seemed like his every muscle relaxed further.

She looked up at Jack, and there was a smile on his face. He knew he was giving Sam what he needed and that satisfied Jack.

Jack's world revolved around pleasing them. To the outside it might not seem that way. Their relationship might seem perverse and one-sided, but Abby knew the truth. The Dom gave. It was his reason for living—to be what his subs needed. Abby had accepted a long time ago that what she needed wasn't necessarily what the world would think she needed. The world didn't have to live her life. The world didn't walk in her shoes.

She gave no apologies for her needs. She'd found two men who fulfilled them and she was happy.

She was alive. She was young.

It hit her suddenly. She was the only one who could decide who she was, what she was. If she allowed herself to feel young, to see herself with all that potential life still left, no one could take that from her.

She didn't have to be old. She could just be Abby. Sam's Abby. Jack's Abigail. She chose her life. She defined herself. That was what her Dom had taught her.

Age was a number, but her soul was a choice. Her life was a choice.

She tugged on Sam's hair as the flogger bit into his flesh and he moaned in pleasure.

She would choose them. She would choose this life. With them.

Every single time.

She leaned close and whispered to Sam. "I love you."

His face turned up to hers. Those gorgeous lips of his curling into a smile. "Oh, baby, I love you, too. So fucking much."

She tugged on his hair again, thrilled at the way his eyes dilated with the sensation. She didn't call it pain. It wasn't for Sam. It was pleasure for Sam. It was connection.

Another slap and Sam nearly sank into the floor.

The world could think what it liked. They knew the truth. Love was love. Love was different for every living human being and it was all right as long as the emotion was the same. Jack would die for Sam. He would die for her. He would give his whole self for the two people he loved. He gave them his everything.

Love was everything. No matter how a human defined it.

And she defined love as Jack and Sam.

She looked up at her Dom. "Please, Jack."

Jack held his hand. "You need something?"

"I need my men." She needed them so much. She needed them to make her feel young and alive and free. She needed them to fly.

"Sam?" Jack asked.

Sam moved fast, getting to his feet in an instant. "I think we should give it to her."

"I think she should ask very sweetly." Jack slung an arm around Sam's shoulders. They looked awfully hot together, their bodies pressed against each other.

"Ask us, baby," Sam said, rubbing against Jack.

She didn't hesitate. One lesson she'd learned was that the universe rarely gave her anything she wasn't brave enough to ask for. "Please make love to me. I need both my men."

"And where do you want us?" Jack asked, his lips curled in a smirk that told her he knew damn well what her answer would be.

"One in my pussy and one in my ass." She wanted to be filled with them.

"Sam, I'm worried I'm not ready for that," Jack said.

Sam fell to his knees and had Jack's cock in his mouth before Abby could take another breath. Unlike her, Sam didn't play around. He sucked Jack hard, pulling the whole thing past his lips and then dragging his mouth back.

Over and over, Sam sucked him hard, taking Jack all the way to his balls. His hands came up, cupping Jack's balls as he rolled his cock in his mouth. Sam's blond head worked Jack over.

She watched her men, her whole body on edge. She wanted to be with them, but she loved watching them. She loved when Jack had Sam on his knees, driving into him from behind. And she loved when they were chest to chest, making love as they kissed each other with such passion she couldn't turn away from it.

And she was a part of that.

She moved close to Sam, pressing against his body. He turned slightly, winking as he gave way.

Abby leaned over, licking along Jack's cock. She looked up and Jack was staring down at her with such tenderness that she wondered how she could ever feel old and worn. Not when she was so well loved.

"I think if I wait another minute, I might not be able to grant your wish, darling." His hands came down, lifting her up. He hoisted her easily into his arms. She loved it when he carried her around like she weighed nothing at all.

Years of marriage hadn't dimmed her passion, hadn't broken them apart. The years seemed to make her love them more. Perhaps she should stop worrying about small lines and wrinkles and find joy in the fact that she was loved each and every day. She'd been given an extraordinary life, something many people never managed to find.

And that was beautiful.

Jack carried her to the bed, laying her down on top of the coverlet. He stared down at her body, his eyes hot with desire.

Sam was suddenly beside him. He wound an arm around Jack's waist and Jack responded, pulling him close. They both stared down at her.

"That's our girl," Jack said.

Sam winked her way. "That is one hell of a woman. And she's ours."

"Damn straight, but sometimes I like to prove it to her." Jack gave Sam's ass a nice slap. "Get into that pussy, Sam."

"I thought you'd never ask." Sam jumped on, throwing his body on top of hers as he took her mouth. He rolled them together on the bed, their tongues working as he ended up on the bottom.

Abby straddled his lean hips and let her pussy sink on his cock. She was soaking wet, but Sam was so big it was always a fight.

Jack's big hand pushed her down so that she was chest to chest with Sam. She looked into his blue eyes. Even Sam had all the little lines that came with age and smiling as much as he did. But Sam would always be young to her. She couldn't see past how much her heart lit up at the sight of him. He'd given her such love and devotion and joy. He'd given her babies to love. He was the one who held her hand while they played and explored.

"My man," she said.

His hands smoothed back her hair. "Forever."

And that was what they had. Forever. Suddenly she knew that nothing would stop her love. Not age or time or anything that came after. Faith was all she needed and she had such faith in them.

She gasped at the feel of lubricant against her asshole.

"I love it when I surprise you," Jack said as his fingers started rimming her.

He was her rock, the center of her universe. She and Sam could have fun and play because Jack took care of things. She could always count on Jack being there.

She gave over, submitting to them both as Jack's fingers stretched her asshole, preparing her for his cock. This was the place she longed to be in—in between them, giving them her all.

She groaned when she felt Jack's cock begin to invade. He was so big. He had to work his way into her ass, inch by inch until she was full, until she simply was one with them.

"That feels so good," Sam said on a moan. "I love feeling him slide against me."

Their cocks were inside her, only a thin membrane separating them. They could feel each other working deep in her body.

"It's heaven." Jack leaned over, kissing her back. "This is my heaven."

It was their heaven. To be together.

Jack tunneled in as Sam pulled out and then they were off. They worked in tandem, perfectly timing every thrust and release. Abby let them work their magic, moving in time with them. Pleasure coursed through her, the orgasm building inside.

Pressure built, threatening to make her scream. It was right there, right on the edge. She worked her hips back, taking every inch of Jack's cock into her ass. Sam slammed his hips up and then she went flying.

She rode the wave as her men found their pleasure. Jack filled her ass and Sam her pussy.

Abby fell against Sam and Jack against her, their bodies a sultry tangle of arms and legs and mouths, lightly kissing. They lay together enjoying the intimacy of mingling.

"See, we're totally the best because we've been doing it longer," Sam said with a smile.

"And we'll be doing it forever," Jack promised.

Abby let her men start to heat her up all over again. She was perfectly satisfied.

Forever was really all a woman could ask for.

* * * *

The Bliss gang will return in *Happily Ever After in Bliss*, now available.

Kitten and the rest of the Texas Sirens gang will return in *Siren Reborn*, now available.

Author's Note

I'm often asked by generous readers how they can help get the word out about a book they enjoyed. There are so many ways to help an author you like. Leave a review. If your e-reader allows you to lend a book to a friend, please share it. Go to Goodreads and connect with others. Recommend the books you love because stories are meant to be shared. Thank you so much for reading this book and for supporting all the authors you love!

Happily Ever After in Bliss
Nights in Bliss, Colorado Book 11
By Lexi Blake writing as Sophie Oak

A man hiding from his nature

Henry Flanders never dreamed his past would catch up to him. After all, the man he used to be is dead and buried. He made a clean break with life in the CIA. He moved to Bliss under a new name. For years he has been living a dream, married to his lovely Nell. Now a miracle has happened, and they have a baby on the way. Life is perfect, or rather it was until a violent cartel showed up in Bliss ready to reap their bloody vengeance on the man he used to be.

A woman shaken to her foundation

Nell Flanders has never met a problem she couldn't handle, but discovering her husband isn't the man she thought was more than she was prepared for. How can she trust Henry, when John Bishop—the ruthless man he used to be—keeps bringing deadly problems to their door? She has a beautiful life growing inside her, and now she isn't sure her marriage can survive long enough to welcome their child into the world.

A reckoning that will shake Bliss to its core

Henry isn't willing to give up on his life with Nell, but it's going to take some Bliss magic to overcome the forces pulling them apart. When the full weight of Henry's past comes to bear on the town and the bullets start flying, it might just be Bishop, and some old friends, who can save the day and win back her heart.

Siren Reborn
Texas Sirens, Book 8
By Lexi Blake writing as Sophie Oak

Cole Roberts and Mason Scott loved each other since childhood, but they needed something more to make them whole. A Dom and a switch, they searched for the right female submissive to settle down with, but a terrible accident tore them apart. Their perfect life shattered, they were each left angry and alone.

Kitten Taylor's past is filled with heartache. She yearns to be part of a family with a Master to call her own. When Master Cole takes her in, she might have finally found the place she belongs. Even though something is missing, she is willing to compromise to have the life she always dreamed of, until Mason returns and shows her just how perfect a threesome can be.

When a killer puts the trio in their crosshairs, Cole and Mason will have to put aside the demons of their past in order to forge a future with the woman they love.

About Lexi Blake

New York Times bestselling author Lexi Blake lives in North Texas with her husband and three kids. Since starting her publishing journey in 2010, she's sold over three million copies of her books. She began writing at a young age, concentrating on plays and journalism. It wasn't until she started writing romance that she found success. She likes to find humor in the strangest places and believes in happy endings.

Connect with Lexi online:

Facebook: Lexi Blake
Twitter: authorlexiblake
Website: www.LexiBlake.net
Instagram: www.instagram.com
Pinterest: www.pinterest.com/lexiblake39/

Made in the USA
Las Vegas, NV
19 November 2025